Daniel Shand's debut novel, *Fallow,*
His second book, *Crocodile,* was shor
for Best Second Novel. His short fictio
(*New Writing Scotland, Gutter, 404 Ink, Popula...*)
he was the winner of the Saltire Society International Travel
Bursary for Literature. In 2021, he was the Jessie Kesson Fellow
at Moniack Mhor.

Praise for *Model Citizens*

'Shand has fashioned a gripping and original
story – and he writes like a dream'
The Times

'All this rich world-building constructs a framework for
sharp questions about consciousness, identity and death,
played out against the threat of an imminent and apocalyptic
end to the comfortable, if pressured, existence Shand's
characters have grown to depend on ... [it has] the pace and
dynamism of a thriller, the metaphysical curiosity of the best
science fiction and some judiciously-planted charges of wry
humour ... his social commentary is funny and on target'
The Herald

'*Model Citizens* is a dazzling novel, combining the
imaginative boldness and emotional clarity of Daniel
Shand's previous work with a torrent of provocative
ideas, and a tremendously broad satirical scope. This
is fiction that's equal to the strange times ahead'
Edmund Gordon, author of award-winning
The Invention of Angela Carter

'A consumerist hellscape is brilliantly evoked ... the cloned
self as ultimate consumer product is a compelling idea and
Shand has such fun with it that the reader gets carried along'
The Irish Times

MODEL CITIZENS

DANIEL SHAND

corsair

CORSAIR

First published in the United Kingdom in 2022 by Corsair
This paperback edition published in 2023

1 3 5 7 9 10 8 6 4 2

A CIP catalogue record for this book
is available from the British Library.

ISBN: 978-1-4721-5666-2

Printed and bound in Great Britain by Clays Ltd, Elcograf S.p.A.

Papers used by Corsair are from well-managed forests
and other responsible sources.

MIX
Paper from
responsible sources
FSC® C104740

Corsair
An imprint of
Little, Brown Book Group
Carmelite House
50 Victoria Embankment
London EC4Y 0DZ

An Hachette UK Company
www.hachette.co.uk

www.littlebrown.co.uk

For Gill and Helen

ONE

It was the junior's first birthday. That day, he became one year old. Nobody at work recognised the date, but the junior knew, and back in the home they shared, so did his senior. To the junior, 'one' seemed like a nice round number. If anyone asked how long he'd been going, he could now say, 'About a year.' He smiled to himself as he went about his working day, then left at clocking-out time. A whole year in the world with no issues and no complaints. It felt good, to be one.

The air smelled hot and dusty; another scorcher in an endless line of scorchers. Guys sold sliced fruit and canned soft drinks from barrels full of ice. Trams slid by on gleaming rails. The street was full of bodies, full of other juniors and seniors crammed onto the pavement. He recognised a few folk from his shift, but he didn't go with them. Today, he had plans. Moving through the crowds on the Dalkeith Road, going against the grain, he requested help from his system. It asked him: *What do you need?* He replied: *I want a lift.* He stood on the kerb for a moment, feeling his system access the field around him. A few moments later, a speeding bike crested the hill.

The courier's shirt was dark with sweat. 'Buchanan?' he asked.
'That's right.'

The junior climbed up for a backie and the courier set off, weaving into traffic and coasting beside a passing tram. There were others going by bike too, most of them heading in the junior's direction: towards the north of the capital. He stood firm on the stunt pegs, holding the courier's shoulders, watching Edinburgh as it went by. On corners, he leaned into the curve. He eased back when the courier braked.

'Busy day?' the junior asked.

'You wouldn't believe it,' the courier replied, shaking his head.

His system informed him of the time: *18:30*. He needed to reach the pub by quarter to, because his senior expected him by then. Alastair, his senior, needed him, so he couldn't be late. The evening in question had been in their shared calendar for a few days now: drinks with Caitlin, his senior's girlfriend. That morning they conversed quietly with each other over breakfast, after she left for work. What might she want? Why all the secrecy? Alastair told the junior Caitlin probably wanted to get married. They were at that stage in their relationship.

On North Bridge, the traffic looked likely to block itself. A tram sat in the middle of a busy intersection, preventing movement, and the courier was forced to bump up onto the pavement. People there stepped aside. The junior hissed through his teeth but didn't complain; they were now running late. His system told him: *18:38*, and the pavements and roads across the bridges were rammed.

'Is a diversion alright?' asked the courier through heavy breaths.

'Just get me there,' he answered. 'Five minutes.'

He closed his eyes as the courier veered sharply to the right, swooping round a Step-Stone van to head downhill towards the parliament building.

'Come on,' he whispered. 'Hurry up.'

He wasn't sure if he felt quite as optimistic as his senior did. As far as he could tell, Caitlin was not happy, and certainly didn't appear to be in a proposing frame of mind. As long as he'd known her – one year already – she'd been off. Partly, the junior was to blame, but mostly the fault lay with Alastair.

Time pressed on. The courier brought them past Holyrood and up into Leith. He stood for the sharp incline, rocking the bike from side to side, but it seemed likely they'd be late. The junior tried not to get pissed off; the guy was doing his best. He started to feel a little queasy, a by-product of letting his senior down. The area where a stomach ought to be felt empty and unsettled. His head hurt. The desire to do right by your senior got baked into every part of you, and when things went wrong, you paid a physical price.

He started to say something to the courier, but before he could speak, they rounded the hill and were flying.

'Hold tight,' said the courier.

'I am,' he replied.

They were going faster than the vehicles, than the trams, speeding downhill, warmth rushing across the junior's face. In among the air, he could sense the field too, its power and data flowing through his body like water through a sieve.

He stood outside the pub, close to its window, and watched his senior sitting alone at a table, his legs jittering where they rested against the stool. He took tiny gulps from his glass. The junior knew how his body would be feeling, because it was his own, in a way. The junior had the same hands, the same chest, the same face. He knew how their shared throat tightened up from nerves, how their guts went cold under stress. The junior was one, Alastair was thirty-one. At first, they'd been identical, but a year of different lives had caused their looks to diverge. Now, his senior seemed pale. He wore dark rings around his eyes, as well as an untidy beard. His hair was sheared short, because who would see it?

The junior went inside, unwilling to let him stew any longer. 'Sorry I'm late,' he said.

Alastair looked up from his glass. 'There you are,' he said. 'She's not here yet.'

'No,' said the junior. 'I know. You needing a drink?'

'I'm okay,' said Alastair. He looked at his glass again, then reconsidered. 'Aye, please.'

As the junior walked towards the bank of lockers, he submitted an order via his system: *a pint of Guinness and one Junior Meal.* He felt the cost debited from Alastair's account and his system replied with a PIN for one of the lockers. On the other side, he could hear staff arranging their order, then the lamp above his locker flashed green.

'There you go,' he said.

'Cheers.' Alastair's first drink was already gone. 'How was work?'

'Fine,' said the junior. 'Normal. Loads of long routes, but fine.'

The junior knew his senior did little with his days, so didn't bother to return the question. Only so much you could say about scrolling on your mobile, pulling up streams, killing time. And plus today he'd have been anxious about this meet-up with Caitlin.

The junior took the stool beside his senior and picked the Junior Meal off the tray. The guilt from his lateness was gone, replaced by a serious hunger. After undoing a few buttons, he slipped a hand inside the collar of his shirt, drawing the fabric back to reveal his shoulder. He felt around the peak of the collarbone, which he then compressed. A small compartment opened up along the upper reach of his shoulder, a darkly shining reservoir leading down to his inner parts.

Alastair watched the procedure. 'What do you think she wants?' he asked.

The junior shook his head. 'Could be anything.' He took the sachet in his hand and squeezed it gently, so the jellyish liquid inside rose to the opening, viscous and pale brown. He tipped it up, letting the Junior Meal slide into his reservoir. The stuff tickled a little as it glugged down, but soon a pleasing fullness entered him.

'I said, didn't I? I think she's going to pop the question.' Alastair closed his eyes. 'I think this is it.'

'Maybe,' the junior nodded. 'But that's good, isn't it?'

'It's not good,' snapped Alastair. 'It's a total hassle.'

'You've been together a long time,' said the junior, doing his buttons back up. 'What? Eight years?'

'I know we have, but still.'

They were quiet for a moment. 'Well I don't care what you say. I'm excited.'

'Good for you. You're not the one getting asked.'

'Aye,' said the junior. 'Whatever you say.'

Ten minutes later, Caitlin arrived. She had her work coat on, standing near the entrance, looking deep into her mobile so you could see its light spread across her neat features. She was tall, with excellent posture, and wore her dyed-white hair just off the shoulder. For a moment, she rocked on her heels, then glanced up, saw them, and came over.

The junior couldn't help it. He carried residual feelings for her, almost like those for an ex – half bitter, half fond. He remembered what it felt like for Alastair to fall in love with her. All those long afternoons in the pub she worked in, doing things to make her smile, needing to believe she thought about him when he wasn't there. Barely eating, barely sleeping, all his skin desperate to press her skin. Those memories were his too.

'Hiya,' she said as she neared the table. 'Sorry I'm late. Another nightmare. Can I get you anything?'

Alastair said no, tipping his glass. The junior shook his head. One sachet of Meal was enough, just as the advertisements claimed.

'Fine.' Her eyes scanned the room. 'Give me a second.'

'Did you notice,' said Alastair, once she was out of earshot, 'how nervous she was?'

The junior watched Caitlin cross the pub floor with confidence, her face back in the mobile. 'Hm,' he said.

'Listen, just play it cool, would you? Don't go sticking your beak in. I need to get my head together.'

The junior played with the empty sachet before him. 'No worries.' Across the room, he could see Caitlin waiting in front of the lockers. She would be buying red wine, like always.

Back when you still got visible staff in these places, Caitlin used to do bar work. Alastair met her as a punter. A refugee from Fife, the ruined peninsula, he received small monthly stipends, deposits he quickly transformed into pints in Caitlin's pub, located on a corner near his damp bedsit. Unlike some, she carried no bigotry against those who required assistance after fleeing their destroyed homelands. The junior remembered watching Caitlin move around behind the beer taps as though he'd been there himself.

Her wine glass landed on the table as she huffed into the stool across from Alastair. Her mac weighed down her shoulders.

'Bad day, then?' Alastair asked.

'The worst,' Caitlin replied, glancing quickly at the junior, offering him a small portion of distaste.

Another painful shift down at Arts Systems, according to Caitlin. This guy in her office, this Otis character, had been acting up again. When Otis started, they spent a lot of time laughing about his weirdness, his fashion-consciousness, his constant girlfriends, but now it appeared to be wearing on

6

Caitlin. She said, 'And the work itself is endless, just endless. I think I'm finished one thing, suddenly I've got something else on my desk.'

'That sounds terrible,' said Alastair.

'Aye,' agreed the junior. 'Really bad.'

She met the junior's gaze for a second time. She squinted a little. 'How would you know?' she asked.

'Well . . . I don't. It just sounds bad.'

She necked a quarter of her glass.

It also turned out there'd been this gallery visit, where they needed to investigate the reflective qualities of the glass used for framing purposes. Dealers were asking for a certain brand, more reflective than normal, because some in Arts Systems suggested viewer engagement increased when the public got a good, healthy eyeful of themselves alongside their artwork. Caitlin didn't like it. Everything else was fair game, but this felt like a step too far.

'But I'm blethering,' she sighed. 'Sorry. How are you? What did you do today?'

The junior sensed his senior tense up at the question. He didn't like to reveal to Caitlin how he wasted his days at home while the junior went to work. 'Oh, this and that,' he said. 'A few pies in the oven.'

Caitlin nodded. 'Right.'

They each stared into their glasses, their eyes cast downwards, and the junior felt such an awkwardness to be there. He looked across the bar, yearning for something interesting to focus on, but nothing came to him. 'Step-Stone was a pain in the arse today too,' he announced. Neither his senior nor Caitlin responded. 'Joe Pegg's been getting on at me again. Well, you know what he's like, Al.'

Unlike Alastair, Joe Pegg worked alongside his own junior; something that was still pretty rare. At first, it was unheard of, but then Charline Mossmoon was on one of the interview streams and she said how she didn't laze around while her junior worked. Instead, she doubled her output. You started seeing all these think pieces on the content feeds for and against Mossmoon's proposition. Some wrote it was an example of good practice – Why not be more productive? Look at Kim Larson, the World's Father himself. Was it not Larson's manic early period that helped him perfect the technology that led to junior production in the first place? – whereas others argued that Mossmoon's story was nothing more than boasting, and bad-faith boasting at that. What about quality of life? What was the point in the whole junioring enterprise if it didn't provide humanity with the promised levels of free time? The argument blistered across the field in the hours after the interview ran, some calling Mossmoon a moron and others, those with juniors, wondering if she might be talking sense.

But anyway, Joe Pegg was one of those who had taken on Mossmoon's wisdom and both junior and senior clocked in to Step-Stone daily. A decent boss, Joe Pegg, with one fatal flaw: you felt sorry for him. His stats on the field were low in *prestige* and *health*, but decently high on *determination*, which was enough to pull him up to middling rank. They rode a tandem bike to the office, Pegg and his junior, both stuffed into race-grade leotards. Watching them pedal up the road was enough to remind you that it was sensible to apply for your junior as close to thirty as possible.

That morning, Pegg gave the junior a hard time about his own stats – Alastair's stats, really – saying he needed to hit their numbers more regularly. 'I suppose he's looking out for us,' the junior added, 'but man, he's a moan.'

Caitlin watched him, then shook her head. She said, 'I've been having these chats with Elaine, actually.'

Alastair jumped on this, clearly keen to move past the tension that existed between his girlfriend and junior. 'Oh,' he said. 'That's good. She likes you, doesn't she?'

Caitlin nodded. 'She's a good boss. But she's pestering me just now ... There's a job going.'

'Oh right?'

'Yeah. It's a pretty big deal, actually, and she wants me to take it.' The relaying of this information seemed to unlock something in Caitlin; her expression softened somewhat and she sighed.

'That's great news,' said Alastair. 'So what's the deal now? Do you have to apply, or is it a done thing?'

Caitlin nodded. 'It's a done thing. If I want it, it's mine.'

'And what does it involve?'

'Well, it'll be a secondment. This other agency needs someone from Arts Systems to consult on PR.'

'That's amazing,' chipped in the junior. He couldn't help it.

Caitlin paused. 'Is it?'

'It sounds like more responsibility, more excitement ... I don't know?'

'Well,' said Caitlin. 'What if I tell you the project's based out at Uist? What if I tell you the secondment involves setting yourself up there for, like, three years? Does that sound good?'

A silence fell on the table. After a moment, Alastair said, 'Wait. What?'

'It's true,' said Caitlin.

'I don't know what you're saying here,' said Alastair.

The junior felt confusion radiate from his senior. Perhaps his own mind was a little sharper, because he thought he could see where the conversation was headed.

'It's a good offer,' said Caitlin. 'Elaine wants me for it, and I want to take it.'

'I'm sorry if this comes across as mean or whatever, but I'm not happy about this.' Alastair shook his head. 'I'm not happy one bit. Three years? Uist?'

'The Scolpaig spaceport,' said Caitlin. 'I still have to confirm it for definite, but I think I'm going to.'

'But what about me?' asked Alastair. He put his hand out on the table. 'What about us?'

'Al,' she sighed. 'We're done.'

'Done?'

'We've been done for a while now. We both know it, don't we?'

'I didn't know it!' exclaimed Alastair. He looked briefly to the junior, who kept his eyes firmly on Caitlin. 'Why am I always the last to know?'

Caitlin frowned. 'Al, I'm tired of being a third wheel. I'm tired of *him*, hanging around the flat like a ghoul. The ghost at the feast. You know how I feel about juniors.' Now she met his eye. 'I'm sorry. I'm not prejudiced, you know that, but it's not for everyone.'

The junior shook his head. The less he said, the better. She didn't like the junior, it had to be admitted. They'd carried on a long conversation, Alastair and Caitlin, through his late twenties, about whether he'd go in for junioring. Caitlin was a few years older and could have signed up whenever she wanted, but hadn't. Wouldn't. Was turned off by the entire process of copying oneself and living beside the result.

'But I asked you,' said Alastair. 'We spoke about it, for months it felt like. I always told you that once I turned thirty, I wanted to go for it. I said I'd be silly not to, with the scheme Pegg worked out for us, didn't I?'

'You knew you would do it from the start, but you made me talk about it for long enough that it was like we'd agreed. I realised whatever got said, he was coming.'

'That's not fair.'

'It's true, Al. You know it is. And the thing is, if it worked out like you said, then fine. Fair enough. If you got your precious junior and suddenly you were happy and successful and making the most of your life, then fine. But that's not what happened, is it?'

The junior sensed his senior bristle at this. He didn't take criticism lightly. They were trying to work on it, for the benefit of his stats.

'Hey,' he said. 'Come on. Things *have* changed since he came. Things *have* got better. I've got all this free time, I've been making plans. My stats went up, you can't deny that.'

'I don't—' Caitlin began, before pausing to lower her voice. 'I don't care about your stats. I've never cared about them. When we met, what sort of stats did you have then?'

'I had fuck-all stats,' he replied.

'Exactly,' said Caitlin. 'And—'

'But it's only been a year. That's not long enough. All I need is to get them a little higher, then who knows what'll happen. If you get high on prestige, you might end up with a stream of your own.'

Caitlin sighed. She shook her head. 'All you do is sit at home. You sit on your arse and sit on the field. You're barely living, Al.'

Another silence, the truth and pain of that last comment poisoning the air between them all. The junior sniffed, then jerked into motion. He said, 'I should head back to the flat. This isn't anything to do with me.'

'I asked you *both* to come,' said Caitlin. 'You need to hear this too. You're part of him.'

He became aware of his senior slowly nodding. His face was nearly resting on his chest, but still he managed to bob his head.

'I thought you were going to ask,' he said, quietly. 'I was nervous, because I thought you were going to ask me.'

'Ask you what?'

'I thought . . . I thought you wanted to get married.'

'Oh,' said Caitlin. 'Oh, Alastair.'

Soon afterwards, she left. She wouldn't be coming home with them that night. She had a room booked in a hotel somewhere and her suitcase was already there. They watched her go, following her purposeful stride through the door, along the street with the other pedestrians, disappearing into the swell of bodies behind the window. Outside, an old senior pushed some sort of wheelbarrow through the crowd, full of damaged electrical equipment, broken toasters, mulched blenders, ancient frayed cabling. Others were jostling past him, tripping on the barrow.

'She won't take it,' the junior said. 'She's just upset.'

Alastair nodded. 'I think she will.'

The junior decided to be honest. 'Aye. Probably.'

Alastair breathed in sharply through his teeth. 'Think of the stats, mate.'

This was all he could think of, even now? 'What do you mean?'

'Think of how it'll look on the stats, getting dumped.'

They spent hours there, long after most of the clientele left. Alastair pulled up orders on his mobile – pints and shorts of whisky – and the junior went to collect them, returning the empties to the appropriate space. Those trips represented nice breaks from the mood back at the table.

He brought the next round over. Alastair accepted the drink to his hand without looking up. He said, 'I feel sick.'

'Do you know what day it is?' the junior asked.

Alastair shook his head. 'Tuesday.'

'What *date*.'

His senior burped.

'It's my birthday.'

'What? No, it's not. My birthday's June the—'

'Not yours, mine. A year ago today I came out the plant.'

Alastair stared at the junior below wonky eyelids, then shrugged. 'Were you expecting a card?'

His senior was unsteady on the way back. The junior put an arm round his shoulder to help, assisting him through pockets of street people, the ones hidden away during sunlit hours. Here were the gangs of vagrants, messily dressed, wearing combinations of ill-matched clothing, all of them scarred around the mouths and eyes. At one point, he had the sensation that this giant bloke was following them: a huge beefcake in a long, greenish jacket, wholly bald, and despite the size of him, able to creep. The junior kept seeing his shiny pate bob above the crowds, always in the direction they walked, but told himself he was being ridiculous.

They came to their home street. On one side was a row of sandstone tenement apartments, on the other a tiny park with swings and a roundabout where children ran around in the day, groups of motherly juniors chatting on the benches.

They went up the close, into the flat.

'Hello?' they said together.

No response. They moved from room to room in the darkness, opening doors softly, peering at the lack of Caitlin inside. They stood together in the bedroom, and the junior had nothing to say. This mirror of himself, the person in whose image he'd been made, sighed and watched the floor.

'Listen, man,' he said. 'It'll be alright.'

His senior opened his mouth to respond, to fire back that no, it wouldn't, but before he could speak, a crash came from the far end of the flat.

They surged out, together, dashing along the hallway, pushing by each other at the kitchen, to emerge into the empty living room.

'Caitlin?' asked Alastair.

But no one was there. All they found was the coffee table upended, on its side, the little candle and the cracked cactus pot on the floorboards, a few dusty books splayed out beside them.

Unable to explain this phenomenon, they wrote off the sound, disregarded the tipped table, and took themselves to bed. The junior waited outside the bedroom door to hear his senior snore, then went to the box room to indulge in his equivalent of sleep. For a long time, for hours, nothing moved in the living room, not even the particles of dust suspended in the moon's light. The very definition of an empty room.

Then, for a few moments, a spark appeared, up near the ceiling. A sound too. A man's voice asking, 'What?'

It was like the room held its breath. A few minutes passed, then the spark returned, a tiny molten spot hanging above the mirror in empty space. Next, it connected itself to another point at the base of the bookcase, a string of light hanging in the air. The voice spoke: 'I don't know!'

The beam existed for a count of ten, then moved itself around. It consolidated into a shape, an amorphous blob, which then formed the outline of a person. It was the figure of a man. If pushed, you would be forced to call it a ghost.

The man, the ghost, blinked. His mouth opened. He took a step forward and held out his hands, pawing through something unseen. He moaned or growled or hummed. If Caitlin or Alastair or the junior were present, they would have seen right through this spectre as it grasped at the air and created small sounds of consternation and anger.

He said, 'It can't be right. The controls are set all wrong.'

He took another step forward, then vanished before the other shoe could drop. Silence, again. Nothing.

14

TWO

A tall figure moved through the crowds, towering above the other pedestrians on the street. He had watched the junior and senior enter their tenement, then he departed, heading south. He stomped uphill now, away from the shore, aiming for the hulk of volcanic rock that dominated the city's CBD, a maze of skyscrapers and luxury housing blocks. Even this figure seemed small as he passed under that crazy architecture: inverse pyramids, columns of bubbles, frozen fountains of cool, flat glass, pale on the panes facing the moon.

The man barged through crowds, stopped traffic when he stepped from the pavement, making his determined way towards the few patches of green beyond that antic centre. The southern neighbourhoods were more spread out, more leafy, more free of billboards and argon lighting and noise. In time, he came to one building in particular, a great villa formed from bricks of pale rose: Summerfield House.

The 97ers moved in two years back. The summer before last, during yet another season of scorchers, they banded together from their separate groups, a member having stumbled across the abandoned kiddy home during a futile shroom hunt. They arrived by night, smuggling themselves inside; not that anyone watched out. These were upper-middle-class lands, and the building was blanked as an eyesore. No one observed the darkened figures rush blind across the Meadows, carrying packs and satchels and towering rucksacks. No one heard the rattle of canteens and jerrycans and foldaway cutlery, as night by night the new inmates massed through a broken cellar window, slipping in like gas.

Now, the building's interior was as ruined as ever. In that evening, room after room was filled with collapsing bunks, springs poking out their mattresses to snag socks and skin. Rooms held rusty bathtubs wrapped in bedsheets to protect against tetanus, held fetid hovels rank with black mould. Here, there was no full connection to the field; their only concession to the age was a single bulb wired atop the gusty roof, positioned to bring power to the lower places. Data was forbidden. Most rooms' walls crinkled with pasted tinfoil, a useless defence against that all-encompassing field. Data moved through them, whether they liked it or not; content and streams and pure data swam in three dimensions, choking every corner of the building, dying out a half-mile above in weak air.

In the two years since their occupation, the new inhabitants had leaked into all areas of Summerfield, taking up all spaces. On every floor, these squatters plotted and schemed. They smoked black-market rollies and popped Smurf. They held séances and used Ouija boards in vain attempts to contact their long-dead heroes.

For the residents of Summerfield House, the 1990s would never die.

The building had been constructed in the late Victorian period. Originally purposed as a home for the city's runaways and orphans, Summerfield had initially been administered by a cruel and esoteric brotherhood. After those priests departed, the building moved through various other incarnations, before sitting vacant for long, long years. Now, in an upper room, a meeting was in progress. The 97ers were non-hierarchical by design, but human nature dictated that a few chunks of cream would rise to the top. Assembled there, in a space once put aside as a schoolmaster's garret, were three: Hirst, Mandelson and Spencer. All were aware of a great rumbling from below, as several members moved a castor-legged snooker table from room to room, its journey's purpose unclear.

Hirst, their leader, was the only one standing, his back to the other two, facing the cramped window. One of the few Anglo accents heard within the building, he grew up rural. His family eked out a living in flooded Humberside, marsh-sifters and hunters of eels. The 97ers' leader was rail thin, his features those of a rodent.

He said to the window, 'Fine night tonight.'

Behind him, Mandelson and Spencer scratched runes into the tabletop. At his words, they raised their heads from the surface, from carved-out *97RULESOK*s and other glyphs, from pubes of tobacco droppings, from smudged pencil shavings, from the apple core Spencer had lately munched. He was one hundred per cent, dyed in the wool, complete and utter city scum, Spencer. Pure dregs, his DNA, and proud of it. In his veins ran the adrenalised consciousnesses of vandals and glue-sniffers and mince-eaters. He was gigantic and muscular and on his knuckles were written: *CRAP* and *PISH*. His skull was hairless. Spencer could not give a single solitary shite about whether or not the night was fine, so said nothing.

Mandelson, a little different. She was minuscule in Spencer's shadow, spring-haired and lean. A refugee from the ruined peninsula, growing up in Fife just like Alastair Buchanan. If she had a feed, and if her feed was linked up with Alastair's, there'd be connections in common. They all knew each other, mostly, or were friends-of-friends, the survivors. Her entire family were carbonised, and Mandelson never quite managed to overcome that teenage devastation. She bolted up some mornings from night terrors of frosty firth water, dreaming horizons ablaze like in the cartoons her mummy used to stream. Steely, you would say. High on *determination*, if her stats were accessible.

She went to stand behind Hirst, to peer through the bottom-heavy glass. Fair enough, a nice night. 'Uh huh,' she said. 'And?'

'Just an aesthetic judgement,' said Hirst. 'Nothing else.'

Calling from the table, Spencer: 'Take a photo if you love it so much.'

'Ha,' said Hirst, dryly.

The corners of this attic room were stuffed with detritus, items and material brushed back from the centre at some earlier date, left in heaps: coils of matted dust, emptied meal sachets, miscellaneous scraps and leaves and shards suspended by hidden cobwebs. Into one pile of mess, Spencer threw his used-up apple core.

Hirst tutted, coming away from the window. 'Have you got to act like that?' he asked.

'What?' sneered Spencer. 'It'll just rot away. That's the whole benefit of fruit. No rubbish.'

'Fair enough,' said Hirst, sweeping away mess from his own place at the table, 'but it makes you look like one of *them* lot. Wasteful.'

'Aye, aye,' said Spencer, mashing his vast fingers into an interlocked club. 'Dry your eyes.'

'Are we getting on to the meeting?' asked Mandelson.

Hirst leaned back in frustration. 'I'm just about to, if this one wasn't playing the clown.'

With that, Spencer heaved himself up from the table, untold kilos of solid muscle, creaking the boards as he went rifling through the rubbish pile for his browning core, brandishing it like a pearl within his paw and then crunching it whole. 'Waste not,' he said.

The others watched for two, three ... then Mandelson: 'Are we done?'

Hirst got to it. He unscrolled the rolled-up message, delivered that morning by drone, sent by one of their compatriots within JNR, the place where juniors were born and monitored.

The drones were a clever bit of kit, put together by an Anglo 97er, recipient of a shipment of infant AI chips, now largely out of fashion. Once popular among bereaved parents, these chips were not designed for full junior development. Rather, the infant chips contained a generic sort of babyish personality that could be installed within inanimate objects, such as teddy bears, to ease the tortuous transition away from parenthood. Popular for a while, then understandably reviled, it turned out these chips could be hacked into drones, the destination programmed in via the mother impulse, sending the flimsy helicopters whizzing through the sky like bawling daddy longlegs. This one example had arrived a few hours previous, tapping at a window to be retrieved by Hirst, who stole the message while swatting away the crying, needy drone, squawking for milk and maternal comfort from the very coordinates it'd arrived at.

Hirst read the scroll before them. He already knew what was written there. 'The junior's well established at Step-Stone,' he said. 'He's been there a year now and everyone seems to like him well enough.' He folded up the little scrap, weighing it down with a tankard made from bone, and closed his eyes. 'How did they look to you, Spencer?'

Spencer shrugged. 'They were sitting together in this pub. The senior keeps drinking, keeps drinking all night. Then they walk home together back to their flat. They looked fucking normal, like nothing.'

'What we need,' said Hirst, 'is an *in*, and I think the job's the way we do it. We need to get someone into Step-Stone, to grease the wheels. Then we can turn the screws on this Alastair and find out what he's hiding.'

The lights were fading. Tankard and turnip core and busted wristwatches made shadows across the tabletop. A deep crease worked its way into Mandelson's brow, her pupils fixed on the trapped paper. In her heart's heart, in the childhood bedroom kept hidden beneath the bared teeth and uncombed curls, she nursed a tenderness for other refugees. Christ, she shared a hovercraft with them, did she not? Despite them all being strangers, all blackened with soot but unburned enough to be worth saving, they huddled down in those bobbing crafts, the firth's spray invading each time they crossed a wave. They kept together and shared blankets, whispering soft consonants to each other, the entire estuary lit up by the hundreds of ships. Was that not meant to count for nothing? This senior, he must've been out there too, seasick and scared.

Spencer, on the other hand, cared nothing about this fucking dude, this dude and his posh-cunt junior. For him, the senior was a black silhouette with a white question mark held within its limits. Would always be so. If there was anything he hated, posh-cunts was it. There was no jealousy. Spencer wanted to be on the field like nearly all conscious minds wanted to be on the field, but the other shite, they could keep it. The twenty-four-hour gyms and recording the exercise so you could log it for stats, those pipes – flumes – into your house all hours of the day and night, clogging it up with what? With fuck all. Spencer considered the others round the table posh-cunts too. He tuned into that frequency all his lot possessed, the inaudible hum of being looked at down someone's beak.

An example: one season of boyhood, babyfat Spencer found himself signed up for Brazilian jiu-jitsu lessons in this hall, its floor blackened by plimsoll scuffs. The instructor, this wang with a goat beard, called Spencer a natural. Spencer kept going. He excused himself from normal duties, saying to the mates he was helping his grandad do up a speedboat – a speedboat?! – down the garages at the back of Hong Kong Kitchen. A sort of truth: at the end of lessons, the hall began to fill with the sweet reek of frying rice with prawns and eggs and little hard chunks of pork. Kept going, got better at the moves, kept getting partnered with this one lad Chris Hobson. A funny lad. Posh-cunt funny.

Chris wore one of the higher belts, blue or orange or something, and he said to Spencer he owned these pads you could use for kicking against, but it needed two of you, and Spencer said something to the effect of, aye that sounded good, but it must be a pain in the arse if it's just you, and this Chris said that yeah it was a bit, so did Spencer want to come round for a shot that night?

So in the early evening, out they went to the bigger houses down Lymond Road, so close Spencer could have arced a pebble across the railway bridge and chances are he'd have hit a mate doing Smurf near the tracks. These houses, man. Like something off an old-worldy stream. Kept thinking a butler was going to pounce out and toot a horn. Chris Hobson took them up a driveway and Spencer noticed the pebbles, the stones. The little pink sharp ones like on his grandad's driveway at home. Huh, he thought, just the same. And then they were up to the place, which was very lavish, very ornate, and Chris went right on in, and the windows were taller than a person and stuck out from the front of the house in three parts, showing off the orange glowing insides, this vase of some white flowers.

And the next bit was all a confusion as Chris went marching into different rooms, asking has he got time to show Spencer the jiu-jitsu pads before supper – calling Spencer by his old name, before he got gifted with Princess Di's – and a woman's

21

voice answering, saying *what what, slow down, I don't know where you are, what are you saying?* This was Chris Hobson's ma, who came springing out from one of the rooms, brushing up greyish hairs that still looked good, smiling at her son and then staring at Spencer, who used his special senses to zero in on the corners of her mouth, on her eyes' creases, seeing everything he needed to; seeing himself in that flurry of expressions as they processed him.

'Give us a minute, would you, petal?' the mother asked.

Spencer went out. He nearly waited. He spent three whole minutes kicking stones with the toe of his size-ten plimsoll so they shot straight down the drive. The exact same chippings, same as the ones eight-year-old Spencer tried to draw on pavements with, the results so disappointing compared with their chalky promise.

Through the large, closed door, some sort of row was going on, ma versus son. Spencer nearly waited. He just about did, so nearly waited to hear whatever the excuse ended up being – that Chris needed to get his tea now, that posh-cunt grans and grandads were coming – then instead, stooped to scoop a pawful of gravel, thereafter showering them across the window in a brief, glassy shower of hail.

Next week at Brazilian jiu-jitsu, nothing got said on the matter, and during sparring, Spencer got this Chris Hobson in a vicious gogoplata, a gogoplata so extreme he felt Hobson's panicked heartbeat in the bone of his shin. A wide circle of lads opened up around them, quiet staring lads, and the only sounds in the room were Hobson's hissing nose-breaths and the squeak of his plimsolls, plus Spencer's deep, simple laugh. Never went back to the BJJ. Didn't want to, plus was banned. An example.

He now retrieved the message from below the horn tankard, rolling it out with two fingers. 'So what?' he said. 'What do we do with this?'

'I'm trying to think,' spat Hirst, 'if you'd shut your fat mouth for a second, and let me think.'

'Think then!' said Spencer.

In this building, there was little understanding of night, or rest, or sleep. Dim lights burned all hours of the clock, some inmates working nightshifts no one requested of them, waking insane and tight-eyed at sunset and blundering around in one-piece pyjamas, boiling up rumbling vats of porridge as others snoozed in their bunks and tubs. All night, long games got played, cards mostly, but also hide and seek, or mousetrap. The true insomniacs skinned up over wavering candles, a slow leak of tears glossing their eyeballs, the last two years existing for them as one unbearable yesterday.

In a cramped back kitchenette, two of the nightwalkers kept each other company. Insignificant low-rankers, they enjoyed little oversight from the likes of Hirst or Mandelson, and with no one to tell them when to go to bed, they fell asleep wherever exhaustion found them. Now, they played darts, despite the smallness of the room. Their tools were so blunt that good shots often ricocheted back from the board and were lost under the free-standing oven, or within the pile of soiled boilersuits blocking the outside door of the pantry. Both of them were young, barely out their teens, and Albarn especially was small. Perhaps five foot on a good day, a day of stretching out. Creutzfeldt-Jakob towered over him, a great gangling lad of knucklebones and extreme Adam's apple. Because of the game, they never had to meet each other's eye.

'I'm thinking of getting out,' said Albarn, messing with the flights of his dart. 'I'm so bored.'

Creutzfeldt-Jakob took ages to measure his shots, stroking the air repeatedly, squinting. 'Oh right.'

'Aye,' said Albarn. 'I keep thinking, what are you doing with your life, man?'

'I think that every day.'

Thunk. A clear miss. Creutzfeldt-Jakob loomed across the tiles to retrieve the dart, Albarn taking his place. The board hung above his head. 'Well you know what I mean then. I keep thinking, there's all this mad world out there and I'm spending it here, with you lot.'

'So what'll you do then?'

'Dunno. Anything. Be one of them drivers for Step-Stone.'

'Wouldn't fancy that.'

'No. Well, me neither. But anything. I don't think the world's as bad as Hirst says.'

Albarn: double-fifteen. They swapped. There was no end-game here, no score-keeping, no winding down the numbers to absolute zero. There was only the current dart, only the treble-twenty to aim for, or the bull.

Creutzfeldt-Jakob again, with his measured moving of the dart, back and forth. He said, 'I wouldn't let Hirst catch me saying that.'

'Hirst,' snapped Albarn. 'That ponce. Why does he get so het up for anyway? Look, I get it. I get that the world's fucked and juniors are evil and—'

'I think you're oversimplifying the message. No one's saying the juniors are evil.'

'You know what I mean.'

'Do I?'

Albarn looked to his colleague's skeletal hand, the shot still untaken. 'Well, aye. It's all about things were better in the old days, isn't it? Were they though?'

Creutzfeldt-Jakob took it. The dart pranged against one of the board's radii and rocketed backwards, somersaulting, landing within the cast-iron sink, rattling around and scraping on the bare metal.

From through the wall, a low moan came: 'Siiilence.'

24

The players looked at each other for the first time that night, wary. They had thought they were alone in this back-room quarter.

Creutzfeldt-Jakob went to retrieve the dart. He whispered now. 'But you wouldn't want to go out and be a norm, would you, Albarn? You wouldn't want to deal with that pressure.'

Hissing: 'What pressure?'

'All that field bollocks. Putting everything up and that.'

'I don't know. I used to like it, when I was a kid. I mind of going out to the beach with the family and they'd set up a mobile to record it and—'

But before Albarn could finish his reminiscence, a further sound came to trouble the players. They paused, breathing in the reek of rotten boilersuits, crockery caked with hardened sauces, the carpet of muddy bootprints leading from door to oven to board.

From the outer door came a scuffling, as of vermin.

Creutzfeldt-Jakob placed a finger to dry lips; Albarn nodded.

Together, they crept through the dinge, beneath the bare bulb, to scoop away the heap of shitty clothing that blocked the door. The scuffling continued.

Creutzfeldt-Jakob pictured any second the wood flying back as a shiny black boot punted in the door. Albarn thought of a fox, a good omen for his upcoming freedom. Instead, they opened up to a girl, a woman, kneeling there, looking up open-mouthed, caught in the act of tricking the lock. She stood. 'Alright?'

'Alright,' said Albarn.

'Alright,' said Creutzfeldt-Jakob.

'What you wanting?' sniffed Albarn.

'Is this Summerfield House?' asked the stranger.

'Might be,' said Creutzfeldt-Jakob. 'Who wants to know?'

The woman scowled. 'Me, obviously.'

They let her in. She came into their hiding place and looked around. Nice clothes on her, Creutzfeldt-Jakob noticed, nice fashionable gear.

'You lost or something?' asked Albarn.

'No, I'm not lost. I was looking for Summerfield and here I am.'

'What for?' asked Creutzfeldt-Jakob. They'd had it drummed into them by Hirst that strangers were to be distrusted. For all Creutzfeldt-Jakob knew, this was a secret agent. Not government, obviously, but who knew what private interests might come calling in the small hours to bamboozle a trusting party member?

'*What for?*' she echoed. 'What do you think for?'

Creutzfeldt-Jakob shrugged.

The stranger rolled her eyes. She shook her head, swallowed, then produced the magic words: 'I'm looking for ... education, education, education.'

And with that, they were off. Albarn and Creutzfeldt-Jakob dragged her by the hand, pulling and jerking the stranger, a friend now, out of their hovel, finding broom handles and pans to rattle off walls and exposed piping, calling out, 'Education! Education! Education!' to the population still awake, rousing others, and despite the late hour this was cause for celebration. 97ers burst out dressed in curtains, in rancid finery, in kilts of perished rubber, in nicotine wedding dresses, in top hats of faded card, in soleless brogues, in bathmat capes and shoelace ties, bearded, skin shining from four-day grease.

A conga line brought the stranger through the darkened maze, her face showing surprise at the sudden influx, all through the lower corridors to the old drawing room. One wall of this vast space was taken over entirely by what had once been its fireplace; now a television sat in the hearth, programmed to play VHSs endlessly, washing the great table and tech wall in the flickering lilac of *Titanic* and *Saving Private Ryan*. A confusion of bodies in this light as everyone fought for the honour of educating the stranger. A great, leather-bound tome was chained to the table: *Mullay's Almanac 95–00: UK & Ireland Edition*.

'Any mobiles?' someone asked her. 'Any screens, any tablets, any phones?'

She brought a skinny piece of kit out from a pocket and handed it to the questioner. At once, they clambered up the ladder clinging to the tech wall, a surface reaching high, tiled in the cracked faces of mobiles and other screens. This one member tottered as they pulled a hammer out from the pocket of their boilersuit, a long bronze nail from their shirt, positioning the stranger's mobile into a suitable gap, before driving the nail into its screen so all below could cheer at the sharp *schok, schok, schok*.

Then someone else: 'The name, the name!' and it was Creutzfeldt-Jakob himself nearest the almanac, Creutzfeldt-Jakob who elbowed away brothers and sisters to grab hold of the tome's edges, leaning over it for prominence. When they backed off, he closed his eyes and spun the pages, poking his index nail down at a random entry, gifting her a name of the era, just like all others had been assigned.

'From now on . . .' He paused. 'You'll be called Dolly, as in the sheep.'

The crowd continued to buffet the stranger – Dolly – through the rooms of Summerfield House, more and more joining them, wakened by the racket. Soon, Dolly would be forgotten by most, one face among many, no one keeping a record of admission, but in the madness of three, four a.m., there was protocol to respect.

Only Hirst took an interest in the fresh recruit. Only Hirst came calling in the morning, having caught wind of her arrival, keen to discuss a proposition with the 97ers' newest member.

From a nearby room came the soft burble of the infant drone, where it hung from a pulley, rocked to sleep by a pedestal fan set to *SCAN*.

Hirst nursed an infamous hatred of the junior class. Something to do with gangmasters down on the fens who bussed in small towns' worth of abandoned juniors to his family's locale, pricing out honest hard-working seniors who'd sieved the land for one generation at least. Needless to say, there were zero juniors in situ within the 97ers. All of the assembled ranks were seniors to a man and woman, though rumours persisted that Shearer, for example, flirted with junioring in her previous existence. Folk in her old profession made good money and could easily take the hit if they wanted to. Shearer expressed furious indignation – *as if I'd get one of them fucking things made of myself* – but that was the nature of rumour. The rest were safely beyond suspicion, hardly any of them compos mentis enough to have held down a job of work for longer than two birthdays.

In truth, few of Summerfield's inhabitants shared Hirst's zeal. Most were just after free board, happy to swallow whatever ideologic price the leaky roof cost. On some level, Hirst realised this. He knew his cause attracted recruits drawn mostly by the possibility of chaos, by the cell's relaxed attitude to substance abuse. Even his trusty lieutenants, Spencer and Mandelson, did not live and breathe the cause like he did. He knew nearly all of them, even now years free of it, were absolutely desperate to get onto the field and scroll some content. When you grew up within that sort of thing, it never left you, but Hirst was different. In his early life, his family worked too hard to interact with the field; he felt no real attachment to its pleasures.

This lack of conviction in his underlings didn't cause him much concern. To make a real change, he knew, all you needed was a single individual. All you needed was someone with enough belief, enough power of will, to create a whole new world. Or rather, to force open an older world, a better world.

Having left behind the new recruit, he walked to his private quarters, a little way off from the others. His was a small, clean room, the only example of such inside Summerfield House. It contained an iron bedframe knocked back into shape. The bed was neatly made, with the sheet and rough wool blanket tucked at the corners like parcels. A desk was squared against the wall, the drawers below full of the exact right quantity of pants and socks. On top of the desk, he kept a photograph of good old Tony B, shaking hands with Noel inside No. 10, 30th of July 1997, beside a framed compact disc sleeve of *Urban Hymns*. From below the bed, he pulled out a locked strongbox, containing his one guilty pleasure.

Hirst had set himself against the world beyond the house's walls. If people there preached connection, he isolated; if they preached health, he binged; if they preached fitness, well ... The old ways died hard. Shirt off and towards the window, he limbered his joints, glowering at loafers in the parklands. He began tugging and wrenching apart the secret implement, a coal of exertion relit in his breast, hoping beyond hope that neither Mandelson nor Spencer would overhear the rusty wheeze of the chest extender as he operated it, grunting, snarling, counting.

As he worked, he told himself: you are a soldier. You are a soldier for your class. Every day, he reminded himself of the high, high stakes. The world marched closer to oblivion, content to circle down the drain in a wash of onanism. He saw himself as a single groyne, one length of timber designed to hold back wave after wave of greed, of ego, of vice. At times, it felt insurmountable, but he would do it; he knew he contained the power. All of the drop-outs and loonies and weirdos nestled in the hive below him, they were his children. They were his children, and he would see his children right.

THREE

Who hasn't, in the middle of a long, dull journey, wished they could remove themselves from its boredom? Who hasn't, during a lengthy flight, say, felt so sick and ill with the hassle of the procedure, at the careful timing of airport arrival and security processing, that they've thought: this whole ordeal would be much better if I simply wasn't present?

Who hasn't driven long distance and wanted to plunge their motor into the central reservation out of the desire to experience something, anything, other than oncoming autoway asphalt?

Who among us hasn't ogled with contempt their fellow commuters on trains, trams, omnibuses of all description, biting back fury at bad music streamed at full volume, or stains on the seating?

Who, during those moments of frustration, has not hallucinated a door-shaped portal – an archway in the air, its edges perhaps glowing green – through which the commuter might step, delivering them *immediately* to their destination, the journey having been scissored out of their life like an edit, the removal of something tiresome that we, the travellers and spectators of our own travelling, find too dull to even think about enduring?

These were the questions that led to the foundation of Step-Stone and its regional imitators. The geniuses behind

Step-Stone didn't invent time travel or teleportation technology, but they got pretty close.

Outside Step-Stone's Edinburgh base, a few days after Caitlin's departure, the junior leaned on the low wall that encircled the building. What a day. What a scorcher. Behind him, the stagnant pond simmered, its artificial heron bobbing slightly. The hills behind Step-Stone looked aflame from the intensity of the gorse; the air tasted metallic, full of dust.

He was dressed in Alastair's very best gear, the real highlights of his wardrobe. Alastair had spent a good fifteen minutes preening at him that morning, plucking his hair just so, dabbing down the eyebrows with a wet thumb, running a pencil round the inside of his belt to make sure the shirt sat flush. The junior understood. He got it completely. Getting dumped, that could play absolute havoc with your stats. What worse taint was there than that of the dumped? The rejected? Just the mention of it might lose you multiple points on *prestige* or *influence*, never mind the resulting stigma, which would also mess you up, leading to a vicious circle of poor social standing. He would put in a good shift at the office, then Alastair had scheduled a gig for him with some pals that evening. They needed to show the world that the dumping hadn't changed them one bit.

Far off down the road, the junior spotted Joe Pegg and his own junior huffing uphill on their tandem. At that, he went in through the automatic doors, right below the giant, red, faintly backlit letters that spelled out:

STEP-STONE

The junior's first duty that day was to be present during integration. As a relatively new addition to the Step-Stone team, he could answer any questions that fresh batches of juniors

31

and seniors might have. The juniors rarely had anything to ask, given that they could remember precisely the work their own seniors did at the company; they usually looked extremely bored during these sessions.

This morning, he sat at the back of the conference room while Pegg and his junior busied themselves at the front. A dozen people were sat in front of him, spaced out from each other, facing Pegg as he took his usual stance for the start of these sessions, feet set wide apart and empty palms cupped as though he were handling udders. The junior knew that the boss became nervous in these last moments before beginning his spiel. He said good morning to everyone, making eye contact with all present, smiling desperately, then explained how the morning would proceed.

'So what's Step-Stone all about?' he asked the room.

The group didn't respond. They weren't supposed to.

'Step-Stone began out in good old America, where they asked the question: why don't we unravel . . . what it means to travel.' Pegg paused for effect. 'People enjoy that,' he chuckled. 'Most of the time people enjoy that. So our colleagues out in good old America, they were like, how can we make getting about a bit easier? For the consumer, I mean. How can we take the stress out of getting from A to B? And they had this idea. What if you could go to sleep in your own bed and wake up where you needed to be? Imagine that. Imagine how that would change . . . travelling.' The Peggs shared an almost teary look. 'All across the world, busy people tuck themselves into their own comfortable beds, sleep sweet dreams, while overnight dedicated Step-Stone operatives transport those customers to where they need to get to, leaving them fresh to start a day of calm, wholesome productivity, full of vigour and peace.'

'That's beautiful,' said Pegg's junior.

'I appreciate you telling me that,' said Pegg. 'Thank you so much. Where was I?'

'Step-Stone's core values,' said his junior.

'That's right. Folks, listen, I know you've got about as much time for corporate mumbo jumbo as I do, so I'll give it to you straight. Step-Stone is all about convenience. That's it in a nutshell. We're about convenience, and we're about using the latest pharmaceutical and transportational technologies to get as close to teleportation as we're going to, in any of *our* lifetimes anyway. Am I right?'

Someone at the front said, 'I remember all this.'

'I know, I know,' smiled Pegg. 'But we've done core values, so if you don't mind, let's move on to the customer journey?'

The person shrugged.

'So what is the Step-Stone customer journey? Let's say you decide to go on your holidays, or you organise an important business face-to-face on the other side of the country. Nightmare, am I right? Aye, total nightmare, agreed. So, what do you do? You come to Step-Stone. You tell us where you're coming from, where you're going to, we send you a tiny little sugar-coated pill via flume that you take once your bags are packed, once you're snuggled up in your bed, and the pill knocks you out. Later on, our highly trained delivery operatives arrive, uplift your luggage, uplift you, and stow you carefully – very carefully – in one of Step-Stone's trucks. Is it comfortable? Okay, full disclosure, no, it's not really very comfortable, but what do you care? You care not one jot, do you, because you're out of it. You're dreaming sweet dreams, well past the boredom –' he drew the word out, so that *dom* sounded almost like *doom*, '– of long-haul travel. We deliver you to your hotel room or rented property and BAM, you wake up fresh as a daisy, ready to get on with your business or pleasure. All that's left to do is dispose of the sanitary shorts you've been obliged to wear, which are of course organic and recyclable.'

'You've got a good way of putting it, Joe,' said his junior.

'You might have guessed, but I'm very proud of being part of Step-Stone. I bought shares you know. It's true. But anyway, let me say something. I can feel a sort of tension hanging in the air just now. It's the m-word, isn't it?'

Pegg closed his eyes, nodded, and took a seat, leaning with one elbow on the table, world-weary.

'The old m-word raises its head at this point, I'm afraid. It makes sense, I hate to admit, because when you boil it down, who in their right mind takes a sleeping pill and knocks themselves out after giving a pack of strangers access to themselves in such a vulnerable position?' Pegg sighed. 'I get it, folks. Believe me I do. It's the m-word, isn't it? The old m-word raising its head. And fair play to you for thinking it, because believe me, I understand nobody wants to get molested. I understand. Nobody wants to get molested by the drivers they've given access to their home. I'm the last person that wants to get molested in my sleep. I shudder imagining that.'

Here, Pegg shivered to prove how much he disliked the thought of being molested by Step-Stone staff.

'Because, deep down, we all know the temptation those drivers are operating under. Constant, endless access to sleeping Step-Stone customers? They'd have to be saints not to consider it, which is why each of our drivers is obliged to accept weekly doses of anti-arousal medicine. What could be simpler? Another tiny wee pill, and problem solved, no one gets m-worded, Step-Stone customers sleep easy as they're driven all across these great countries of ours. It means only a senior can drive for us, but that's a small price to pay.'

'Listen,' said the disgruntled person in the front row. 'Thank you, honestly, for taking us through all this. I do appreciate it, but we know what we're doing. We've gone through it before. We—'

'I am required,' snapped Pegg, 'to run the full debrief. I have instructions,' he paused, 'from *America*.' He waited to see if the person would respond, then said, 'Thank you.' He sniffed. 'Where was I?'

His junior consulted the tablet. 'We've still got to do the inverse productivity pyramid.'

Pegg smiled. He whispered. 'That's my favourite.'

Just then, someone knocked on the door of the conference room. A small man's head popped in. He looked at them all, then asked, 'Room for one more?'

The one more, another new recruit, was a young woman who appeared to have gotten dressed in the dark. Some buttons of her shirt were slotted into incorrect buttonholes; her hair was combed from just above the ear.

'Hiya,' she whispered to the junior, slipping into a chair beside him.

'Get yourself settled in,' said Pegg, loudly. 'Take your time, please. It's always great to see a new face here at Step-Stone Edinburgh. There, get comfortable . . . excellent, excellent. This is Alastair Buchanan's junior you're sitting beside. One of our best guys, don't listen to what folk say about him.'

Pegg's junior turned himself around, doubling over slightly, and snorted.

'Just my little joke,' said Pegg. 'Alastair's junior doesn't mind, he's a good sort. Salt of the earth. Right. Well. I'm sorry, but you just arrived at what's probably the best bit of my debrief. But that'll have to wait. You folks don't mind me skipping back to the start, do you? No? Grand. Cheers. So. Ladies and gentlemen, what is Step-Stone all about?'

*

Once Pegg's debrief was over, the group dispersed. The junior lingered outside the conference room. To his surprise, he found the new recruit lingering beside him. They watched Pegg and his junior head down the long, blue carpet and saw them exchange some words right as the corridor bent, Pegg shrugging, the junior patting his senior's shoulder in a display of solidarity.

'He gets emotional after these things,' explained the junior. 'Never thinks he's done a good job.'

The new recruit grimaced. 'I can see that.'

Down the corridor, Pegg had his hands on his knees, taking visibly deep breaths. His junior looked back at them, trying, it seemed, to hurry his senior out of view. Someone came out of another meeting room to check what the noise was. You could see the junior attempt to apologise.

'I'm Dot,' said the new recruit. 'Nice to meet you.'

'Nice to meet you too,' said the junior.

He helped Dot to parse the timetable she'd been issued, showing her where to find certain rooms or certain individuals. She tucked her hair behind an ear to focus and smiled at the junior.

'This must be fun for you,' she said. 'Helping out new people.'

'Sort of,' said the junior.

She left then, running late for an IT set-up, sending back a small wave as she went in Pegg's direction, disappearing round the bend.

When she went out of view, the junior realised his head felt heavy, like a flu coming on; that period before you even realise you've got the bug and the tubes behind your face feel like they're holding weight. Except it wasn't a cold, it was Alastair in there. He could feel the senior in his sinuses, clogging up the pipes, causing the wee slight ache inside his head. This was how you knew your senior was watching. Back in the flat, Alastair had a stream set up, and the junior sensed it, knew the connection existed, knew everything he saw was being seen twice.

Alastair's voice came to him: *What was that all about?*

The junior resisted. He scowled. *How d'you mean?*

What are you being like that for? 'Sort of'? Is that the impression we want to be making today?

I was just saying, you know, it's not that exciting.

Be nice, alright? Be gracious, okay? Mind your Ps and Qs, and don't go contradicting folk. Alright?

I understand, said the junior.

Aye, he did. Aye, Alastair, he understood. The junior knew the rules the same as he did, so could Alastair give him a break for even just a second?

The junior calmed himself down. He tried not to care about his senior's observance, his meddling. Everything he did was in service of his senior and their stats. He tried also not to dwell on the little surge of something tight in his belly, caused by the shininess of Dot's pearlescent, waving nails.

One perk of helping with integration was you were excused from normal duties, so that you could help with transitions as much as possible. The junior headed for the canteen. Largely, the building was empty. A few bosses wandered by, eyes glued to tablets, the junior having to dive out the way as they barged past. The canteen too was quiet; at Step-Stone, breaks away from desks were quietly discouraged.

He went for a Junior Meal from the machine, feeling the cost be debited from his system. Over to the seats, where a group of drivers were hunched. They were huge men, the drivers, vast fleshy backs a metre wide, their grey tops pinching round the armpits. Feet of chairs stretched outwards when drivers sat in them. The anti-arousal medicine made drivers mostly bald, all of them big and soft around the middle.

He skirted by, a little frightened of their placid hugeness. Across in the far corner sat a group of route-planners that the junior didn't recognise. He killed some time browsing the field in his mind, experiencing the day's headlines, until it was time for normal duties to resume. Upstairs, in routing, he found himself scheduled with another junior, Shun. Their room was taken over by four displays, two featuring feeds of passenger stats: heartbeats and breathing rates and depth of sleep. The other pair streamed driver POVs.

Shun asked, 'Alright?'

The junior nodded. 'Everything going okay?' he asked.

'Aye,' said Shun. 'Fine.'

The junior's second screen, the driver's stream, showed a door, a bright yellow door, and you saw the driver's hand bring a pass up to the lock, to scan themselves in and enter. One of those boxy builds of the early millennium, the walls looked insubstantial even through the stream. The driver called out, 'Hello?' and a boy emerged from one of the rooms. 'It's a Step-Stone uplift,' the driver said.

'Oh, that'll be Mum,' said the boy. 'Come on.'

The stream showed him follow the boy upstairs, all the lighting carrying a tinge of ghostliness, something lost in the transfer from camera to field to screen. They went into the customer's bedroom, where the woman was laid out on top of a large bed, wearing the Step-Stone eyemask and pyjamas with its logo on the breast. The pyjamas were bulky round the hips from the sanitary shorts.

'There she is,' said the boy. He could only have been twelve. 'Help yourself.'

The woman breathed loudly through her nose, one arm raised above her head like a gesture of greeting. You zoomed right in on her dreaming features as the driver ducked to lift her and he came close. For a moment, the screen went black. You needed to watch out for this. Who knew what went on when a driver's stream was compromised?

'Everything alright there?' the junior asked, leaning forward to the microphone.

The stream returned as the driver stood, and he said, 'Fine.'

The video swept down the woman's form, now held in the driver's arms, and you saw there was a tattoo on his left wrist: a scorpion. She was cushioned against his broad tummy, sound asleep, lips parted. He took her gently down the staircase and the boy did not come out to check.

The driver called out, 'That's us off,' to no response.

Next, they saw the back of the van, the Step-Stone truck. An emptiness down the centre of the storage compartment, dark, and on either side transparent windows where the feet of those inside showed through, stacked ten tall, all the way down the length of the vehicle. The driver stepped up into the space.

'Christ,' he said. 'My back.'

The traveller was allocated a space on the bottom rung. A little pedal sat under the compartment, which the driver toed, allowing the sleeping suite to slide out: a thin rubber mattress, pillow, and a panel screwed to the side that read:

IN RARE EVENT OF WAKING MID-TRANSPORT
PLEASE DO NOT SCREAM OR CLAW

He placed the woman down on the mattress and slid her inside the block. Some of the windows were empty. This was only halfway through the uplift portion of the driver's shift. He would pick up travellers from across the city and drive them out of town, where an incredibly complex network of other drivers would become available to the algorithm that dictated his journeys. Some travellers would be exchanged at Newcastle, Birmingham, others taken all the way to London. He would accept cargo travelling from the remains of the West Country; sometimes he'd pass the whole truck over to a fellow driver on layover in Leicester, stopping at a Step-Stone Bothy until he was rescheduled back to Glasgow, Aberdeen, cosmopolitan Uist. It boggled the mind. The sheer choreography of making it come together. The junior loved to think of the sleeping travellers coursing through the autoways of the countries.

Then, the driver hauled himself up into the truck's cabin and the stream showed the vehicle pull out into traffic, and you could only imagine the sensation of responsibility that driver must've operated under, all those souls in his care.

A light mist moved through the city. The scorcher had soured, turning dark and overcast, and everywhere a humid mugginess clung. Juniors on the street looked uncomfortable in raincoats. Seniors sweated, and dark stains showed through on their shirt-backs and armpits.

He felt glad to be heading for the gig. Things in the flat were sour too. Alastair didn't want to talk about it, about Caitlin. He wanted to watch streams and eat lo-kcal ice cream and pull up certain forums on the mobile to read. The junior did his best. It was his job to make sure his senior kept on the straight and narrow, to put on a good face down at Step-Stone, to come out on nights like this and help with the stats.

Ed and Marcin – Marcin's junior, rather – waited on the pavement for him, outside Charlie Bucket's. A poster on the wall outside read:

2020 VISION: OLD TIME FAVOURITES

Tall slim Ed, Caitlin's brother. The junior felt a little scramble of irritation coming from Alastair's presence inside him. Ed of the latest tech and flash trainers and him married to gorgeous

Syd and them doing so well these days. Never saw a shaving rash on folk like Ed. Ed did not sweat in the heat.

Aye, the junior thought, but he's been good to us. He could easily have cut off contact.

Alastair, miles and streets away, seemed to communicate: *And I should be grateful?*

Marcin a better sort. More humble. Stocky and trustworthy and looking like he'd dressed in a hurry. Marcin, the senior, still smoked illicit organics even after all these years. They'd been flatmates, Alastair's first ever, introduced via pub pals in the early days of the city. There was a whole web of them at the time and Marcin had a spare box room. They were good pals. They'd spent most evenings together and Marcin did impressions and knew a lot of good information from uni. He looked different most of the time, hard to pin down physically. His head seemed to change shape and his sallow skin was clarified differently each day.

'There he is,' said Marcin's junior.

Tall slim Ed squinted. 'Some weather, eh?'

The junior brushed himself off. 'Aye. Awful.'

'Shall we go in?' said Marcin. 'I'm getting soaked.'

They walked inside. The floor of Charlie Bucket's was bare concrete, its insides done up all retro with fake posters pasted to the walls, advertising gigs from the designer's imagination. Folk handed their coats in to the cloakroom and a wee chap was by the door checking your mobile's ticket. You could pay extra for a proper paper wristband too, if you wanted to indulge in the old ways of doing things.

The three of them passed through to the darkened room. Ed went to the bar, while the junior loitered beside Marcin at the rear of the crowd. Some pink lights shone across them. He looked through the heads and could tell the vast majority were juniors, with only one or two seniors like Ed in attendance.

Even the word *crowd* stretched its definition. Large spaces hung between individual clusters and you could see most of the stage, even from the rear. A little buzz of irritation leapt in his neck, down his spine. It didn't come from him; he had nothing to be annoyed about. He sensed Alastair thinking: *Remember the stats.*

The junior hurriedly tapped Marcin on the back. 'Nice to see you again,' he said.

Marcin smiled. 'Aye,' he said. 'You too, pal.' He looked on expectedly for a moment, then turned to face the stage, where one sound guy was playing with a guitar.

'What've you been up to?' the junior asked.

Marcin kept facing the stage, where the sound guy played unheard strings. 'Not a lot, mate,' he said. 'Not a great deal.'

Ed returned from the bar, carrying a single beer. 'So what is it then?' asked Ed. 'This band? Some of your old shite, Marc?'

Marcin acted as keeper of legends, obsessed with cultures from the long-ago. Go round his place and you'd get film posters behind frames – Day-Lewis, *Goodfellas*, non-CGI pictures – and plus he'd slide out a compact disc and remind you of how things used to sound. Marcin said the 97ers hadn't got everything wrong. Things were just better then. The junior understood, nearly. He liked the Strokes and Vile Acts as much as anyone, but Marcin could get obsessed.

'They're covers, mostly,' said Marcin.

'Covers, eh,' said Ed, taking a sip. 'No imagination these days. I remember when—'

But before Ed could tell them what he remembered, something in the back of the room disturbed him. Everyone in Bucket's turned at the sound of a door being violently thrown open. It was a boy. Hard to tell the age because a bandana covered the bottom of his face. He strode onto the concrete floor of Bucket's and looked around, shoulders back. He cocked his head. Someone nearby asked him, 'Everything alright mate?' then the noisy stranger left, backing out through the door he'd used, closing it behind him.

'I was saying,' said Ed. 'I remember when folk used to play originals.'

Fucking blowhard, the junior thought – or rather, Alastair thought. The junior himself had no issue with the brother, not really, but apparently Alastair thought different. Fucking blowhard wank, he thought, unable to avoid his senior's vibe. But Ed was fine. He was daft, a bit poncey, but basically fine. Not worth breaking sweat over.

'How've you been anyway?' Ed asked the junior. He widened his eyes, in order to signal the business with Caitlin. 'I was speaking to the old man earlier. He's distraught. He thought you two were the real deal.'

'How's he doing?'

Ed's cheeks burst out. 'Fine, I suppose. I worry about him mentally.' A sip of beer. 'Down there on the farm, all alone.'

And then Marcin shushed them. The lights went down. A few kids walked onto the stage and picked up their instruments – a guitar, a bass, the small one behind drums. The bassist said hello into his mic and told them the name of the song, then they started to play. Immediately, Marcin's head was going, down by the junior's shoulder. He bobbed it in time with the percussion. His lips were pursed as he clicked his tongue.

'What's this band called again?' the junior asked, but no one heard.

They were good players, the kids. One of them had done something with his hair so it stood on end. Not gelled, because the hair was still fluffy. They did the thing where you couldn't tell what the lyrics were. At the end of the first song, they posed in the lights and everyone took photographs, even Marcin who generally frowned on such behaviour.

'That's a good one,' he said, looking at his mobile.

The junior felt a swell of information pass through him as the crowd's images leapt onto the field. He couldn't see the photos, but a definite wave made its way through Bucket's at that point, ebbing then receding. For a while, the band messed around, tuning and detuning their guitars so the amplifiers picked up feedback. At this, Marcin cupped a hand round his mouth and whooped.

'So what's he been saying?' asked the junior. 'Your dad.'

Ed shook his head, eyes to the stage. He leaned a little to the side so the junior could hear better. 'I shouldn't say. Probably a family matter, eh?'

The junior heard the word *family* and remembered a Christmas down in border country, not long after Alastair first started seeing Caitlin properly, him on his stipends and her getting by on bar work. His first visit to the old man's farm and his first with anything like a family since the disaster. He left Marcin back in the flat for a lonely fortnight and went down into the wilds. Caitlin's mother was still going then and the pair of them lived in this red wooden house, but big. This big huge wooden house by a river, almost hidden by violent greens, and Alastair walked across the ford from the car park in a daze, having never really heard birdsong or seen a river's skin punctured by teeming insects.

The family were inside drinking wine around a table – Caitlin's old man, her mother, Ed and Syd. Small lights hung around the place. A wood burner sat against a wall and the smell of stewing food came through a doorway.

They were pleased to see him. The old man leapt up from the table to offer him a hand. He said, 'We've been waiting.'

That first band finished up, a really loud number with the same chord coming again and again, fast. The singer repeated the same word over and over, louder, then they were done. For a while after, they did fake jumps and some people came forward to take close-ups.

'That was magic,' said Marcin. 'I was hoping they'd play "Melt Away", and they did.'

'Aye,' said Ed. 'Good band.' He went for another drink.

'He looks just like him,' Marcin said to the junior. 'The lead singer, doesn't he?'

The junior had zero clue what he was on about, but he said, 'Aye, he does a bit.'

Marcin came a little closer. 'Is everything alright with you and Ed?'

The junior shrugged.

'I just thought, what with Caitlin and all that . . .'

'It's fine. Ed's fine.'

Marcin's face changed, as was its habit. The jowls dangled and the beard sprung. 'I can't believe she just went away. Puff, she's gone.'

The junior couldn't think of anything to say, but understood the necessity of a response. What played well on the stats? Being humble. Not holding onto grudges, definitely. Being the bigger man, always. 'Some things just end, you know? Sometimes it's just the right time.'

Marcin smiled. He understood.

As they waited, a commotion started up, coming from the corridor they'd entered by, the same place the bandana boy burst through. You could hear shouting and scuffed feet and after a while, two new figures entered, one with a full-on horror mask, the other covered up around the mouth like the chap from earlier. A few punters noticed them, but these two made less fuss. All they did was hold the entrance doors of Charlie Bucket's closed behind them, leaning back against it so whoever was after them couldn't get in.

'What's going on there?' asked the junior.

Marcin shrugged. 'It's not like I want to pry or anything, but what happened, man?'

'Looks like something's going on outside,' the junior added.

'Uh huh,' said Marcin. 'We've been worried, me and the senior, you know?'

'It's fine,' said the junior. 'Honestly man, I'm getting on. I am.'

'Where is it you're going?' asked Ed, looming over once more. Two beers this time, to save time.

'No place,' said the junior. 'I was just blethering.'

'Ah,' said Ed. 'Fine.'

The second band were starting up, these four lassies wearing all cowboy things: plaid, denim, tassels. One of them set up a flat machine. A pedal steel, Marcin called it. They did their posing right at the start, waiting for the lights to hit just right, then picked up banjos and guitars and pretended to play. Everyone snapped their mobiles.

'What's going on back there?' asked Ed, thumbing to the folk blocking the doors.

'Who knows?' said Marcin.

'Just young ones playing,' guessed the junior.

The second band started proper and it was pure country, a bit of folk here and there. The singer's voice was high and pure and warbled in the right places as the band played some numbers the junior recognised vaguely. Then, a loud shout from behind, and the intruders were gone, the doors standing open and one weedy staff member peering in.

'These are boring,' said Ed. 'I hate this stuff. Country.'

Marcin scowled, tapped his foot.

Ed drank deep, spilling some of his spare. 'I liked the first ones better.'

The junior felt Alastair's irritation build. He started to get hot around the lower back, under his pits. What was Ed's deal? Why go to a show and stand around slagging the bands?

Well, thought the junior, say something then. Say: easy on mate, it's just cover bands.

Alastair thought back: *Aye very good, and how will that play on the stats?*

If there was one thing guaranteed to fuck you up on the stats, it was aggression. Male aggression especially polled poorly. The metrics did not respond positively to a man acting out in that way and you might see yourself lose multiple points from a badly handled altercation. There were guys at Step-Stone, blue-collar types maybe working in the depots, that the junior knew via field only, and their stats were doomed to languish in the lower reaches since they insisted on beating each other up at weekends. They did everything else right. Nice houses, filled with good-looking ornaments and technologies; nice partners, plus willingness to engage with good-quality cultural products. These guys were streaming obscure gangster dramas and should have been sitting in the upper echelons of the stats, but they let themselves down. You saw it time and time again. They spent the week eating healthy, exercising, streaming and sharing all the ideal content, then binned all that good will by throwing a punch on a Friday night. Well-known streamers got filmed without their knowledge, laying into someone or other; their stats nosedived, they lost their sponsorships. What a waste, the junior always thought. The refugee mindset kept him in check. Even though his senior washed up in a city only a few miles from home, he never felt safe enough to actually display the anger boiling away inside.

He watched the country band finish up. People started to move around in front of them, meaning the show was probably over. He caught someone's eye – a woman's. She stood still as others walked around her, her shoulder bumped by people passing, and she looked so intently at the junior he felt unnerved. Where did he recognise that face from? He tried to roll through his recent memory, but nothing obvious appeared. Then she came closer and he realised: this was Dot, the new-start at work.

'Give me a second,' he said to Ed and Marcin, who were arguing about the second band again. He moved against the crowd, ducking past taller men, until they were close together. He said, 'Do I recognise you?'

She smiled. 'It's Dot.'

'So it is.'

'I was just going and I saw you, so.'

'Same.'

A little moment of uncertainty. He was probably bothering her, and plus Alastair inside was asking: *Is this the girl from work?*

'Did you like the bands?' he asked.

She nodded. 'They were good. I was meant to be coming with pals, then they said they couldn't make it, but I thought, I've already paid.'

'I'm with them two.' He flicked his head back towards Ed and Marcin. 'So how've you been? Did you get settled into the office alright?'

'I did. I did. You were a good help during training.' She laughed. 'You always think those things are going to be awful, don't you? But then they're okay.'

He asked where in the company she'd ended up and she explained. She was a desk hog down in customer acquisitions, just like Alastair when he first started. Often the first rung on the Step-Stone associate ladder. She liked it well enough, but it seemed like a boring gig. There was this one manager, Zivko, who even on her first day had treated Dot really poorly and gave her a horrendous hard time about using her AUX-9 comfort break code too often, even when it was a biological necessity.

'He sounds like a fanny,' said the junior.

Dot laughed. 'He is a bit, yeah.'

And also, what a hassle she'd been having with housing too. The junior knew how bad things were in the city these days, how scarce accommodation could be, especially during July and August, the festival months, when a good portion of the inhabitants packed their things in storage and moved to the Lothian complexes built for this specific purpose. Dot's housemates caused her trouble. They were smelly and took Smurf, but it was still better than when she lived with her ex.

'Your ex?' asked the junior.

'Yeah,' she said. 'My ex. That's how come I'm at Step-Stone now.'

'I didn't realise—' he started to say, but suddenly Ed was barging into the conversation. Tall slim Ed with his fucking jaw and hairline, and this anger came from the junior now, not Alastair, who as far as the junior could tell was taking a backseat to see how the Dot situation would play out.

'Hiya,' said Ed. 'How's it going? Good, yeah? Great. Listen, we're going to make a move. Are you coming?'

Quickly, the junior explained they were going but would probably get a drink somewhere else, on the way home or whatever. Did Dot want to join for a bit? Fine if she didn't.

She looked at the junior, then up at Ed. 'Absolutely,' she said.

Outside, the evening's murk had deepened, grown soupy and dreary. The sky felt very close to each of them as they left Charlie Bucket's and found themselves part of a disturbance in the street. As they came through the corridor, they heard shouting and sirens and pounding feet on pavement. They emerged into a swell, many bodies jostling and elsewhere the shouts of Honey Bee peacekeepers struggling to maintain order. The junior thought: of course, those guys in bandanas.

'Oh,' said Marcin. 'What's all this?'

'Some sort of protest,' said Ed.

'Well obviously,' said Marcin.

They were hemmed in outside Charlie Bucket's, within a small area formed by the bollards at the entrance. There were perhaps two hundred people before them on the short stretch of road and they all covered their faces and carried placards and blew horns and seemed angry and upset and energised.

'What's it for?' asked Marcin.

No one knew. No one knew anyone who'd mentioned protesting, no one knew about something on the news streams that might have riled folk up.

'Let's go,' said the junior, and they made their way through the scrum.

At some point earlier, the streetlamps had been killed and now the only light came from flares and the torches built into the peacekeepers' helmets. Chants started here and there but died out as the group moved through the crowds. A huge percentage of the people around them were juniors – you knew it even with bandanas and masks in the way – and the junior felt a great surge of information, of photographs, of video, being sent into the field. It was like standing atop a tall cliff, creeping to the edge, and wind from the sea sweeping up to meet you. In the wave of data moving through him, the junior felt his connection to Alastair die.

Nearby, a back lurched towards them, someone pushed from their front side, and Dot stumbled close to him. He said, 'Are you okay?' and she said, 'Yeah.'

Around the Big Hotel, they lost Ed and Marcin. Ed would be heading for the tram depot up on Waverley anyway – him and Syd stayed beyond the bypass – and Marcin kept his Old Town rooms despite the cost. So they were alone, Dot and the junior, and the crowds were thinning out anyway, only handfuls of people filming the scene on their mobiles.

'Wow,' said Dot, when they were out the worst of it.

'Wow,' agreed the junior.

'I didn't know about that,' said Dot. 'I wasn't expecting it.'

'Well,' said the junior. 'No, of course not.'

'I just meant—'

'It's fine.'

They went downhill and the junior felt giddy. Something about the music, the riot, this person walking quick beside him. He recalled the early days in the city, when Alastair was emerging from the worst of his fear, when the memories of the disaster were slipping; certain early evenings contained a similar giddiness. He said to Dot, 'Will we go for a drink then?'

And she said, 'Yes please.'

FOUR

A little over half his face felt cold. The rest of it was warm. When the air entered Kim Larson's nostrils, it was cold. When it left, it was warm. Cold air in, warm air out. Through his eyelids, he saw an orb of veiny reddish light: the sun, sat in the window across from him. It was bright enough to make him want to squint his closed eyes. He did this for a moment, then remembered and relaxed those muscles again. He kept all the tendons of his face slack, purposefully loose. His jaw hung below the rest of his head, the lips parted. He could sense the wrinkles on his forehead touching each other. Now and then, parts of him started to hurt. Usually joints. When this happened, he thought to himself, *That's a sensation*, without judgement or movement and the pain quickly diminished.

The meditation came as a prescription from a doctor friend of his. A few years back, at Larson's eighty-fifth birthday party, he got talking to her near the punch bowl. He explained that recently he'd been having trouble sleeping. In the daytime, he felt broadly fine, but when bedtime arrived, he found himself gripped by a powerful anxiety, a sensation that the world was deeply flawed and that he himself, was responsible for the dark pip at the centre of it all. 'Normally I'd write that off as standard paranoia,' the doctor friend had said, 'but in your case Kim, it might just be true. You've got the body of a man two-thirds your age. This isn't physical.' She suggested he ought to try being quiet and still for several minutes at a time, every day. Which he did, haphazardly at first, but with increasing regularity as he entered his ninetieth year.

Air came in and out, heated to various temperatures. Time passed. He pushed away thoughts and feelings until the watch on his wrist pulsed, telling him to open his eyes. At first, the light blinded him, but he soon adjusted. The window showed a wide expanse of turquoise Pacific, with small puffs of cloud bobbing along on top. He looked at the view and knew he felt bad.

Behind him, someone coughed. He swivelled round in his chair and was confronted by a dozen people standing in a row on the far side of his office.

'Good morning,' he said.

'Good morning, Mr Larson,' one of them replied; he didn't care to remember names.

They wanted their day's instructions, it turned out. He dispensed orders to each of them, after asking what their roles were exactly. They seemed pleased enough with his requests and filed out of his office one by one. When they were gone, the room looked extremely empty. He liked it.

He walked through the corridors of his facility until he found a door he recognised. The plate read: *Deborah Stock*, and he went inside. Stock glanced up from her desk and said, 'Morning, Kim. How are you?'

'Pretty good,' he said. He leaned against the wall. The office looked like all the offices in the facility: clean and well-decorated and lit by huge windows. He owned every one of them and enjoyed coming and going as he pleased.

'Can I help you at all?' she asked.

'No,' he said.

'What's on the schedule for today?' She tapped around on her machine and rattled off their morning responsibilities. Stock was his second-in-command and they tended to keep similar routines. Sometimes, when he was up against the blank faces of his employees without Stock at his side, his mind went blank.

He nodded. 'Sounds good.'

Stock sighed. She took her glasses off. 'What's going on, Kim?' she asked. 'You're out of sorts.'

'I'm fine,' he said, shrugging. 'Honestly. It's just one of those days. I've got a bad feeling.'

'You should speak to the warlocks,' Stock suggested.

'Can you set it up?'

'Sure,' she replied. 'And we're still on for tonight?'

'Deborah,' he said. 'We're still on for every night.'

He trusted his gut less and less these days. Thinking back to the early years, up until his fifties really, everything had been slapdash and off-the-cuff. He came up with an idea and didn't think it through; he simply pursued it until it was realised. That felt like a young man's game. Now, possibilities clouded his vision. He began to see invisible paths reaching out from every choice he made, no matter how small. If he ate fruit for breakfast, he'd pay for it at eleven with indigestion. If he stayed up a little later to work on a project, the next day he'd be a zombie. He relied more and more on people like Stock to run ideas past, Stock and the vast reserves of experts at his disposal.

Today, he sat down with one of them. For a long time, Elliott Svaasand had been tasked with monitoring clues from the environment; Larson wanted a team analysing the data continuously, running metrics every day, making predictions. These were his warlocks.

'Can I get you anything?' he asked Svaasand.

The man across from him shook his head. He looked

nervous. A single strand of his greased-back hair had sprung upward like an aerial. 'No,' he said. 'I'm fine.'

'Alright then.' Larson drummed the desk with his fingers. 'So how are we looking?'

Two of Svaasand's fingers clutched at his Adam's apple. 'Pretty good, by all accounts.'

'Excellent news,' said Larson.

'Yes,' nodded Svaasand. 'Yes, I suppose it is.'

Larson decided that next, he would be quiet. All his life, people spoke about him as a genius of technology – the juniors, the field – but what they didn't realise was that he was a people person. He knew people inside and out. You couldn't copy something unless you knew the source material well, and because he knew people, he decided to be quiet.

Svaasand nodded again. He opened his mouth, then closed it.

Larson narrowed his eyes a little. This could be read as a smile or a scowl. He knew exactly how he looked when viewed from across a large, polished desk. Air came into his nostrils shortly before leaving them. Only he could hear the sound it made.

Svaasand chuckled. He said, 'That's really the long and short of it, boss.'

Any usual person, any normal person, they would respond now. Larson felt the urge. It came directly from his deepest mind: when someone speaks, you speak back. But there was something he wanted from Svaasand and he would not budge until it came to him. He decided to tilt the corner of his mouth. As he did, Svaasand coughed. Next, he leaned forward just a touch in his chair. 'I've got a bad feeling, Elliott,' he said.

Relief flooded Svaasand's features; Larson couldn't help but be pleased with the effect.

'Oh,' said Svaasand. 'I see.' He grimaced. 'That's unfortunate.'

'Yes,' said Larson. 'It is quite.'

'Is there anything I can do to alleviate it?'

'You could start by being honest with me.'

Larson thought himself the master of this; the pull-back and reveal. Hold something in for a while, retain it for one, two, three . . . then let it fly. The words leapt across the shiny table and walloped Svaasand, whose head seemed to jerk back from their impact.

'Honest? I am being honest, boss. Things are looking, more or less, pretty good.'

'I know they aren't, Elliott. Do you think I got where I am by being slow?' He pointed to the wide window behind himself. 'That world is fucked, is it not?'

'Well . . .' Svaasand licked his lips. He ran a few fingers across his aerial, only serving to provide it with further spring. 'It depends on what you mean by the word . . . the f-word.'

'You can say it,' laughed Larson. 'I think I'm old enough. It's fucked, isn't it? I can feel it.'

It was his own fault, really. You didn't get to sit where he sat without cracking skulls over the years. You crack enough skulls, people catch wind of the x-rays. Naturally, they want to avoid their own skulls being cracked, so they do their best to stay on the right side of the cracker. They avoid upsetting the cracker, avoid committing themselves to anything much, so that if a situation turns out poorly, they might have a reasonable expectation of their skull remaining whole afterwards. Check the records, I said nothing of value, why should my skull be cracked?

Larson could see this dilemma play out across Svaasand's handsome features now. If he said something definite, something concrete, he would be liable for whatever actions emanated from his speech.

'Things might be . . . a little bit effed,' he admitted.

Larson pressed him. 'On a scale of one to ten, please. One being a picnic in the park with a blowjob afterwards, ten being lava pouring through your peasant village.'

Svaasand puffed out his cheeks. He thought about it. 'Maybe a five?'

'Elliott . . .' Larson warned.

'I'd say maybe, perhaps, an eight, if I was pushed, which I suppose I am being. Pushed. Let's say an eight for argument's sake.'

'An eight.'

'A *light* eight.'

'But an eight, nonetheless.'

'If you like.'

'It's either an eight or it's not. Would you like to downgrade your answer to a seven?'

'It's an eight. Eight, eight, eight.'

'Eight.'

'Eight.'

Larson leaned back in his chair. 'Was that so hard?' he asked.

'No,' said Svaasand, with an expression that indicated it had been very hard indeed.

'So what does an eight mean?'

Svaasand blinked. He put a finger to his nose. 'An eight might mean lots of things. Lots of different things.'

'Elliott . . .' he said again, causing his employee's eyes to cross themselves.

'Fine, okay, let me think.' He stared into empty space for a couple of beats then appeared to steel himself. 'We may have run a couple of models for what an eight might look like, okay? That may indeed be part of the work me and the warlocks have been doing recently, modelling an eight. An eight has all kinds of issues associated with it. Let me finish! I'm not fudging, okay? An eight, as we've envisioned it, might involve a certain degree of sea level increase. An eight might involve a sort of release of some nasty fumes currently lurking under the permafrost upstairs in the Arctic. An eight might involve an unmanageable amount of heat from roughly forty degrees north to forty degrees south. In all honesty, no, we wouldn't be very happy about an eight.'

'And you're saying an eight is what we have.'

'Yes, in a way, I am.'

'I need you to show me,' said Larson. 'I need to see it for myself.'

They came to the laboratory where the warlocks worked. Svaasand entered first and Larson heard him whisper a hurried admonishment to whoever was inside. He followed behind and found two young men on the floor, one of them riding the other like a pony. When they saw him, they leapt up, pushing each other out of the way to stand with their backs to the nearest desk.

'So it's literal horseplay,' he said. 'This is what I'm paying you for, Elliott?'

'I'm sorry, boss, I really am. I'll deal with this later. Come on, come through.'

The horse and his rider did not glance up as Larson passed; they looked so closely at the tiled floor that he could see down the backs of their shirts.

Svaasand led him into the inner sanctum, to the Holy of Holies, where they carried out their predictions. Larson recognised it; the room looked like most of the other computer labs that made up the facility. He recognised too the room's atmosphere, which was identical to most of the rooms he entered: a hushed silence, a tension in the air, everyone trying their best to appear casually busy, no one looking at him as they might with any other guest.

'Mr Larson is here to check up on some of the predictions we've been doing,' said Svaasand. 'He knows you're all working hard and he wants to show his appreciation by being interested in it.'

A few of the men and women glanced in his direction. One or two smiled with thin lips. He knew they hated him. It didn't matter to them that everything positive in their life flowed out of him; because he bossed them around, they hated him. He could see and feel this truth without being hugely concerned by it. There had been a time as a younger man that the world's distaste frustrated him. What do they want from me, he used to ask himself. I gave them everything they needed, everything they wanted, everything they asked for, and still it's not enough. He saw himself as a skeleton, vast as a landscape, with all the world's creatures picking over his bones like carrion birds. He saw himself as a tureen of liquid that they supped from, cup by cup, until nothing remained but the container.

He ignored their glances and followed Svaasand through to a smaller room, his personal lab.

'Here's the machine,' explained Svaasand, switching on a vast viewing screen.

'Looks good,' said Larson.

'You should know,' said Svaasand. 'You bought it.'

He messed around for a while, until the screen showed a revolving graphic of planet Earth. The two men watched it turn, like a vision beamed in directly from the moon's surface. You could see the green and ochre continents covered by cloud swirls, large swathes of ocean slowly edging round before their eyes.

'So now I'm going to run an eight,' said Svaasand, touching the screen. 'And we'll see.'

Larson watched his employee enter some information into the screen. Then they sat back and watched the planet carry out its natural rotation. They watched the land around the equator turn brown and crispy; they watched beaches and tides surge inland, creating new islands and deltas; they watched smoke rise from the globe's edges, plunging out and dissipating in the darkness of space; they watched the poles spring into horrendous life.

Larson observed for a few moments, then said, 'Turn it off.'

'We've only just started,' explained Svaasand. 'This is only stage two of an eight. We can—'

'Turn it off,' he repeated, raising his voice.

Svaasand reached forward to freeze the image in place.

'I said turn it off,' he said. 'Turn it off, now.'

Svaasand scrambled to blacken the screen, hunching over the input until it went dark. Afterwards, they sat together in silence. He couldn't believe the things he'd seen, the destruction, the carnage. Really, it was the last thing he needed.

On the way out, he found the two young warlocks that had been tomfooling when he arrived.

'You two,' he said. 'Come with me.'

'Is everything okay?' asked Svaasand.

'Everything's hunky-dory,' he replied.

He passed the day in a fugue. He went in and out of meetings, usually with Stock at his side, and did a good job of being present. It helped to have her there to translate the language he couldn't quite grasp, to explain for others the things he mumbled. After one long, number-laden discussion, he drank a decaf with Gerald Krause, someone high up in the marketing department, he reckoned. He found it hard to keep track.

'Did you know the world's ending?' he asked Krause.

Krause laughed. He was a tall man with a deep chest. The noise was substantial. 'I didn't know that. I thought we got it fixed.'

'It's true,' he said. He tipped the decaf to the side to look at the bottom of his cup.

'Well I think that's excellent,' Krause said. 'I think that's thoroughly excellent news.'

Larson could think of nothing to reply, except, 'Why?'

'People spend a lot of money when they think things are hopeless, don't they?'

This confused him. It didn't sound correct at all. 'That doesn't sound right,' he said.

Krause shook his head. 'People put on serious weight during times of stress, because they're stuffing their faces with caramels and baked buns. It's a known fact. We know all about it in our expertise. The destruction impulse forces the organism to expel its resources so they might be picked up afterwards by the rest of the herd, the pack. Everyone knows that.'

Larson didn't think he'd heard that theory before. It seemed wrong to him somehow, but who could argue with expertise? 'I didn't realise,' he said meekly.

'Oh yes,' Krause assured him. 'It's very true. You might be surprised to learn ... remember the big drought, was it maybe ten years back?'

Larson remembered it well.

'There has not been a better quarter in terms of junioring before or since. Record numbers applied, record numbers of juniors went into the world. It was a boom.'

'I see,' said Larson, but he didn't see. What he saw was a burning world, slowly turning. He zoomed in on the burning world and saw a little miniature of himself placed on top, choking in the smoke and ashes.

'I assume you're talking figuratively?' asked Krause. 'What is it? Are we running low on some resources?'

'Yeah,' nodded Larson. 'Something like that.'

After the meeting, he went back to his office alone. The two warlocks were sitting outside where he'd left them, gripping their knees, watching the wall across from them as per his instructions. He liked to see people following the rules he set out for them. In his experience, when things went wrong, it was usually down to a too-many-cooks situation. Too many individual minds trying to force their opinion in where it wasn't wanted. One strong mind did a better job than a suite of substandard specimens.

'You two,' he said as he walked by. 'Come inside.'

They were both juniors, the horseplayers. They were young men, each in their early thirties, each with the unmistakable hum of junior physiology. Not that it mattered. He treated all races, all examples of the species equally, being in a sense their father. They went down into the chairs on the far side of his desk and the blond one started talking right away, like sitting released some plug in his gullet.

'Mr Larson, sir, I'm so sorry. We're so, so sorry,' he gabbled. 'Me and Jim were on our break and blowing off steam. We just—'

He held up a finger. He didn't want to listen to what they had to say.

'It's true, sir,' said the one called Jim. 'Honestly, it was. We didn't mean to be disrespectful to you or your work. That's the last—'

He kept holding his finger upright, kept pointing it towards the ceiling above. Eventually, young Jim looked at the finger and stopped his yammering.

'That's better,' said Larson. 'I don't like to listen to people talking unless I've asked them to, and I haven't asked either of you to speak, so.'

'No,' said the blond one. His friend nudged him in the ribs.

'Listen,' said Larson. 'I don't care if you want to get down on your knees, in the dirt, and pretend like you're horses. If that's what gets you off, that's what gets you off.'

Both men nodded. They started smiling.

'I mean this in a purely personal capacity, of course.'

They continued smiling, nodding with further vigour.

'As a businessman, however, what am I supposed to do? I'm supposed to witness employees riding each other like horses and just pass on by? I'm supposed to take that in my stride?' Their faces fell. The pull-back and reveal, reliable as always. 'Let me ask you a question. Think very carefully about this, your jobs may depend on it.'

'Please,' said the blond one.

'Go right ahead,' said Jim.

He rolled his tongue around inside his mouth, tasting the shape of the slippery lump. 'Do either of you know where in the world I was born?'

The two juniors froze. They blinked their eyes a hundred times between them. Both looked like they wanted to stand up, put on their jackets, and walk out into the pale afternoon.

'I suppose,' said the blond one, 'that where you're born doesn't *really* matter. What really matters is where you come into your own, and I'd have to argue you came into your own—'

'I'm not talking metaphors here, son,' he said. 'I'm talking geography.'

'Understood, completely,' said the blond junior. He looked to his colleague. 'You were saying the other day how you knew a fair bit about Mr Larson, weren't you Jim?'

'Was I?'

'You were.'

'Oh,' said young Jim. 'It might have slipped my mind . . .'

'I was born in Scotland,' said Larson. 'I lived there until I was twelve years old. I was brought up by my aunts.'

He spoke the truth. He lived the first decade of his life in a small, clean tenement building in a city south of the ruined peninsula, which at the time was whole and green. His parents died within a year of each other, both before his second birthday, his mother succumbing to breast cancer and his father jumping into the Forth the following New Year's Day. In other words, an abandonment. His father did not want to care for young Kim, did not love him sufficiently, so selected abandonment instead. It was just one of those things. They happened now and then.

Of course, he didn't remember his parents. He didn't care to think of them much. However, he did reflect on the time spent with his aunts, Fiona and Claire, the ladies who adopted him as a tot. They moved in with each other in order to share the burden, and, as he grew, they took the time to remind him of the hardship his arrival caused them. They explained to him clearly the financial burden he was, bemoaning the experiences he'd caused them to miss out on.

The one good thing they did for young Kim, other than provide nourishment and shelter, was to let him come along on the annual trips they took. Big groups of their friends congregated in various villages on the west coast and had fun drinking together, listening to music, playing card games he couldn't keep up with. He spent time watching the ocean. He watched the water move, expanding and contracting, bulging like breath.

'Fascinating,' said the blond junior.

'I think I did know that, actually,' said Jim.

'It's a nice country,' Larson observed. 'Wouldn't you say?'

They both agreed with the fullest enthusiasm; Jim looked liable to sprain his neck from nodding.

'We have facilities out there, you know? We have places waiting to be used.'

'Sure,' agreed Jim.

'It's a known fact,' agreed the blond one.

'If we needed to make a journey, there's places in the home country that would be as good as any. As good as anywhere else in this world.' He went quiet for a while, not in order to intimidate the juniors, purely because he needed time to think.

You got some of your best thinking done when people were watching it happen. 'Okay,' he said, eventually. 'I guess we've covered everything we need to. Does all of that make some sort of sense?'

The two juniors agreed that it did. Then he realised they didn't know yet.

'I should add that you're both dismissed, as of today.'

'What?' one of them asked.

'As of this second, I mean. You're both gone, lads. I'm sorry, but it's decided. When you leave this room, there'll be a muscular gentleman waiting to escort you outside.'

There followed a brief period of pleading, of passionate reasoning, most of which he was able to surf through on autopilot. He saw but did not experience the anguish in their faces. He watched one of them burst into tears, his face red and shiny and wet, and he thought: *That's a sensation.*

The day turned into night. He sat in front of the big window and watched the sky and sea turn satsuma coloured. He thought about the wrecked world, about all the little pieces of himself that scurried across it. Some men, they want a legacy. Some men want a legacy, so they shoot their stuff into a womb and give their name to what crawls out. He didn't need that; a significant portion of the population owed him life. His field hung across the land like a thick fog, powering everything, beaming data into all corners of human experience. The word *Larson* was written on the very molecules one breathed. His legacy was assured.

But it wasn't his fault. He inherited a fucked planet. It came pre-fucked, so who could blame him if he made it a little fucked-er? Was he supposed to dedicate his life to growing organic muesli plants on a kibbutz somewhere? If anything, he'd helped the world. Nearly all the field's power came from renewables, didn't it? He'd done his best to right the ship, and still they would blame him, he thought, the little scurrying pieces of himself.

He leaned over and pressed the command that made blinds slide across the window, cutting away the landscape, inch by inch. Watching it all disappear, he experienced a measure of grief inside his chest; he found he didn't want to leave it all behind.

At the end of the corridor, light shone out around the edge of a doorframe. Larson knew this doorframe well; he walked towards it in this manner most evenings. Most evenings, he ambled down this corridor completely unobserved, leaving all mobiles and most other devices behind, technologically stripped. The walls in this area of the building had special lining to stop the field encroaching in any way, shape or form.

The doorframe's light made a sort of sideways staple, an image that had been burned into his neurons through repetition; when he saw the shape, he began to feel aroused. His mind recognised the shape and sent signals to the fleshy parts of him that said: *get ready*. He came to the door and opened it, stepping inside.

The room within was bright and unwindowed. Its décor was different to every other space inside the facility, resembling more than anything else a family living room from the early millennium. None of the contemporary fittings could be found here, only an old-fashioned viewing screen, some flat-pack bookcases, an overstuffed couch.

'Hello Kim,' said Deborah. She sat on the edge of the couch, flicking through a magazine.

'Hi Deb,' he said.

They didn't say much to each other in these meetings, at least not at first. There was little point; they'd covered every piece of business during the day. The only subjects left on their minds were the things that could not be said. He walked over to the armchair and took off his signature baseball cap, throwing it onto a pillow. He unbuttoned his shirt and slid it off his shoulders. There had been a time when undressing depressed him. He didn't like to look down at his greying chest hairs, his purpling stomach, his nuts. These days, he didn't pay it much mind.

He was now naked, except for the necklace he wore every day of his life: a loose chain that carried a slim black lozenge, equipped with a button that would respond to only Larson's thumbprint. Hardly anyone knew he owned this object and carried it on his person 24/7, but it was his most prized possession. Next, he stepped over to a short ottoman and opened it up. It contained a huge quantity of pristine white nappies. He selected a pair from the top and stepped into them, securing the fastening at his hips. They fit him snugly. The comfort around his groin was like a pair of soft cupped hands supporting his genitals.

He sat down beside Stock. He leaned against her, resting his head on her shoulder. She closed the magazine.

'We're going to have to make some plans,' he said, eventually.

'You spoke to Svaasand?'

'Yep.'

'It's not looking good?'

'Deb, it's looking bad.'

'Well, Kim,' she said. 'We'll need to make some plans.'

Larson nodded. It felt good when Stock told him what he already knew. He explained to her he'd been thinking of the old country. He'd been thinking of the slowly beating waters that gave him his first big idea: an ocean in the air.

He said, 'Deb, I think we have to go. There's only so much time.'

'Then we'll go,' she said. 'It's been on the back burner for a while now. Tomorrow, I'll pull up the list and start contacting people.'

He nodded. He plucked at the waist of the nappy, ran fingertips through belly hairs.

'I want to go from Scolpaig,' he said. 'That's where I want to go from.'

'Then that's what we'll do,' she said. Her voice was soft, maternal. 'We have something in the works there, we can piggyback.'

He righted himself, sitting back on the sofa, closer to the cushion. He shifted around, straightening out the nappy. The two of them looked at each other and Stock glowed with warmth, as he expected her to do.

'Baby's hungry,' he said.

'What's that?' she asked. 'What are you saying?'

'Baby's *hungry*,' he repeated, a nagging whine creeping into his voice.

'Well if baby's hungry, then he'd better get fed,' said Stock, shifting closer to him, her glow increasing, a powerful radiator's heat bursting over him. In that high temperature, he could ask for anything, anything at all, and feel completely and utterly at ease.

Later, after he'd cleaned himself up, he went to his private rooms on the eastern edge of the facility. His kitchen was reliably stocked with bio ingredients, but the staff were asleep, so he cooked himself some toasted bread and butter. He wore a bathrobe and ate the food while watching some of the news streams, some of the financial round-ups. He saw his own stocks charging up the charts, towering above the competition. That felt good. That helped.

When the toast was gone, he put his fingers in his mouth to

suck off the butter. As they were in there anyway, he pressed onto his tongue and created a long, loud whistle. The sound rang through the apartment shrilly. He waited. He paused, then heard a thud from a far-off room; the muffled landing of his animal.

You could sense it moving along the corridor, his animal, his invention, and then it was there, standing in the doorway.

He raised a hand, and it came forward to smell.

FIVE

Alastair slumped back into the couch. The Calcyon One viewing screen was blank. Not even its little owl logo showed up, just a great rectangle of nothingness.

'What the . . .' he whispered to himself, staring at the blank screen, where only a moment before a live stream of the group leaving Bucket's had played. He turned the screen off then on again. He went into the hallway and checked the field uplink, the little box nestled beside their flume. A small light winked green, meaning: *you're part of it.* The field's slogan, repeated often: *you're part of it.* He pulled up the locator on his mobile. It showed a map, with his junior represented as a little red J, exactly where he was supposed to be.

Back to the couch, where he threw himself down. All around him were empty meal sachets – Ultimate Gumbo, I Dream of Tagine, Pork Supper – zero-kcal beer tins, plus the evidence of masturbation. He was unwashed, unshaven, wearing clothes he'd never be seen dead in on the field. He noticed all this accumulated mess in a physical sense, but his eye passed over its implication, because he knew he was fine. He was doing well. Don't worry about the loss of stream, he told himself. The junior probably went to a place with bad field coverage. The pub probably lined its walls in lead paint, blocking out proper bandwidth for streaming. Probably.

He sat for a few seconds. He felt itchy. His left shoulder began to ache slightly. He sniffed.

But what if the junior turned it off on purpose? Was that possible?

Alastair leapt up and went back to the hall, to the cupboard there, finding the info pack JNR sent him. Was there anything there about self-censoring the live stream? The pack contained a slim booklet, full of images of juniors and seniors enjoying themselves, sharing canoes, picking grapes. There was a photo of a junior's face, all pastel shades and attractively shining cheekbones, vacantly smiling off into the middle distance, and text explaining the important technology that went into crafting a junior's features.

Alastair sighed.

He walked through the rooms of the flat, looking at items he hadn't looked at for a while. Lots of Caitlin's things, still in place. He'd heard, after a breakup, you were meant to dispose of the departed party's possessions, out of fear they'd depress you. He didn't get that. Caitlin's stuff – her puffy shower ball, her old running shoes – he didn't connect them to her somehow. So they were still present, everywhere, in this house he could no longer afford. The rent was enormous, and plus there were bills every month for Honey Bee, for Pyreol, for all other domestic services.

As he walked, he began to itch again. Around the kitchen doorway, he smelled this odour. It crept into his nostrils, and it was the smell of his old man. Whatever specific deodorant he'd used and his scratchy clothing and his fruity beard oil. Alastair shivered, moving quickly along the dark hallway and into the comfort of his filth nest, among the sachets and other rubbish. He picked up the mobile and scrolled. He scrolled solidly for twenty minutes, losing himself in the flow.

Across town, people were protesting about something or

other and a few contacts were checking in, the field showing them below the bridge, their faces covered with hankies or something. He felt a small blow of envy. A protest was exactly the sort of thing he should be getting himself involved in, or sending the junior to anyway. The gig with Ed and Marcin played well on the stats, but it wasn't anything special. Loads of folk sent their juniors out to watch music, to see art or attend book launches or whatever; only a select few got involved in riots.

And now there was this Dot character, who Alastair recognised from Step-Stone. Someone to keep an eye on, he thought, especially if the junior felt the need to turn off his ... But no. An accident. Just an accident.

He watched something once, years ago, probably a pop-science stream fronted by a celebrity intellectual, that said we don't really care about getting things. It's actually the waiting, the wanting of the thing, that turns us on. The desperation for the thing. He could vouch for that. Christ, the things he'd wanted. The viewing screen in front of him, for example. It stretched two metres corner to corner, taking up an entire corner of their living room. It could link you up with your choice from the thousands of stream broadcasters. Its blacks were a deeper, truer black than tar. It was too large to get delivered by flume, so some actual guys came round with it in a van. They carried it up the stairs one day, long before he juniored, and dumped the bulky package in Alastair's hallway, blocking the cupboard. It had *Buchanan* in big letters on the side. The day it arrived, he stood admiring the box, relishing the culmination of a delicious process.

That process began with starting to feel dissatisfied with the previous viewing screen. Noticing, during movies maybe, or a celebrity house tour, that some of the colours were a little off.

See, they'd streamed *Inside the Mansion: LuAnne Box* when him and Caitlin were visiting her brother, and the pinkness of Luanne's mansion really, truly popped on Ed's viewing screen, and the blue of LuAnne's junior's eyes sparkled, so that when he and Caitlin came home, he streamed *Inside the Mansion* on their screen and compared the popping of the pinks and the sparkling of the eyes. Their model was an YR30, whereas Ed and Syd owned a YR32. That was the first step: gentle dissatisfaction.

The part that came next involved sort of casually browsing catalogues for the newest models, looking up reviews on his mobile, ascertaining the resolutions and added features of the YR36, or even the Calcyon One, if he wanted to push the boat out. On the field, everyone agreed those were the big daddies of viewing screens, the biggest bang for one's buck. But the price of those things. It was insane. Ridiculous. He would flick the reviews away with his thumb and get back to whatever he and Caitlin were streaming and be like, What's the problem with this? This is fine. And he would forget about the issues with the YR30 for hours at a time, until he got back to thinking about the money.

He worked hard, didn't he? He put the hours in at Step-Stone, when others chose to shirk their responsibilities. And besides, it was a false economy, wasn't it, to buy cheap? Consider the poor destitute person, who could only afford the thinnest of jackets, which went on to become destroyed in a matter of weeks, meaning said person had to buy another coat, when if they'd been able to afford proper, waterproof outerwear in the first instance it would probably have lasted a lifetime. That was Alastair's bind.

He now knew he *needed* a new viewing screen, that much was clear, so the only real decision was whether to go cheap and end up spending more in the long run, or go expensive and make a saving. When you looked at it like that, it was easy to approve the spend, to order the Calcyon One, which had all sorts of functionality built in that the YR models didn't, and then, because the Calcyon One was too large for the flume, to get leave approved from work and wake up bright and early – too early probably, considering the deliveries didn't start until 08:00 – wake up bright and early and wait. And that morning of waiting was the whole entire process shrunk down.

He made a decaf, fresh from the pod, and pulled up a news stream. There was Nye Morgan reading the headlines. It was the real deal too; you didn't usually get juniors on the news streams. Good old Nye glowered into the camera, describing the previous day's happenings, the foreign atrocities, and good old Nye talked about an upcoming event in the capital, giving out the stream details, and he wore a little sardonic half-smile that told you this was sponsored content.

The old viewing screen looked like a piece of junk. You could barely make out the strands of Nye's signature black beard. It didn't give you the names of the interns milling about unfocused in the background of the shot, so you couldn't pull them up on the field and see their feed and make a judgement about their stats in relation to your own. In fact, nothing got synced to your mobile, so if Nye said that partisans were massing on a border somewhere, you had to manually search for it on the field and try to work out which was the best page to read more about the partisans, if the border was even somewhere of interest. It was pathetic that he and Caitlin had made do with this old technology, and in fact, as he waited, he felt sort of proud of himself for having rejected the newest models for so long. Some people out there, people like Ed, had to have the best of the best. They got new mobiles on release day. They queued for trainers. So what if he was buying the best of the best now, when they'd endured the previous viewing screen for, what, four years? That was fair. That was justified.

But then at the end of Nye's round-up, something came up about Australia and all the problems they were having down there with the weather and the fires and Alastair began to experience guilt. The living room felt small and cramped. He went to the window to check for the delivery van. There was nothing downstairs except parked cars, a few small children playing in the park with their parents' juniors. He thought about what the cost of the Calcyon One could have purchased for the poor Australians. The mosquito nets, the sandbags. It was the sensation of having eaten something gigantic and absent of nourishment. A vast hollow creamcake of a sensation, and with the calories uploaded to the field so you then dealt with the shame of everyone knowing your excesses.

But come on. What was he playing at? It was a telly at the end of the day. Everyone needed a telly. You couldn't be in the world, not properly, if you weren't able to access the news streams or whatever. He watched the children playing. It was a good neighbourhood, if a little run down. Some people, people like Ed, lived beyond the bypass with their gates and moats. Alastair was hardly Prince Lucas or Princess Xi.

That good feeling carried him until the guys arrived with their van and hauled the box upstairs and left it in the hallway, with its crisp corners and various taped barcodes on its sides. The unpacking was another part of the process, perhaps the most important of all: the compressed bark cushioning, the protective plastic wrap on the screen. He unpacked at half-speed, relishing each moment, folding the packaging up and replacing it in the box, measuring the wall so he could slide the hanging clasps into place. And then, the apex: switching on.

He pressed the pad. For a few seconds, the screen stayed dark, apart from a small orange animation at its centre: an owl marching down a never-ending road. The Calcyon Owl. Inside its technology, the machine linked itself up to the field for power and for data. This was what the owl's march represented. In time – in no time at all, really – a little house appeared at the road's terminus and Alastair said, out loud, 'There it is,' and the little owl went inside the house and the animation zoomed in on its welcome mat, which read *WelCyon!*, and then the screen came to life and all Alastair's fears were put to bed. The pinks and blacks! The menus! His favourite streams were already pre-loaded onto the homepage. He chose *News* and it was like he'd installed a window into his wall and on the other side sat good old Nye Morgan himself, reading the headlines. You could see every follicle on Nye's distinguished face. The entire pane was alive with information and content and he fumbled in his pocket for the mobile. It knew he was the proud owner of a Calcyon One and all the information he needed – the guides, the manuals, the data agreements – were autoloaded in a manner of such simplicity and ease that a sort of luxuriant palm closed his eyes for him.

Caitlin came home later and agreed it was a good piece of technology, but wasn't he worried about missing the time from work?

'No,' he said, even though it was a matter of some concern. There would be raised eyebrows the next day, for sure, but it was worth it. Some things you took the flak for, you took the hit on your stats. All that would turn around once he got Shun and the rest of the team around for a film night, and they saw the nicely decorated flat, how their furnishings were ethically sourced and sustainable. He would pull up a foreign language movie from the field and they'd all watch and comment about it on their mobiles and the lost day would be forgotten.

In total, the excitement of the viewing screen lasted many, many days. Perhaps a week. After a week, anything could become usual. After a week, even the newest thing, the newest item of technology, melted into the background of daily life. He spent a good three days marvelling at the Calcyon One, really truly noticing every time it exceeded his expectations, every time it gave him something he didn't know he wanted. The day after work, for example, when he was scrolling on the mobile, waiting for Caitlin to get home, and he read something about the 97ers and he couldn't quite remember who they were and as he started to type *who are the 97e ...* on a new tab of his mobile, the Calcyon One sprang to life and the little orange owl waved to him and pulled up a heavily animated video where a guy in a bedroom told the camera the whole story of the 97ers, where the group had formed, what its aims were, etc. It was so easy that he wasn't even listening. He was merely relaxing in his ease.

But it went. The luxury waned. The feeling of having arrived at the end of a long, tiring journey, much as the little cartoon owl had done on the animation, began to fade. The satisfaction of having worked hard for the money the Calcyon One cost, he forgot. Soon, within a week, the viewing screen was part of the furniture and he expected it to meet its side of the bargain. He began to notice when it delayed a little on start-up, or when a few lines of transmission flickered or warped. Once, during a stream of comedy, live comedy, the screen went black for three, four seconds and they missed a punchline. It wasn't much, but it got logged inside somewhere. He didn't want it to; he couldn't help but pop that indiscretion on a little list, and even though he didn't realise it, the list would grow over the years and be present at some future date when Caitlin's brother upgraded to the YR45, say, with all-new features. The remembrance of the missed punchline would float up in his mind, dull, barely legible, as damning as a crime.

But still. But still. This was the nature of life, wasn't it?

77

You worked, you spent. What else was there to do with your money, other than use it to buy things that made you happy for an un-infinite length of time? Was that so wrong, that your happiness was un-infinite? You couldn't blame the viewing screen, or Calcyon themselves, for the fact that nothing lasted forever.

And anyway. That was a viewing screen, or a telly as he'd called them over on the peninsula. A telly was a telly. Fun for a bit, but there to perform a function. A telly was nothing, nothing at all, like a junior. It was nothing like a junior, he told himself, but even still, there were times he wondered whether he'd made a mistake in allowing himself to be copied.

After another ten minutes, Alastair heard something. The room by now was quite dark and nothing illuminated him except moonlight and the faint glow of the mobile's screen. He heard a single footstep come from the direction of the kitchen. The solitary pat of a shoe, heavy with its body's weight, landing on tile.

He scrolled a while longer. Someone needed money to help one of their Aussie relatives. He scrolled further and didn't hear anything else, but became convinced he was no longer alone. You couldn't say why, exactly, but you knew when a place was inhabited. A human sense, surely, but now clearly misfiring. He put down the mobile. From his position on the couch, he peered through the open door, down the corridor. Everything stayed dark; nothing moved.

'It's my imagination.' He said it aloud to himself, but quietly, just in case.

He did not believe in the supernatural. He carried no religion. In the suburbs of his childhood, God and Jesus were for streams, not real people. Your great-great-grandparents ... even they probably only got it at school, for Easter or Christmas or whatever. The world was what was real. But then why was he shivering slightly? So much like a footstep, the sound, but it couldn't be, because he was home alone. He knew that. No back doors, obviously; nowhere for anyone to get in. Ghosts were a superstition. Science had proven that, hadn't it? He felt very scared, very alone. More than anything, he wanted Caitlin to come through the front door, all breezy and disorientated from a day of work, but still smiling when she saw him.

I'll just check, he thought. I'll go through and check and that can be the end of it, and there won't be anything there because there's nowhere to get in and I know there's no one there, and at most it'll be a mouse. At the very most.

He got up and left the room. A light flickered on the hallway floor, coming from the kitchen. Maybe the microwave's display. Maybe the washing machine's display.

He waited on the threshold. There was a household hammer, wasn't there? It was probably stored somewhere inaccessible though. For a second, he considered finding it, but what would he do with a weapon? Kill an intruder, like an American? No, he'd be too embarrassed, cause you'd have to double-check they *were* an intruder in the first place, before you even swung ... and anyway! He was alone!

He went into the kitchen and saw someone stood there.

A man, and also not a man.

The man's form bristled at its edges, spiky from electrical current, and you could see the fridge through his torso. He was sort of hunched over, slouched at the shoulders, staring down into the sink and not moving, not talking.

Alastair froze. He was not afraid. Instead, all he thought was: *huh.* So death wasn't the end after all. Lives continued beyond and everything he believed in was bullshit. He knew all this because a dead man stood there in his kitchen. He recognised it as a dead man, cause it was the old man, his dad. The same dad who got himself crushed by a collapsing semi-detached sixteen years ago, whose junior got himself vaporised as he worked nightshift out at the ethylene plant. That was how come he knew.

It had been a time of dogs. A time *for* dogs. A fortnight where dogs roamed the land, unleashed, unowned, free to come and go as they pleased. A time where dogs ranged wild, genuinely happy, sometimes panting, allowed to maul without discretion. Hordes of pugs, battalions of German shepherds, big long crocodiles of beagles moseying nose-to-tail, swarming poodles. Within hours of the disaster, they regressed to feral states, losing collars, growing mad tufts of fur in unexpected places, teaming up in inter-breed gangs to steal meat, to corner feline victims, to howl. A good time for dogs.

It was a time, too, for rubble. Such shapes of rubble. No one realised how many forms rubble took til then. Whole streets formed of nothing but smashed teeth of rubble, out-of-town malls razed to amusement parks of rubble with stringy iron rope bursting free like spiders' legs. Rubble meant dust. Sometimes the collar of a T-shirt became necessary as a make-shift mask when darting from one place of hiding to another. Sharp rubble, dull rubble. Abstract art rubble and rubble that was basically grain. Packs of dogs scurrying across rubble, barking at cracks where the smells of juicy bodies leaked out.

What else? A time of fires, certainly. The unbelievable variety of fires the world hid, all of them waiting to burst forth at any time. You got the sense that the natural state of the planet was to be on fire, that the purpose of all human civilisation had been to quell those flames. Stalks of fire reaching to the sky, turning black as they birthed taller smoke towers. Low-lying, invisible fires in certain valleys, wanderers at first thinking their legs had brushed by nettles before understanding it was too late. The homestead on fire: a classic image. Everyone knew what it meant when they saw it. Lumps in the throat at an all-time high, a record high for the area.

They all came to appreciate that the sun behaved weirdly when buildings and structures were gone, even more so when dust and smoke were introduced to the mix. If you could tear yourself away from the fear of dog attacks, of flash fires, of rubble slips ... the mad shit those suns would get up to. They swelled with the blood of the world. They lurked for hours down near the horizon, red eyes bursting in contact with distant mountaintops. Clouds of particulated matter passed overhead and lit themselves up like fresh bruises.

A time, one supposed, for freedom too, though it seemed churlish to acknowledge it. Some were ready. Some had been waiting entire lifetimes for accountability to vanish, and out came the ropes and knives and vans with upholstered backs. Some finally gave into temptations that had plagued them since adolescence, and naturally the most vulnerable suffered. For the vast majority though, there was indeed a queasy freedom to be found among the carnage.

A time for screaming. A time for running barefoot.

Alastair thought of that first morning, the survivors of the neighbourhood wandering the ruined street in various stages of undress. Carol Aitken held bloodied baby clothes to her chest, Frank MacIntosh squawked over and over: *The field's no working the field isnae working,* waving his mobile's screen to prove it. Alastair's own mum and dad were gone, he knew. They'd been asleep upstairs when the tremor came down the A92, crumpling the road like foil, reaching their home and collapsing it sideways. Alastair, in the garden sneakily vaping, was saved. He didn't see the bodies, but knew they were demolished. The old man's junior was working nights out at the ethylene plant. You had to assume he was away now too.

Later, Alastair would grieve, but for now, in the queer dawn of hot fires and helicopters passing, he felt little. He needed his parents to tell him what to do. Out on his ruined road, with neighbours flailing around, he didn't know who to stand beside or what to say. He wasn't wearing trousers or shoes and he worried about what his pants would show. His Vile Acts Grand Bullring Tour T-shirt was torn from oxter to waist from getting over the ruins of the kitchen wall. He could sense lots of dusty material across his mouth and eyelashes.

The neighbours made their way to the old high school building, where many others assembled. Carol Aitken disappeared en route, saying something about the baby, and Frank MacIntosh was jogging back and forth in the crowd outside the school, still trying to tell folk about the lack of field. Someone got the doors open and they all rushed in. He went alongside a stranger. Their arm was busted up but the skin hadn't broke. You could see all these sharp parts moving below the surface.

Someone else pushed him out the way, from behind, and he slid down the wall, pulling his legs in to stop them getting trampled by the surging bodies. Already the dogs were starting to howl. Dogs howling, the impotent scream of fire engine sirens, helicopters rotoring, bare feet slapping on tiles. He'd just give up. He'd huddle there in this school, his own old school, and afterwards they'd find his fossil skeleton like those poor bastards out in Pompeii. Even in that moment of acute terror, there was an understanding of afterwards. This would pass. There would be a future time where whatever-happened was resolved, he just wouldn't be there to witness it.

A hand slapped his mouth. It belonged to Mrs Birdie, the mum of his friend Jayden. She was furious. 'Get up,' she said.

'Where's Jayden?' he asked.

She looked at him. 'Get up.'

He pushed himself up the wall. Mrs Birdie's big arm went

round his shoulders and protected him into the crowd. In close, he could hear she was humming, very softly. He felt thankful for the feel of her terry dressing gown.

The people congregated towards the main hall of the school. Someone would be waiting there to tell them what to do. A figure of authority in suit and tie, or emergency gear, a clipboard with everyone's names printed out and plans being made for a return to the status quo. Loads of those silver blankets. Hot drinks. Naturally, nothing of that description presented itself. It was only locals; no one from the outside could get in. People rushed around, trying to see who else had made it. The walls rung with shouting and crying. For the first time, Alastair smelled real fresh blood in volume.

'What happened up your way?' he asked Mrs Birdie. She lived near the playing fields with Jayden and the stepdad.

'I don't know, son,' she said. 'I was up early for work and was just away for a shower and I started feeling something. All the walls and that were shaking. I had to sit down for a minute cause I thought it was me, then a photo falls off the sideboard, so I knew.'

Such a weird feeling, too, being in the old school. He was in fourth year up at the new-build and hadn't been back here since the middle of second, when it shut down. Damp stained the roof. Areas of wallpaper bulged from whatever ruin was stored beneath. Tiles peeled off the floor in places where no one convalesced. Just complete and utter abandonment. Around him, cheeks shone from tears, genuine adult men sat on the floor with their legs stuck out like teddy bears. Mums ran and pushed at full speed, turning bairns' faces up to check for genetic connection.

He said to Mrs Birdie, 'What'll we do?'

She shrugged. 'Just wait and see, I suppose. They've got helicopters out, haven't they, so something's got to happen.'

They spent the morning in the hall as the numbers there grew. Someone found a source of water in the chemistry lab and basins of cloudy water got passed through the crowd. Eff-all to eat though, only messy gulps of the warm chemistry water. By the afternoon his stomach ached, his eyes blurred from the dust in the air. These older teenagers, ones he sort of recognised from the school, started saying they were going to see what was going on. He wanted to go with them. Not out of bravery, but to be away from the madness forming in the school hallways, from the constant crying of the damaged and scared. When he saw the teens meeting by the big doors, he slipped away from Mrs Birdie's gaze and went near them. They paid scant attention to the skinny fifteen-year-old with ripped band-T and naked legs.

Outside, waves of dust passed down the street like curtains. Streetlamps were switched on, even though it was midday. The sky formed a single, purple blanket. From demolished gardens, dogs continued to call to one another, announcing the dawn of a new era: their own. Off in the distance, a naked man shuffled along solo.

One of the lads said, 'Let's see what's happening over on St Clair Street,' and Alastair and the boys made their way out the school grounds and into the road proper. The reek of fires choked his sinuses as they passed the broken villas in this nice bit of the neighbourhood. Entire roofs were missing, fallen into buildings below. Certain houses smouldered, while in others jets of water shot out from the ruptured pipes inside. They all turned their faces away from one garden, containing a person chopped in half. The street the lad suggested would normally have taken no more than a few minutes to get to, but fallen lamp posts and crashed cars hampered their progress. Soon, he got lost in all that mess. Soon, he found himself completely alone.

He remembered that his mum was gone, his dad was gone, and began to run.

Now, he went into the kitchen to be beside his old man. The air tasted funny in there, like metal.

He said, 'Hello,' and wondered if the old man would acknowledge him. He wondered if this was a passing haunting, a brief glimpse into the next life, something even he would struggle to believe in the morning.

The ghost looked away from the sink, to his son. Shock slackened his face. He said, 'What?' then, 'No.'

SIX

For a long while, Alastair thought he didn't miss his family. How could he, when they were just two among thousands? Three, counting the junior of his father. His own personal grief felt weak and measly compared to the national tragedy it occurred within, one that touched everyone. Two individuals lost, versus hundreds of thousands lost. All of them just utterly gone. No illnesses or saying goodbye, just thousands of streams unplugged at once.

So when people asked, when they found out he came off the peninsula, he said: *I don't miss them*. Partly a lie designed to shut down further conversation, further probing. In those days, peninsula refugees carried a certain stigma. Some might call you a freeloader, or a leech. When are you moving back then? Someone has to get over there and sort things out, shouldn't it be you, a young healthy chap? So he said no, he didn't miss them. Partly true too though, because he hardly did. Two lost; hundreds of thousands lost.

The word you'd want would be *numb*. A numbness. An injection into, say, your jawbone, with the meds creeping out through your mandible, your cheek, nearly into the ear itself. Like that, except all over, all over outside and in. Impervious to pain. Once, in the little bedsit, he held on to a hot pan handle for three, four, five seconds, then put it down. He looked at his palm. A blister the size of a small apple erupted, a blister he barely recognised. He felt numb. How are you doing, mate? I'm fine, I'm doing away. I'm getting on, I'm no too bad, I'm easy-osay, awch I'm alright like, I'm good, I'm grand, I'm doing away, could be worse – ha ha ha – I'm fine, I'm super, how are you?

This is what I am, this is who I am: I am fine.

For years, he suspected he was due a crack-up. A crack-up lurked beyond the horizon for him, cause of course he knew about emotions and expressing them and how when something's unsaid it festers in the mind. He wasn't a halfwit; he knew. Just past the horizon, this great fat toad of a crack-up waiting all puffed up and smiling, opening its mouth day by day to swallow him up. He knew it. It was obvious. Even Caitlin tried with him. They moved in together at, what, twenty-five? She used to say to him, if you ever want to chat about it, the disaster and your place in it, you know I'm here to talk, I'm here and open and willing to listen without judgement. In not so many words. She asked: is everything alright, pal? And he said: I'm fine. He said it every day.

He started at the college, doing techy stuff and folk there didn't even clock him as a refugee. He got sad around holidays. It felt like an irritating warm wind. But sadness he could eat for breakfast and forget about, down it with a Scrambly-Eggy sachet and a decaf and be on his way. What got him was the anger. The fury. That was what blindsided him and turned out to be the crack-up's eventual shape. He always imagined he'd end up a classic depressive, crying on his side near a portable heater, drinking strong cider under his quilt. But no.

It started with folk in the street. Pedestrians. People not walking fast enough, or getting in his way. Dawdlers. The ones stepping out of shops and looking around like they'd never seen the sky before, juniors and seniors both. It sent him doolally. He started muttering under his breath. *Morons. Clowns. Fucking idiots.* Caitlin said to him: what's the problem, just walk round them. Just stop, let them go. She spoke sense, of course, but he couldn't help himself. He seethed. On his way to the college, he did these huge obvious movements around dawdlers to put them in their place. These fucking clowns. A few steps later and he was like: what was that about?

After pedestrians came inanimate objects. Pointless little things sitting on stupid shelves. Crap stuff leaning against annoying walls. Going for the toilet roll and the sheet not tearing along its perforated line. The time it took for a previous incarnation of their screen to load stuff. It gave him a stomach ache. He got heartburn trying to reattach the roller blind in their bedroom. The lace on his trainer split and he went cross-eyed for a few seconds, hunched over, warm blood pooling in his forehead.

He couldn't concentrate down the college. Someone would say something, anything, just a daft comment, and he'd be livid. He'd be imagining beatings. He'd be rehearsing pulling a bat out from a parallel universe and swinging it around, crashing it down on skulls, forcing it into soft faces, generally losing his mind. He dropped out, or stopped turning up. He went on the computers various places. At night, cold sweats woke him and he went through their flat checking for electrical faults.

How dare they? How dare they go? Go away, just like that. Click your fingers. Wake up. Goodbye. Over and done with. What right did they have to pass over beyond where he couldn't reach? Listen, you make a baby, that's you signing a contract. Yourself, child, the universe: all cosignatories. Everyone signs it and everyone agrees that you're on the hook til this one turns eighteen, got it? Shagging's a dangerous game if something conscious comes out at the end of it. So how dare they pass over beyond?

One night in particular, he woke to the sound of laughter. It must have come out of a dream cause once he wakened, laughter was impossible. Caitlin lying next to him, out for the count, and he went around the flat breathing shallowly, checking for something. Rain fell. He went to a window to see the darkened playpark across the way. His teeth chattered, making the same noise as the rain on the glass. He rested his brow on the window and said their names quietly, since he didn't trust himself. He said their names and asked: how could you do this to me? How could you leave me behind? Probably they were together in heaven or nirvana or whatever. I wish you took me with you, he thought.

So it was anger that got him in the end, the explosion still reverberating years and years later. He survived the blast, the ethylene plant rupturing and all its underground pipes and systems catching and fucking the entire peninsula up beyond all recognition. Imagine all the body's veins catching fire at once. He survived the blast, and its aftermath, and he wandered the land's ruined skin. Even now scared of dogs, nervous of staffies in the street. Even now wary of open flames and a huge fan of sachet technology, loving the ease of slipping Chicken Luncheon out from the silver pouch, so inorganic, so separate from hydrocarbons and gas and fire opening earth like paper.

It took weeks to reach safety and a lot can happen to a young man in weeks. He can experience a lot of shit in a few short weeks.

The ghost of his father turned to face him, there in the kitchen. Sixteen years since he'd seen the old man and now Alastair tasted the substance of him; the air around felt a little thicker, a feeling like chilli spice on his tongue, the scent of a hot hairdryer.

The ghost asked, 'What's going on?'

'I've fucking lost it,' he announced. What would be next?

Maybe now would come the cider under the quilt, lying sideways on a bare mattress in a carpetless flat. 'That's it,' he whispered. 'I'm done in.'

The ghost stepped back. 'What's going on?' it asked. 'Where am I?'

Alastair shook his head, then, at speed, he walked away, out the kitchen, down the hall past the bright orange flume. Shaking his head the whole time, like: no. No way, no chance. No chance am I going along with this. Your brain couldn't go insane if you didn't allow it. He wouldn't accept it, no. In the living room, he turned on the lamps. Lamps were good. Lamps made it seem proper, like a room from a stream. Were there candles? Candles might help.

He turned and the ghost stood there on the periphery. The old man, waiting, looking inside, a little bit lit-up from no-place. 'Who are you?' the ghost asked.

Alastair looked back. 'No,' he said.

The best bet would be to get the place cleaned up. Cleaning up would help with going mental; cleaning up proved you were a proper person. He started on all the sachets, discarded and folded and scattered round his place on the couch. Chicken Luncheon, Veggie Medley, Dinner Delight, Morning Hamper. He cradled sachets in his arms and made a pile.

'Where am I?' asked the old man. 'I was just ... I was at the plant.'

The ghost had the same appearance as Alastair's dad, but that made sense, since it'd been dredged out from his memory. The big beard, the dark eyes, the wiry shoulders. Thirty-nine at time of demise, built like an old-fashioned fisherman. He remembered his dad's junior heading off for the nightshift on that last evening, the last evening of Alastair's first life, saying cheerio to them all and whistling down the hall, away to wait for the shuttle.

'I feel weird,' the ghost said. 'I feel like I'm coming down with something.'

Alastair wasn't listening. He didn't have time, cause he'd just thought: the junior will be back soon, back from the gig. He'd forgotten about the stream shutting down and all that. They would have words about it. He might have to remind the junior how this all worked, who was in charge and where his bread got buttered.

'Something's wrong with me,' said the ghost. 'I was just up at the plant and something started rumbling.'

'Shut up,' said Alastair.

Once the sachets were disposed of, he went around dealing with the packaging. Packages came constantly through the flume: his pills, his sachets, toiletries, wee gadgets, old-style books that he unwrapped and placed on shelves, clothes for the junior (only the best, cause your stats could take a pummelling if you sent them out looking shabby, if they weren't wearing something modern, on-trend). All of it coming in daily and all of it packaged up in materials. On top of the flume sat a switch: *IN/OUT.* He turned it briefly to *OUT* and deposited the packaging.

The ghost followed. It asked, 'Who are you? Where is this?' It seemed to be growing in intelligence, its voice strengthening.

He polished the living room up. He used the hoover for the rug. He lit some of Caitlin's old candles. How long did psychotic episodes last? Hours? Days, possibly? All he needed to do was keep a handle on the little things: the flat, the junior. You keep a handle on the wee things, keep them under control, run a tight ship, then the big things fall into line. Soon enough, the ghost would disappear, and he'd be left in peace and able to be like: wow, that was trippy. I just about lost it completely but now, now I'm fine.

'What are you doing?' asked the ghost.

He nearly went to answer it, then thought better of it.

Talking back would be asking for trouble. Instead, he turned on the Calcyon One and watched the wee owl do its thing before trawling through streams for something to watch. He went past all the thumbnails, all the ads, all the titles designed to demand his attention. Look at this, look at this, look at this though, but look at this.

He went for Nye Morgan in the end. Good old Nye. You could trust good old Nye even in these times. There he was: good old Nye. Dark, tanned, really handsome. Nye's face boxed into the corner of the screen so you could see the footage he was reporting on, which seemed to be another riot or a protest some-place else; a bunch of dossers kicking off and throwing things and Honey Bee peacekeepers trying to calm things down.

Alastair felt the air crackle as his father came close, as he entered the living room and stood gloomily in the middle of the floor. You could see the armchair through the ghost's jeans, though the outline was a little blurry, its colour bluey-green. The ghost stood there and watched Nye Morgan reporting and put its hands in its pockets and rocked a little on its heels. The dad used to do this in life. Never wanted to sit down and watch the streams with wee Alastair. Come and watch this, Dad, he'd say, and Dad would go, Naw, I'm away out in a bit. Rocking on his heels, rummaging in his pockets for lost items. Always something on the go. Always away out in a bit, a few minutes in the future. I'm here now but in a moment I won't be.

'That's Nye Morgan,' the ghost said. 'He looks old.'

On the Calcyon One, some protesters were climbing a statue. They were trying to raise a flag but there was no wind and the fabric hung limp at the lead climber's side.

After a few moments of watching, Alastair slipped the mobile from his jeans pocket. He could only stomach a few moments of watching before he got the itch for his mobile. From there, he pulled up some news content and read more about the protest raging on his own personal doorstep. These folk were crowding up in the Old Town, half an hour's walk away.

'His hair's all grey round the sides,' said the ghost. 'Poor Nye. How's that happened?'

On the field, lots of his Step-Stone colleagues, and old friends too, posted stuff about the protests, the riots. Some thought they were a good thing; others felt the protesters were being irresponsible. Mostly, folk tested the waters, hedging their bets a little. You couldn't go too far in the early hours of something newsworthy in case your statement ended up going against the eventual grain. You couldn't take the risk.

Marcin, on the other hand, posted photos from the gig; Alastair looked at his old friend, at Ed, and himself. The junior, stood smiling with Alastair's pals. He looked good. Alastair felt proud.

'I mind of him when he did the sports,' said the ghost. 'He was a funny chap, Nye Morgan. Always coming out with these jokes.'

He saw an interaction with one of Marcin's photos. A little tick mark, meaning someone had acknowledged the image, and he checked and it came from Caitlin, from Caitlin's own thumbpad. A little green tick, meaning: *yes, I have seen you*. It felt good, despite everything, to have been seen.

'Who the fuck are you?' asked the ghost. It seemed he'd snapped out of his fascination with Nye Morgan and he was near Alastair, looking down with a scowl. 'Who the fuck are you, eh? What am I doing here?'

Alastair paid it no mind. He trawled through the notes of interest and outrages and reviews and everything else the mobile afforded him, the field's power, its data, coalescing inside his palm.

And then, suddenly, the front door went. A key in the lock and footsteps on the floorboards and the junior going, 'Hiya.

That's me back,' and Alastair and the ghost gazed at each other in surprise.

A sort of stand-off: three men in the room, hands poised at their sides, the eyes of each moving from one to the other slowly, carefully. Two of them copies of each other, the third a ghost. No weapons, sure, but a question in the air: who's going to strike first?

Alastair, in the end. 'You're seeing him?'

The junior swallowed. 'Aye.'

'I thought I'd lost it,' he said. 'I thought I'd fucking cracked.'

'I can see it,' said the junior. 'What is it?'

'I don't know. It just turned up, in the kitchen.'

The junior nodded. He said, 'I've been hearing things. Little noises, like. I didn't think.'

Alastair nodded. 'Me too.'

The ghost moved towards the junior. 'So you've got your junior, eh? Some game this is. Two against one, I suppose.'

'It's Dad,' said the junior.

'I know,' said Alastair. 'I know it is.'

'Our dad.'

They went off together. They shut themselves through in the bedroom away from the old man. The ghost, the ... whatever it was. Alastair kept thinking *ghost*, really the only way for his mind to categorise it, now he knew he wasn't tripping. They shut themselves away and stood together and spoke quietly and Alastair could see his own anxiety reflected in the face of his junior. The same pale worry in his slackened mouth, his bright eyes. They spoke quietly and asked each other what was happening to them, asked what the *thing* was, asked were they imagining it? They remembered ghost stories from their shared childhood. They remembered a pure ancient stream of *A Nightmare Gesture*, remembered skimming through *The Shining* on a reader. The thing in the house brought none of the same sensations; this wasn't a spectre or ghoul. They were not afraid of their father.

Then, a thought. 'What if it gets out?' asked the junior.

'Aye,' nodded Alastair. 'Right.'

They found it drifting through the rooms. It moved like a person, using doorways, and appeared unaware of its condition.

'Let me out of here,' it said. 'People will be looking for me. I'm due back at the plant for nightshift.'

They said for it to come and sit down with them and it blinked. You sensed the ghost's confusion. 'Aye, for a minute,' it said. 'Then I need to get going.'

They sat down together, the ghost between the two of them, and Alastair said, 'Tell me your name.'

The ghost scowled and laughed. It said, 'What're you on about?'

'Say it.'

'Well, it's ...' It looked around. 'I mean ...'

'You don't know it.'

They waited together for a while. It was pure improvisation, but it helped that they worked with one mind. They shared glances and had all the same references and Alastair appreciated his junior's presence.

'Thomas,' said the ghost, eventually. 'Tam.'

'Alright,' said Alastair. 'Thomas what?'

'Boo ... Byoo ... It's something like and-and. An-an ... Buchanan.'

'That's right,' they said together. 'You've got it.'

The ghost looked really pleased. He beamed at them. 'I remember.'

'Do you know who we are?' asked Alastair.

'Some clown and his junior,' said the ghost.

'My name's Alastair,' he said. 'Alastair Buchanan.'

The ghost stood up and walked straight forward. He said, 'Ha ha, very funny. How did you know that's his name?'

'That's *my* name,' Alastair said. 'Our name, I mean.'

'You aren't funny,' said the ghost. 'Yous aren't being fucking funny if you think you are. One minute I'm at my work and the next I'm sitting here with you two jokers saying your name's my boy's name.' He paused. 'I don't think so.'

They explained to the ghost that they felt confused too. They also had zero clue what the story was here, honestly.

'Yous must be in your thirties though,' the ghost reasoned. 'My boy's fifteen.'

'I'm thirty-one. Last time I saw you, I *was* fifteen.'

The ghost's eyes narrowed. 'When did you see me?'

'Just a night,' said Alastair. 'A normal night. We were watching something, me and Mum. The junior-you went off for the shuttle and the senior-you needed to get some sleep, upstairs in bed. You won't know this, but something happened. The plant you worked at blew up. Something happened. Some explosion or something. Dad, it destroyed everything. The whole entire place. All the gas underground caught and blew up and whole entire towns went down. It was . . . You won't know this, but it was a disaster, an actual disaster. Everyone died. You and Mum died in the house. It fell in. I'm sorry, it did. Thousands of folk died, Dad.'

'I didn't die in the house,' said the ghost. 'I wasn't at home, I was working. I didn't die. How could I have died if I'm here?'

There were no funerals for those lost on the peninsula. Imagine the logistics of it for a start, and plus by the time Honey Bee got them out, resettlement became priority number one. But there could be no doubt the old man died. Their house brought down to rubble, and the junior out at ground zero, swallowed up in a ball of flame that caused weather anomalies as far as mainland Europe. Flights cancelled, snow in late spring, several species of bird entirely disappearing from human knowledge. No one escaped the blast. Some consolation at least that those working at its epicentre would've felt no pain.

'I don't know what to tell you, Dad,' said Alastair. 'You did. Both of yous did.'

The ghost sat down on the floor. All you could see was the head of it, resting above the coffee table. It started crying. It said, 'I remember going into the plant and doing my work, then nothing. I feel like I've been away for a long while. I feel lost. I remember this feeling like flying. I was flying through some sort of darkness. I was flying a half hour ago. I'm not myself.'

It cried harder. It sobbed, even. It kept saying, 'God,' and, 'Oh Jesus,' and despite the strangeness of the situation, Alastair's main reaction was embarrassment. No one wants to see their old man cry. Things were badly wrong if you saw your old man weep. His dad hadn't been a tough sort. Not a bully or a big drinker or a rager, but he'd been distant. Always on the way out, a few minutes in the future. I'm here now but in a moment I won't be. Rocking on his heels, playing with the edges of his beard, searching his pockets for something lost. Alastair never saw him express much beyond humour, irritation, or mild happiness.

'So your mother's away too, then?' asked the ghost.

'Aye,' said Alastair. 'But if you were the junior ...'

'I know,' said the ghost. 'But even so. I knew her. I knew her years. Listen. I knew her fucking years.'

'I'm sorry,' he said.

After a little more conversation, the ghost passed out. It fell into a kind of sleep on the floor of the living room, tired from emotion. They left it lying there and reconvened in the kitchen. Alastair poured out some whisky and the junior said it wanted some too, wished it could join in.

'So it's his junior, then,' said Alastair. 'Not the real one.'

The junior nodded. 'Depends on your definition of real.'

'You know what I mean.'

'Aye. I do.'

'What happens . . .' Alastair thought about it. 'What happens when we go?'

'That's a big question.'

'What happens to you,' he asked, 'after I go? Is it the same? Is it instant for you?'

'When you go,' said the junior, 'I go. It happens the same, right away. Like that.' He snapped his fingers.

'So explain *him*, then.'

'It's the field, isn't it? He's living in the field.'

Alastair knew this. He needed the junior to say it too. 'It's his memories and data. They're all up there.'

'I didn't know it was possible.'

'It isn't. It shouldn't be.'

They watched each other across the breakfast bar. Each saw an appearance of extreme tiredness in the other's face, a twitchy look, darkness below the eyes. Each blamed the other for the apparition on the living room floor; the junior for his senior's humanness, Alastair for his junior's juniorness. They blamed each other and thought: it's here because of you. It's you that let this thing into the world.

'I didn't ask to be made,' said the junior. 'I'm here because you wanted it. You asked for it.'

Alastair nodded, drank. 'I know.' Then he shivered.

His dad lay out on the floor, a few walls away. His own dead dad, curled up animal-like, dreaming whatever ghostly dreams its un-body picked up from the field. His dad, imagine it. A dream come true. More than anything else he wanted to put down the glass, leave the junior behind, and go through to him. To lie down too, lie down in the blank space in front of his father's stomach. He imagined the arms growing real, meat forming from the electricity, muscle and bone and heat making arms to sneak round him.

Sixteen years, he thought. I've been solo for sixteen years.

For a while after the disaster, he carried these fantasies. They involved chance occurrences, such as his mother and father sneaking out on the night of the disaster, nipping to the shops perhaps, meaning they weren't destroyed in the collapse and were merely lost. Obviously, this did not come to pass, but he never stopped hoping. And now, his hope had been realised, in the worst way possible.

You're fine though, he told himself. You are fine. Human beings are able to process anything. This he knew. The human brain adapts to new situations with surprising ease, withstands pain and makes suffering a process you can, if you like, opt out of. He would not give in.

'Anyone at work,' he said, 'Ed, Marcin. None of them find out, okay?'

The junior nodded. 'Agreed.'

'We need to think this one through.'

They were quiet for a while, unable to talk to even each other about where they'd found themselves.

'I'm going to bed then.'

The junior nodded and Alastair drained his glass, leaving it in the sink. He passed the junior, before pausing in the doorway.

'I'm going to get them for this,' he said, without quite knowing what he meant.

SEVEN

The morning was fine. Hot air rushed to Caitlin's cheeks as she left the hotel and went out into the street, sweat emerging in the corners of her brow. Her brain felt foggy, despite the morning sachet of Fruit Cubed, despite her long, cool shower. Her eyes were dry and she got irrationally angry with the crowds up on the main drag. You had to push on the main drag; there was no kindness there. Once you were off the backstreets, you put your bag out in front of you, your head down, and squeezed into the masses of suits-and-trainers. Trams passed, bikes passed, little pools of absence formed around panhandlers, the mobile in your free hand drew information from the field, saying which cafés were doing special offers, which breakfast places did take-away, which of the cyclists would be willing to sack off work if you gave them a better rate for a ride to the office. Mornings like this made you remember the quietness down in your home village, the squeaks local birds made, the river's gurgle. But you held your breath and pushed into the crowd.

At least the tram was quiet. She used Saltirely ones, those being a bit dearer but more nicely done up inside. There was air con in the summer, unlike the others. Trackstars were especially bad, some of them like rolling shanty towns. In a rush, a Big Mad Alec's Big Mad Tram would do. Those carried lots of adverts though, meaning extra hassle linking your face before you'd be allowed to board. It was already nine, so she started work on the move, after plugging in her drinks from the night before: a few glasses of minibar wine. The mobile gave her back the info in terms of kcals and units and a flush went to her cheeks as the incriminating info went directly into the field.

A message came through. Caitlin saw the tiny avatar of Elaine, her boss, and some text began relaying, but she killed it before it appeared in full. If she didn't read, then she couldn't participate.

There was plenty of other nonsense to deal with anyway: miscommunications that had festered overnight; lengthy forwards from higher-ups, full of data, tacit justifications for salaries; people wanting meetings with her where a question would be raised and discussed and turned over and broken into sections and laughed about, then argued about, questions rephrased, bucks passed – is this maybe a marketing issue, as opposed to systems? – and ultimately all would place a pin in the question. Something to think about. An action point. There were messages where the other party added nothing, pieces of communication designed to move the onus back to Caitlin, the situation unchanged. There were idiot fool questions, something the other party could have pulled up from the vast banks of data that Arts Systems managed, but it was always easier to Q Caitlin, wasn't it?

The Saltirely's vents piped cool air across her face. All around, the business classes were talking. Somewhere, a few carriages down, an accordionist had managed to sneak themselves aboard. You weren't supposed to be able to do that on Saltirelys, something about the passes; she didn't know how it worked. When gaps formed in the blabbering of passengers, distant squeezy moans filtered through. An ancient rhythm.

Most mornings, she thought to herself: *Why don't I pack it in?* Just to herself. Just quietly, behind the lips. Why don't I pack it in, for all the good it's doing me? A sort of mantra, the most unhelpful sort of transcendental meditation going. Why don't I pack it in? Why don't I pack it in? Why don't I pack it in? Over and over: a sore to be pushed against, to relish its small, bright pain.

Why didn't she pack it in? She'd liked bar work well enough, hadn't she? Those dim, damp afternoons where stained-glass light crept over the few hold-outs leaning by the pumps. Big Walter. The driver man. Inchworm. That smell. Wood, real wood, and last night's disinfectant. Sweet beer. They looked after her, the hold-outs. She didn't think they were eyeing her backside when she reached for whiskies, and once, when this young guy came in, shoeless, bleeding from places on the skull, trying to clamber atop the bar, it was Inchworm that got the young guy down and swept him out the door like a human conveyor belt.

She didn't miss it ... She missed it a wee bit. Sort of. She didn't miss it, except nights. There were some nights in bar work she revisited often. The crush of bodies, all of them swaying to her attention. This lad – who maybe was Big Walter's nephew, now she thought of it – kissing her down in the cellar. Sometimes she missed that. Who went to bars nowadays? Hardly anyone. A dying breed, the driver man called them, going into the old film speech: *we are at the end of an age, we live in a land of weather forecasts, and here we are, we three, perhaps the last island of beauty in the world*, Inchworm and Big Walter snickering behind their glasses.

And then came the business across in Fife. The explosions and fires and it was all anyone spoke about for days, weeks, months. No telly in the pub but punters ran streams on their tablets or mobiles and everyone agreed: a crying shame what'd happened to those people. You saw them in the streets sometimes, these poor individuals, after the refugees were brought

102

across and housed, sometimes scarred on the face or head, blotched red across the scalp. Some of them started coming to the Shackle, and it was only Inchworm who made one or two snide comments about the stipends Pyreol and Multi-Bio and Honey Bee donated to the cause.

A few years later and a certain group of them were arriving often, after giro day, making a pint last. Caitlin allowed herself a pride that she was helping survivors, though they were paying for the privilege to be fair. A certain group of them, and one member in particular – Marcin's pal – caught her eye, and wasn't there bravery and tragicness about having endured the destruction of an entire county? Wasn't there something to be said for someone with nothing? She stood him bags of crisps, wanting to grow out his shoulders, get them wide and round. One night he started crying, so.

She could pack it all in and go back to bar work. Ha. As if anyplace would take her. She hadn't stood behind a bar since she was twenty-four, twenty-five. But she could do something else. Now, these days, she thought about little but Arts Systems. And she was lucky. Many from uni days toiled. Roz, for example, took photographs out at the rollercoasters, snapping gangs of juniors as they screamed on the ride's downturns, the images going right into the seniors' feeds without them lifting a finger. So many were on pills. Roz herself was prescribed Capsule Bhagavad Gita; Ursula had been supping Liquid Om for who knew how long.

Behind her, a door opened. She turned to see the accordionist creep in, pulling gentle whispers from the box. He was wearing a hoodie backwards, to cradle his payment lozenge. A few reached over to transfer change.

On the mobile, she pulled up her schedule and told herself she was lucky. A series of fast promotions, some out of nowhere, all of them hauling her up the ranks. She left bar work for an out-of-nowhere Arts Systems internship, met folk at parties, became a golden child in the system, first-born of the research drones. Folk liked her, you had to admit. It was a way of being, learned from bar work; you asked questions, developed set phrases that people liked to hear. She was lucky, and that's why she couldn't pack it in. Getting something by luck . . . You couldn't turn your nose up at luck.

Ten minutes to process through security, everything scanned, her eyes greenlit, sterilised tongue depressor administered by machine. Layers and layers of glass – the Atrium – then into a waiting lift. She eyed the others quickly: nearly all juniors and some she knew. She nodded to Piepipe from Allied Figurative Painting, or his junior anyway, who chose the button for her floor.

When you looked a junior in the eye, you did a couple of things. Firstly, and without thinking, you received the information that this was a junior you were dealing with. Easy. It just came. She remembered the early days of junioring, when the first local went up to town to collect their replica, bringing him back on the distance bus and presenting his acquisition outside the newsagents on a Saturday morning. Tiny Caitlin had witnessed this copy of Sandy Bandon, worker at the trout farm, watched it stand around and shake hands, everyone marvelling at the tech. When Bandon and his junior left, the villagers broke into immediate gossip about how much like Bandon the junior looked, but how you knew they were distinct. You knew. Deep down in the senses generated by your small intestine you knew.

Secondly, after that initial assessment, you wondered if elsewhere the senior was watching you too, through their junior's eyes. Entirely possible, at all times. Nothing in the junior's face to indicate their senior had logged in, no expression of concentration or any pain of transmission, so in a sense you were always presenting yourself to twin watchers. Finally, you made the comparison between the junior before you, usually preserving their senior's looks from age thirty, maybe forty, and your own knowledge of how the senior actually looked now, how pale they'd become, how unkempt of hair, how hunched and tired and sad.

Overall, a total headache, but one you barely noticed each time it happened.

In the office, Simone waited. Caitlin shared with this young guy, fairly new to Arts Systems, called Otis. Every few weeks, his appearance changed. New hair, new areas of skin revealed by innovative shaving patterns, new conceptions of fashion. A slim tube running the side of his jaw delivered a constant nicotine steam to his nostril. No sign of Otis this morning though; only Simone, fingers against the outer window, peering.

'Morning,' said Caitlin, sitting down.

Simone turned. 'Oh, it's you.'

'A bit late,' Caitlin admitted.

Even for a junior, Simone impressed. Over six feet and immaculately turned out. On Caitlin's feed, Simone always drew recognition. 'How was last night?' she asked.

'Oh, it was fine. I just—'

Simone nodded. 'Uhuh, listen, I wanted to talk to you. Have you spoken to Juliette recently?'

Caitlin shrugged her jacket off. 'I don't think so.'

'Well I was speaking to Juliette and she's been speaking to Gus, from Dance Partnership, who's been speaking to Literatures Lemuel, and apparently there's this big opportunity going, out west.'

Caitlin stiffened. 'Is that right?'

'Yeah, well so Lemuel was saying anyway. A big opportunity. Lots of moosh, lots of creative oversight. What do you think?'

Caitlin had a talent for expressions of blank indifference. She said, 'I'm not sure. I've only been here for—'

Simone interrupted with a laugh. She slunk into Otis's empty chair. 'Not you. Me! Verse's engagement's been sky-high for years now. I'm killing it upstairs, you have to admit. When people interact with a poem, they're really *interacting* with that poem, know what I mean?'

A quick nod. 'Sure.'

'And I mean, you know how Elaine is with me. She just loves me, doesn't she? She told me I was the best thing to happen to Verse for a decade. Ha. I was at her grandson's baptism, and she just said that, right out the blue.'

'That's great,' said Caitlin. 'If Elaine's involved, you're a shoo-in.'

'Thanks. Yeah, you're right. I'm worrying over nothing. I know I am. I'm a classic worrier, a classic neurotic.'

Caitlin did not think about the message she'd received from Elaine, high up in National Strategies. Elaine's message had not been seen, so did not need to be thought about. For a long time, Caitlin watched Simone's mouth move, the lips drawing over teeth in perfect human vowel sounds, and the formation of those sounds was just as good as the real thing.

'And anyway,' said Simone. 'I'm just getting bored, you know? Just so bored. Bored, bored, bored. You know?'

The figures, the endless figures. Caitlin's screen was crowded by figures. Numbers, percentages, calculations, graphs. Across town in the gallery, each piece was set up for engagement monitoring, and everything generated figures.

Participation got tracked. How long did someone look at a piece of art? Seconds? Minutes? Did they photograph it? Did they look at it with friends or solo, or did they call a loved one over to observe alongside and make comments on the brushstrokes, or simply voice little appreciative hums as they looked? Were the observers juniors or seniors? How far back did they stand from the piece? Was it possible for the algorithm to make a non-judgemental, non-discriminatory guesstimate as to the race/nationality/sexuality/gender of the observer? Was it possible for the algorithm, taking into account any and all peculiarities of the specific viewer, to describe a pithy one-word approximation of the viewer's overall facial expression, i.e. sad, or fascinated? If the art was photographed by the viewer, or if it was photographed alongside the viewer, what happened to the resulting image? Did it go straight to the field or was it edited first? Did the junior or senior, or multiple, smile in the photograph or did they look pensive and moody and perhaps monochrome? What was the relationship between a piece's description and the way it was subsequently interacted with on the field? Was there any metric to determine whether the viewer's interaction with an especially provocative or socially engaged piece was 'put-on', or performed – meaning, did the fact that the viewer was aware they were being viewed them-selves, by Arts Systems and by their own personal miniature Arts Systems-style audience out in the field, have any influ-ence on the pieces they interacted with, or for how long, or for how serious their face was? – and did that in the long run even matter, if engagement metrics were up and the artists and their dealers were getting a good return on their investment in Arts Systems?

And how to tell what the best things were? Well, that was easy: the best things were the ones with the most people look-ing at them.

Otis, lately arrived, coughed, then reached up to mess with the tube in his nose. A small puff of steam escaped.

Nights, Caitlin suffered anxiety dreams of figures. She dreamed meetings with higher-ups where someone said,

Caitlin, run those exhibition figures by us, would you?, and the screen she'd been allocated malfunctioned and started running a stream of *Carlo Valentine's Spongebath Showdown*, except no one noticed so Caitlin conjured the numbers up on the hoof and it was only later that the mistake's consequences revealed themselves, during some big fuck-off launch or whatever. Some mornings she woke more exhausted than the night before, vision messed by endless eyelids – Why don't I just pack it in? – and the very first new-born thought would be of work.

A year and a half back, she booked annual leave. A five-dayer, which raised some eyebrows. Simone, scandalised, asked was she sure? Did she really want to take the whole week? It wasn't like it was even Simone's responsibility to okay the leave, but she started giving Caitlin this hard time, saying it would look bad for a full five-dayer to come out, like Caitlin's holiday represented a departmental moral failing. She took it anyway. Had to have it, this during the height of her and Alastair's ongoing discussion on his junioring.

There were no paternal juniors in Caitlin's younger years; it wasn't in her blood. She was out of old stock, old borderland stock. She grew up down south near the wall. In a word: remote, which made things difficult in terms of junioring. There were few payslip-garnishing schemes for repayment down in the borderlands, and as a result, juniors were few and far between. Her old man would have had to pay outright for a junior if he got one. Lee Weir was essentially a born-again hippy, feeding chickens on his farm and growing high-strength skunk. It wasn't hypocrisy, his field link-up. He needed it for dealing.

On the first day of her leave, she took a Saltirely out beyond the ring road, transferred to distance buses afterwards. The vehicle was near empty, just her, a pair of vagrant seniors politely snogging on the back seats, and the open road. On the east side, the beach came right near the A1's bank. A low green haze drifted out from beyond and one sun column shone on the sunken power station's boxy islands. Her old man was waiting to pick her up. They drove in his van back to the house, which you had to admit was large. She grew up fine, no problems at all, nothing til the mother passed and the less said about that the better. Imagine a combination of the January blues, the post-Christmas slump, and waking up one morning to a video call from the old man with a face made unrecognisable by his shitty field signal and also grief.

'How you doing, sweetie?' her old man asked, out on the porch, after tea. They lit the lamps a way off, to draw the night's moths from their table, her old man helping with the pungent weed cloud he sent to the dark.

She said, 'Fine.' Fine about work, fine about Alastair, fine about the city, about their flat, fine to it all. At this point, her old man didn't know about the junior; she could guess the tight face he'd make in response to the news.

From their position, round the back of the house, the whole valley was presented to them, the pine clumps navy, the big sky fingernail-coloured. Woodsmoke now and then, beyond the old man's weed. It was the longest she'd been home since her mother went, that fucking awful New Year. But this recent holiday turned out fine. They sat out every night and said little and she woke with barely any thoughts at all. Once or twice, she even became restless and irritable; in other words, bored. Now *there* was a novelty.

It had been the same in bar work. Slow afternoons, before anyone was in, where she'd polish every glass with a soft cloth and check nothing catastrophic had happened in the bogs and set up all the liqueurs so the labels sat just so. Such fucking sweet boredom. Horrendous at the time, pure absolute torture, but looking back, a total boon. A total delicious pudding of wasted time. The landlord popped in sometimes. He had this policy about using the field during working hours, wanted his staff sprung to attention, so she rarely risked pulling out the mobile and scrolling or reading or whatever.

She counted her teeth with her tongue. She noticed blinking. She watched the long beams of red and green light from the door's window stretch and span across the floor. She practised different kinds of standing, moving from one foot to the other, holding the taps. She gave meditation a go but it made her remember her faults, so she stopped. Little phrases got stuck in her head, meaningless phrases that her brain ran over and over, things like *Tequila Sunrise*, or *Golden Roasted Oats*, or *Once in a Blue Moon*. A time of earworms and looped choruses. She set up minuscule theatres on the inside of her skull, spaces to rehearse conversations she'd have one day, or to perform autopsies on prior interactions gone skew-whiff. The victories she won in there. Sparkling turns of phrase, hunks seduced, snobs dismissed. At the time, she complained. She said to the hold-outs when they arrived, Christ it's been a slow day, I'm losing my mind here, I'm going crackers, I need to get a radio or something. Now, what she would give for an afternoon of wiping down tables and chanting choruses and listing faults.

She'd left her old man's glowing. Light, and moving with purpose, her clothes fitting well, the muscles in her hips and lower back aligned, locked; she barely felt herself exist.

Otis leaned way back in his chair, clasping his hands behind his head, which today was mohawked by a strip of grey fuzz. 'Want to get a decaf?' he asked.

Caitlin sighed. She did not like to go places with Otis. 'Sure,' she said.

They went out their shared office, passing the vast hive of data goons working silently in the middle of the floor. Viewing screens hung from the ceiling like bats, streaming productivity figures as well as reminders of the upcoming Systems Fun Run, and cringey cartoons about the craziness of office life.

'I'm maybe getting one of those implants,' Otis said. 'Basically, they get a certain level of field into your head so it's easier to access. I really amen't bothered about it one way or the other, but basically it's like why not make it easier if the option's there?'

They waited for the lift. 'Where would it go?' Caitlin asked.

Otis stretched his neck to show a lump of skull just past the spinal column. 'There. It looks like a wee jelly sweet. This lassie I'm seeing has one.'

Caitlin nodded. 'That's good.' There was no need to take Otis's senior into account – he was too young – but she still avoided any sort of protestation. It would only lead to further chit-chat.

In the lift, Otis scrolled his mobile, as did Caitlin. He sniggered at something he saw. 'This is such bullshit,' he said.

'Hm,' said Caitlin. 'I know.'

On the third floor, the doors opened to let someone in. Caitlin glanced up from the mobile as Elaine entered. Just under five feet, severely wrinkled, bejewelled and prone to violent swearing fits, Elaine came from the old guard.

'Hello you two,' she said, peering up at Otis and Caitlin. 'Good morning?'

'Fine,' nodded Caitlin. 'Busy.'

'I bet you are,' said Elaine. 'I won't tell you about the time I've had. We had reps in.' Her eyes bulged to indicate her displeasure. 'Moaning and moaning and moaning about the placement of John Susan in the south gallery. Fuck me, they're a dour lot.'

Caitlin's mouth opened to speak, before closing at the interruption.

'I was just saying to Caitlin, I'm going to get one of them

implants put in. You seen them, Elaine? They're so stupid. I hate them, honestly, but I'm just thinking, if the option's there then basically why not?'

A beat, then Elaine smiled. She said, 'That's good, dear.'

The lift descended; no one spoke. The lift door shunted, and just as they were waiting to exit, Otis having slid in front, Caitlin felt a tiny hand tweak at her sleeve. She didn't look down but felt Elaine's leg come close to her own, and her little gravelly whisper slipped up sideways, asking, 'Have you made up your mind, then?'

You could see Otis's head cock, the right ear turning infinitesimally backward. Then, the doors opened and the cafeteria's noise roared like traffic, and the women's eyes met for an instant, an instant where Caitlin head-shook an apology and wrinkled eyes for: *not right now.*

The little toddler fingers on her sleeve slid round the wrist to grasp just below the watch-line, to ground Caitlin in an instant where she felt herself lift off from the planet, an instant where her head felt full of gas and the skin was tight and shiny and ready to rupture any second now.

'See me later,' whispered Elaine.

More data, more figures, more lines on her screen. Otis's vape went down the wrong way and he coughed noisily and with much production for ninety seconds.

'Ouch,' he said. 'Did you hear that?'

'I did,' she replied.

'Wow.'

She took a sip of decaf and found it was cold. The sour liquid rested on her palate. She looked around the room, at the screens, at the wallpaper, at Otis's confused blinking, then braced herself to swallow.

'I'll be back in a bit,' she said as she stood.

'Yeah,' said Otis. 'Okay.' Then as she was leaving: 'Where are you going?'

'I need to see her. Elaine.'

Elaine nodded rhythmically as Caitlin spoke, as she relayed her answer. In short, the answer was: *yes*, but she felt it necessary to include all sorts of additional information, extra data.

'But so you want to take it?' asked Elaine. 'You're doing it?'

'I am,' said Caitlin. 'Yeah.'

'That's wonderful news, that's ... Come here.' Elaine stood, reaching up to grab hold of Caitlin's shoulders. They were in Elaine's office, right at the back of Arts Systems' building, an unusually shadowy place for a woman of Elaine's stature.

Caitlin sat when directed. She had said what needed to be said; now the future would take care of itself. She barely felt herself exist.

'I can't tell you how happy I am,' said Elaine. 'I so wanted it to be you who took it, and ... Well anyway, that's great. You'll need to be ready pretty sharpish. They want you up there yesterday, essentially. I don't know the ins and outs, but I just heard they have something new that's commandeered everything out there now, something *big*.'

Caitlin smiled. 'That's fine, that's totally fine. I can go whenever.'

'Have you told what's-his-name the good news?'

'I have.'

'And he doesn't mind? Three years is a long time, isn't it? Not everyone would manage.'

'It's not a problem, Elaine.'

Elaine's little wrinkled head tilted. 'No?'

'We're not ... It's just not a problem anymore.'

'I see.' Elaine looked extremely concerned for exactly three seconds, then her face reset. She smiled and started battering away at her machine, telling Caitlin all the details were now going downstairs to HR to get everything sorted out, to arrange a Step-Stone journey for her, and so on and so forth.

'And I'll get someone to look into a going-away party for you,' she added.

'No,' said Caitlin. 'That's okay.'

'You're sure?'

'I absolutely am.'

It was remarkable. She could move through the building like a stranger. Everything seemed unreal to her; all colours flashed in their true, original hues. Doors felt well-oiled as she used them. This unusual feeling was excitement, it was hope. She realised now that something dark and opaque had been slipped over her eyes, years back, and was only now being released. You should've felt that air surge into her nostrils, filling her up, clean and sweet and pure.

She paused at the lifts. You could go up or go down, naturally. She used the button for down, feeling too good to go back to the office and Otis's self-centred talk. Inside the lift, she realised she wouldn't have to see or hear the results of his experiments with implantation. What a result. When the lift opened on the floor below, her smile faltered. In strode Simone, mid-chat on her mobile. She gave Caitlin bored eyes and made a duck's bill of her fingers, meaning: *this person won't stop*. The gesture was designed to make Caitlin feel unimportant, but who cared? Simone could have it. She could have everything she wanted.

'Yeah, yeah, of course. Absolutely,' said Simone. 'You do that, okay, then let me know.' She killed the call. 'My god, I am in demand today. You going for a decaf, yeah?'

'I am,' said Caitlin.

'I'll chum you. I could do with half a Meal.'

They were quiet a while as the lift descended, then both spoke at once. Caitlin apologised; Simone waved her hand. They did it again. Caitlin laughed; Simone scowled.

'All I wanted to say was, I got that job,' said Caitlin. 'By the way.'

Simone's mouth opened up so you could see her really white bottom teeth. Her shoulders seemed to pincer together. 'What job?'

'We were talking this morning about the thing going out west. I got it. Elaine wanted me.'

Simone froze as the lift descended a single floor. She looked ahead into space. Then she said, 'I thought you might. I thought that might be a good fit for you. For me, not so much, but I can see you making the most of that sort of thing.'

'Thanks Simone,' she said.

'I think you'll be well suited to it.'

She repeated herself, thanking Simone as they emerged into the Arts Systems eatery, busy at this time of day, full of familiar faces she wouldn't have to deal with for years and years and years. She realised she was walking ahead, letting Simone trail in her wake. It felt remarkable.

'And so what's it going to be?' asked Simone. 'I never quite found out.'

Caitlin thought about it as she chose some decaf from the big humming machine. A new job, a big opportunity, another go at life, but she didn't know the full story. 'It's out at Scolpaig, at the spaceport. They're running rockets from there again, so they want PR I suppose. They need professional help.'

Simone took a Junior Meal from the display and smiled again. 'Well done,' she said. 'And if things go well, perhaps you'll end up staying.'

EIGHT

Somewhere in Summerfield House, a mouth screamed. Probably attached to a person, this mouth, to a face. Difficult to say, though, where the face, and presumably the body, was located within the building, given all the other high-volume yelling taking place in the early-hours mania of the 97ers' Edinburgh HQ.

In the kitchens, below open bulbs, Boyle argued with Gascoigne about the correct method for peeling potatoes – small knife versus dedicated peeler – the discussion growing increasingly heated, until Gascoigne, armed with the peeler, got his friend by the wrist and threatened to peel the skin there with his implement. Across in the laundry room, among the vats of hot water where boilersuits steeped, someone stirred the nearest vat with a long wooden pole, yelling the chorus of 'Roll with It' at the top of his voice. Elsewhere, anonymous members broke out of sleep mid-scream, tumbling from bunks, eye-whites dazzling in the dark. One young girl – Frischmann – lounged in a hallway chaise longue, pulling the gum from her mouth as long as her arm before letting it snap back to her gritted teeth, while at the hallway's far end a television played the *Braveheart* VHS at full volume. Others simply enjoyed the sound of their own opinions, declared loudly from right down in the diaphragm.

But the scream in question, that particular sound, emanated

from an attic bedroom, right below the eaves of Summerfield's roof. In there, cramped beneath a sharp V ceiling, three members were gathered, plus a stranger, tied to a chair. A muggy space, that attic bedroom, liable to collect all the breath and boilersuit damp from the floors below, the tiny dark windows fuzzed from condensation. Crammed with junk too, like the rest of the place – mannequins and black bags and towers of crates.

The three members crowded around the stranger, making sure his restraints were secure.

'He looks good,' said Beckham.

'Aye,' said Creutzfeldt-Jakob. 'Nice and tight.'

Van Outen frowned. 'Make sure that leg's okay. Do another cable tie to the ankle.'

Beckham obliged.

These three monsters had spent the evening camped out on the recreational parkland the building loomed over, huddled within bushes, looking out for likely victims for this latest scheme. Low-rankers, the three of them, with lots of free time to dream up tricks and scams. Their latest endeavour required a junior, hence the status of the poor, crying individual strapped to the chair before them. They captured him easy enough; smuggling him inside was no trouble at all.

'So what next?' asked Beckham, the lowest ranked of the three.

'What's next,' said van Outen, the highest, 'is we give him the old one-two.'

'Right,' said Creutzfeldt-Jakob. 'The old one-two.'

'Ah,' said Beckham. 'I see. Ones and twos.'

Van Outen waited. A snap of frustration. 'Get on with it then!'

Beckham stepped forward. He paused to scratch at his beard hair. 'You see when you say the old one-two, what do you mean exactly?'

'What do I mean? I mean, you work him over, don't you? You give him the old one-two.'

'Ah,' said Beckham. 'Got it. Say no more. Say no more.' He stretched his fingers backwards. 'And by that you mean ...'

'Oh my Lord! Creutzfeldt-Jakob, take care of it, will you?'

'Sure thing,' said Creutzfeldt-Jakob.

And of course, it immediately became clear Creutzfeldt-Jakob didn't understand what the old one-two was either. He approached the trapped junior, who looked up wide-eyed, mouth concealed by black tape, moving his head side to side. He sniffed, Creutzfeldt-Jakob, bracing himself, and squatted low and powerful. Easy, confident. The junior's eyes bulged above the tape rectangle.

Creutzfeldt-Jakob coughed. 'Give it to me once more, van-O. It's the old two-one, is it?'

'Fucking hell!' exploded van Outen, rushing forward and grabbing hold of his accomplices. 'Yous two are a fucking liability, aren't yous?' He stood them up proper, away from him, so he could work unobstructed. 'All the old one-two is,' he explained, 'is a kicking. That's all. A good old-fashioned battering. Nothing fancy or posh or anything, just a battering. The old one-two. We get a junior up here, give him the old one-two, and see what comes of it.'

They'd been studying, you see, these 97ers. All the free time in the world to study and learn and loaf around and dream up schemes and ideas and fall out with each other, then make up again. Long, long nights needing filled up with talk, because silences were where the doubts crept in. Certain night-time silences made you liable for cracking up, and none of them wanted to go through life as a crack-up. Downstairs, there were crack-ups aplenty: the utterly broken, the dishevelled, the psychotics and paranoiacs and bed-wetters.

Quietness in the night-time should be avoided if you didn't

want to start considering the world outside those walls, about life beyond the 97ers. What was your old ex-girlfriend doing with herself? How were lads from the school getting on in careers and industries? Where had Albarn disappeared to? Worst of all: what was being missed on the field? Jesus, that kept you up. All that content sliding by in the darkness, beyond your thumb, unseen, unobserved, gobbled up by others and not by you. That's how come you talked, and theorised. You made predictions, such as if those fucking juniors are sooking their electricity out of the field, does the process maybe go in the entire opposite way also?

'And plus,' said van Outen, yanking back the junior's head, 'these don't feel anything. No pain. They feel nothing. Isn't in their design, to feel.'

The junior looked nice enough. A peaceful sort of gentleman. His hair was swept over to the side in a way Creutzfeldt-Jakob had seen on adverts for aftershave.

Van Outen brought the base of his fist down gently on the junior's forehead, measuring up. 'The old one-two,' he said.

And downstairs, at the same time, other gatherings took place. In an entrance room, several teenage 97ers used a decrepit games system to play Crash Bandicoot. They huddled together cross-legged like very young children, passing the controller between deaths, giggling when the cartoon animal shouted. In some back-rooms, twos and threes congregated to draw up juvenile acts of sabotage, uncommissioned by higher-ranking members. They planned to glue the locks of certain establishments, to freeze urine and post the resultant yellowy puck through enemy postboxes. Elsewhere, solo 97ers tended their Tamagotchis with great sensitivity.

Above them all, in the usual space, the schoolmaster's garret, Hirst sat with Mandelson, waiting on Spencer. When alone, a small measure of tension existed between them. In his private, barely acknowledged fantasies, Hirst held a candle for his young lieutenant, one of the first members of the opposite sex he'd spent much time with. Barely any females out on the fens – barely any males without pockmarks or trench foot either – so they took a bit of getting used to, in Edinburgh, the real flesh-and-blood women, as well as the metres-high vixens featured on city centre billboards.

He said, 'I saw something today.'

'Oh aye?' asked Mandelson. 'Did you now?'

'I did. I saw something specifically interesting.'

'Go on then.'

'Well, you know me, I like to keep my head down, don't I? I get to where I'm going, avoiding fuss as much as possible. That's my way.'

'You have a fast . . . what's it called?'

'My gait is very, very quick,' he agreed. 'But I seen something today made me halt in my tracks. I was going up the Lothian Road, quick and sharp, and I passed this café. This is a café specialising in colas. You seen it? The Cola Cup is its name, and they do all the old ones. The Pepsis, the originals, the fruity ones such as Lilts. Very nice, whatever. I am going by at my usual stride, when I spy something through the window. I spy a pair of them, juniors, sat drinking Junior Meal colas from big frosty glasses in them window benches. Except no, I amen't spying that, cause instead of drinking them colas, these juniors is necking each other.'

'Is that right?'

'It is right. Brass as you like, in full view of window. I could see it were two juniors going at it, like. All smooching and that. With tongues I expect too. Could you credit it?'

'That's bizarre,' said Mandelson. 'I didn't think that was meant to happen.'

'No, it isn't meant to happen, but it has done. Two of them, going right at it, in window. I'm no prude, you know I'm not. Two lovely young healthy human beings sharing a kiss on a sunny day: no problem. But *juniors*. What does it represent?'

'I'd say it's bad news,' said Mandelson, with scant interest. She didn't care for junioring and all it represented, but who gave a shit if a few of them were kissing?

'Bad news indeed,' said Hirst. 'It represents the species eating itself, doesn't it? A big coiled-up snake munching off its own tail end. What are these two's seniors doing while these two are getting off? Eh? They've made babies of themselves and sent babies off to neck. Delegating romance, is what it is. They're outsourcing the act of love.' A quick flush of rosiness across his pointed nose at this. 'What happens when they move on to the other? Downstairs business and all that? Does that make a kid? Does it fuck.'

Suddenly, a significant portion of the room's air vanished, displaced by the giant figure now looming through the door-frame. Spencer, ducking: 'Does what fuck?'

'Hirst here's seen something that gave him the willies.'

'Oh aye? What's it now, Hirst? A crumpled shirt? Litter?'

Hirst smiled at the insult, a quick sneer. 'Two juniors necking down the Cola Cup.'

'Nice,' said Spencer, his chair complaining as he took a place at the mess-strewn table. 'Get a good eyeful, did you?'

'I saw enough. I saw plenty.'

'Pervert.'

'I saw the end of civilisation conducted across two things of black cola. I saw plenty.'

Spencer slid off his heavy jacket, showing the meaty rounds of his arms, his knee-like elbows. 'Someone's screaming down the corridor.'

'Who is?' asked Hirst.

'Came from Beckham and van Outen's bit. A big huge shout.' Spencer, being a genius of yells and screams, was able to identify the sound as a person in some pain. 'Will we do anything?'

Hirst glanced to the little window. He squinted. 'Nah,' he announced.

'A-okay,' said Spencer.

'How did you get on?' Mandelson asked, impatient with the two men's tendency to become distracted.

'I got on very well. Very well indeed. They came out one of them gig places in the Old Town, in the middle of this riot.'

Hirst straightened. 'Oh really?'

'And Dolly was with them, as per the plan.'

'Excellent.'

'Either of you spoke to this Dolly yet?' asked Hirst.

The new recruit. He'd conducted a proper sit-down chat with her the morning after she turned up; the house tended to be quiet in the earlier hours. Hirst sometimes sneaked out at dawn to jog through the neighbourhood, his heart racing from the exercise but also from fear of being caught by a fellow 97er, prancing round like one of *them*. She seemed good enough, this Dolly, with a history of employment, unlike the rest. She was vaguely sensible-looking, with no facial tattoos or erratic cranial bald spots. She wasn't wall-eyed or hunched. By any chance was she interested in getting involved in something important, straight off the mark? It turned out that actually, yes, indeed, she may well be.

'I haven't properly seen her,' said Spencer, who slept off-campus for private reasons.

'She's a good sort,' nodded Mandelson. 'Seems to be doing well down at Step-Stone.'

'I thought so too,' said Hirst. He stood then, and went to the wall. 'Can you hear that?' he asked.

Mandelson said no, she couldn't.

'It'll be Beckham and van Outen,' said Spencer. 'Whatever they're doing.'

And indeed it was.

Along the corridor, van Outen sweated from his work. As he performed the old one-two, he spoke to Beckham and Creutzfeldt-Jakob, comparing the messed-up junior before him to the mannequins in the corner. 'Think about it,' he heaved. 'You wouldn't think twice about battering one of them, would you, the plastic models? They're made of fibre, card or whatever, so it doesn't matter if you hurt it. You can't hurt it, I mean. It's an impossibility.'

The junior's mouth tape had been lost in the violence. He mumbled, 'Please ...'

'All we're doing here,' said van Outen, 'is messing around with a machine's programming. These machines,' he placed a sharp jab across the junior's cheek, 'are only programmed to accept a limited range of displeasure. Makes sense, eh? You can't programme something for every eventuality. Not possible. So what happens if the wires get crossed, the mainframe gets scrambled? Well, we're going to find out.'

The junior was in a bad way. Liquids seeped out from his head's openings. His chin sunk to the breastbone in a way that struck Beckham and Creutzfeldt-Jakob both as traumatic. Now and then he spoke, little words of pleading or of sorrow.

'Nothing's happening,' said Beckham. 'You're just a cruel bastard, van Outen. It's a waste of time.'

'Aye,' said Creutzfeldt-Jakob. 'You'll just end up killing it.'

Van Outen looked around. He shrugged. 'I did think something would've happened by now.'

'Juniors probably get messed up every day,' said Creutzfeldt-Jakob. 'Doesn't mean something's going to happen.'

'Maybe it's the whole pain thing,' said van Outen. 'Maybe

we're not going far enough. The old one-two's maybe insufficient for our purposes.'

He started to rake through the room's corners, as the junior moaned, as Beckham and Creutzfeldt-Jakob lounged on the bunks, bored. The room contained much to rake through – old dolls, humps of soil, discarded cabling – but van Outen soon found something to catch his interest.

'How about this?' he said, presenting a shiny set of pliers to the room.

'What are those?' asked Beckham.

'Tools or something,' said van Outen, his shadow falling across the junior's slumped form.

Hirst said he couldn't hear anything else. The others sat listening for a moment, then turned away from the southern wall. They were used to odd sounds in the house and barely registered the yells from Beckham and van Outen's quarters.

Mandelson swallowed. Of the three, she was least easy around loud noises. For her, sharp bangs sometimes set off what she knew as the Head Thing. The Head Thing started up without fanfare a couple years back, when she was sat in a cinema, one of the old-fashioned set-ups. She enjoyed the film. It was easy, and funny, and she was with a boyfriend of the time, this muscly lad with good posh glasses. The Head Thing began during the third act, when she felt herself plugged into the drama entirely, like completely focused on the happenings on-screen, not fussing about anything psychological, and the Head Thing appeared from nowhere. It felt like sort of wanting to sneeze. Like being very, very sleepy and feeling your head droop forward of its own accord. Like fainting, except she'd never fainted before and could only guess at what that felt like. A sort of vertigo somewhere between her eyes, a few centimetres outside her body.

She fought it back, wrestled her own mind into control.

Inside, somewhere, she said: you're having a stroke. This is it. The big one. She knew her old granny had stroked way before the disaster, and Mandelson herself found her on the back stair. This was it, she thought, but then the big one didn't come, just the Head Thing. Her ears rang. The pictures on screen grew colourful and vivid and she couldn't understand what the plot was.

She went out into the lobby for a moment, passing by heads in the dark. Pacing on the carpet there, among the moving adverts for films and streams and decaf, she plucked at her neck. Her heart raced, her bowels pulsed, the Head Thing whooshed, and the muscles of her skull contracted and beat.

I'm needing fresh air, she thought, and went into the street.

The crowds were insane outside the cinema. Another scorcher. The Head Thing whooshed. Her eyes wanted to close and her skin burned from cold sweat. A sudden weakness in her elbows, her knees. The Head Thing told her to get away, to escape, that all the eyes and mouths of the passing faces, grimacing and leering, meant her direct harm.

She abandoned the boyfriend with the good posh glasses and went down the road at speed, plucking the neck, checking the pulse. At home, she lay down in the dark and waited it out. In time, the Head Thing seeped away into a low-grade migraine. Not much ready cash at that time, so no hope of accessing Chem & Med, nor of ordering Capsule Om over flume. She nicotined more instead, which sort of helped.

So, aye, an uneasiness in Mandelson around loud noises. Once, a few days post-Head Thing, a wee bairn dropped his toy on a Big Mad Alec's Big Mad Tram and it came back with a vengeance. The whole deal. The whole headrush panic and plucking and shivering.

In the garret, she said, 'They're probably just messing about, Beckham and van Outen.'

'Aye,' said Spencer, peering at her. 'Probably.'

'Anyway,' said Hirst. 'This Dolly. I think we can trust her. A good sort, as I say. She's doing well at Step-Stone. That's them got her set up on fake papers.'

'Fine,' said Spencer.

'Actually, I think I heard something else,' said Mandelson. 'Should we check?'

'It's fine,' said Hirst. 'They'll just be messing about. Them lads, they'll be wrestling.'

'Right,' said Mandelson. 'Okay.'

Spencer got up. He sighed. 'I'll just go and fucking check and get it done with.'

He struggled to maintain patience among the 97ers sometimes. Too much blethering for his tastes. Spencer preferred to get on with a thing and see it done. This wasn't just an issue with 97ers but also with his other contacts throughout the city. Too much blether, not enough action. Blethering was where doubts and anxieties let themselves in. Better to apologise than to ask permission. Or better yet: never apologise, never explain.

Spencer lowered himself through the doorway and out into the hall, ducking to move past a low-hanging light fixture. His shoulder nearly brushed against the walls on either side. It felt good to be big, to take up space, to consume space with your presence. Spencer fucking loved it. He felt like a machine for using up space, for burning tens of thousands of calories. The faces on the lads down the Pit when he did his trick of downing eight beef curry sachets in a row, lining up the crumpled silver as he went, burping and asking: any more?

Despite their violence, the Pit lads were mostly smallish. Mostly rats. You still had to be careful with a rat lad. They could be wiry, full of potential, liable to sneak implements into the matches: little knives and sharp nails and the like. This was Spencer's main income stream now, winning matches down the

Pit. They all wanted to see the big man fall, to end his streak, so his bets ran high. He bet tokens against himself, down in the old garage on Gordon Street not far from where he'd grown up, because he knew. He was unbeatable. He filled corridors, he filled jackets, he filled bedframes. Bath water plunged to the floor when he slipped under. When he shagged, he filled the individual up entirely. He'd broken watch straps, bent spoons, cracked pint pots, bruised lintels, compressed windpipes. After that gogoplata on the posh-cunt Chris Hobson, he'd focused on growing, getting large, gnashing and consuming and swallowing whatever he could get his mitts on. When he stomped into the ring at the Pit and saw whatever pathetic rat lad they'd put him up against, he nearly cried from amusement. It was so easy.

The items he could lift! The objects he could separate against their will!

Sounds came through Beckham and van Outen's door. Sounds sort of expressing fear. He opened up.

And a few moments later, back in the office, Hirst leapt at Spencer's yell coming down the corridor. Mandelson did her best to conceal a slight reoccurrence of the Head Thing as they both piled out, down the hall, past numerous other doors, and into the room where Beckham and van Outen bunked.

'The fuck is that?' exclaimed Hirst.

Much of the small room was taken up by Spencer. He was planted to the middle of the floor, standing over a beaten-up junior, tied to a chair. The low-rankers had crammed themselves into the bunk beds, all three pushed into the lower portion, snivelling, holding each other. Aside from all this, something else stood in the corner of the room. Something Mandelson couldn't believe.

'What've you cunts done?' growled Spencer, eyes moving from the junior to the low-rankers to . . . the entity in the corner.

'What is it?' asked Mandelson, whose Head Thing began kicking in overtime.

The entity in the corner stepped forward. It glowed slightly in the room's dimness, its edges crackled and distorted. The shape of a human, but transparent, ethereal. It opened its mouth and gazed around itself.

Mandelson quickly went out, disappearing into the corridor's dark.

'We were just—' said Beckham.

'It was an idea that—' said Creutzfeldt-Jakob.

'We didn't know what—' said van Outen.

Hirst steeled himself. He crept beyond Spencer, skirting his gravity, and came near to the thing in the corner. It observed him. It watched as he reached out a hand and moved it across the thing's body.

'It feels spicy,' Hirst whispered.

'Spicy?' hissed Spencer.

'Like spicy on my fingers.'

The thing looked down to where Hirst's fingers had touched.

They spoke in low voices to one another, Spencer's breath landing on Hirst's shoulder.

'Is it a ghost?' asked Spencer.

'Don't know.'

'Is it real?'

'Don't know.'

'Are we fucking cracking up?'

'We're all of us seeing it, aren't we?'

'What does it mean?'

'Don't know.'

The thing in the corner began to move. It walked slowly, soundlessly, across the floor, past Hirst and Spencer, towards the slumped figure in the chair. They all held their breath as it considered the poor, ruined junior. It crouched a little, bending at the knee to get to eye level. It started to sob, quiet, but audible.

'You lot have got some serious explaining to do,' said Hirst, his voice stiff with the rigidity of his jaw.

Van Outen spoke. He leaned out of the bottom bunk. 'It was just like this idea to see what happens when you give a junior a bit of the old one-two, how they handle it, see what we could learn. I never thought it would happen. This thing just appears out of nowhere, eh, and starts sparking about.'

'Did you kill it?' asked Spencer.

'Pretty much,' said van Outen. 'I don't know. I reckon. Listen, Hirst, I'm fucking sorry man. We just—'

'It doesn't matter,' said Hirst. 'It doesn't matter.'

Something changed in Hirst's face then, something that scared the low-rankers. The skin encircling his mouth pulled back, his eyes became glossy, and a sheen burst out across his tight features. He moved through the room slowly and fell upon the ghost, bringing his arms around it. The ghost continued to mourn as Hirst yanked at its shoulders.

'Spencer,' he hissed. 'Help me. It's strong.'

The big man lurched to his side to assist in this task. His paws gripped the ghost's body. He grumbled swear words.

'We've got to get it, Spencer,' said Hirst. 'This could be huge. This could be fucking *huge*.'

Back in the office, Mandelson's Head Thing had her down in a chair, head between her knees, focusing on breaths like they were last hovercrafts out. One breath in, then in exchange, one breath out. No one told her to do this. It was a personal solution to a personal problem. She pictured all these breaths getting banked up in her tight lungs and saw measuring them as some sort of compromise.

She too had bad memories of the dog days. A similar

wake-up call, mid-catastrophe, going out into the road, witnessing gore and horror. Everything she saw, she wanted to forget. Deep down, she knew her Head Thing was a response to those visions.

Upon seeing, for example, a little child squashed beneath a fallen wall, she set up an implement outside herself. It was a sort of lamp hanging above her head, a small floodlamp she could control. It dangled invisible above and sometimes contained her consciousness. She used it to watch from. Mostly, she directed its light straight down, onto Mandelson herself, scanning her body and brain constantly, checking for weaknesses and gaps in the armour. She sensed out illnesses before they formed. She watched as she spoke, checking the words before they escaped her lips. The light burned onto areas of her brain that tended towards emotion.

In the garret, she knuckled her temples, stared at the dirty floor, and breathed. One for one. One for one.

It beamed outwards too, this light, which may have been its main function. It watched out for enemies, for anyone snickering behind their hands. It saw disaster around each corner and prevented Mandelson from walking below scaffolding, or feeling alright in rooms where her back wasn't close to the wall, or being truly present during the conversations she had before she fell in with Spencer. She'd had friends, hadn't she? She knew folk from off the peninsula and was doing fine at work, but the lamp stopped her getting close. It shone on colleagues and made her aware of deficiencies and weakness. It told her to steer well clear. Spencer was different. Nothing hidden there. The lamp scanned and showed him as evil, but honestly so. A useful contraption, her lamp, but Christ its maintenance exhausted.

When he first spoke to her, this wall of man, using his skills to sense her dissatisfaction, her powerlessness, her lack of hope, she let herself be convinced. Wouldn't she like to return to an earlier time? Wouldn't it feel good to move back beyond her hurt? Wouldn't she like a place to belong? All of this, he said, he could offer her. There were others out there, others who shared her pain. Afterwards, once inside the cell, it was a piece of cake to rise through its ranks, to find herself suspended above the 97er lowlifes in this tottering garret room. All it took was a brain on your shoulders. All it took was the ability to cut out the parts of you that felt. Mandelson was highly trained in that kind of surgery. She would dissect anything, if it gave her a place to belong.

NINE

In the bright light of morning, the firth's abandoned bridges stretched across the water cleanly and sharply, their shadows darkening the Forth below them. Above, a small chopper passed by, the sound of its blades carrying far and wide. Inside, Larson watched the river slide beneath him, noted the sections of bridge that had fallen away, only stumps showing above the waves.

'Nearly there,' the pilot said in his headphones.

He nodded, though no one was with him in the back. His attention was now on the ruined peninsula's steaming bulk.

They sped towards the city's north shore, the roads there already packed with vehicles and trams, and made their way to the airstrip.

That morning, he had left the rest of the operation west of Edinburgh, at the airport. No one knew he was planning this diversion and his announcement in the hotel caused some consternation from Stock. They were due to leave for the west immediately; the schedule had been approved at all levels for days in advance. All well and good, he told them, but he needed a few hours. The west would still be there when he got back. They probably assumed he wanted a quick tour of the old stomping ground before the grand plans were put into action. They would be dead wrong. The city he saw unfurling below caused him to feel no great affection. In his time, he had choppered over countless small cities, countless towns and conurbations, observing them with passive disinterest. This one, this city of his youth, was no different.

The pilot landed them cleanly at the airstrip and Larson ducked out beneath the slicing blades. He made his way to the terminal where a car waited for him. Leaving the chopper and entering the car took less than three minutes. There was something about the neatness of the operation that greatly appealed to him. Something in his head clicked into its housing whenever well-laid plans went off smoothly.

The car's driver, a junior, read him the address.

'That's right,' Larson confirmed and they set off.

For a long time, for a good many years, he had kept a small property in the city's north. The rent was expensive for the area, but the cost was nothing to a man of his means. The property contained two bedrooms, a kitchen and bathroom. It housed two tenants, both of whom Larson knew well. Through the window of the car, he watched the building's front door, painted dusky grey and with ferrous digits spelling out: *240*. He watched it for a couple of minutes, then said to the driver, 'Find a place to park would you? Get me when I'm done.'

'No worries, boss,' said the driver.

He stepped out onto the pavement and waited for the car to depart. The road was full of traffic and it took a while for him to cross. There were lots of young people milling around. They seemed to be an entirely different species. He didn't recognise the clothes, the haircuts, the attitudes. He ignored them and went up the short staircase to the door of 240. He rapped on the letter box, then waited.

This road he knew well. As a teenager, he used to walk across the city from his aunts' tenement, meeting up with lads from school on the way. They tried to buy pints in the countless pubs and mostly got rebuffed. It felt good to be around the older students though; they strutted about the place with bravado. When the time came to acquire a property in a place no one would suspect, he knew precisely which location to plump for.

In time, the door opened a crack. The inside of the property looked very dark. The woman who lived inside had her face pressed close to the opening, only her left eye peering through.

'Hello,' said Larson.

'Oh,' she said. 'It's you.'

He nodded in agreement.

'I wasn't expecting you,' she said.

'No, I understand. But it's urgent.'

She looked at him for a moment, then cast her eye out onto the street beyond. He appreciated her resistance; part of her role was to jealously guard the property.

'It won't take long, Mrs Bailey,' he said. 'I won't be back again for some time.'

'Fine,' she said, opening the door further. 'But make it quick.'

She stepped back into the shadowy hallway and allowed him to enter. He passed by her closely and smelled her odour: a floral powder floating above rich, meaty stock. She quickly closed the door and stood inspecting him in the gloom.

'You're getting old,' she said.

'We both are,' he replied.

She coughed then, her interpretation of a laugh. 'It doesn't matter what *I* look like,' she said. 'No one sees me.'

He nodded. 'That's fair.'

She chewed something over in her gums. 'So you're passing through then?'

'In a way.'

'I like it when you give me notice.'

'I know you do. That's the agreement, but this is an exceptional circumstance.'

'Aye,' she said, turning and shuffling down the hall. 'They always are, aren't they?'

Together, they went into the back room, a combination sitting-dining room. There were a few lumpy sofas, a rather fancy viewing screen, and a table with one chair. It could be nicer if she wanted it to be, he paid her enough. She continued through into the adjoining kitchen, where sounds of water running, then boiling, could be heard.

He sat down on one of the sofas and called through: 'How has he been?'

'Very poorly,' she replied, her voice carrying through. 'A very sickly customer.'

He didn't know what to say to that. He shifted round to look out the window behind himself. The view stretched out across rooftops, the land sliding down towards the river. You could make out a few flashes of reflected sunlight among the lower roofs.

Soon, she brought out a pot of decaf and put it on the table. 'I had to dig out a second cup,' she said, blowing dust out of the mug she'd selected for him. She grimaced. 'We don't get many guests.'

He laughed, accepted the cup. 'No,' he said. 'I guess not.'

'*Guess*?' she said, approximating his accent. 'You mean *suppose*.'

'Okay Mrs Bailey, I *suppose* I do.'

She sat down on the single chair and crossed her legs. She wore old-fashioned denims and a T-shirt printed with a beach scene, the words *Los Angeles* copied across its palm trees. Her features were narrow, the wrinkles pinched around her eyes and mouth. He visited the property only once or twice a decade; it always surprised him to notice these changes in Mrs Bailey.

She took a quick sip, then asked, 'So what's this all about?'

'I just need to have a quick conversation with him. There's

something big in the pipeline and I'm going to be off the map for some time.'

She nodded. 'It's not just his body, you see. His mind's starting to go too. I don't know if he'll make much sense.'

'I understand.'

She stared at him fiercely for a moment. 'You're not his favourite person in the world, either.'

He smiled. 'I understand.'

Once the decaf was drunk, she tidied away the cups. She took a long time at the sink, facing away from him, and he knew what was going through her mind. What gave him the right to come barging into their peace, to come upsetting the delicate balance she maintained? A fair criticism, he thought, but one he didn't care to tackle. He sat on the sofa and waited for her to come to him, holding the key.

'Well,' she said. 'I'd better let you in then.'

He followed her back to the dark hallway, past the bathroom with its toilet visible through the open door, to one of the bedrooms. She put the key in its lock and turned it.

'Try to speak quietly,' she said, then walked away.

He went inside, letting the door close behind himself. If the hallway felt dark, then this room was like a starless night, deep in the country. Put simply, he saw nothing. Shuffling forward, he brought out his hands to feel for any obstructions, smelling the unusual odour once more. It was a shock every time, this stink, one that brought him back to his early career. Something sweet and sickly like almonds, with a shrill chemical base: batteries, or coins.

'Hello?' he said to the dark. 'Are you awake?'

He heard shuffling within the room's heart, moving fabric, but no voice responded.

'It's me,' he said. 'I'm here to see you.'

A bedspring squeaked, followed by a grunt of effort. He

could hear the body moving around and making little sounds. 'I was sleepy-timing,' said the body.

Internally, Larson shuddered. He hated to hear the sound of it, the babyish tone of its voice, so high-pitched and nasal.

'Can you turn on the light please, Junior?' he said. 'I can't quite see.'

'Okey-dokey,' wheezed Junior, giggling a little in the dark. Larson heard him scrabble around before a small bedside lamp switched on. It cast an orb of light around the bed's head where Junior sat supporting himself on one arm, wearing creased stripey pyjamas. Empty sachets of Junior Meal lay on the carpet around the bed, alongside basins and jugs half full of some orangey gloop.

Junior blinked against the light as Larson fought down the disgust of viewing his only son.

The first junior the public heard about was named James Partridge. James Partridge, the senior, had been a casual friend of Larson's, someone he trusted well enough and whose main qualifications were extreme good looks. Everyone agreed: if this thing is going to fly, we need a looker. James Partridge received a hefty payment when they secured the rights to his likeness, to his genetic data, to his biology. Partridge's junior got presented to the world and all was well, but before James, there were others. Others like Junior.

His room contained a bed, a table with the lamp, a desk with chair and an open wardrobe with clothes hanging inside. The room had no window. On the walls were pictures Larson recognised, because they were of him; early in his life, Junior had combed through magazines and newspapers, cutting out pictures of Larson and pasting them to his bedroom wall. In the middle of everything sat Junior himself, knuckling his eyes and yawning. He looked disgusting. Larson hated to admit it, but there was no other word for Junior. Dressed up in civilian clothes and travelling on the tram, your eyes might pass over Junior and register him as a normal-looking twenty-something man. Passing by him in the street, you might clock a slight eeriness in the air around him but probably not much more than that. If your gaze hung on him a little longer, you would recognise the deficiencies. You would notice his slack, waxy skin. It hung from the structure of his face like loose bacon, greyed and pocked in places. You would notice his hair, very thin and insubstantial, palest blond. You would notice his eyes most of all. They were wide and round like a beautiful baby's, but the irises held no colour. Enormous pupils watched you, dark holes that weren't malevolent in any way but which certainly could not be called human. All of that might be bearable if it wasn't for his attitude. If he looked ugly and behaved in an ugly manner, fair enough. Larson could've lived with that. But no. Junior's heart was pure. He was like an angel present on this earth.

'Are you okay, Daddy?' he asked.

'I'm fine, Junior,' said Larson. He pulled out the chair and set it down at the foot of Junior's bed. He sat. 'How was your sleep?'

'Sleep was ace,' said Junior, nodding and smiling. His lips were a little glossy, from his equivalent of spit. 'I dreamed of an ellingphant.'

Larson nodded. 'That's good,' he said. 'That sounds like a nice dream.'

Junior beamed with such purity, the smile so discordant with the dreadful features around it, that Larson had to briefly look away.

'I didn't know you were coming to see us,' said Junior. 'Mrs Bailey didn't tell me.'

'Well, it was supposed to be a surprise,' he said. 'I didn't want to ruin things by calling ahead.'

Junior nodded. He understood.

For years and years, the boy – what else could you call him? – had known nothing but the interior of this small property. He slept in the bedroom, watched streams with Mrs Bailey, ate a Junior Meal once a day, even though it didn't quite agree with his primitive system. He had no real understanding of the outside world, no knowledge of anything that didn't come to him via Bailey or the screen. He loved Larson more than anything else.

'It's really good to see you,' he said. 'I do worry about you, you know? I wish I could be here more often to sit down together like this.'

'But you've got to work,' said Junior. This concept had been explained to him often.

'I do,' said Larson. 'Unfortunately, I do.'

'Because you're the world's father,' said Junior excitedly. 'You're not just my Daddy, you're everyone's Daddy.'

'That's just a saying, Junior,' he said. 'I'm not literally—' As he started to contradict the boy, Junior's expression began to darken. He didn't much like being told he was wrong. It wasn't his fault; he operated with the facilities of a roughly six-year-old child. 'Well, it's a nice expression anyway, isn't it?'

Junior nodded, hard at thought, then jerked up onto his knees. 'Can I wear your hatty, please?'

Jumping back a little at the outburst, Larson's fingers went to the brim of his cap. Instinctively he wanted to bat the boy away, to raise his hand and smack at the advancing Junior. 'Of course,' he said. 'Anything you like.'

He took off the cap and flung it onto the bed, where Junior greedily snatched it up. He popped it on top of his head, where it perched like a party hat. Junior's cranium was unusually large and domed, an error they ironed out in later models.

'Look at me,' said Junior. He pushed his shoulders back and

made guns with his fingers. 'I'm Daddy and I'm going to blow you all up.' Loud screeches of laughter erupted from his moist, pink mouth; Larson fought a grimace into a grin.

'That's very funny, Junior,' he said.

There was nothing wrong with Junior, not really. He was simply born before his time, created before the technology had been perfected. The primary issue, the fatal flaw in Junior's construction was that he'd been dreamed up from scratch. In the early days of junioring, before they'd even called it that, Larson's aim had been to create a new being. He wanted to take all their advancements in AI and robotics and fashion a man out of the ether. That turned out to be a dead end, Junior being the result of that disastrous misstep. It was impossible, it turned out, to make something from nothing. The results were horrifying, macabre, nauseating. You needed a body to copy your junior from, otherwise you entered nightmare territory.

'You can keep that, if you like,' he said.

'Thank you kindly,' cooed Junior, up from the bed now and moseying around the floor like a cowboy. Standing upright, you saw Junior was tall and lanky, stooped round the shoulders with a pendulous pot belly. When he passed behind Larson, the hairs on the back of his neck sprung up.

'I've got some big news for you,' he said.

From behind: 'Big news. Big news.'

'That's right. I'm going to be going away for a while. I'm going to be taking a trip.'

If it was possible, the room seemed to darken. The lamp's small orb shrunk in on itself and Larson felt himself vulnerable. He heard Junior stop pacing behind him, sensed his gaze fall upon Larson's exposed head. The boy was strong; tests at the time had shown he could overpower a well-trained biological male nine times out of ten.

'Why?' asked Junior, his voice thick with something.

'It's for work,' said Larson. 'You wouldn't understand.'

There was silence in the room for a while and he held his breath. Then, he felt hands creep onto his shoulders. He felt Junior's fingers slip into the opening of his shirt. They were ice cold.

'I can go with you?' he asked, a few inches from Larson's ear.

'That's not going to be possible, Junior.'

'I can go *with* you?'

'Look, come around here where I can see you. Come and sit on the bed.'

The fingers drew away sharply with a sensation like a knife slicing his skin. For a moment, he wondered if the boy would try to attack him, and what he might do in response. But no, he was being ridiculous. He turned in the chair and saw Junior backed up into the corner, into the deepest dark, palpating the cap between his claws.

Larson opened his arms. He opened them wide.

Junior watched him, then rushed forward, gripping his father in a tight, chilly embrace.

'There there,' he said, rubbing the nodules of Junior's back. 'It's okay.'

Junior broke away from him and sat at the edge of the bed. 'I thought you were coming to take me,' he sniffed. 'Mrs Bailey says one day your Daddy will come and take you away from this. From the dark.'

'We've been through it,' he said. 'Junior, it's dangerous out there. You don't know the things that go on outside this house. You don't understand. There are terrible men out there right this second and they'd do awful things to you if they found you. When I made you—'

'When you birthed me.'

'Okay, when I birthed you. When I birthed you, it had to be secret so that the bad men couldn't hurt you.'

Junior worked at the material of his pyjama bottoms. He started to moan.

'Please be quiet,' said Larson. He tried to keep his tone light, but the moaning continued. Junior became increasingly upset, shaking his big head, screwing up his eyes, tugging so hard on his bottoms that his navel became visible. 'Shush,' Larson said.

A bang came at the door. 'What's going on in there?' asked Mrs Bailey.

'Nothing.' He went to the door, opening it an inch. 'Give us a minute, would you?'

'I don't want you upsetting him. If you go upsetting him, I'll be the one left picking up the pieces.'

'Look! I—' He fought his temper down. He sucked on his teeth. 'Please, Mrs Bailey. Let me have a little more time, in peace.'

She glared at him for a moment, then vanished.

He turned to the boy and said, 'Let's start again.'

It didn't take long to realise their mistake with Junior. Before animation, his appearance looked pretty good. It wasn't until life surged into him that they recognised how badly they'd miscalculated. Not only did they recoil at his physical appearance, they quickly understood that his intellectual capabilities were severely diminished. In a few weeks, they were changing course, looking into replication rather than production, but the awkward question of what to do with Junior remained. At that early stage, no one quite had the stomach to euthanise their experiment. 'I'll take him,' Larson had said. 'He's my responsibility.' Stock warned him that no one could know, that the outrage would be tremendous, that –

'I've already said I'll take him.'

With Mrs Bailey dealt with, they now spent time together. Larson helped him tidy up the discarded Meal sachets. He poured all the orangey vomit-equivalent into one large jug. They took opposite sides of the duvet and made the bed.

'There,' said Larson. 'That looks better, doesn't it?'

'The room's all clean now,' confirmed Junior. 'Now, it's sparkling.'

They sat together on the end of the bed and Larson described how he spent his days, something that always interested Junior whenever he found time to visit. He wanted to know what Larson ate for breakfast, what his own bedroom looked like, what he watched on the streams. He kept his face close to Larson's, hoovering up the information like calories, gorging himself on Daddy's secrets.

'Junior,' he said. 'I don't want to upset you again, but you should know I'm going to have to go soon.'

Junior nodded placidly. 'You're going on a journey soon.'

'That's right,' he said. 'Well done.'

'Thank you.'

'Now I want you to be very brave when you listen to this next part, okay?'

'Okey-dokey.'

'I'm going to be going on a journey and I don't know if I'll ever be back. Do you understand that? Does that make sense to you?'

'Yes.'

'And I'm feeling very worried about leaving you alone when I'm gone. I'm worried about all the bad men outside the house. I'm worried about what they'd do to you if they found you.'

Junior giggled. 'It's fine. Mrs Bailey keeps me safe.'

'But what happens if Mrs Bailey stops getting her money, huh? What happens then?'

He stuck out his bottom lip and sniffed. 'Money . . .'

'Do you understand what I'm asking, Junior?'

Junior scowled, the loose skin around his eyebrows

contracting. 'You'll look after me,' he said, smiling at this new understanding. 'You'll look after me, won't you, Daddy?'

Larson sighed. He put his hands out on his knees. It had been silly to expect the boy to understand, but he wanted to give it a try. If anything, he owed Junior the attempt. 'Let's have another hug, shall we?'

Junior nodded furiously. He dived into Larson's chest, pushing his head into the breastbone, moving aside the device hanging from his necklace. Larson clapped him on the back, taking one last look at the depressing bedroom. It would be good not to have to come here again, not to have to deal with Bailey, not to be reminded of his own boring, provincial childhood. He wished he could have given Junior a better existence, but his hands had been tied.

'I'm sorry,' he said. 'I don't know if you understand that, but it's true.' He laid a hand on the boy's neck, across his icy skin. 'Things didn't work out how I wanted them.' He ran the hand up towards the nape of Junior's head, brushing away the babyish hairs. 'If I could've made it different, I would have.' Underneath the hairs was a panel, dark and shiny. 'I'm sorry, Junior,' he said, placing his thumb against the glass.

Mrs Bailey had boiled up more decaf, but he didn't want any. He stood in the middle of the living room and looked around. His skin started to feel itchy. He wanted to get away.

'I'm going to hit the road,' he said.

She stood up. 'Let me know in advance next time,' she said.

'There isn't going to be a next time.'

A small jerk of surprise showed in Mrs Bailey's face, but she didn't allow it to live long. 'No? You won't be seeing him again?'

'I won't.' He took out his mobile and confirmed the payment he'd lined up earlier that morning. 'You're going to find a large sum of money in the usual account, Mrs Bailey. You should consider this your severance payment. By next month, this property will be sold and you'll have to get somewhere else to live.'

Mrs Bailey stuck out her jaw. Her eyes nearly closed. 'Oh really?'

'Yes, really.'

'You're going to find someone else to do this work, are you?'

He shrugged.

'I doubt it. I doubt it very much. You know I'll go to the streams, don't you? I'll be on the streams by this evening.'

'It's all in the paperwork, Mrs Bailey. If you talk, your life won't be worth living.'

'And what about the boy?' she asked. She took a step towards him. 'Who is it that's going to look after the boy?'

'That won't be an issue, Mrs Bailey. I want to thank you for the years of service you've given to me. It's been very much appreciated.'

He could feel the fury radiate out from her. The room grew hot and close and he knew he ought to leave. Checking the mobile again, he called his car back.

'I'm going to go now,' he said.

'You scumbag,' said Mrs Bailey, but he ignored her. 'I'm going to tell him you've abandoned him. I'm going to tell him right now.'

He walked by her and into the hall. He passed the closed door to Junior's quarters and went straight to the exit. 'Goodbye, Mrs Bailey,' he said.

A light drizzle fell on the street outside. The pavement and road were shiny with moisture and the car wore tiny dots of light. As he walked away, he heard a panicked scream from inside the property.

So, she'd found him then. That was okay though, because the remains wouldn't last long.

*

At the airstrip, the chopper waited for him. Like with his arrival, the transfer was utterly seamless. He stepped out of the car and walked up and into the aircraft without expending an iota of unnecessary energy. They ran through the usual safety protocols and he buckled himself in and wore the ear protectors.

'Let's move it,' he said to the pilot, through the mic.

'Yes sir,' he heard from his headphones.

The chopper took off, surging out of the airstrip and across the water. The river looked dark now, made of metals. Way out in the sea, beyond the land, were vast banks of rotating windmills, indistinct from distance and heavy atmosphere. He would need to check, but he suspected he owned them. It felt good to see his machinery working, even at a time such as this. He liked to imagine the mills sucking all that power out of the wind, snatching up the earth's potential and funnelling it right into his own personal field.

They passed over the water and went out across Fife, avoiding the congestion above the city. The country below them smoked still, most of it cracked and blackened. Whole fields bore nothing but ash and cinders, the remnants of villages were little more than heaps of rubble, entirely still. No life moved underneath the chopper; not even gulls could pick sustenance out of this ruined land. It was a pity what happened to the people of the peninsula. He felt for them, for those who died and those who survived. You heard terrible stories about those times, and he regretted his part in what happened to them.

He looked down at the dark earth and in a burst of light saw a flash of Junior's face. It beamed like a light from God, pure goodness shining out, and said, *You'll look after me.* The glossy lips mouthed the words with pleasure. *You'll look after me, won't you, Daddy?* At times like this, he found his fingers acting of their own volition, sneaking beneath his collar to worry the black button he carried there. But he wouldn't use it, not yet.

'Everything okay back there?' asked the pilot.

He coughed. 'Yeah,' he said. 'Yes.'

'Sorry, sir. I thought you made a sound.'

The towers of Edinburgh were just visible on the horizon as they touched down again a few minutes later. Another transfer to a car and into the hotel where his people waited. There were all sorts of trucks and lorries parked up outside and employees were coming and going, loitering in the lobby. He made his way through them, trying to avoid meeting anyone's eye, before picking up his security team. Whenever he travelled, this morning being an exception, he liked to have heavyset men nearby, in case anything went wrong.

'Where's Stock?' he asked one of them. 'I need to speak to Deborah.'

They led him through the hotel, completely crammed with his own personal staff, and into a meeting room at the rear of the building. Deborah sat alone at a large table, working on a tablet.

'Leave us now,' he said. 'I'll call if I need you.'

She stood up. 'Where the fuck did you go, Kim? Everyone's been waiting, everyone—'

He sat down in one of the chairs. Now he was close to her, he could finally relax.

'What's wrong?' she asked. 'What's happened to your face?'

'Nothing,' he said. 'I'm fine, Deborah.'

'You're not *fine*. Look at you. Have you been crying?'

'Of course I haven't been crying. Just . . . Just fill me in on what I missed.'

'You haven't missed anything. We've all been killing time since you disappeared. Where did you go?'

He sniffed. He felt better already. 'I had business to take care of. That's all anyone needs to know.'

'But—'

'That's all anyone needs to know.'

She frowned at him for a long time, then took her seat. They ran through their plans for the upcoming days, how they would move this mass of people and material out to the spaceport on the west coast. It seemed he had indeed thrown a spanner into the works, but the works belonged to him and were his to disrupt as he saw fit. Because it came down to precisely that. None of them, not even Stock, understood the pressure he was under. They only saw a small portion of the enterprise, a tiny peek behind the magician's curtain. He felt sure if they could see what he saw, if they could appreciate the multitude of plates he personally spun, they would blow their brains directly out their skulls. They too would reach into their collars and press the button hidden there.

TEN

Another scorcher. Yet *another* scorcher.

The feeling of your shoes sticking to the pavement as you walked; either your soles or the tarmac softening in the morning heat. Having to bring a hankie out with you, because of forehead sweat. A fashion for baseball caps. For years now, everyone shearing their hair extremely short. Linen shirts; shorts an accepted part of formalwear. Vendors on corners selling iced water and bits of melon and cups of strawberries and making a killing, apparently. At any one point, sixty per cent of the populace suffering from fungal infections in their groins, armpits, or underneath the breast tissue. Sandals, over time, losing their stigma. Constant little altercations at tramstops and pedestrian pressure-points, bickering, a general furious vibe ever-present on the streets at rush hour. Even juniors disliked the heat – well, those whose seniors couldn't afford the Cool Water upgrade, which you needed to select at point of purchase and for some reason couldn't be added afterwards. Alastair's junior, being one of those, couldn't stand it. He pushed his way through folk outside Step-Stone, feeling the crowd's sweat and cooling liquid wick off onto his bare arms.

This morning, there was a picket line outside the offices. The junior couldn't tell, from the signs or the chants, what the problem might be, but he crossed it anyway. There was no one he recognised in the crowd, so he crossed it. He half expected there to be some kind of explanation on the internal systems but no one mentioned it to him, so he carried on like a normal day. If something was amiss, someone would say.

All the usual faces were there: Gavin, Shun, Lena, Lyle, so he treated it like a normal day. He spent the morning checking drivers' routes, making sure those within his remit were where they were supposed to be. It was painstaking work, dull work, but at least it kept his mind off the mess he'd left behind that morning: the ghost in a daze, Alastair moving through streams and moving through content, ignoring the presence beside him. At least checking small geographic details kept his mind off that.

At break, he went down to the canteen for something to do. A group of drivers lurked in a dim corner, up from their subterranean garages. They played a simple card game on the table and drank sugary colas and ate chocolate bars. The other Step-Stone workers left a moat of empty tables around them. No one liked to be reminded of the procedures drivers underwent to become suitable for their occupation.

The junior looked around the tables and spotted her, the new-start. Dot, hidden away beneath the stairs and waving to him. A small shiny clip held her dark fringe to one side and she cupped a mug of decaf between two palms. She said, 'You're looking well today.'

'Not much rest last night,' he said, taking a seat.

'That's my fault, keeping you out late.'

He nodded. He wasn't sure what to say next. He felt nervous. 'Did you get home alright?'

She shrugged. 'No, I got murdered on the way home, I'm afraid. It's very sad.'

'What a pity,' he said. 'I'll miss seeing you at work.'

'Oh, will you?'

'Is there going to be a funeral?'

'I suppose so. A horse-drawn procession, very regal. So you'll miss me then?'

'I'll try to make it,' he said. 'I might be busy though.'

One of those smiles from her, her mouth twisted and falling down at the side. 'You've got a busy schedule, yeah?'

'Yeah.'

'I'll bet. You're going to be pretty bored around here once I'm gone.'

'I don't think so. I'll just find someone else to sit with at break. Maybe the drivers.'

Dot blew surprised bubbles into her decaf, pulling the mug away to shake her head and carefully swallow. 'You're funny,' she said, swatting him on the hand he'd let wander across the tabletop.

They talked about work, the junior asking after that Zivko fellow, whether he kept giving her a hard time about her AUX-9s. Zivko, it seemed, still acted the royal bastard, monitoring Dot's comfort breaks like a prison warden, wanting her chained to her machine near constant, being sniffy about her lack of viciousness in securing sales. She told the junior about her home life too, about the troublesome flatmate and their bad behaviour. Their latest escapade involved swallowing a dose of Smurf large enough for a food meal and pulling up the flat's carpets at three a.m.

'Sounds like you're having a nightmare in general,' the junior said.

'I could do with another one of those drinks, actually,' said Dot. 'Fancy it? After work?'

'Maybe,' the junior said.

He said he'd think about it, and Dot looked disappointed. He chewed it over as they blethered and he really, really wanted to go. He wanted to be alone in a public place with this woman and make jokes and see her eyes crinkle up. He wanted to walk through the hot, pre-teatime city in sunglasses to meet her someplace and enter the bar and look around for her. But it wouldn't suit Alastair and he couldn't get past that. The urge to help his senior, to put his needs first, coursed through every part of him. At the bottom of him was love for his senior. Love made up his core.

'Look at these two,' said a voice behind him. 'Nice and cosy down here.'

Lyle Gardener. Lyle fucking G, who even the junior disliked. This wasn't a residual feeling, like for Ed, picked up in his programming and surviving despite his resistance. Lyle G was an absolute piece of shit. One of the junior's first shifts at Step-Stone, after Alastair departed, Lyle had called the junior 'the runaway's copy' and painfully tweaked his nipple, gurning his sleazeball smile so there could be no comeback. He was only fucking joking mate, can you no take a joke, like? He existed to give all of them a hard time and pretend like it was good fun.

'A right little cosy pow-wow.'

He slipped into the seat beside the junior, who said, 'Alright Lyle?'

'Aye, uh-huh. So who are you then?'

Dot introduced herself.

'I know you. You're one of Zivko's desk hogs, aren't you? A new-start, eh?'

'That's right.'

'Fresh meat,' he said, giving the junior this sharp elbow into his ribs. He never sat still, always shuffling round in his strappy jacket, drumming fingers, sniffing. Narrow-shouldered and shorter than he seemed, sometimes wearing an ironic sideburn. 'This one'll be all over you, I bet.'

Dot shook her head. 'He's been good, actually.'

'I bet he has, I bet he has. This one's famous for sniffing out the fresh meat, I should let you know.'

The junior tutted. He shook his head.

'Is that right?' asked Dot.

'This one? Oh aye. An absolute horn-dog, this one. A slave to his friend downstairs, shall we say. Famous for it. Well known for being a horn-dog.'

'Lyle . . .'

'What's the matter?' Lyle leaned forward and mooned his skinny face towards the junior. 'What?'

'Just pack it in, eh?'

'Aw,' said Lyle, pouting. 'Aw, he's so sensitive. Such a *feeler*. She knows I'm just messing about, don't you Dot? You're the only one here being a jessie.'

'Aye,' said the junior. 'Fair enough.'

'Watch out though, he does have a missus,' Lyle added, winking to Dot. 'They've been going steady for ages now, ever since your senior swam across, eh? You got her trapped good and quick, didn't you?'

The junior played with his fingers. He couldn't say anything; Lyle kept tight with the higher-ups and went out with them on Fridays.

'Look at the pair of you,' he smiled. 'A right pair of downers. I'll leave you to it, thanks.' And he leapt up and shouted at someone across the canteen, snaking away between chairs.

The junior exhaled. He said, 'I'm sorry about him.'

But Dot just shook her head. She didn't care about Lyle and his jokes. She said, 'So you'll think about it, aye?'

After break, he processed data: driver tags and routes and uplift locations and stop-offs and impromptu rearrangements. The information came out of the system; his role was a double-checker, providing confirmation that everything the system produced was acceptable. And it was. Every single time. Constant accuracy, creating a job that would push you nearly to tears with its repetitiveness. The junior remembered Alastair's joy at finally getting out of sales and then doing routing for a single morning and wanting to hop straight through one of the smoked-glass windows. Juniors fared a little better. As a junior, your mind responded well to figures. Probably your programming was all done in figures, he supposed, so it made sense. The bosses liked it when folk juniored, cause productivity took a marked swing upwards. Your numbers improved, the company's stats improved, your own personal stats improved. A win-win, he guessed.

Later, he was due to switch to monitoring. He went along the corridor where Gavin waited outside the observation room. They said, 'Alright?' to each other and leaned on the wall to scan in. The junior stole a glance at his colleague. He wondered what Gavin got up to with his senior at nights. They probably had a good time together, gaming or whatever. They probably didn't deal with ghosts or absent girlfriends. A nice guy, Gavin, but fairly dull. Sort of weak around the chin and the junior knew the senior once had surgery for varicose veins, which gave him the willies.

Once inside, they worked on separate duties. The system recognised them – again, easier if you were a junior – and set up their roster for the day. A few dozen uplifts each, a similar volume of drop-offs. Their role was to act as insurance against the drivers. Even though they'd been neutered, there was no guarantee one wouldn't go rogue and make off with a truck full of victims.

The junior scanned his roster. One of the names leapt to his attention. The font switched to bold, twenty-four point.

Could it be her? Really?

He checked the details again. *Caitlin Weir: Edinburgh to North Uist, 11:10.*

He started to panic. Caitlin Weir? Their Caitlin? Surely not. Surely a conflict of interest there?

'Gav?' he said.

Gavin, distracted, sorting out his roster: 'What?'

He looked at the name for a second. 'Nothing,' he said. 'Nothing.'

The stream showed the driver pull up outside a building the junior recognised: the Travelpod hotel down by the old Haymarket building. The stream showed, from the driver's POV, him lurch out the cabin and move through pedestrians on the pavement. They avoided him, deferentially averting their gaze and letting his bulk pass. He entered the hotel and approached the reception, where he spoke to the junior on desk.

'Step-Stone uplift,' he said. 'Caitlin Weir. Room 3003.'

The receptionist checked the details and said, 'Go right up.' You could see the look of fear in their face as they gazed up at the driver.

Likewise at the lifts, where those waiting to board let him go ahead, motioning they would take the next one. The numbers ticked upwards and all you heard on the stream was the gentle rasp of the driver's nasal breathing, his vision swooping over the interior of the lift.

Along the corridor at an amble, checking door numbers until he found it: *3003*. He knocked. 'Step-Stone uplift,' the voice said.

There should only be the traveller inside, but policy dictated you announce before entering. He paused for five seconds, then used the chip from reception. The room was dark despite the hour, curtains drawn, and barely six feet across. A body lay out on the small bed tucked beyond the shower cubicle. From the doorway, only the feet were visible, pale toes poking out of the Step-Stone pyjama set.

The driver set to work. He walked forward and ran his eyes down the sleeping form, and it was her. There, lying out on this bed, their Caitlin, sound asleep, her hands crossed on her chest, the Step-Stone pyjamas a little too baggy for her so she looked oddly childlike. Her pelvis bulged from the sanitary shorts she wore below the bottoms. So, so peaceful. The junior recalled mornings where Alastair woke first, Caitlin being a weekend heavy sleeper, seeing her laid out on their shared bed. She had very shiny eyelids, filmed by the night's grease, and her hair was all over the shop. Those mornings he'd make a pot of decaf and watch wee kids play out at the park and wait for her to wake naturally; they might go for a walk or whatever, and he barely thought about what sort of viewing screen they owned or what nonsense was kicking off on the field, what disagreements or arguments, and all he wanted was to be close beside her as she moved from sleep to waking.

The driver bent. You saw his arms scoop up Caitlin below the neck and knees, big fleshy fingers emerging from below, cradling those joints of her, and the unavoidable comparison was with a corpse. All this time on monitoring and he never saw the resemblance before.

Wake up, he wanted to say. Wake up and get out of there, but of course she was in no danger. After breakfast, she'd have taken a little sleeping pill and conked out and she was in no danger at all. The driver gently scooped her and took her away, back to the lift and out to the truck, where he toed the pedal beneath an empty compartment, allowing the sleeping suite to slide out. He placed Caitlin down on the skinny mattress and went back inside for her luggage, and the junior thought: you can't just leave her there, stacked in a truck in a loading bay, like cargo. You can't do that to her.

*

After Caitlin's uplift, the system flashed a reminder for him to move on to the next name on his roster, the next sleeping passenger waiting somewhere in the city. But he couldn't do it, couldn't tear his eyes away from the screen showing the driver drive.

He monitored the feed as it showed the truck go beyond the suburbs and into the tech parks bleeding from the city into the surrounding greenbelt. The autoway was largely empty, aside from distance buses running the Skye route and other Step-Stone trucks coming back towards the capital. Legacy pathways, the countries' autoways, and rarely used by average punters. The junior watched the road flow beneath the driver's eyeline as they went further and further west, and at a certain point they crested a hill and the ruined peninsula lurched into view across the water. A blackened slip of land, lightly smoking, drawing the eye like an absence – something rubbed out.

'What's that you're on?' asked Gavin, leaning across in his chair.

'Just checking in on this drive,' he said quickly.

'What for?'

The junior watched the road, the driver's hands on the wheel. 'Just a feeling,' he said. 'I got this feeling.'

'Hm,' said Gavin. 'Better watch yourself.'

You never knew when a higher-up might decide to sign into your profile and observe your work. If they found you slacking off, or doing something unassigned, there might well be consequences. He watched the driver proceed for another few minutes, then pulled up the next uplift on his screen.

He knew how long to leave it, since everything at Step-Stone got scheduled to within an inch of its life. Her route was four hours, as the crow flew, out past Glasgow and the western shores, across the bridges and terraformed waters to the old islands – what had once been islands – each now basically a city in terms of population. Cosmopolitan Jura, flattened Mull, the Coll Autoway reaching through fields of corn like a line of thread. Four hours as the crow flew to her destination, but with drop-offs in outer Glasgow, in Tyndrum, in Oban; Craignure uplifts, Dalmally uplifts, uplifts all over the shop. So more like six hours to her destination, and he was there, six hours later, just before he was due to scan out.

'I'm just going to check on that driver,' he told Gavin, who was finishing up.

'Whatever,' Gavin said, tapping and swiping.

He pulled up the stream to see the driver cruise through the Uist streets, past the plate-glass towers and shops, the pavements decked with juniors going about their business. The driver cruised until he found the stop, which the junior already knew: Flodday Towers Luxury Hotel and Bistro. On the stream, you saw the driver enter the hotel, where the proprietor – curly hair, paisley shirt – was marching about the foyer. His eyes widened when he clocked the driver.

'Step-Stone drop-off,' said the driver. 'Caitlin Weir.'

'Ah,' said the proprietor. 'Yes. Let me see.'

And all the usual checking-in bollocks carried on until the driver went out to collect Caitlin and there she lay, inside her narrow suite, content and safe. The junior watched the driver pick her up and carry her inside, into the lift, into her new room. He placed her on the bed and the proprietor brought her suitcase up alongside him.

'Never quite got used to this,' he said nervously.

'Sign here,' the driver said, bringing out his screen.

'Right,' said the proprietor, pushing his fingertip across the glass. 'Thanks.'

And the last thing the junior saw was Caitlin laid out on this new bed, a nicer place than the one she'd left behind, and even though this was not his Caitlin – his own body had never touched hers – the inherited feeling felt so strong that he pushed back from the station and stood up as the driver loped down the hallway. Stood up and held a crooked finger to his lips, because there she was: gone.

The picket line held its place outside the offices. A smaller group in the early evening, but still loud. The junior loitered in the foyer, making up his mind. He promised Dot he would think about it, so he thought about it. The *right* thing to do would be to go home. Go home, and help Alastair out and tell him the news. A good junior: out like a shot, practically sprinting up the road, finding someplace with bio ingredients, sorting out his senior's tea, all while looking sharp and fashionable. He put his hands in his pockets. He chewed his lip. He watched the picket line shout and wave their placards and thought it must be nice to be out there, believing in something. They weren't workers, he realised; more of a protest than a picket line, really. But they shared bottles of something with each other and patted each other's backs and seemed to be enjoying themselves, despite the anger.

He took his hands out his pockets and went through the doors, through the line, where they called out to him, and then to the pavement. Dot waited on the wall by the ornamental pond. She fell in line as he walked by.

'Good shift?' she asked.

'Fine,' he said. 'A bit weird.'

'You're not still thinking about that Lyle, are you?'

'No, I just saw someone I know when I was monitoring.'

'Oh,' she smiled. 'That *is* weird.'

'Yeah,' he said.

They walked together and found a bar somewhere, and even though neither of them acknowledged it, they selected a quiet place on a side street with little passing foot traffic outside. After he got her a drink from the bank of lockers – he sensed the cost be debited from Alastair's account – he asked how her day went and she regaled him with a description of the tediousness of selling journeys to the general public, how slow they were, the silly questions they asked. He remembered all this from his senior's early days in the company. He laughed along at things that weren't even that funny, wee jokes she made or silly voices.

'You know what?' she said. 'I've never been on a date with a junior before.'

Not many had, really. You heard stories about back-alley places you could go to shag someone's junior, but seniors rarely crossed the barrier publicly. Women did it even less frequently. A mild taboo about it. Not immoral as such, but certainly mucky, questionable, low.

He looked at her for a bit. She sucked her drink and grinned, champing the top of the straw.

'A date,' he said.

She shrugged. 'Well?'

He shrugged too. 'I've never been on a date with anyone before.'

'How old are you?' she asked.

'My senior's thirty-ish. I've been out for a year.'

'Oh,' she said. 'A younger man.'

'I'm brand new.'

She pulled on her straw and released it, so a tiny speck of soft drink spattered his neck.

'You'd better watch it,' he said.

'Or what?'

'Things might get nasty.'

'Oh,' she said. 'I'm scared. I really am.'

'What about you, then?' he asked.

'I'm older,' she said, 'both ways.'

160

'And where're you from? What have you been doing with yourself?'

And he noticed she got a little squirrelly at the questions. She drew something on the table using the liquid from the bottom of her glass. She said, 'I'm from all over. I've been doing everything.'

'But really though?'

She squinted. 'What does it matter?'

'I don't know. It just does, doesn't it?'

She leaned back. 'I've done different things, I suppose. I went to uni, I did history. I had a good time, got out and couldn't get a job, couldn't get *anything*, so I had to move home. Eventually worked something out and I was doing these admin things for places like Honey Bee, domestic services, and I got pretty high up too. I liked it. It was going well for me, but I ended up somewhere else and they ended up doing a compulsory junioring drive and for whatever reason I wasn't into it, so I had to go.'

'Right.'

'So that's why I'm at Step-Stone being a desk hog.'

He nodded along, then said, 'But I thought you said it was cause you broke up with someone.'

'Did I say that?'

'Aye.'

She smiled, a little icily he thought. 'Maybe that was part of it, but mostly it was because the company went with juniors over me.'

'Sorry,' he said.

'Not your fault. Just the way of the world.'

As she told the story of her journey to Step-Stone, he couldn't help but see a different side of her emerging. A different, harder side . . . But that made sense. Probably everyone got steely when they spoke about being laid off.

He apologised again and she told him not to worry about

it and he sensed a shield go up between them, a shield made of jokes and banter. She seemed a touch nervous, as if she too realised she might have let something slip.

A while later, the junior felt something: a little tickle emanating from the place where his neck met his head. Something worming into him and he knew it was Alastair beginning to monitor his stream. He'd been due back hours ago and, even if the ghost was taking up his time, by now he must be seriously cheesed.

The junior's system proposed a decision: let your senior in or shut him out.

Across the table, Dot spoke, and he felt so good watching her speak. Dot spoke and if Alastair logged in, then the junior was ruined. Big questions would follow and what could he say? On the other hand, he could stand up, get out, walk away. Tell his senior there'd been a work emergency, forcing him to stay late. A bit dodgy, but plausible.

Dot spoke and he listened and inside ... inside he shut it down. He felt himself reject the incoming connection. A firm, polite *no* that made him feel instantly nauseated. Unlike losing the link outside Bucket's, this had been a decision made by him.

'Are you alright?' she asked. 'You've gone pale.'

'I'm fine,' he said. 'Keep going, what was it you were saying?'

'No, you're not fine. You're ... God, you look awful.'

He stood up. His vision pulsed. He took a step to one side and felt his arm tighten, the muscles of his hand go numb. 'I need the toilet.'

Walking quickly, he crossed the bar, drawing looks from its few patrons. In the bathroom, he leaned against a wall, reeling. If he could breathe, he would've needed some fucking lungful right now. He leaned against the bathroom wall and tried to rearrange his internals, tried to calm down the processes now spinning wildly out of control. He felt a touch better.

He went to the mirror. He gasped when he saw the face looking back at him: Alastair. His senior. A liquid analogous to tears sprung up across his eyeballs.

The lowest of the low, he told himself. You're scum, to have let down your senior like that.

When he returned, a third party had joined them. A woman of his own age, with a head of bushy curls, sat alongside Dot. The first thing he noticed was her clothes. They were ill-fitting and oddly matched, as though fished out a bin at random. The next was a flicker of recognition; someone from his senior's past, perhaps? He watched from across the room and saw Dot and the newcomer deep in conversation, their heads close above the table, whispering urgently to each other. It didn't matter though. He was off. This would be the end of it. He would say a quick cheerio, thank Dot for the good time, then get away. Nip it in the bud and knock it on the head. That face in the mirror, he couldn't deal with. He didn't have the stomach for the path he'd found himself on.

'Alright?' he asked.

The two of them looked up, Dot and the stranger.

'You feeling better?' asked Dot.

'Yep,' he nodded. 'But listen, I need to get off. I need to—'

'I was just saying to Mandy here what a lifesaver you've been up at the work,' Dot said.

'Oh,' he said. 'Really?'

'So I'm told,' said Mandy. She spoke with the junior's own voice, with Alastair's, the accent of the lost peninsula. He could swear the voice was familiar, as though he'd heard it once, long ago. There was also some similarity in the two women, a familiar expression in the way their eyes ran across him. Something predatory that caused an excitement.

'I was just going to say,' he said. 'I need to be getting away now.'

The new woman, Mandy, she pouted. She said, 'But Dot's just been saying what a laugh you are. Apparently you're the best laugh in the whole job.'

He shook his head. 'No. Hardly.'

'We were just going to get another round,' said Dot. 'You're not going to leave us to drink by ourselves?'

'Go on,' said Mandy. 'What's another half an hour?'

So he agreed and took his seat and they got in more drinks for themselves and Mandy was introduced as a friend from uni. They'd shared some terrible dive housing in the capital's southern zone. They said to him he should've seen the state of this place, all these bodies crammed into too few rooms and people up carousing all hours of the day and night, and levels of hygiene and sanitation at low, low levels, and the antic inhabitants being basically the worst kind of housemates you could wish for.

'That sounds tough,' said the junior, thinking the level of detail they provided didn't seem to correspond to a past memory. The women spoke as if the recollections were fresh.

'But it was fine,' said Mandy.

'We made do,' said Dot.

'There were only so many lassies, so we got a bit of breathing space,' said Mandy. 'The things we got up to ...'

'Don't!' squealed Dot, squirming there on her stool.

The junior realised what a performance this was, the words designed to elicit the exact response he currently experienced. 'I should get going,' he said. 'Honestly, I—'

Mandy's eyes flicked to the wristwatch she wore. 'Just a few more minutes,' she said. 'I was just getting into those memories. I was just remembering all that stuff me and your Dot used to get up to. It really was anything goes in them days, wasn't it Dot?'

'It certainly was.'

'The stories we could tell.'

'Do you want to hear some stories?'

He sat very still, then jerked his head forward. A nod.

They smiled at him, then each other, and Mandy said, 'We used to get up to all sorts, Dot and me.' Her eyes sparkled as they bored into him. 'We used to go out together and pick up strangers, from pubs or clubs or whatever. Just anyone that took our eye. We had similar tastes, didn't we Dot? We used to go out and see what caught our eye and we'd dance with him and these chaps couldn't believe their luck, could they? Imagine it. Dot and me appearing and getting ourselves all over you. Imagine it. We used to pick them up and take them back to our house. We had this bedroom we shared, didn't we Dot? It was all good fun. All good clean fun. We'd get them back to the bedroom and get them stripped off, Dot and me, both together, and then we'd get stripped off too, so everyone then was stripped off. All three of us together, us and the chap, and Dot and me were like hungry for whatever he had. Didn't matter to us, did it Dot, long or short? I remember your Dot being very, very hungry sometimes, weren't you, love? Ravenous, like. Both of us were, I suppose. It didn't matter who it was. We just wanted what he had. We shared it out between us, even though we were really fucking greedy for it. That's friendship, isn't it?'

The junior swallowed. As the woman spoke, everything else began to melt away. His sphere of knowledge narrowed to this table, these words, the sets of sparkly eyes watching him.

'I think he's liking it,' said Dot.

'I think maybe he is,' said Mandy. 'I think he's liking these stories. Do you want to hear some more?'

Another tight nod. He wanted some more.

'Maybe he'd like to hear about all the places Dot and I would put it? How does that sound?'

Yes. That sounded fine. He wanted it.

'Maybe he wants to hear about the things we said? Maybe he—'

And then the questioning stopped. Mandy's lips tightened and she looked beyond the junior to something behind him. He wanted to hear some more. As she cast her eyes above his head, her expression changed. It unsoftened, hardened up. Her eyes dried. He saw Dot. She also looked beyond him. She was also changed.

A shadow fell over the table. It fell across the whole table, the junior and the women too. He pivoted round to a wall of greenish leather, a single button perhaps an inch from his eye.

'You took your time,' said Mandy.

The wall spoke: 'Sorry, I was dealing with the thing back home. How's he keeping?'

'Oh, fine. We've been having a lovely old chat. Christ, I feel sick.'

The wall took the stool beside the junior. A man, gigantic and bald, full of good cheer. He rearranged the glasses on the table and said, 'She been telling you all her dirty stories, pal? You being a bit of a perve, aye?'

'I'm sorry,' said the junior. 'I don't know what's—'

'This is my bird you're talking to,' said the giant. 'D'you like talking dirty to other men's birds?'

Quickly: 'No, no. I didn't realise. We've never even met before.'

'This is what gets me about some of these juniors. They think they can just swan round, chatting up strangers' birds, getting off on their dirty stories.'

Dot and Mandy were smiling again, but different kinds of smiles.

'If I was another sort of chap, I'd be murdering you right this second,' said the giant. 'Another sort of chap comes in here and sees some cunt getting his jollies to his bird's dirty stories and he hits the fucking roof, doesn't he? He kicks off immediate.'

The junior nodded. 'Sorry.'

'He's sorry,' said the giant. 'Well, I suppose that's the end of it, then. My mistake. He's fucking *sorry.*'

'I just,' said the junior, 'I just never realised. I didn't know.'

'Leave it,' said the giant. 'I'm over it. I'm past it now. You've got good taste, that's all. Cannae hold it against you. Just can't. But make it up to me, eh? You've gone against me, so make it up to me?'

'Aye,' said the junior. 'Anything.'

'Come out to my van with me.'

'What?'

'Come out to my van. It's just outside.'

'No.'

'I've got some puppies in my van,' said the giant, his voice heavy with irony and quickly losing its cheer. He whispered, 'Come out to my van and see the fucking *puppies* I've got in the back of my van.'

And the junior let himself be levered out of his seat by the man's big hands and the two women came along and sure enough, outside on the street, there sat a van, bashed up and parked below a streetlamp.

He went with them, silent, and allowed himself to be escorted inside.

ELEVEN

It took some doing, but even Nye Morgan seemed to have his feathers ruffled. His face, cramped into a wee video-in-video corner, showed genuine alarm at the viewer-submitted content featured on this stream of *Nye Morgan's Eye Vision*. The footage showed the recorder's wellington boots as they splashed around their flooded lounge. The Anglo hurricanes, it seemed, were getting worse. Alastair killed the stream. He nearly pulled up *Inside the Mansion*, but selected *Background Ambient Tones* instead. He couldn't deal with anything substantial. Anything substantial caused his head to ache. In the next room, the ghost spoke to itself, chanting away in low murmurs about nothing of any substance.

The junior hadn't come home. Alastair waited up until the early hours, trying to connect to the junior's stream every few minutes, unable to access it even once. It was now the morning after, and still no word. The junior would be due at work soon and all Alastair could think of was the stats. Missed work would fuck his stats up significantly, perhaps beyond the point of recovery. He took out the mobile and scrolled, which made him feel better for a while. He scrolled and the anxiety got better, so he pulled up the locator once more. It showed the junior as a little red J on the map, somewhere beyond the large parks in the capital's leafy south.

Fine. Whatever. He'd gone out with a Step-Stone colleague – Gav maybe – and went back to their flat. He should be happy, but still, he couldn't shake the horrors that flitted around him.

He went in to see the old man. The ghost stood in the box room, facing the wall, speaking incessantly. It whispered non-sense little phrases and snatches of gobbledygook, over and over.

Alastair sat down on the bed and said, 'What are we going to do with you?'

The ghost stopped its blethering. 'I'm so lost,' it said.

'I know you are,' he replied.

'I want to go home,' it said. 'Back to the old house and see your mum and dad.'

'Me too.'

'I loved them so much.'

'I know. Me too.'

He began to realise just how limited his options were. He couldn't alert the peacekeepers, or Chem & Med; there was nothing the care industries could do for him. He considered getting in touch with JNR, via the link that came with the junior's introductory pack, but struggled to imagine himself describing the situation to whatever hapless individual staffed their helpdesk.

Another thought did occur to him though. Surely, if this had happened to him – his father's junior's data reanimated on the field – surely then, it must have happened to others too. What were the chances of him being an anomaly? Low, surely. *Surely.* So what if . . . What if he put together a wee recording, just like the poor flooded Anglos on Nye's stream, a recording of him and the ghost to be sent to Nye, or uploaded directly by himself. Might that draw the attention of others like him?

He mulled it over as he watched the ghost. It wrung its hands and paced the room, clucking its tongue. This would make good footage, he thought. They wouldn't know what hit them, the viewers out on the field. He imagined the recording catching people's attention and spreading like wildfire across the planet. Imagine what that sort of advocacy might do for the stats ...

She woke in the lap of luxury. It was the sort of awakening that might feature on an ad for high thread count bedding or posh soap: one hand facing up from the pillow beside her, the knowledge that yes, she felt entirely well-rested. Caitlin breathed in, then smiled. Getting ready in the roomy bathroom was an absolute pleasure too. She peed, then cleaned herself beneath a powerful shower. Every surface gleamed. Stray droplets formed perfect pearls on the shower door. She tasted some water and stretched.

Downstairs, she searched for the breakfast room among reception areas and guest lounges and conference suites. She found it after a short while, and with it the first moment of consternation in her stay. A sign attached to the doors of the dining hall read: *Closed for Private Function.* A bit annoying. She wanted to be well-nourished for her first day, but resolved to find something elsewhere. As she passed by, she looked into the hall and, to her surprise, spotted several faces she recognised. Not friends or colleagues, but big names, big business names from the streams. Weird, she thought, stepping out into the morning sun.

It took no time to source food in a café down the road. The place was littered with brasseries and brunch spots and bars. She ate a porridge sachet with a strong decaf and looked out at the city around her. Day one of the Uist secondment. She didn't have much info to go on, so pulled out her computer and ran through the HR messages. *Present yourself at 09:00 on the 18th of October.* There was to be an induction speech by someone high up; it seemed they were gearing up for something significant.

She felt pleasantly nervous. All that nonsense about packing it in and going back to bar work, just stress. She knew it now. Stress made you want to smash up your surroundings, then craft a new thing out of the wreckage. And anyway. At least she was away now, from the flat and from Alastair. The Step-Stone journey marked a line in the sand for her. She took the little pill and fell asleep, waking up in her whole new life. He could live with his junior forever, as far as she was concerned. Let them stew there in their filth, sitting round in their pants watching streams and checking stats. They wanted different lives; so be it.

Caitlin held her pace as she made her way through Lochmaddy. She didn't want to rush, to build up a sweat, and plus the shuttles out to Scolpaig were notoriously crowded. All the advancements they'd made and still the transport ended up oversubscribed. A large group of people waited by the tram terminal and she joined them, holding herself hard in the core, shoulders back. You never knew who was watching.

She overheard one woman say, 'Yeah, apparently he flew in last night. No idea why,' and her companion responded, 'I don't believe it. No chance.'

She wanted to ask what or who they meant, but felt eaves-dropping might not be the best introduction.

A low whistle sounded and the shuttle slid down the boule-vard towards them, reflecting towers in its darkened windows.

The main issue was getting the ghost in line. It didn't want to comply with his directions, didn't care about where it stood in the flat, and would slip into reveries, its eyes going vacant as it stared into a place Alastair had no access to.

Instead, he spoke to his old man, describing moments from their life together to catch its attention and move it into areas where lighting was favourable. He reminisced about their back garden and all the time they spent there, cooking on barbecues, playing swingball hour after hour. The ghost nodded, it followed, near to the living room window, and Alastair got out his mobile for the footage. He filmed the ghost from all angles, moving around to record how the background showed through.

He said, 'I know this will seem weird or whatever, but what I'm filming here is the ghost of my dad. Or his junior, we're not sure. We've been hearing these strange noises for a while now and then the night before last, it appeared. Just in the kitchen of my flat. I know if you're watching this, you'll think I'm hoaxing, but it's true. Maybe you'll think I'm mad but . . . well, I don't know what to say about that.'

The ghost watched him filming and took a step forward. Alastair took a step back.

'The last thing it seems to remember is the night he died, my dad. He was working out at the gas plant when it blew up and that's all he remembers. We think it's the field. We think he's somehow living on the field. He's see-through, obviously, and he crackles a little bit.'

He walked around the ghost, catching it from all sides, and it seemed only bemused by the attention. It asked Alastair, 'What are you doing? Why are you filming me?'

Next, he set up the mobile to record himself, away from the ghost. He sat in a chair and spoke directly to the mobile. He said, 'Something isn't right here. Something's gone wrong with our technology that's allowed this to happen. It isn't right. We shouldn't be able to come back after . . . I'm making this to let you know what's going on in this world. I mean, safeguards should be in place to stop this, if this is what junioring and the field can do. Someone needs to address it.'

He killed the recording and thought about whether there was anything else he should say. He expected it to come out as more of a grandstand, but he didn't know how to achieve that. Didn't know the methods for ranting passionately. The footage would speak for itself, he decided. He used software to combine the two clips together, the ghost and his own message to the camera, then played the result through a few times. It felt amateurish compared to most videos you saw on the field, but the ghost was undeniably effective on film. Surely whoever saw it would be affected by the strange phenomenon and would immediately share and spread the evidence.

By now, he was late for work. An hour late at least, but this took priority. He uploaded his video to the field and began sharing it as widely as he could. He pinged it to *Eye Vision*, knowing good old Nye would take an interest, and also spread it around his personal outlets. If this paid off, it might not matter that he'd missed work. In fact, he might never work again.

The tram came to a gentle stop and Caitlin alighted, along with the rest of the tram's occupants. They emerged onto the plaza of the Scolpaig spaceport, wide, clean, surrounded by domed structures and vast warehouses. She followed a portion of the crowd into the main entrance, a cavernous atrium busy with people coming and going, ascending on escalators and milling by. She went to reception and introduced herself. The boy working gave her a pass – security level 2 – and some instructions: head to the Strugatsky Room for induction.

'Thank you,' she said.

Inside the room, people had already arrived. They helped themselves to decaf and breakfast sachets and either took seats or chatted. Caitlin knew no one, so found herself a space and pretended to take notes. This would probably be a standard intro session, with lots of nice messages and talks about positive thinking and staying energised in business. She'd probably get to the meat later on; this would be something mandatory, to be endured.

Others started to take their seats around her and she was

this close to striking up a conversation with the person beside her, when one of the doors at the front of the room opened. In walked a burly security official in dark suit, shades, with a bald head. Another one entered. A third, then a small man wearing a baseball cap. A fourth security official followed, along with a severe-looking woman, reading a tablet as she marched. This band of newcomers busied themselves. The security guys took position around the room's perimeter, by the doors, by the window, while the plainclothes couple headed for the refreshment table. Those seated continued to chat among themselves, but Caitlin became aware of a hushed quality to the speech. Clearly, a person of some significance was present. She twisted in her chair to get a better look. She didn't recognise the woman; the man's face was obscured by his cap.

'It's not,' someone behind her said.

'It is,' said another. 'I *told* you.'

The room became quiet. They all faced front and no one, it seemed, had the courage to talk. Caitlin waited. Eventually, they presented themselves. The baseball cap man came down to the front of the room, holding a cup of decaf, then pulled a table to the centre of the open space. He perched on a corner of the table and she realised: *Kim Larson*. Kim fucking Larson.

He smiled around and sipped some decaf. He said, 'Hi.'

No one said anything back.

He took off his cap and placed it behind him on the table. His hair was white and overlong and his face was deeply cracked and wrinkled, though he looked a few decades younger than his actual age. He wore a neat, grey beard. 'Hello?' he said.

A few of them mumbled hellos back. Caitlin kept her lips sealed. She couldn't believe it. Kim Larson, here, in their neck of the woods. The man who brought them juniors and the field; worked on them all, anyway. The World's Father, they called him. More powerful than any of the old-style politicians had been, more famous than Elvis or Santiago or Susie Ex or the Bonobo Child. Kim Larson. Here.

'I wanted to start,' he said, 'by saying thank you. I appreciate we've sequestered you from your normal duties here, so thank you. I say this to everyone present in this room, for being brave enough to be here today.'

A hum grew in Caitlin's ears. Kim Larson looked at them all personally, each in turn, and he smiled warmly and authentically and noticed every single one of them.

He said, 'I want to take you on a journey.'

A response came back from a staffer on Nye Morgan's team. A standardised reply that read:

> *We appreciate you taking the time to submit content to Eye Vision. We couldn't do what we do without the help of our valued contributors. It is with regret that we must pass on your submission. After considered discussion within our editorial team, we rejected it for the following reason(s): ... HOAX/ DOCTORED FILE ... Please don't hesitate to submit other, better content in the future.*

He checked the details. The response had come only fifteen minutes after his original message.

Okay. So he wouldn't get the message out via the mainstream media. Whatever. He'd been putting off checking his own personal outlets, waiting to let momentum build, but now he pulled them up, his online presences, his hubs and portals. He stared at the mobile. There were no updates, no notifications, no interactions. It didn't make sense. He dug around for a moment and found that the video was gone, deleted direct from the source without any explanation, any apology. That happened now and then, fair enough, but his video didn't contain anything truly problematic.

He tried again, throwing the file up on the field. He waited a few moments and checked. Already it had been removed. No apology, no explanation.

He sat back, letting the mobile rest at his side. In the hallway, the ghost walked by, singing a song beneath its breath. It went back and forth, like a bear in a cage. Alastair's knee started to go; his whole lower leg. He felt the big fleshy muscle of his calf jerk into cramp. Clearly the powers-that-be did not want his evidence out there. That much felt obvious. A thought occurred to him and he went to the mobile. He pulled up his social feed and started a simple textual message, explaining the situation he found himself in, an admission that he realised how bizarre it all sounded, and a request for help and advice. He went to upload, but the box was greyed over. He thumbed it once, twice, three times. Nothing.

Truly panicking, he went from room to room. He felt light-headed, queasy. He spoke to the ghost, saying, 'They've got me. I tried to put it on the field and they noticed and I'm blocked in. I can't get anything out.'

He checked on the junior. His J still hovered across the same location on the map. What the fuck had happened to him? Why wasn't he working? Alastair fought his breath down into a reasonable state. He hissed between gritted teeth.

Fine. Okay. Forget about it. The whole idea was a dud. Whatever. He'd pull himself together and get into the office and take it from there. See if he could dig up anything on where the junior went, apologise for the missed morning, try to negate the negative hit on his stats. He found a mirror in the toilet and looked into it. Bits of beard grew thickly from his neck and cheek. Bruised skin bulged around his eyes. His bristly hair stood up all over from lack of maintenance. A grim state of affairs.

'Come on,' he said to the reflection. 'Get it together.'

Then he realised the time. Just after eleven. Just after eleven and he hadn't heard the flume go with his medicine. He went out to check, passing the ghost, and saw the delivery slot sit there empty. Even though it was pointless, he opened the transparent lid to check. A breath of stale air blew against his face.

Kim Larson took another sip of decaf, smiled again. He said, 'Believe me when I say that you are all lucky enough to be present on a day that will go down in history. I mean that, I really do. All the advancements we've made will pale in comparison to what you're all going to achieve. And you should feel lucky. Accept that emotion, right now. I encourage it.'

He paused, presumably to allow them all to appreciate their luck. Caitlin glanced round. Everyone watched him with wide-open eyes, lips slightly parted.

'For a long time, perhaps my whole career, I've been interested in improvement. I looked at my environment and saw deficiencies. I saw problems that seemed, to me, to be entirely solvable and set out to fix them. I saw people working their fingers to the bone, and thought, why don't we make helpers to assist them? I saw information and data and power inaccessible to the common person, and thought, why not make those resources available everywhere, all of the time? That those two ideas went hand in hand, well that was just kismet. I saw a population chained to the dirt in their reliance on disgusting, dirty fossil fuels. Now, we have our field and only one or two nations worldwide burn anything that comes out of the ground. Things have improved for humankind and you'll excuse my vanity if I say I had a little something to do with it.'

Spontaneously, a round of applause began in the meeting room. It started behind Caitlin and she felt compelled to join in. Larson looked surprised, but he nodded to allow the interruption. He squinted a bit, which was a sort of smile.

'Thanks,' he said. 'Thanks very much. I appreciate that, I really do. All I've ever done has been in service of you,' he continued, pointing to a random worker.

Larson paused. An expression of pain crossed his features and he cupped his chin.

'Which is why the subject of our work here causes me such distress. You see, I've come to the conclusion that I've reached the end of the line, *vis-à-vis* being able to help humanity any further. It's a shame, but my research suggests it's true. You see, despite all our good deeds and work, this planet is, in a word, ruined. It's done. It's ruined and there's nothing you or I can do about it now. We gave it a good shot, but it's done. Look at the planet, look at Australia, look at where I live, out west. Everything's burning, and if it's not burning, it's underwater.'

Caitlin felt the crowd's mood shift. If before they were adulating, now they were confused. Perhaps Larson was building up to something, a revelation about new technology or systems to reverse the problems he described.

'And believe me, I've tried. I've had the boys and girls sweating day and night to work something out, but it all comes back the same: we're ruined. No matter what I put into the machine, the same product comes out the end: ruin. I'm seeing certain expressions before me now. Certain looks of concern or displeasure. Well, let me tell you, you can stop that now, because everything's A-okay. You see, we're going to leave all of it behind.'

A breath of stale air blew against his face, and he really started to freak out, because if the flume had a problem and his pill wasn't coming through, then he really couldn't make it out. There was just no chance, none at all. Game over, done and dusted.

'What's wrong?' the ghost asked. 'What are you shouting for?'

'Something's wrong with the flume. It's blocked or broken

or something.' He had his arm wedged into the pipe, searching around for whatever might be messing with his access. That happened, every so often. Perhaps a neighbour ordered a bulky parcel and it got wedged downstream and now all Alastair's deliveries were backed-up elsewhere.

'I think someone's looking up,' the ghost said, from through in the living room.

'What?'

'No. Never mind.'

He stormed through. The ghost stood by the window, peering out. 'I thought I saw something, but it's fine.'

Alastair stood beside his old man and looked down. 'What did you see?'

'Those lads, down in the park. See them? On the swings? I thought one of them was using binoculars on us, but maybe not.'

True enough, a pair of men sat there down in the playpark. It was empty of children and they perched beside each other on the swings, rocking back and forth. They wore dark fleeces and woolly hats and seemed to be conversing quietly with each other. Alastair watched them and wondered why two grown men chose to use the swings when plenty of benches were free. Why two grown men hung around the park anyway, without children or even dogs. Then one of them glanced up, the smaller and skinnier of the pair, glanced up to their window and held Alastair's gaze despite the distance. He nodded to his friend, who also looked upwards and locked eyes with Alastair and watched.

'Fuck,' he hissed, spinning away from the window. 'Get away from there. They'll see you.'

The ghost nodded and plodded away, coming to a stop in the centre of the room.

'You said they were looking with binoculars?'

The ghost held his hands up to his eyes, replicating the motion. 'Aye. I think so. Something like that, anyway.'

'Jesus,' said Alastair. 'So who are they? Why are they watching us?'

The ghost shrugged. 'It's a coincidence.'

'Is it fuck. They're ... they're ... Well, I don't know, but they're someone. It's the videos, Dad. It's cause I put you on the field.' As he spoke, Alastair pressed himself against the wall, beside the Calcyon. He felt coldness gather within his palms and he coughed from surprise. It was saying the word. *Dad*.

'You put me on the field?'

'To find out why you're here.'

'I see.'

And then he realised: the flume, his pills. This was all connected. Out there, someone had been alerted to his posts, his videos, someone who didn't want anyone else finding out about the ghost. The men in the park, the blockage in the flume, it all fit.

He pulled out the mobile and checked the junior. His J remained unchanged on the map. He tried to get inside his head, to pull his stream up on the mobile. The screen circled for a bit, attempting connection, then cancelled. He was still blocked. Who could he talk to? He knew he was losing it, but by how much? He needed outside eyes on his situation and for someone to tell him he was exaggerating. Marcin, Ed, someone from Step-Stone.

He practised the words in his head: sorry to bother you mate, but I think the system's out to get me.

No fucking chance.

He went through all his contacts, then saw her name.

A person sitting in the front row raised their hand. Caitlin noticed the security guys by the door stiffen, as if anticipating threat, but naturally it was just a question. Kim Larson nodded to the woman, who asked, 'So you're saying we should abandon the planet?'

Larson chuckled. 'In a way, I suppose I am, but that makes it sound very cynical, very utilitarian. Instead, picture this. Imagine you're on a desert island, an actual palm-trees-and-sand desert island, way out there in the blue ocean. Imagine also that the island is sinking into that blue ocean, bit by bit, sinking away and you and your ... friend are watching it sink. What's better? For you to stay there and go under together, and get eaten by sharks or whatever, or your friend to make a swim for it, to swim out into that blue ocean and see if there's another good-looking island somewhere near by? To find that island and then send word back to tell you to swim also? I know which I'd prefer, and it's the latter, by a long, long shot. There's no point us all going under, when hope might be out there, waiting.'

A few other hands shot up, which made Larson scowl. He picked up his baseball cap and wrung it briefly.

'This wasn't supposed to be a Q&A, I'm afraid. I know you'll have lots of questions but there are people better equipped to answer them than me. All I'm here to do is say hi, give an overview, and set you on course, alright? You have the headline now and—'

As Larson spoke, a handful of people – four or five – stood up and walked towards the door. The security guards looked to Larson and he shrugged; they were allowed to leave. This is my chance, thought Caitlin. If I don't go now, then I'm in. She saw a fork in the road ahead of her, but felt unable to rise from her chair.

'That's okay,' said Larson. 'We anticipated that. This is a complex project and it's only natural that a percentage of people won't have the stomach for it.' He motioned to the back of the room and the severe woman strode towards him. 'Our resources are limited right now so I can't sit round and chit-chat as much as I'd like to. I want to introduce my colleague, Deborah Stock, who is so much better at the nitty-gritties and the daily so-and-sos than I myself am. Give them a wave, Deborah. Excellent. Excellent.' He put on the baseball cap. 'I'm so proud of you all, believe me. Obviously, none of you in this specific room are engineers or scientists, but you have an important role to play in the work we'll be doing. It's your job to manage the optics of our mission, to make sure it plays well on the street and in boardrooms round the world. We can't take everyone and we need to make sure those *temporarily* left behind keep reputations in check. The wheel must turn, after all.'

The room was quiet. Deborah Stock looked nervous.

'Excellent,' said Larson. 'Excellent. I'm going to go now. Thank you for listening.' He stood and the security guys swung into action. They surrounded him, escorting the small figure to the door. Then, as it was opened for him, Larson turned back. 'You have seven days,' he told the room, with a wink.

Soon, the day turned to night. Alastair was too scared to use any field-powered lights and instead sat in darkness, huddled on the couch, lit only by the ghost's glow. Now and then, he crept across the floor, hands trailing the carpet, to crouch by the window and spy on the park across the way. The men remained into the evening. They moved off the swings and were, variously, lying on the benches, using the seesaw, and aimlessly kicking the roundabout around. They didn't seem to notice him watching, but he supposed it didn't matter. They were there to make sure he didn't leave the block. They couldn't care less if their target knew.

He checked his stats. The work absence system must have uploaded by now, because, as he feared, he'd taken a substantial hit. Christ. A whole day down the pan, and unable to leave the flat and feeling the withdrawal of his pills. Couldn't get the junior, couldn't get through to Caitlin, no one out there looking for him and his stats going down bit by bit. He couldn't even stomach streaming anything, or scrolling on the mobile, and that lack of engagement didn't help his numbers one bit.

'I wish you were really here,' he told the ghost.

'I am here,' it said.

'I wish you were here to tell me what to do. I never know what to do.'

The ghost nodded.

They were quiet for a while, then Alastair said, 'I never learned how to shave.'

The ghost looked confused, then understood.

His mobile lit up: Caitlin. He thought she wouldn't do it, but she was returning the call. He answered and said, 'Hello?'

'Hi,' she said. 'What's up?'

And he found he couldn't say. He couldn't voice it out, even to her, this person who he'd shared so much with. Instead he asked how she was, what she was getting up to, if she liked the new thing. 'I just wanted to check in,' he explained.

At first, she spoke quite matter-of-factly, describing the new gig in plain terms. She was out west now, right at the heart of all that advanced tech they ran out there. She lived in a hotel, all paid for, and felt excited by work for the first time in ages. He said that was good. She didn't speak for a moment, then came out with it. She said she'd had the weirdest day ever. Just the weirdest day that he wouldn't believe. First morning on the job, guess who turns up? Guess who's running the show out west?

'No way,' he said. 'You're kidding.'

'I'm not. Him.'

'So what is it?' he asked. 'What's the project?'

There was a silence on the line as Caitlin turned the question over. 'I'd better not say,' she said, 'but when he told us, I thought I might pass out.'

'Like on the rollercoaster that time,' he said.

No response, but he heard her blush across three hundred miles.

'Shut it,' she said, audibly smiling.

They ended the call on good terms, with Alastair requesting her address to send an old-fashioned post card. He wished her all the best and Caitlin returned the sentiment. She hoped they could be friends, when she got back.

'See you soon,' she said, as he killed the line.

In the dark, alone, he nodded. Larson was there, *the* Larson, only a few hours away. Now, he could see a light.

TWELVE

Beyond the watching strangers in the park, past the tenement hinterlands and above the city proper, an anomaly was flying through the air. The night-time ruckus roared away below, everything lit up fairylike and magical, but one noise rose above the others at this high elevation: the cry of an infant. Bizarre, among the skyscrapers and tower blocks and manic sugarwork buildings, to hear a baby fuss, but true enough, there it was: a colicky hiccup soaring between glass walls, a high keening scream coming from who-knew-where in the dark. Only the sound for now, careering among the upper floors, heading south, until a shaft of light, projecting an ad onto low-lying smog, captured its source: a daddy longlegs sort of contraption, fitted with whirling blades, moving quickly but clumsily, dropping then rising a few feet at a time, and crying, crying, crying with the voice of a babe.

The drone lurched messily onwards in fits and bursts, until it flew free of the higher buildings and soared across the Old Town. Onwards, over parkland browned and crispy from recent scorchers, into the sandstone streets of the upper classes, crying still, the utter despair of a lost or abandoned child screeching and searching for its mother. Down below, via open windows, a few listeners heard the sound but already it was gone, passing over, locked into the location it wanted more than anything else in this world.

Ahead, Summerfield House, and the drone knew Mama was ahead of it, waiting, soft and smooth-skinned and warm, with heavy delicious breasts and a cloth to wrap the drone in, to swaddle it, and hush it to sleep and be present as the drone slept. In the drone's tiny mind, it had been lost for so, so long and now the moment of reconnection and nourishment lay across a few feet of sky. It zeroed in on an open window in the building's upper floors and surged straight and true towards it, wanting Mama, wanting milk, wanting skin-on-skin and maternal heat, and as it came near, a hand reached out from the open window to catch the drone and snatch it inside.

In the same building, on another floor, the junior faced a difficult decision. Either he could live, or he could die. At the moment, both options offered advantages and disadvantages. For a day, he'd been with the 97ers and wasn't sure how much longer he could hold out. He was now extremely used to the face of Spencer, the gigantic features the only consistency in the past twenty-four hours; every so often the dinner plate-sized skull appeared over him to administer a fresh burst of pain.

'You're gonnae give it up sooner or later,' Spencer's voice said. 'Why not make it sooner? Save us both some time.'

What did they want? It was tough to say. Their demands changed hourly, so all the junior could do was deny them the latest thing they requested.

'Save us both some time,' Spencer repeated. 'I would if I was you.'

And on top of that difficulty, there was the issue of his swollen-seeming head. Thoughts moved slowly up there, trickling among busted passageways, getting caught up in areas Spencer's knuckles had ruptured.

He whispered, 'I don't know anything.'

'But your old man was there,' said Spencer. 'You've got to know *something*.'

Strapped to the gurney, he couldn't quite shrug, so shook his head instead. 'No.' From his position, he wasn't able to see Spencer, who he guessed sat somewhere nearby in this shabby room, in this house of horrors. They'd dragged him in by his armpits the night before and all the inhabitants came out to leer and pluck at him as he passed. It was pure *Texas Chainsaw*, like on that ancient stream. There were cannibals here, skin-wearers, inbreds and outsiders and the junior felt such a fear of them. He'd heard of the 97ers – everyone had – but he had no understanding of their true nature.

Spencer's voice boomed. 'You ask me, I'm being pretty fucking fair right now.'

The ceiling the junior faced showed blooms of damp, browned lines where leaks peeled back its paper. What a stink in the place, the whole building: vinegar and mould and rancid fat and the choke of dust.

'A lot of chaps, they come into the pub and see a dirty junior cracking on to their missus, they hit the roof. They get much, much nastier than me right now. They murder that junior right there, on the spot. They twist that junior's neck off his shoulders so all the gunk inside spills out. Me, I'm a fairer sort. I like to make a deal with the junior cracking on to my bird. Fair enough, he's made a mistake, but that's not to say we can't work out a deal, eh?'

The junior didn't know what to say. He suspected he wasn't supposed to. His true fear, deep down, was that Spencer didn't want anything from him. That his only desire was to cause the junior pain and the show of interrogation was just to give the torture a context. But then why all the palaver of getting Dot to trick him? And where was Dot, his colleague, who they'd called Dolly in the drive back, saying well done Dolly, you got him good and proper?

'This is a long old chat we've been having now, son,' said Spencer's voice. 'You've forced me into a corner I don't want to be in. I'm a busy man. That city out there's waiting on me so I can *rule* it. Understand? That's how come I want this wrapped up. No one wants you to die, do they? No. Course not. So just speak. Just do it.'

The junior croaked. 'And say what?'

'Say about your old man, about your senior's old man. We know all about it, we just need it confirming. We just need it down in black and white. We know he was there the night it happened.'

'What?'

A loud sigh. A rasping breath and the sound of huge palms slapping knees, then the face reappeared, blocking out the entire ceiling. The junior saw every pore gape. 'You no listening? Your ears no designed for fucking hearing, eh? I'm saying: tell us about your old man, the night of.'

'The night of what?'

'The night of *what*? The night of the big fucking kaboom, of course. You thick or just pretending?'

The junior felt a hand close around his knee. At first, the contact brought some comfort, then his body recalled the events of the past day and everything stiffened. The material of his leg tensed. Spencer had this thing for joints. Joints were where talking came from, he'd said.

'I honestly don't—'

Pressure grew around his knee, around the cap. Spencer's hand compressed it, bit by bit.

'Really, I promise, I—'

Spencer smiled. Many of his teeth were blackened and unevenly spaced. The junior felt the pressure on his knee increase, build up, and he thought he felt some connections squeak against themselves.

'Please,' he said.

'We know all about it,' said Spencer. 'My boss upstairs. Now he's a real nasty bastard. He makes me look like the tooth fairy, Hirst does. I've seen him eat little mammals alive and bleeding, just for fun. He doesn't care. He drinks blood for a laugh, Hirst does. And this boss of mine's been doing some research on the disaster and he knows a thing or two about your old man. He knows your old man's at ground zero when it all kicks off, right there in the control room that set the fire. We're not stupid, us citizens, we know stuff. Folk like you and your old man and all them lot, your Step-Stones, your Honey Bees, your Kim Larsons, you think you can pull the wool over our eyes, but not now.'

'I was ...' The junior coughed. 'I was only a bairn.'

The pressure released. He felt his knee bloom out, away from the giant's grip.

Spencer shook his head. He stroked his chops with a display of disappointment, weary friendship. He said, 'Everyone knows, mate. Everyone knows the disaster was an inside job. It's common knowledge, out there on the street, it's just your average punter doesn't give a shit. He's sorry about all the folk that died, aye, but he likes his field, doesn't he? He likes not having gas running under his feet. He likes being linked up every hour God sends. But he knows. He knows what Larson did, what your old man did. Not enough folk using the field, so they do in the competition. Tell us what went on.'

'I don't—'

But before he could release another denial, Spencer was upon him. He leapt onto the gurney like a cat, landing delicately, with his knees either side of the junior. The hands again, holding his head, holding it like a melon. Spencer pushed big teeth against the junior's ear and whispered threats of violence that came right out of horror stories, straight from fairy tales, as he pulled on his head's lobes as if he wanted to twist them apart.

And as the junior writhed and jerked, his system presented him with an option. It wasn't textual or verbal or voiced in any way, but he became aware of an option open to him. He could die now, if he wanted to. Or perform whatever a junior's equivalent might be: stop functioning, end programming, cease to exist. His system recognised the pain and panic he experienced, calculated it was equivalent to a life or death situation, and offered him an out.

Spencer gripped and whispered and crushed him. The things he said! The images he spat! The junior could've fainted from them.

His system nudged him. *Do you want to go now?*

But he was so young. Only a year old. All he'd done so far was live and work and there were things him and Alastair spoke about doing. Alastair. His senior. He recalled the first morning at the JNR plant, sitting there nude and alone, being tested, being measured, being probed. The day of his birth. At first he'd known nothing, then the person processing his birth showed him a screen. On the screen, a series of images had flashed by at rapid speed: numerous intricate grids with different blacked-out sections that updated several times per second. He watched this happen and a variety of sensations passed through his mind. A concept of selfhood coalesced around his eyes and he became hugely embarrassed by the exposure of his chest and stomach and genitals; he realised he was nude. At once, he covered the genitals with his cupped hands. The person processing him presented a pile of folded clothes: a flannel shirt and pair of dark jeans, some pants and socks. She'd handed them to the junior and he'd dressed, starting with the pants and jeans. Next, he pulled the shirt down over his head, but paused midway through. He slumped back on the stool, arms raised and held by the sleeves, his nose pressed into the shirt's stomach. They were pre-worn and contained an odour that overwhelmed him. He could smell a body, and the effect was astonishing. Pure love flowed into him through his nose and mouth. He smiled into the darkness of the shirt's insides. They explained to him this was the smell of his senior, the smell of home.

He knew it was all programming, all automatic, but you couldn't deny it. You couldn't deny the feeling that was at once *you* and also *not* you. Returning to a place and finding it still there, even better than you remembered.

No, he told his system. *I don't want to go now.*

Fine, the system said, *have it your own way.*

When it became clear the junior wouldn't break, Spencer gave up. He heaved himself off the gurney and brushed his hands together. He showed no embarrassment over the things he'd told the junior. 'You've got some gonads on you, son, but wait til Hirst gets his hands on them.'

It wasn't this Hirst that came next, which calmed him slightly. It was Dot. She entered his vision slowly, looking round as if scared, and whispered, 'What have they done to you?' She put her cold fingers to his face, pressed them to areas of his bare torso that Spencer had ripped at. She said, 'I didn't know it'd be like this.'

'You fooled me,' he said. 'I thought it was a ... you know.'

'I'm sorry.' She looked it too. She nearly cried. 'They said they wanted to talk to you. I didn't realise.'

He sniffed. 'Right.'

'But listen. I overheard the big one. He said he was away to get Hirst. To get some sort of machine to use on you. I really think you should tell them whatever you know.'

'I don't know anything.'

'You must.' She smiled. 'You must know *something*. Why else would they want you?'

'I don't.'

'Please, for me. I don't want to see them use the machine on you. I don't want to see what that boss will do. I'm on your side, honestly.' She came so close, he could feel her eyelashes flutter against his cheek. 'Tell them what they need to know and I'll get you out of here, tonight. I'll take you back to my place. I'll look after you.'

'It was ages ago. He was my old man. If he was involved, I don't know.'

'Please,' she said. 'I don't want them to hurt you.'

But there was nothing for him to say. He didn't know anything about a conspiracy, he didn't know anything about the disaster, except what it took from him.

Dot left. She said goodbye, and begged him to reconsider. He knew the game they were playing, but it felt nice to be fooled.

For a while, he was alone. Once or twice, he sensed an incoming connection. A tiny tickle down in his neck and he wanted to say *yes*, but he didn't have the strength. In his condition, the system prioritised vital processes and a data link to the field came second to sucking up its power. He wondered if it had been his senior. It must've been. No one else knew how to get to him. No one else had access.

He heard a door slam open and something with castors get pushed inside the room.

'Rise and shine,' called Spencer.

He appeared in the junior's eyeline, a surgical mask spread across his nose and mouth. The other one came with him, the curly-haired woman from the bar, all her flirtation gone.

'We didn't want it to end like this, but you've given us no option,' Spencer said, his voice a touch muffled.

192

'You had to do things the difficult way,' said the woman. She snapped a latex glove as she slipped it on.

'Too right, Mandelson,' said Spencer. 'Too right. This here, my electronic friend, is our final straw.'

The junior pushed his head sideways and saw what Spencer was slapping: a boxy piece of machinery with many cables bursting from one side, a blank display on its front.

'This piece of kit does a very special job,' Spencer continued. 'It lets us suck up your memories to view at our leisure.'

Mandelson put on the second glove, all business. 'Whenever we want.'

'It's not our favoured route,' he explained, 'cause this here gets us life, if we're caught. Bruising you up a little, giving you the old one-two, what's that? A few years, and that's if Honey Bee even chases it up, which they won't. So what do you reckon? Like the look of it?'

The junior looked at the box, at the cables. The screen was glossy and dark.

'I should say,' said Spencer. 'The reason this gets us life is the process kills you, or whatever killing is for your lot.'

The junior nodded. He felt too exhausted to speak.

'Righto,' said Spencer, full of good cheer. 'Let's get started, shall we? Nurse! The implements.'

The junior felt them work on him. He felt one of them open up the slot in his shoulder and a sound told him they'd turned on the machine. Spencer said to expect a little pinch, but he felt no pain, felt no pain as they took some cable and fed it into his body, through his feeding hole. He was aware of a certain sensation: a weird tension around his breastbone. Spencer explained this was the tricky bit.

'The body tells us to go down,' he said, 'but we want to go *up*.'

They worked together, Mandelson at the machine, Spencer

over him, feeding the cable in, and now he did feel that pinch. Whatever they were doing, his body did not appreciate it. Whatever pipe they fed the cable through, it was not designed for upward motion.

'Stop,' he croaked. 'Please.'

He heard the woman laugh. 'So now he's talking.'

'He doesn't like the feeling, does he?'

'He should've listened.'

He felt the cable worm its way through his insides, inching through the neck. Everything inside him fought against it, but the leering giant to his right kept feeding it in, kept forcing it towards the final destination: his skull and all the materials it contained.

'I don't want it,' he said. Again, something similar to human tears welled up around his eyes, partly from physical pain, partly from emotion.

'All you had to do,' grunted Spencer, 'was talk. That's all we needed. You could be home right now, eating an electric biscuit.'

Inside, he felt the cable reach a barrier, right behind his mouth. He felt it push against something that offered considerable resistance.

'We're there,' said Mandelson. The box was turned on properly now and the junior saw it showed video: a camera positioned on the end of the cable, so they could operate on whatever blockage stopped them accessing his mind.

'Righto,' said Spencer again. 'Start the saw.'

And Mandelson worked the machine and he suddenly became aware of a whirring inside himself, a high-pitched whine that came through his mouth as though he spoke it. Oh Christ. This was it. He wished he'd taken death when his system offered it. Anything would be better than what he was about to experience.

'Cut away,' said Spencer, holding the cable secure, clamping his hand over the junior's shoulder. 'It's been nice,' he told the junior. 'Let us know if there's a heaven.'

And the junior knew what he had to do. He made the decision in those few micro-seconds, the brief moment of time where the saw approached his inner mind and began to scuff its very edges.

'Stop,' he said. 'I'll talk.'

'I've heard that one before,' said Spencer. 'Keep going, Mandelson.'

'Seriously,' he said. 'There's something you want to know.'

'Aye, aye. Whatever you say.'

The saw cut into something inside his head and he felt like he flew. He felt himself pushing through air, felt a kind of cold wind blowing against him, rushing against his wet eyes. He said something, mumbled it, forced it out before the procedure could finish him.

Spencer, close now. 'What was that?'

He said it again.

'Hold on,' said Spencer.

'Eh?'

'I said stop it!'

The saw spun to a halt and the machine beeped. The junior lay facing the ceiling, staring at the patch of damp, feeling the cable lie heavy against his insides. Spencer came into his field of view, his eyes wide with excitement.

'Say that again. Say that one more time.'

In his quarters, Hirst used an illicit wrist strengthener: a small device, fitted with a coiled spring that he squeezed. He tried to ignore the burbling of the drone in the corner and concentrated on the muscles of his wrist, tried to live inside them as they protested and burned. He squeezed, again and again, and a good motivational tool was to imagine it wasn't the strengthener you squeezed, but something else. Maybe like a hand or an arm or a neck. A fleshy item, one with interesting bits of hardness inside, with a bit of give. He imagined it was one of those items he squeezed, over and over, compressing, watching veins worm out from his fist.

The drone hiccupped. It was home now, contently babbling, and Hirst had already digested the message it transported, all the way from the far-flung outer places. An interesting message, one that forced him to fish out the strengthener from under the bed and get to work. He compressed; he considered.

For a while now, he'd been turning a thought over in his mind. A thought about how it was a shame they couldn't harness technology in the way their enemies could: the big companies, whatever remained of the state now, the juniors themselves. All of them fitted themselves into the field like gears in a machine and everything they wanted done got done. Them, the 97ers, they were hamstrung by physicality. Sure, they went out at nights and destroyed field bulbs, they graffitied certain buildings, but all that looked like increasingly small beer to Hirst. Small potatoes. The conversation happened on the field, which they shunned, so they were outside it. But now ... but now he'd received news that someone on the other side had entered their realm. One of the big wigs, the technocrats, the World's Father himself, physically present in their corner of the world. No one else knew. Not Barlow of the 97ers Anglo or Matthews of the 97ers Cymru. Those jokers were light years behind him, squabbling over the scraps from his table.

He squeezed the device, he crushed it. His wrist wanted him to stop, but it was only a part of him and he controlled the whole. What would they do? What *could* they do? They had van Outen's ghost, that was something. He pictured them unleashing the pathetic spook in a room full of them, full of the powerful and the privileged, saying: look what you've done.

Look at what you've done to us. You've destroyed the sanctity of death. They had the junior too, this disaster worker's son, who might give them something. If they got evidence the disaster was an inside job, that rounded the package up nicely.

He squeezed the device, he crushed it. He imagined skin and soft hairs below his fingers, squashy blood, some meat. Every time he squeezed, a lump of muscle leapt out from his upper forearm. He liked seeing it. A little piece of himself that he forced out through sheer will. A result he caused to happen.

In the corner, the drone carried on, laughing sometimes, screeching. Hirst watched it, its propellers spinning jerkily, though it didn't fly. He thought about taking it apart. He felt so strong, he thought about breaking the drone into little smashed-up bits and seeing what that felt like. He could even jump on top of it, if he wanted to. He could climb up onto the bed and leap across the cramped room and land on the drone and destroy the stupid fuck intelligence inside it.

The strengthener went back into the strongbox, along with the chest extender, a framed photograph, some magazines. These were things that might ruin Hirst, if Mandelson or Spencer or any of the others found out. He got himself dressed, into his pants, his jeans, his boots, his vest, his jacket. Then he approached the drone, listened to it gurgle for a while. He took the toe of his big polished boot and leaned it against the side of the drone.

It giggled.

'Are you laughing?' he asked. 'Are you laughing at me?'

Perhaps the tread of his boot tickled, because the drone giggled more. Hirst smiled as he pressed his boot down into it, into its mechanism, bending back a single propeller.

'Ow,' said the drone, in its high-pitched voice. 'Ah!'

A knock came on the door. He paused, waiting a second. The person rapped again.

Spencer. He could be quiet when he wanted to. Hirst had seen the boy walk unnoticed through crowds, moving above ignorant strangers, light on his slab feet. My protégé, Hirst thought, as the lad ducked inside.

'You'll want to hear this,' Hirst said, pointing to the drone.

'You'll want to hear *this*,' Spencer countered. 'The junior's talking. We were gonnae scrape him, but he started up. Guess what the senior's got at home?'

'That drone came from out west,' said Hirst. 'A certain someone's come for a visit.'

The two of them stood together in the austere room, these two old friends, beginning to see a plan knit together.

The next morning, morale in the park was running low. The two Honey Bee agents were becoming increasingly cold and tired after a night spent outdoors. Luckily, they could rely on the weather, which was uniformly warm; the sun rose eventually and burned the dew from their fleeces.

'I fancy a decaf,' said the first agent, a senior. He sat on one of the park's swings.

'Go and get a decaf, then,' said the second, a junior. He sat on the other swing.

'Couldn't you go?' said the first.

'Nah,' said the second. 'Not for me.'

'Well how long are we going to be?'

The second sniffed. 'How long's a piece of string?'

'This hardly compares.'

'Go and get a decaf then. I can wait here.'

The first agent, the senior, pushed himself on the swing for a bit. He felt tired, even though he'd been allowed a nap in the back of the car, his junior partner not requiring sleep. When would this target show himself? When would he be able to go home?

'Nah,' he said. 'I won't bother.'

The junior agent pulled the mini binoculars out from his pocket and checked the upper flat. 'Still no sign. Nothing all night.'

'He's not there,' said the senior agent. 'He's snuck out and we've not noticed. Just my luck.'

'He hasn't. We would've seen.'

There hadn't been anything, nothing at all through the night or morning. Neighbours came and went but no sign of the target, or this ghost he caused such a fuss about. There had been a Step-Stone uplift – passenger and large suitcase – in the early hours, but they checked with the eerie driver and it was for another flat. Rather them than me, the senior agent thought. Those vans gave him the heebie-jeebies.

'So how long do we wait then?' he said now. 'Until one of us passes out?'

'We wait,' said his partner, 'as long as we wait.'

The senior sighed. 'I hate these jobs. I hate watching out for mouthy pricks. Why can't they just keep their heads down like the rest of us?'

'Because they get delusions of grandeur,' said the junior agent. 'They think they're going to change the world and get themselves a little slice of attention. They think everyone's going to call them a hero and their stats will rocket and they'll get commissioned to stream or write or whatever.'

'I could be in my bed just now,' moaned the senior agent. 'I could be laid out like a whale.'

'You'd be in the office just now.'

A pause. 'Well, anyway. Let's head back there now. We'll get ourselves a nice cup of decaf and let the boss know it was a waste of time. A dead end. The fucker's flown the coop. Write it up, pass it on, job done. Have a nice sit down, a nice latte, a nice—'

'Shut up. Look.'

'What?'

'There. On the road.'

Through the parked cars, they noticed a van idling outside the target's flat. This messy old banger, self-driven, barely electric, humming and rattling and disturbing the peace. It was full of folk, full of weirdos. Three of them in the front seats, all decked out in old-fashioned gear, dirty and messy, just an absolute state, and one of them was gigantic, barely fitting within the van's cabin.

They watched two of them, the two blokes, pile out and scurry up the target's path and –

'They've done the door!' exclaimed the senior agent. 'Look, they've knocked it in.'

'Just wait. This might play well for us.'

'But who are they? They've done the fuck—'

'Just wait.'

So they waited. They waited and watched and the woman driving seemed to be talking to someone in the covered back. She turned her head often but of course they couldn't hear what was said. The junior agent took out his binoculars to observe the upper windows and after a few minutes he said, 'They're in.'

'What are they up to?'

'Not sure. They're walking around in there, but I think you're right.'

'How am I?'

'I think he's pissed off. They've gone in looking for him and, from what I can see, he's gone.'

'Motherfu—'

They waited a while longer. They waited for the two weirdos to reappear, and when they did, they looked livid. The smaller man kept pushing the larger, shoving against his back, but this made no difference to the larger's stride. They got into the van.

The agents watched them bicker. They seemed to be directing their ire towards whoever sat in the hidden rear of the vehicle.

'Let's go,' said the junior agent. 'We'll get back to the offices and let someone know. Feed it up the chain.'

Which was exactly what the other agent had been saying this whole time, this whole time. What a waste. What a waste of prime hours, and if only he'd been listened to then the palaver could've been avoided. He had a good mind, after his decaf, to let someone know about his partner. He couldn't get away with ignoring good ideas for a second longer.

In the back of the lurching van, the junior did his best to grip hold of the pole he was handcuffed to. The 97ers drove fast. He felt them take corners without braking, swerving and bumping over lumps in the road. By listening to their arguing he knew Alastair was safe. They ignored him now, after calling him every name under the sun when they returned. He didn't care. He didn't care because there wasn't anything they could tell him that he didn't tell himself. You scumbag. You coward. All it took was a little pain to break you, to make you betray your one and only. The van rocked him, its side slammed against his back and the handcuffs wore at him. The discomfort felt good.

I should have let the system take me when I had the chance, he thought. I should have taken the proper way out.

As he thought about it, his system offered him something else. Again, it didn't present as textual or verbal. Strictly speaking, it was an emotion; a feeling in his gut that, if he wanted to, the option existed for him to connect to his senior.

That made no sense. None at all. The connection ought to be one-way. A senior shouldn't be living within the field in the same way a junior did.

But he responded to his system anyway. He said: *yes.*

Immediately, he began to shut down. It felt a little like the rest protocol he entered at night. Now, his system shut him down and for a while all he saw was darkness. It panicked him, though it didn't last long. After a few moments, the darkness greyed. Fuzzy blobs of light formed around him, areas of brightness in the black. Soon, they resolved into patches of distinct vision. He was seeing! Seeing through his senior's eyes. But what did he see? Nothing much, at first. A wide section of sheet metal, a few inches above the senior's eyes. It looked like he might be hiding somewhere. A secret place in the flat perhaps? A cupboard in the downstairs close?

He felt his senior sigh. He felt the sensation in his own breast and it floored him. His first ever sensation of true, human, organic life. A plug of air coming in to squeeze the nostrils, his belly bulging with accumulated breath, then its release. The air tickling his lip as it escaped, passing over his lips, just reaching his chest and arms. He felt a little pain around his left shoulder, under the armpit, and it felt delicious, sweet. He felt a weight in the lower torso, the heaviness of the guts. He felt some heartbeat in his ankle, his temples, a little in his eyelids too. He felt air coming in and going out and the sensation was bliss.

And then the senior turned over and the junior turned over with him. He turned to lie on his side in his hidden area and his vision passed over the sign attached to the senior's cell:

IN RARE EVENT OF WAKING MID-TRANSPORT,
PLEASE DO NOT SCREAM OR CLAW.

So that did it. He knew. His senior was safe. Right now, he was being delivered to a place unknown, but safe, whole, in one single piece.

THIRTEEN

In the time of dogs, the boy learned to run. At school, they taught him sports and he performed them without ever experiencing enjoyment. It did well for your juvenile stats to participate, to join in, to excel even, but he was too far removed from his body to be truly present. In his fantasies, his body became disconnected from his mind. In daydreams, the mind was stored in a jar or uploaded to the field itself, separate from the traitor that was the slowly dying flesh of the body. Do without it. Cut away the excess. Trim the fat off everything but the thoughts and knowledge and consciousness. Distil that consciousness down into a morsel and let it exist forever in formaldehyde or wires. The school took them on cross-country runs and the boy hid in the woods with his friend Jayden, emerging once a reasonable time passed. He beat the system. He wouldn't be forced to coexist with the body.

In his home with his parents, he made the connection between mind and field as close as possible, holding screens up to his face so his eyes burned from the light; in his ears, connections for audio. He lay out in bed and if the screen was close enough, if the sound was loud enough, you were in there. You were under the field like an ocean. There was no barrier, no delay. You were in there. Boredom did not exist. He fed the mind as soon as it hungered. As soon as it wanted, he provided.

He was in there. He forgot his toes, his hair. Cut out the middleman. Place the mind where it wants to be. Let it sit in a vat of pleasure and dispose of the body, that carrier of diseases and cancers and plagues. At school, they taught him sports but he feigned sickness. He stayed home. He fed the mind whenever it wanted, whenever it hungered. It was a matter of seconds. A thought occurred and the field responded.

Then the bad night and the bad morning and going up the school with Jayden's ma, leaving with the older kids and getting lost among the debris, seeing a passenger trapped inside an early-morning tram, beating on the glass, silently screaming for release. It amazed him how quickly the world changed, how quickly passive background revealed active antagonism. He learned to run. He learned it quick.

He couldn't do it at first. His lungs felt shrivelled up and barely able to bring in a cup of breath. The backs of his legs pinched. Mouthfuls of drool clogged his gob. But he learned. Mist or smoke lay across the ruined streets, an ambient rustle of fires followed him always as he ran. A few days later, when the dogs started massing, he learned to sprint. The first one he saw: a blue-eyed Weimaraner sniffing bricks in an arcade. He stood in the opening until it looked up. It watched for a moment, then the eyes turned. The old systems kicked in and the boy legged it.

He got fast quick. When he ran, he rarely had the energy to remember the lost parents. When he ran, it was all debris. It was dodging sinkholes and fallen masonry and cracks in the road. Sometimes, he saw strangers on horizons and he ran from them. Sometimes, he wasn't quite fast enough. He ran through aisles of superstores, swiping whole shelves of abandoned dry goods into bin bags. He ran through open spaces, watching the sky for helicopters or Honey Bee peacekeepers. When he ran, all that existed was the running. The feet, in stolen trainers, connecting and reconnecting with the pavement, were a sort of machine he could set off, then ignore. The lungs took up so much attention, keeping them filled, maintaining their capacity. He felt everything. He noticed pains in his knees and hips when he was losing steam. He felt everything. He noticed areas tight and knotty in his back, his bum, his thighs. He listened to dogs howl in the distance and laughed at his freedom. For energy, he gorged on superstore spoils: chocolate biscuits, canned crisps, long-life plant milks. He felt everything. He was alive.

In time, his running took him to the coast, away from his homeland. Here, he saw a true crisp sun for the first time in weeks. Across the firth, it hung above Edinburgh with clear edges, round and real. For days, the only way to tell day from night had been the smoke mottling yellow, instead of mauve. He met the coast and everything else was pure luck. Salt wind blew against him and he spied a camp near the beach, the first he'd trusted to enter, and found out about the rescue mission: hovercrafts coming, that night, to take them away. A band of other kids his own age looked after him, a boy and two lassies. They let him lie down in their tent and, when he woke, they said his legs moved in his sleep.

Now, in the back of the Step-Stone truck, Alastair felt the same life in him. Perhaps it was the restriction of the sleeping pod, but his body rattled with energy and he couldn't help but remember those running days, the ones he hadn't experienced for many years.

He waited until he felt the truck stop and heard the driver slam the cabin door. It might be an uplift, but he wasn't sure. He waited again and heard nothing else, so assumed the driver must've stopped for lunch or a piss. In a rush, he pushed against the head of his cell, knuckling the wall there to drive his feet against the base and force the sleeping pod out its housing. He found himself in the narrow corridor of other travellers, stacked high around him, their toes resting against the windows.

So far, so good. Now, for the ghost.

They stored luggage beneath the travellers' area on these trucks and Alastair worked quickly. He emerged from the back, blinking in the light, and saw they'd pulled up at a remote charging station and café. Another Step-Stone truck towered beside his own; presumably the drivers would be across in the rest stop, filling themselves up. He snuck along the truck's side and located the luggage compartment, opened it up and found his suitcase inside. A huge black monstrosity, belonging to Caitlin.

He tapped the side. 'Alright in there?'

The ghost inside swore. It said, 'Let me out.'

'Aye. In a minute.'

Then they were off, and at first he walked quickly, looking around for whoever might be on his tail. He soon realised the danger was most likely behind them. Here, in this Highland services, no one sought them out. All they needed to do was make it west, to Uist, to Caitlin, and to Larson. Of course, he felt bad for the aged gent next door, the aged gent he'd been forced to menace. Mr Hannermann, who'd lived in the building since long before they took up residence and seemed like a good enough sort, for all he knew of him. He shouted when Alastair barged his way inside and explained clearly what he expected: for Mr Hannermann to get the fuck into the back bedroom and lie the fuck down cause this was a robbery and if he so much as moved a muscle then he would know all about it, yes he would. Then he arranged an express uplift from Step-Stone and waited for the driver to arrive. A short while later the pill and nappy rushed down Mr Hannermann's flume, neither of which he made use of.

A nice day up the Green Welly, he realised, sweating as he

dragged the suitcase behind him, up past the autoway ramp. The hills behind the stop glowed from the strength of sun and he made his way towards the restaurant and the privacy of the bogs. Once inside, he found a free cubicle and released his old man. Now there was a sight, the ghost folded up inside the suitcase.

His dad stood. He wobbled a bit. 'Christsake,' he said.

'I'm sorry,' said Alastair.

He blinked. 'Where are we then?'

'Up north. I didn't want to stay on the route any more, just in case.'

'That's smart.'

Alastair nodded. 'Ta.'

'So what now?'

'Well, first things first. We'll have to get you back in.'

The ghost shook its head. 'I can't.'

'You'll have to.'

'What for?'

Alastair gestured around himself. 'I can't have you walking about. Folk would stare.'

'Let them stare,' said the ghost. Same in life. Didn't give a shit who looked. The mad stuff Alastair remembered him wearing, even out the house. T-shirts with holes all over, women's shorts.

'Aye, but staring's one thing. What happens next? What happens when they come for us again?'

It took some time, but the ghost saw sense. It wanted to be a team player, so it stood inside the suitcase and folded itself up to fit, so Alastair could bring the zip home. He strode out the cubicle and almost ran into the man standing outside: a tourist in waterproofs, a floppy hat. They stared at each other. The tourist peered over Alastair's shoulder to the empty cubicle: where was the other speaker? Alastair looked into the cubicle too.

'Everything okay?' asked the tourist, nervously.

Alastair could only shrug as he left the bathroom, leaving the tourist staring confused into the open pan.

The place bustled with others just like him, the bathroom listener. This place represented the heart of the tourist trade, the massive conveyor belt that lifted travellers up from the south and deposited them in the far places: the ex-islands, the mountain cities. The world was represented here, all of it. A vast array of screens described fried breakfast in all tongues and a waiter busily slotted decafs into a bank of ordering stations. In the shop, you could buy ornamental whisky with your face on the label. A thought occurred to Alastair as he watched a tourist churn his own fudge. How to make the next leg of his journey? He needed to get to Uist soon, or else he'd miss his chance to confront Larson. He needed to show the world what the bastard had done.

After watching the tourists, he needed food, so negotiated the suitcase through the queues and ordered breakfast, finding a table near a bank of windows that looked out across the land. Hitching a lift would be best. Even ordering the food had been a bit of a risk, given the order came from his account via the field, where anyone might have access to it. The breakfast was good. He ate it quietly, listening to the chatter behind, feeling comforted by his lack of understanding. You could feel invisible when you didn't understand what was being said. You disappeared a little bit, even from yourself. He ate his food and watched the land and listened to the small sounds of discomfort from inside the case.

The scorcher was turning, as they tended to. Off in the distance, storm clouds were closing in. A wall of them approached, tall, dark, weighty. They looked fat with moisture. He ate his food and drank some decaf and soon the weather was upon them. Soon, the clouds hung above and rain began to patter against the windows. Small at first, then bigger. Eyeball-sized droplets thudded at the glass, specially reinforced for such an occasion. He could barely make out the surrounding lands through the blanket of falling rain. None of the tourists noticed the change in weather. They were used to it.

He tried to huddle near a road sign by the entrance to the autoway. The metal provided a little shelter but he was still battered by rain, by wind. Nothing good came past. Many local buses, but they wouldn't stop for a hitcher, nor would the massive distance buses, the field-powered personal motors. Alastair grimaced as the wet seeped into his shoes and socks, feeling hopeless. He looked down the nearly empty autoway and wanted to cry. What was he thinking? What was wrong with him? He should've reported his old man as soon as he showed up. Where did this madness come from? He didn't want to change the system, did he? He wanted to be home alone, working on the stats, building up the junior. That was all he wanted, and now he stood by an autoway entrance, soaked to the bone. The breakfast soured inside him and all the milky decaf lay heavy in his stomach.

'What am I doing?' he said aloud.

No one heard it because there was no one to hear.

He remembered the bed at home, with Caitlin. He closed his eyes and remembered his eyes being closed. The smell of unwashed bodies beneath those blankets, curtains shut, music playing somewhere. He'd given it all away. He had something he needed badly and gave it away like it was worthless.

He opened his eyes and saw a truck by the roadside, its indicators flashing. He had no time to think, because of the rain, so clambered up onto the steps. The driver peered at him through the messy window, which then lowered.

'Alright?' he asked.

'Sort of,' said Alastair. 'I was looking for a lift.'

'Where you going?'

'Upwards. Uist, if you're heading that way.'

The driver looked at him for a moment. 'Well,' he said, 'close enough anyway. Get in.'

Alastair climbed inside.

'All set?' asked the driver.

'Yep, all set.'

The driver delivered produce to the businesses up this way. Anything too large to be sent by flume, anything needing special temperature control, anything bulky or awkward. Just now, in the back, were many chilled carcasses going to the hotels in the far-off places. He described them to Alastair: beef joints and pork legs and bags of chicken breast. Not much call for that lot in the cities these days, but the hotels still relied on them. The hotels up this way did a roaring trade, no off-season anymore, and their guests demanded meat on tap, day and night. The trucker, going by Ger, based himself outside Glasgow and left behind his family to haul meat up and down, as far off as Stornoway. The hotels needed him, so he drove.

'Must get boring,' said Alastair.

They were an hour or so in and he was still soggy, but warm. The roadside desperation began to fade.

'It doesn't,' the trucker said. 'It gets easier, if anything. A lot of folk say you must get bored but I don't, because I like it.'

'Oh,' said Alastair. 'Right.'

The trucker was a short man. He sat upon an improvised booster cushion to get a good view in front. Something of the terrier about him.

'I like getting away from home, I mean. Wife going on, kids

going on. No thanks. They offered us the chance to junior but I said you can keep it. Let this junior do all the driving while I stay home and get my ear nagged off? No thanks, I said. You got one?'

'I do,' said Alastair. 'Yeah.'

'Well then excuse me, but you're a mug. You should see the things I've come across in these places.' The little trucker grinned and pointed ahead of him to the oncoming autoway. 'I've picked up all sorts on my tos-and-fros.'

Alastair nodded. He was thinking about the junior. Something else in his life he'd fucked up. Poor thing. Stolen or something, he guessed. It happened. You heard stories about folk's juniors getting picked up and sold on and forced to work elsewhere for no money. You heard stories.

'They say, but Gerry, you can stay home, let the junior do your drives for you, it comes out your pay packet but you get all this freedom. Nah. No thanks. I never wanted freedom, thanks. Freedom's for mugs. I'll take the cash, thanks. I'll take the driving, thanks.'

A thought occurred to Alastair. 'D'you ever come across those Step-Stone drivers?'

This seemed to set something off inside the trucker. He jumped up on his booster and gripped the wheel. He said, 'The worst of the worst. They think they're *it*. Everyone in driving hates them, giving it the big "I am". Think they're kings of the road. Won't make the effort in services or anything, sit in their own little corner, just cause they've had their balls cut off.'

'I don't think they actually cut—'

'It turns my stomach, it does.' He faced Alastair for a moment. 'Like I'm less just cause I'm not moving people about, cause I'm moving food and meat.'

Fine, Alastair thought. Whatever. He didn't much like the trucker. He had a sneaky way about him, but what choice did he have? He tried to change the subject, to get him off the hated Step-Stone drivers. He asked what sorts of things he'd picked up on his tos-and-fros.

'All sorts,' was all he said. 'All sorts, my friend.'

After a while, the trucker wanted to know where Alastair was headed. How come he didn't travel by Step-Stone or another service? How come he sat himself down at the side of the auto-way in the rain?

'I'm skint,' said Alastair. 'I'm starting a new job up there.'

'Nice bag for someone that's skint,' said the trucker.

'I saved up for it.'

'No need to explain yourself,' he winked. 'Only saying.'

Quite soon, the heat of the cabin and the rocking of the truck made him dozy. They were so high up, above other vehicles, and he felt his head tap against the window as he faded away. He didn't sleep much these days. The pills that came via the flume played around with his chemistry and, as a result, he woke often in the night. He told Caitlin it felt like surfing along a few inches below the surface, never truly falling into the deepest reaches, never fully resting. But there was something about that cabin. The hot air pushing through the vents, the lurches as it drove across uneven autoway. Out like a light and plunging down to areas he hadn't accessed for some time. He dreamed and in the dream, he went back to Caitlin's dad's house. This big huge wooden house down by the river, almost hidden by violent greens, and Alastair walked through the water, the wetness up to his neck. He walked through the river and up to the house and the old man leapt from the table to offer him a hand. He said, 'We've been waiting.'

In his sleep, he became gradually aware that the truck had stopped. His body missed the comfort of forward motion and he began to rise back up to the waking world. He blinked.

They were no longer on the autoway. Tall evergreens stood on either side of the track they were parked up on; the trucker wasn't in the driver seat. At first, he assumed this might just be a toilet break. A quick five minutes for the trucker to run into the trees to do his business. That must happen all the time, so he waited.

He comfied himself in the cabin seat and watched the trees. The track continued onwards, winding away into these remote forests. He waited, then heard footsteps outside the truck, some gravel crunching. So the trucker was nearby. Perhaps the vehicle needed a bit of maintenance; maybe the oil needed to be topped up. He heard footsteps, then a side door slamming. Something about the light reminded him of his time on the peninsula, those running days, and he swallowed. Saliva pooled in the bottom of his jaw. The trucker wasn't going to try it on with him, Alastair told himself. He wasn't going to slide a hand across the cabin and grab him by the knee. There was no chance, just none.

Outside, he caught the trucker coming round the side of the cabin. He looked guilty.

'We having a stop?' asked Alastair.

'Nah, not really,' said the trucker. 'Get back in.'

'I thought I'd stretch my legs.'

The trucker glared at him. His mean little face narrowed. 'We aren't stopped. Just a bit of maintenance.'

'I'll get in when we're going.'

For a moment, the trucker continued to glare, then he marched around the truck, out of sight. Alastair heard him messing round with something back there. He could hear him mutter away to himself as he worked, a nasty little stream of whispers. Whatever was going on, he didn't like it, so he went off to see.

Rounding the truck himself, he found the trucker kneeling

in the grass with Alastair's suitcase before him. He was busy undoing the zip and when he got it open, he fell onto his back. He swore, then twisted himself up into a crouch.

'You were trying to rob me,' Alastair said.

The trucker wiped his face. 'What the fuck's in that bag?'

'I can't believe you were just robbing me,' he said.

The ghost unfolded itself from the suitcase. It looked around gloomily.

'Oh Lord,' said the trucker. He wiped his face from brow to chin. 'What the fuck. What the fuck.'

The three of them stood there off the track, beside the vehicle. The trucker wouldn't leave his face alone, continually mauling it with his palm. Alastair couldn't tell how to play this, how to make it work.

'Listen,' said the trucker. 'I'm sorry. I really am. I didn't know you had . . . whatever that is. Listen, I really am.' He stood up, remaining slightly crouched at the hips. 'Let me just get back into that truck and I'll let yous alone.'

'You're not leaving me here,' said Alastair. 'I don't even know where we are.'

The trucker spoke, but didn't take his eyes off the ghost. 'Listen, we've all made mistakes here. Let's just draw a line in the sand. I'll get back up into that truck and we'll say no more about it.'

The ghost stepped out of the suitcase and onto the grass. It mumbled a word that no one heard.

'It's like a hologram or something,' said the trucker to himself. 'That's all.'

'What we'll do,' said Alastair, 'is I'll get him back in the bag, we'll get the bag back in the truck and we'll keep going. No one needs to know.'

The trucker's eyes flicked to Alastair. He nodded.

'Alright then,' Alastair said, and he helped his father down into the case. The old man went willingly, kneeling, folding himself in two, and as Alastair started on the zip, he heard the cabin door slam. The truck started up. He turned, and the last thing he saw was the driver's wild eyes staring through the window, passing by, away and onto the road, leaving them there in unknown country.

He watched the empty road for a bit and thought: at least the rain's held off.

Nearing dark, and they traipsed down an overgrown pathway. Dried-up brambles cut him and pulled on his clothes while his father breezed by. From the trucker's abandonment, they walked and walked, heading in a direction he vaguely recognised as west. He'd turned his mobile off before they left the capital and he was hesitant to use it now.

'How are you doing?' he asked his father.

'Fine,' said the ghost.

'It's easier for you, I suppose.'

The ghost didn't look back. 'None of this is easy,' it said.

Despite the situation, it felt good for the two of them to be together. Every so often, he caught himself taking the apparition for granted, then he'd think: this is my old man. Who else before him spoke to a dead father? None. No one. Every so often, he thought back to the early days after his father juniored. Those summers when he was free of work and they spent hours talking. He had not recalled those times for long, long years.

'I can't do this much longer,' his dad said.

'We'll walk a while and see what comes up,' said Alastair.

'I don't mean the walk. I mean all of it.'

They paused there on the pathway. There were no living things around them here, nothing crept in the dry hedging, nothing flew above.

'I don't get it,' said Alastair.

'I feel like I can go, if I want to,' said the ghost. 'I've got this feeling.'

'Well don't.'

'It isn't right, that I'm here. It shouldn't have happened.'

'But you need to stay. You need to stay, and we'll get up there and show this man what he's done. It's going to be explosive, you get that, eh?'

The ghost shook its head. 'I don't care about that, son. It doesn't matter to me, cause I'm not really here, am I? This isn't me, it's only a part of me. It doesn't count.'

Alastair felt a clog form in his throat. He said, 'It does count.' He couldn't look the ghost square in the face; he wasn't able. Instead, he noticed its arms extend and he shuffled forward to be close to it, daring to touch its approximation of a body for the first time. It stung, where their skin met.

'Just a bit longer,' he said. 'We'll get it done.'

'Just a bit longer,' his father sighed.

Then they broke apart and brushed themselves down and continued, the ghost ahead. Alastair smiled to himself. He felt safe.

By the time full dark descended, he knew they were in a bind. A good few hours walking and nothing of any substance had shown itself, no home, no town, no well-used road. He began to panic a little. What if they were driving themselves into remoter and remoter places? What if he died out here?

He stopped. 'Wait a second,' he said.

The ghost paused.

'I'm thinking,' he said. 'I'm thinking we need to get the mobile on. We can risk that they'll see it, on the field. We need to aim for something, cause this is daft.'

He turned it over in his head for a few seconds, then pulled the mobile out his pocket and turned it on. The screen sprang to life and a wave of relief ran through him. Now that was good, to see the pixels flood with light and pop out from his palm. Pure relief, and instantly, the mobile connected itself to the field and sucked up power and data from the air around them. Notifications littered the screen, but for now he ignored them. He pulled up a map and let it locate them in the world. It showed the surrounding lands, the greens, the waters, and up ahead a little named village. A place to aim for at least.

He explained it to the ghost, then killed the mobile. The screen blackened and became an object again, one he hid inside his pocket. He'd been present on the field for such a short period, he was sure no one would have caught it. And probably no one was looking for them, so it was fine.

They continued on, across pathways snaking through the trees and hillsides. Often, Alastair was forced to stop and rest, but as slow as their progress was, he knew the village remained out there waiting and they would find safety within, or at least a place for shelter.

Hours passed and it became true night. A handful of stars poked out, and then the ghost said, 'Look.'

Headlamps flashed down the road; someone was driving towards them in the dark. They paused on the roadside and waited for the vehicle to round the corner, and when it did, they saw it was a sleek black thing, windows tinted, like a dark cat speeding through the narrow lane. It came nearer, then crunched to a halt on the far side of the road.

'Oh,' he said. 'Right.'

The doors flew open and two men slipped out from the driver and passenger doors. They wore dark fleeces and shades and seemed strongly built. One of them was a junior.

'Evening, gents,' the junior said, as he crossed the road towards them.

His partner came after. 'Out for a stroll?'

'Bit dark for a stroll,' said the first.

Alastair looked at them both. 'We're not looking for trouble,' he said. 'We're just heading to the village.'

'Aye,' said the junior. 'That's what we thought.'

'We assumed as much,' added his partner.

'I just wanted to ask though,' said the junior, 'what's the story with your friend here?'

Everyone now considered the ghost. All three men eyed him for a moment.

'It's a fair question,' said the partner.

Alastair sighed. 'What do you want?'

'What do we want?' asked the junior. 'Well, we're just driving through the country, as is our right, and my friend and I spot you two walking down the road, and we say to ourselves, now there's a strange-looking individual. Don't we?'

'We do.'

'So I'll ask you again. What's the story with your friend here?'

'It's a fair question.'

Alastair shook his head. 'It was you two in the park, wasn't it?'

They both shrugged, these two strangers. They shrugged, and grinned. 'We get to a lot of places,' said the junior.

'We try to spread ourselves around,' said the senior.

'No harm in that.'

'None at all. None at all.'

Alastair nodded. 'You were in the park and you were watching the house.'

They shrugged again. 'We see a lot of things,' said the junior.

'I can't help but notice,' added the senior, 'that you're dodging the question, sir. Because we were asking about your friend here, and you moved onto parks and who was or wasn't in certain parks.'

'I get it,' said Alastair. 'I understand.'

A flash of realisation crossed the senior agent's face. Alastair recognised it as phoney. 'I know who these two are,' he said. 'These are the two jokers putting videos up on the field saying that this friend here is some sort of spooky monster *returned from the grave.*'

'So they are!' said the junior. 'Excuse my French, but what a fucking coincidence.'

'Remarkable.'

'The world turns in funny ways, doesn't it?'

'It does.'

He could make a run for it, couldn't he? Dive out into the trees and keep sprinting, bury himself somewhere hidden. But the ghost, his father. He couldn't leave him behind.

'So what happens next?' Alastair asked.

'I like this guy's proactive attitude,' said the junior.

'He's got an excellent attitude.'

'What happens next,' said the junior, 'is we all go together into that car over there and have ourselves a little drive. We get ourselves buckled up nice and tight into that safe vehicle and we go for a drive. There are people out there, important people, who have a special interest in meeting you, young man.'

FOURTEEN

As they drove, the junior indulged in his equivalent of sleep. The option was always open to him, regardless of circumstances. Sitting, standing, cuffed in the back of a rocking van, he could slip into it. He retained nearly full consciousness during these dips, the main difference being an increased awareness of the field. In the equivalent of sleep, he felt the field, really felt it. His system required access at all times, but in sleep, he was able to appreciate the process. Parts of him opened up and let in the charged particles of power, the waves of data. Imagine a summer's air heavy with pollen, little unidentified specks glowing in low sun, those items blowing through you, giving you all the energy you need. No dreaming for juniors though, just a dulling of the lights, a heaviness of the extremities, and an opening up.

They stopped now and then. His kidnappers were still furious, snapping at each other up front. He kept his head down though. He knew he needed to go as unnoticed as possible, to avoid them losing it completely and finishing him off. More than anything, he tried to avoid listening to the whimpers coming from the large dog carrier at the far end of the van. There was no way to see its inhabitant, but the voice did not sound canine.

They pulled over; he woke. In his system, he checked their location and saw it on a map of the country. They were driving across the new lands, based on the data they forced out him, the fake earth built across the sounds and sea lochs of the west. The 97ers pulled over on the new lands and left the van to piss. As for the junior, he'd asked his system to recycle its waste. No hint of a Junior Meal for some time now, so it wasn't an arduous task. In the 97ers' absence, he allowed himself to shift around a bit on the van's floor, among manky brown carpet and blackened tools. Every so often, a sort of tubular wrench rolled out from somewhere and knocked against his foot. He couldn't help but think of it as a weapon. Now, it rested against his ankle. To see what it felt like, he dragged it across the floor towards him with the sole of his shoe. It felt good to have the wrench a little closer.

Outside the van, he heard one of them speak: '—and get a move on, would you?'

Another, the woman: 'Shut the fuck up.'

They were close by, a few feet away from him through the van's metal. He dragged the wrench nearer so it nestled into his groin.

'Why's she taking so long?' he heard one of them ask. The older, the boss, the Anglo one, whose speech was sharp and clipped.

'It's different, eh, for a lassie,' said the big one's voice. Spencer the torturer.

A silence followed. Then, 'Yeah, I know that, don't I?'

If the junior knelt up, he could shuffle the wrench behind him. Then it sat below his back, hidden. It felt good to have it there. He wouldn't use it. Sometimes you wanted a weapon close by, just for the feel of it.

'Finished?' he heard Spencer ask.

The woman. 'What does it look like?' She had the same voice as him and his senior. She spoke with his accent, the one from the peninsula.

'Get a move on then,' said Spencer.

And then the van's doors opened and he felt the lurch of the big one climbing in. The junior waited for the vehicle to start, but nothing came. Instead, he heard boots crunching round the outside of the van, and the back doors unlocked and the boss hauled himself inside. The doors slammed shut. 'Let's get going,' he announced. 'I'm sitting back here.'

If the other two were confused, they didn't show it. The engine started and they took off, back on the road. The boss, the one calling himself Hirst, surfed the van's movements, hunched over, as he found himself a place to sit, back against the wall, legs out in front. Just like the junior. Direct across from the junior.

He asked, 'Comfy?'

The junior stared at him. 'Aye.'

'Good. I wouldn't want you to feel uncomfortable.'

'I'm not.'

'Good.'

The junior knew this man hated him. Complete disgust poured out as he watched the junior, smirking, his slim jaw moving. The expression was: how dare you? How dare you sit like that and share the air I breathe? How dare you exist? The junior watched as Hirst folded his fingers in his lap and crossed his legs at the ankle. He was all wiry muscles, tense and stringy. You could see him working land, this man. Working land like an animal, combing through mulchy earth with strong fingers, wrestling live fish out from cold waters, biting into roots.

He sneered. 'Get a good look?'

'Nothing much to see back here.'

'Well don't look at me, anyway,' said Hirst. 'Look at your feet if you need something to look at.'

The junior nodded. He looked at his feet, still aware of the vision across, trapping him in its beam.

*

Spencer, driving, couldn't shake the feeling they were making a big mistake. The intel was good, fair enough. One of their lot out west sent confirmation on the drone: *Larson's here. If you want to do something, now's your chance.* But the thing was, he didn't trust Hirst not to fuck it up for them. He gripped the steering wheel. He drove. For now, keep going. For now, do as you're told.

He started wondering how long he had left in this game. A good few years now, running with the 97ers and to be honest, he was getting sick of it. Sick of the politics, sick of Hirst's nonsense, sick of spending time in that rotten hole of a house. He didn't give a toss about bringing back the 90s. He didn't give a toss about juniors, not really. They were fine. They were machines, who cared? Back in the old days, they spent time sneaking round places at night, messing up the lives of the posh-cunts. They smashed up electrics in businesses and flooded office blocks: the good times. He missed them. He put on a good show giving that junior the old one-two, but he'd prefer a proper opponent. Even down the Pit, the rat lads weren't proper opponents. They were distractions. With his size, he could plough through them like butter. Even this Larson, the World's Dad, he wasn't an opponent, cause Spencer didn't care about him. No one was a true opponent to him and there was some sort of poetry in that. He enjoyed it, in a way. The biggest cunt, with nothing to beat.

But keep driving, aye. Keep going for now and keep your thinking under your hat where it belongs. He thought: I'll see how it goes. I'll keep my cards close to my chest and see how it plays out. Try to find something I care about. Money, he could take or leave. Didn't want fame; couldn't care less about it. Everything physical he could steal from the world by force. He thought about the gravel on his grandad's drive. He thought about the posh-cunt held in his gogoplata. Aye, he thought. Some more of that, please.

Beside him, Mandelson sat stock still. No one cared to notice, but nothing of her moved. Every part of her held still and tense. Her Head Thing was rushing on like a bastard, an absolute bastard. Everything above the nose felt swollen, blocked, five times the size, but she held it together. At times, she wanted to open the van door and disappear, but she held it together.

At the last stop, she went off into the woods at the side of the road and pretended to piss. Didn't even get her jeans down. Just stood there in among the trees, watching. What were they doing? What were they doing out there? They had nothing. Absolutely nothing. The ghost those low-rankers conjured up in their bedroom: so what? They'd lost the senior and his old man. They had his junior; they had fuck all. She'd bent and let a mouthful of spit spill onto the forest floor: a frothy puddle between her feet. Hirst was going to get them killed, she knew it and now, sat beside Spencer in the passenger seat, she could feel the big man slip away. Something had shifted in him. He didn't have the spark anymore. She knew he would abandon them at the slightest opportunity. All she had wanted was a place to belong, a family, so how had she ended up with this pair?

Her Head Thing bloomed inside her brains. She was back on the peninsula, in the camp, waiting for rescue. They slept in tents that the wind blew right through. They ate expired sachets. They killed dogs out of necessity. They waited for lights in the firth. And the worst bit? The absolute worst bit of this whole ordeal that Hirst was putting them through? She knew him. She knew the junior. Nearly fell over that night in the bar with Dolly when the clown came back from the toilets. Nearly toppled right backwards, because wasn't this the same boy that came running into camp one morning, half his hair missing, bites up and down his skinny legs? Wasn't this the same boy they made space for in camp? The running boy. The one who could barely speak from his thirst and hunger? And she recognised him, sat there in the bar, and lying on the gurney at Summerfield, nearly getting his brains fried by Spencer. One of her own. One of her sort. A refugee from off the peninsula. That junior sat in the back now, the absolute spit of the running boy, just with a few years of life on him, a few extra stone. The absolute spit of him and she would've let him fry. And for what? Some inside info on the disaster? Who cared now, all these years after? Sabotage, accident, cover-up, whatever. She wanted it away, in her past where it belonged.

And back behind the pair of them, Spencer and Mandelson, trusty lieutenants, Hirst seethed. He sat with his spine rigid to the side and watched the junior and seethed at it. This specimen. This affront to all things right and proper. What he needed was so close to his grasp, he could feel it. Could feel his fingers slipping round the neck of what he needed. The whole world. If the whole world had a single neck, you could slip your fingers round it and have all that power there for your usage. Down in the fens, shame had been bred into him. It slipped into him with the water, but was soon to be washed away. Soon, all eyes would be on him, then they would see. They would all see then.

'I suppose you think you're dead smart, don't you?' he said to the junior. 'I suppose you think you're cock of the fucking walk, don't you?'

The junior opened its mouth.

'Don't answer me. I can tell just by looking at you. I can tell you think you're fucking *it*. Absolute arrogance.'

The junior shook its head.

'This is my problem with your lot. Some folk say we're prejudiced or xen-phobic or whatever. But we aren't. Someone like me, he hates arrogance when he sees it. Hates a toffee nose when he sees it. Hates pride. Why am I meant to sit there and let all you juniors walk all over me, while I sit there and take it and say thanks very much for the pleasure? Why am I meant to sit there? Aye, you can talk.'

The junior spent a moment thinking. 'I don't feel like I'm arrogant.'

He spat. 'Imagine the arrogance of thinking you can copy a human being. That's not natural, is it? Even you can admit that. They think they can replace us, wipe us out. Not on my watch, friend. No thank you. These Kim fucking Larsons think they can obliterate a whole class, because understand that this is class fucking warfare, friend. It is. I am a soldier for my class. I would have worked every day given, until they shipped juniors in and priced me out.'

'That's a shame,' said the junior.

'A shame? A *shame*? Kicking your toe against something and it gets stubbed, that's a shame. Losing a pencil's a shame. What was done to me is called purposeful genocide.'

The junior nodded. It said, 'It isn't fair.'

'You heard that?' called Hirst. 'This one's saying it isn't fair.' No response from the dossers in front. 'Of course it's not fair. Nothing's fair. But I'm going to make it fair. You know what I've heard about? Want to know? I've heard about this. It's two healthy adult humans, sat in different rooms, alone, and in another room their two juniors is going at it. For no reason. They're shagging each other while the humans sit separate. What is that? It's fucked up beyond all recognition. That happens. We're sleepwalking into destruction, friend.'

The junior didn't reply.

'I've heard about humans and their juniors going at it, too. You come home from the shift and your senior's there waiting on you. Wants to put it in you. I've heard about it happening. It does. It'd make you nearly cry, friend.'

'That sounds—'

'Do not interrupt me,' hissed Hirst. He looked around

angrily for a moment, then jumped to his knees and shuffled towards the junior. He grabbed the front of his clothes. 'Alright, so we haven't got your old man's ghost yet, fair enough. We missed it. My mistake. But we do have that one there.' He nodded to the dog carrier. 'We'll get Larson on the disaster, and we'll get him on the fucking ghosts, won't we? And then it'll be different, yes it will.'

He spoke with so much energy that he felt splits form in his lips.

'Then we'll see how it goes, when it's *me* on the streams, when it's *me* getting the big stats on the field.'

The junior shuffled back. Hirst let him go, sighing, slumping down to his original position. Hirst called out to the front, asking for the time, asking how long til they got there.

Not long, came the response. Not long at all.

'Tell us where he is again,' Hirst said. 'Tell us exactly.'

The specimen scowled. 'I can't.'

'Tell us where he is,' he said, 'or else ...'

And the specimen glared at him, controlling its anger, then went into its dreamy state. Its eyes turned cloudy and its shoulders slumped. They knew its senior was heading west too, all they needed now was precise confirmation.

The specimen blinked to life. 'He's there,' it said. 'Nearly there.'

Hirst smiled. 'That's all we needed to know.'

He got himself up and shuffled across the back of the van, to his deputies. Big strong Spencer and wily Mandelson, his most trusted associates. He saw them as his children, in a way, and thought that after this was all over, they should be rewarded. Spencer with some good resources, weapons, tools; Mandelson with his personal affections.

He put his head between them and whispered. 'It's found itself a weapon back there.'

'Take it off him then,' said Spencer.

'I think we see what it does,' said Hirst. 'More likely to be honest if it thinks it's armed.'

Neither of them spoke, then Spencer shrugged.

The road lay ahead of them. In the distance, city lights paled the sky.

A plan formed itself in the junior's mind. In time, the van would stop; this he knew. They would arrive at the destination he'd given them, close enough to Alastair that he could find him and warn him, far enough away that they wouldn't be able to get there on their own. One of them would come into the back to release him, and he would use the wrench. Hopefully it would be the woman. She was the smallest of the three, the easiest to take down. It might not feel good, but it would be survival. Next, he would go running, following the GPS in his heart to find his senior, then say: they're coming for you, and then he would do it. He would take the option in his system to die. Because he knew that the events of the past few hours had made him unsuitable for life. Baked into him, into the coding of his DNA-equivalent, his very machinery, was a single motive: keep your senior safe, protect his stats, and he had failed. To save his own skin, he'd given away his senior; now every component of him cried out to be shut down.

'This do it?' Hirst shouted from the front, his voice full of excitement.

'Yes,' he called back. 'They're near here. The ghost too.'

'Perfect.'

And then he felt the van slow, creep to a halt, and he bashed against its side as it swung round for parking. They'd arrived. He saw himself represented as a little J-shaped dot on a map he could imagine, layered over his vision, as well as Alastair somewhere beyond. In the front, they readied themselves, killing

228

the engine, sliding out. He heard their footsteps outside and he heard Hirst say, 'You get him, Spencer.'

So it was to be the big man. That cut his chances, but he would try. He had to.

The back doors opened, but any light from outside was blocked by Spencer's bulk. He lowered his bald head into the space and said, 'Ready?'

The junior nodded.

Spencer came forward on his knees, causing the van to sink. He held the tiny handcuff key between two fingers like a pin.

'No funny business, mind,' he said.

'No funny business,' said the junior.

And then he was over the junior, sucking up the air, and getting him by the wrists. The junior heard the key turn in its lock, a few inches behind his back. His hands were free and instantly he went for the wrench, reaching behind himself to feel for the cold metal, getting it in his grip, tight, and jumping to his feet.

He swung the tool upwards, right from the floor, upwards as hard as he could, using all his strength, swinging it upwards to connect with Spencer's jaw. It didn't seem much like a weapon anymore. The wrench passed through the air and he watched Spencer's head barely move from the impact.

Oh Christ, now it would come. Now the punishment would really begin. He scuttled away. He crawled on hands and knees to be away from the rage, when it came.

He watched. He watched the man's paw reach to where the wrench met his face, touching the bone there, and for a moment their eyes met. A sort of understanding passed between them and Spencer went down. He actually buckled, and the junior couldn't believe it. Could not believe his fucking luck! Must've hit a nerve or a pressure point or something, cause the big man went down, hitting the floor hard, the great bald dome lying there exposed before him.

And he went. He went like fuck, over the body, standing on its back, and into the free air outside. He saw the other two standing by the van, over on the pavement, and they watched open-mouthed as he flew off, their faces blurring past him and they did not even reach out to grab him, such was his speed.

He ran. He ran and ran. In this body, he had never run like this, but he remembered the running days of his senior. He remembered the lost days of constant speed and bringing your knees forward like you were kicking through walls, using the arms for extra motion. Those running days existed for him too. They were his memories to access and align himself with as he pushed past surprised faces on the pavement, elbowing folk out his way, and he ran and ran, moving onto the road to be free of people, throwing his head back over his shoulder to see if those bastards were following, those nutters. But no. No one came. He slowed a little, kept checking, kept running on that road, and in his haste didn't notice a sound high in the air above. A humming sound of spinning blades, a little infant's murmured breath, gurgling.

They watched him go stumbling away into the crowds, the drone zipping out from the van where Spencer released it. He sat up, letting his legs dangle out the opening and said, 'How will we track him down?'

'That baby will come back,' explained Hirst, 'in time.'

Spencer nodded. He looked to Mandelson, who returned the gaze then quickly looked away.

'Let's find a place to set up,' said Hirst, suddenly all business. 'It'll know where to find us. I'm its mother now.'

Spencer went to work removing their stuff from the back of the van: battered cases, boxes, the dog carrier containing van Outen's ghost. Someone should check on that thing, he thought, lining the items up on the pavement. He knelt down to peer through the cage's front.

'Boss,' he said. 'Come and see this.'

Hirst marched round to him. 'What?'

He pointed into the cage. 'Look.'

Hirst came down beside him. Together they stared into the crate. Suddenly, Hirst's breath came fast and hard through his nose. Spencer heard its rasping.

'What the fuck?' Hirst asked.

Inside, the ghost was barely there. Its form was so insubstantial that in the cage's darkness you could hardly tell it existed.

'Get it out,' hissed Hirst. 'Get it out now.'

Spencer opened the latch, the door. He put his hand into the ghost and tried to bring it forward but his hand moved through its substance.

'You can't,' he said.

'Move,' said Hirst, jabbing him aside. '*Move it.*'

People were staring. This trio of madly dressed weirdos with all their stuff piled out on the side of the road, blocking the high street, one of them screeching and abusing, presumably, the dog inside its cage.

'*Easy,*' said Spencer, eyeing the spectators.

'It doesn't matter,' said Hirst as he raked at the air inside the cage. 'Fucksake. *Fucksake.* Come out, you little shit, come here.'

As Hirst clawed at the ghost, all he did was draw parts of it into the air. Spencer watched as it broke apart from Hirst's agitation, its barely visible mouth opening up as Hirst's fingers pulled and it turned to floaty sand, dispersing on the field then disappearing into a matrix that faded too.

Hirst stood up. He stared at the cage. He kicked it a little bit with the toe of his boot.

'What happened?' asked Mandelson. She hadn't seen.

'It sort of vanished,' said Spencer.

'How?'

Before Spencer could do anything about it, Hirst was on his

feet, punting the cage away, and was up against Mandelson right there in front of everyone. Right in her face, and he'd never seen the boss like this before, nearly levitating from total anger, his fingers quivering, his jaw leaping from his neck.

'*I don't know!*' he screamed, actual screamed. 'But it's gone, alright? It's gone.'

Mandelson didn't react. She stared him down. 'That's not my fault.'

'It's both your fucking faults,' he said. 'I'm trying to make this happen and I'm dealing with you two morons every hour of the day. Christ! It's gone, Mandelson, alright, happy now? It's gone gone gone.'

People on the pavement moved by now. No one would interfere in case they took a hit on their stats. You couldn't tell the right side to pick from a distance.

'Easy,' said Spencer again, quietly.

'I am easy,' Hirst said below his breath. 'I'm easy like a Sunday morning.'

He moved away from Mandelson, a little calmer. He walked around among their stuff, righted the cage and closed its little door. He stood tall and coughed.

'Get after that junior,' he announced. 'Get after it *now*.'

When he felt safe to stop, the junior did, inside a deep, covered entrance to some kind of apartment complex, grey and concrete. He went inside, among a few parked cars, to be away from anyone that might see him on the street. The 97ers were far behind but he still felt wary, didn't want to dally in the open, just in case. He found a spot in the rear where he crouched down and settled himself. Everything inside him moved at speed. Quick thoughts morphed into each other, no space to think between them. He needed to find his senior, needed to pass on the warning, then die.

He tried the trick again, there in the car park.

His system shut him down and for a while all he saw was darkness. It didn't panic him this time, because he knew. On the field, his consciousness reached out, throwing its arms wide to find its partner and soon it connected. He linked up with his senior and they were joined, except he saw nothing this time. His senior's eyes saw nothing, only black, so neither did he.

He spoke it out loud: 'Hello?'

For a moment, nothing, and a huge hopelessness nearly crushed him, nearly drove him into the ground where he crouched.

Then a voice returned to him, coming from where? From inside himself? *Who said that?*

He recognised the voice's tone, its rhythm, its scratch. Him.

'It's me,' said the junior. 'It's me.'

Where are you?

'I'm here, I'm near you. Alastair, you're not safe.'

The voice faltered. *How can I hear you?*

'I don't know.'

Where did you go? I thought you were gone.

'These people took me. I don't know. They wanted Dad. They think he did the disaster.'

I left you.

'I told them about Dad. They wanted Dad.'

I tried to get it on the field, about Dad. They came after me. I think it's the disaster.

'It's the 97ers. They're nuts. They're coming too.'

You need to get me out. I'm in this car and there's something on my eyes. They're going to do me in.

'I can't. I'm finished.'

What?

'I'm finished. I'm going to go. I'm going to die.'

You need to come and get me. You have to.

233

The junior felt himself shake. He couldn't do what his senior asked of him. There was no worse feeling. 'I fucked up,' he said.

It doesn't matter. I did too. It was the stats, man, I got all messed up.

'I can't, I just can't. I let you down.'

A long, long pause, then the response: *Please. I need you.*

The junior killed the connection, because he couldn't bear it. The cost was too high. He killed the connection and opened his eyes and stood. Pulling that shirt over his head, at the plant. Pulling it over his head, and before that moment he was barely present, barely alive. It made him human, the love. A system formed him. A system pushed him out through the plant and gifted him memories and a body and a mind, but it was the love that made him. The smell of himself, the confirmation. Could you fake that, or code it? Or did it come from somewhere else entirely?

FIFTEEN

Another morning in the boutique hotel and Caitlin, again, couldn't get in for breakfast. Another sign, or the same one perhaps, hanging on the door read: *Closed for Private Function.* She peered in through the windows and saw every table stuffed with people in suits, talking and eating and sipping decaf. Many, many more than on the other morning, too. She shook her head and took off. Today, time was pressing. She'd been set up with someone who would be her co-worker on the Larson project and they were due to meet up on the tram, to say hello and get to know each other. Sarah Lovett, transferred from somewhere south of the border.

At first, on the tram, she couldn't find the new colleague. There was a crush to board and in the mess of people it was hard to pick out anyone resembling the photo of Sarah they'd sent over. Then she spotted her – Sarah's junior – waving from the next carriage down.

They said hello to each other and squeezed into a spot by the rear doors. An awkward way to meet a colleague, but nothing about this project felt normal.

'First day then?' Caitlin asked.

Sarah shook her head. 'I've been up for a while now, getting settled in. I heard I missed the announcement speech the other morning?'

'You did, yeah. It was something. People walked out.'

'Really?'

This was one of those situations where you didn't know quite the right thing to say, to the person and to their senior, who might be watching from home. This Sarah might be a die-hard Larson lover and if Caitlin said something disparaging . . . On the other hand, if Caitlin went too heavy on the pro-Larson comments, and this Sarah thought he was a nut, that wouldn't be ideal either. So she said, 'Overall, yeah, an odd one.'

Sarah nodded. 'Got it.'

They stared at each other for a moment, then both laughed. 'He's *bonkers*,' Caitlin whispered.

'I know, I heard. Someone told me this rumour that he sleeps in the gel they make juniors out of. The jelly from the cast, or something? He has this big vat that he sleeps in at night with a tube for air.'

Caitlin could believe it. 'Sounds about right.'

'I suppose that's what it takes though,' said Sarah.

'What is?'

'Well, you know, sometimes it takes an unconventional person to make amazing things happen. If no one was willing to think outside the box then we wouldn't have the things we do; the field, everything.'

'Right.' Caitlin nodded. 'Yeah, you're right. So what about this plan?' She made an explosive sound with her mouth and mimed upward projection with a fingertip. That sort of thing worked well. You weren't saying you disagreed precisely, but the levity could be taken either way.

'What do I think of the plan?' asked Sarah. Her eyes widened like she was considering the right words to describe something so outlandish. Instead, she said, 'I think it's remarkable.'

'Really?'

'I think it's remarkable and I think it's brave. These men

and women are willing to put themselves at risk to find a better world for us.' She shook her head. 'It's breathtaking, honestly.'

Caitlin nodded. 'Yeah,' she said. 'I agree.'

In the offices, a large open-plan area had been provided for them to work in. Their job, such as it was, involved researching announcements that had played well, historically, in the public sphere, announcements that resulted in stat and profit increases across the board. The big question: how to tell a population something problematic without making it seem problematic. They pulled up texts from the field and ran them through software to analyse word patterns and incidents of specific rhythm and breath. They looked at fonts used, font sizes, plus which services you could use to broadcast the message. Did it play better to speak to people directly, via their feeds, or release it as a package to the news streamers? Currently, the thinking in the team was that a video would play best. Something full of images of progress and scientific success. Or alternatively, a sort of tongue-in-cheek clip that made it clear the makers thought the idea of making a clip was really passé and dull but nevertheless here it is, take it or leave it, it's up to you. The message came down from on high: this must not be characterised as an abandonment. Larson and the others, blasting off: not an abandonment. The heads of various companies and their close friends and families, leaving the planet behind: not an abandonment. Or else, call it an abandonment, but do it in a way that makes it clear being concerned by abandonment is retrograde and childish and excessively sentimental.

For reference, Caitlin and Sarah pulled up the reveal of the first junior model. An old example but very much the keystone comparison. A little different too, in that by the time the news came, everyone and their dog knew about juniors; the official announcement functioned as confirmation of what they already suspected.

The clip began as black. Pure black. Then slowly, a little glint of light opened up within the black. A little sort of star, off in the distance.

'That's actually what it's like,' Sarah's junior said, leaning across. 'The first thing you see, a star thing, far away from you.'

Caitlin raised her eyebrows to acknowledge.

The little star gradually widened and the music rose and the star opened up until the screen was white and the camera did a complicated swoop and switch to show you'd just travelled through the iris of a junior laid out on a white-sheeted table. Its face looked up towards you, smiling slightly, and the face and its expression seemed so pure and honest and wholesome. And also there was the fact that, even on camera, you knew in your gut that this was not a fellow human being looking back at you. What looked back at you was similar but different, right down in the depths of the cell, in the DNA – or lack thereof. He became famous, this first junior that anyone ever saw. Number one: James Partridge. Loved by all who met him or read about him or experienced him on the field. He looked back into the camera and smiled slightly and a voiceover said, 'Welcome to you.' Cut to black.

Very effective. Huge, huge engagement on the field. Record-breaking engagement and everyone loved it. Everyone loved James Partridge's junior. *Welcome to you.* It felt good to hear that. Everyone wanted to be welcomed back into themselves. They all felt dislocated and adrift and it really resonated to be invited back to yourself.

But that was easy. Anyone could release information about something nominally positive and be guaranteed stats on the field.

'It's good info,' said Sarah, 'but is it really relevant?'

'No,' said Caitlin. 'Probably not.'

For reference, they pulled up the famous case of the Retraction of State. Why not go big, they reasoned, and what was bigger than the announcement that the government would no longer function in the manner you'd grown accustomed to.

'It's a biggie,' agreed Sarah. 'A real big one.'

Before the official information came down the pipeline and got confirmed as one hundred per cent legit, there was the famous interview: the well-known showdown between Kevin Hollander and Ariel Smith. Kevin Hollander, a sort of proto-typical Nye Morgan figure, operating back when visual media lingered in that awkward half-terrestrial, half-stream hinter-land. His interview programme went out on normal television, watched by hardly anyone, then got recut for the majority who streamed it later on. He attracted most of the bigwigs in terms of politics, but getting Smith to appear on the show was still something of a boon. She seemed uncomfortable on screen, distracted, looking directly into the camera now and then. Hollander grilled her for a while on domestic matters, which you could skip past, fast-forwarding to the bit where you saw her head dip into her hands.

'—is basically that it doesn't matter anymore,' she said.

'I think it does matter,' Hollander retorted. 'I think it matters to your constituents and your—'

'You aren't seeing the bigger picture, Kevin, because essentially, as of next week, the state will no longer exist.'

On the clip, you could see a look of bemusement cross Hollander's fleshy face. He flushed a little. 'I don't think there's any need for hyperbole, Minister.'

'Who's exaggerating?' said Smith. She tossed back her long grey hair. 'I'm not afraid to say it. We received a message yes-terday evening explaining that the government, and parliament, will shortly be dissolved.'

'But—'

'Permanently.'

You could see Hollander glance up behind the camera, where presumably a producer gestured something to him. 'Is everything okay, Minister?' he asked.

'Yes,' said Smith. 'Of course it is. The PM's explained – will explain, I should say – that it's an excellent decision. It's a decision that's going to allow us to move with the times, keep ahead of technological development at every turn. It's become increasingly clear that the current situation is outdated and stale. A lumpen donkey, as my colleague recently described it.'

Hollander swallowed. 'So it's just ... gone? Who'll collect the bins?'

'Kevin,' sighed the minister. 'Do you really believe that there aren't a hundred companies out there just waiting to spring to life and take care of the jobs we do, at a small percentage of what it costs us? We, the government, have decided that we, the government, have monopolised these services for too long.'

Again, Hollander looked to his producer for help. None came. 'I'm not sure what to say.'

'There's a first time for everything.'

'If this is true, what you're telling me, then there's going to be outrage. People will march in the streets, won't they?'

Smith shook her head, gave Hollander a withering glare. 'Dry your eyes, won't you, pet?'

And that became the slogan of the state's retraction. *Dry your eyes, pet.* Apparently, Smith improvised the line, genuinely irritated at Hollander's sentimental reaction, but it quickly became official, finding itself on materials delivered to every household in the country. Dry your eyes, pet: the only way is up. Dry your eyes, pet: we're doing things our *own* way. Dry your eyes, pet: get with the times. People responded to the slogan in ways no one expected. During debates, all it took was a quick *Dry your eyes, pet* to shut the opposing side down entirely. No one, even dyed-in-the-wool statists, wanted to be accused of having moistened eyes, of being maudlin.

'It's a great example,' said Sarah. 'Smith really got out in front of the narrative.'

'I can't imagine Larson wanting to announce on a stream though.'

'No, probably not.'

They spent the morning like this, pulling up announcements almost at random and checking them for suggestions or tips. By lunch, Caitlin felt her eyes shrinking into their sockets. She told Sarah she needed a break and went wandering through the long airy corridors of HQ. The place bustled, with people coming and going, but all she wanted was a place that served food; a sachet would do. As she walked the white tiles, her mobile went, and a message came through. She was required, it seemed, elsewhere in the building. A meeting invite for something taking place within the next few minutes.

From the upper corridor, you could face out into the empty black Atlantic. They had pushed back the water from the western border, but a darkness remained out there, lurking. Featureless, except for the launch apparatus sitting a few miles out. From this distance, the blast site looked almost like a children's playground, all poles and coloured metals.

She walked by the long expanse of windows, towards what she now recognised as Larson's impromptu office. His name was printed on a sheet of A4, sellotaped to the door. She knocked. For a while, there was no answer, then a voice said, 'Come.'

Inside, Larson and Deborah Stock stood talking together over a large desk, referring to materials on a machine before them. Security guys ringed the room and in a sub-office she could see a few suited executives relaxing in comfortable chairs.

'Hi,' she said to the room at large.

Larson and Stock looked up. Stock smirked and Larson scowled.

'Who's this?' he asked.

Stock said, 'Not sure.'

'I got a meeting in my calendar,' Caitlin explained. 'It just said "brief" and to come here.'

'Well if it said come here,' said Stock, 'then you should be here.'

Caitlin wasn't sure how to respond. 'Good,' she said.

Larson finished up whatever work was being processed on the machine. He clapped his hands and something in his expression changed. He became the World's Father again: kindly, beatific. 'We like to check in with everyone working on our projects,' he said, gesturing for her to approach the desk. 'I like to keep an eye on all the moving parts.'

'I see,' said Caitlin.

'Remind me what your role is.'

Caitlin explained her purpose and he nodded along, making little listening noises. 'That's right, that's right,' he said. 'Excellent.'

She described their work of that morning, pulling up old announcements and analysing them for effectiveness. 'We had a look at the old Hollander clip, the Retraction of State one.'

Larson blinked. 'I don't know it.'

Caitlin doubted that. She doubted it very much. Larson became one of the key beneficiaries of the announcement. 'And Sarah and I – Sarah Lovett – we were wondering about the possibility of an in-person reveal. Smith really got ahead of the narrative on that one.'

Larson's eyes narrowed and he glanced in amusement towards his colleague, this Deborah Stock. They appeared to have a deep connection, these two, and Caitlin felt thoughts fly through the air between them, unvoiced. You heard certain rumours about Stock, such as she was the brains behind the operation, that everything Larson said in public had been pre-approved by her, that they were in a secret, long-term romantic relationship. You heard certain rumours that there was some weird sex thing between them. Who knew what the billionaires did in the places they kept private, their little field-blocked quarters?

'I think she's trying to recruit you, Deborah,' said Larson.

Stock tutted. 'I think she's trying to recruit *you*.'

Larson laughed. The sound was quiet, gruff. 'That won't be happening, I'm afraid. Oh Lord, no. No. My face doesn't appear on any of this. Got it?'

Caitlin nodded.

'In fact . . .' He looked around. 'Give us a moment, will you, Deborah?' He marched towards the sub-office, where the executives lounged. 'Go and take a walk, will you?' he asked them.

The executives filed out, past Caitlin, who stared at their bare feet. They followed Stock and only the security guys remained.

'Come in here a moment,' said Larson, from the sub-office.

He motioned for her to close the doors behind her, to block their conversation from security. Larson sat down in one of the vacant chairs and Caitlin made to follow, before pausing mid-step. She stared into the corner of the room.

There was something in there with them. It lay on the floor behind the chairs in a space that had been hidden to her. A chain round its neck connected it to a large metal link firmly attached to the office wall. It was the size of a large dog, though more feline in appearance. Utterly hairless, its skin extravagantly wrinkled, and without ears or tail. It lay there impassively on the floor, blinking, watching Caitlin.

'Don't pay any attention to that,' said Larson. 'It doesn't mean you any harm.'

He wanted her to take the other free chair, but that would

put the animal to her back and Caitlin couldn't stomach that. This was a species she'd never experienced; she felt a powerful misgiving at allowing it the advantage. It opened its mouth to yawn, revealing rows of sharp teeth.

'I said don't pay it any attention,' said Larson, a little short. 'It's just an invention. Don't worry about it.' He patted the seat across from him with urgency. 'Sit down, would you?'

So she sat. She put the creature to her back, and sat, and felt its cold stare tickle the rear of her neck.

'There,' said Larson. 'That's better.'

Caitlin nodded. Better, sure.

'I'm not sure you've got your head around this whole thing correctly,' said Larson. He smiled at her, the corners of his silver moustache upturned. 'I think you and your colleagues might be getting a little lost in the weeds, so to speak. Let me make myself clear.' He shuffled forward slightly. 'By the time this gets announced, we will be long gone. We will not be around to be used by yourself in whatever scheme you cook up, okay?'

Caitlin nodded, again.

'By the time the public knows about us leaving, we will have left. My deepest, sincerest apologies if I didn't make myself clear.'

The animal in the room made a sort of moan. It sounded like an old door being opened.

'I get it,' said Caitlin. 'I understand.'

Larson seemed pleased. 'That's all, then,' he said. 'I'll let you carry on. We're all very busy.'

When she turned, Caitlin saw the animal was now upright, standing, reaching nearly chest height. It had raised a paw to lick. Its tongue was black.

She went back to work, back to the office where Sarah had arranged them some lunch. Junior Meal for Sarah, Yes It's

Cassoulet! for Caitlin. Sarah decanted the Meal while Caitlin squeezed hers absent-mindedly.

'Not hungry?' Sarah asked.

'No,' she said. 'Not really.'

They resolved to get back to it. They only had a few days to work on this and they needed to present their findings to the rest of the team by the day after tomorrow. In Caitlin's absence, Sarah went through their records and pulled together more likely sources, setting them up to be played through, or read, in the afternoon.

She selected the first video and the room's lights automatically dimmed. The clip showed a stage, the sound of an audience in the background, and a man entering from the right. He talked for a while, pacing around the space with confidence, then he revealed the piece of technology he was announcing. The audience sounded impressed. He walked around for a bit longer, then bowed. He waved to the audience. They cheered. Caitlin watched him disappear behind a dark curtain; she squeezed her Yes It's Cassoulet!.

Sarah pulled up a piece of text. The software immediately highlighted the pertinent areas for them and began to read aloud. It spoke with the voice of Angela Angela, a popular streamer. The text informed them of something new, a fresh development. It laid out how things before, things that once might have been considered pretty good, had actually been utterly shit. Pre-announcement, the reader had been living in an age of darkness, but the new thing, the fresh development, was about to change that, forever. It made you feel hopeful and grateful and made you really want to experience the fresh development. Caitlin listened to the text's excited speech; she compressed her sachet.

Sarah pulled up another clip. In this one, several people joined together to reveal the introduction of the Honey Bee peacekeepers, explaining in detail how they would be a force for good in the world, how the mistakes of the traditional police forces would be eradicated in this newer, fairer approach to law and order.

Sarah pulled up another clip. She pulled up text.

'Sorry,' said Caitlin. 'I might need to dip out for another minute, if that's alright?'

Sarah looked over in the dimmed room. 'We do need to get on with this.'

'Just a sec,' she said, walking out of the office, dropping her sachet into the waste bin on the way.

In the hall, she breathed in. She gulped down air like cold water.

She found herself a bench outside, within the vast gardens that surrounded HQ. People passed by her on electric carts, others seemed to be taking part in an outdoor meeting, just beyond the reach of her hearing. She brought out her mobile. It was full of information that she instantly banished. Couldn't deal with it, not now. Instead, she dialled into Arts System and waited. Someone answered.

'Hello?' said Otis.

What was Otis doing answering? She'd been trying to get through to Elaine.

'It's me,' she said. 'Caitlin.'

She could hear the nicotine steam interfere with Otis's vocals as he said, 'Caitlin! How's it going, dude?'

A pause. 'Fine, Otis, it's going fine. I was sort of hoping to speak to Elaine.'

'I can't believe you just left us behind,' Otis said, full of excitement. 'Everyone's been missing you loads. Did I tell you I got my implant finally?'

'Did you?'

'Yeah, I did. It's totally rubbish, I love it.'

'That's good.'

'Yeah, and I—' He spoke to someone else in the room. 'It's Caitlin. *Caitlin*. Hold on, I—'

Someone else came on the line, after wrestling the phone from Otis. 'What's the problem?' they said. 'Something going wrong out there?'

'Hi Simone,' said Caitlin.

'If you've changed your mind, it's too late. None of *us* can be bothered schlepping out west to mess around with the yokels.'

'How are you, Simone?' she asked.

Simone went on to describe in great, precise detail exactly how she was, about the continued successes she enjoyed in Verse, about the strides she kept making in engagement, about how everyone upstairs basically worshipped the ground she walked on. She was, in a word, excellent.

Caitlin found herself nodding along, smiling. 'Can you pop me through to Elaine, please?'

The sound of a constrained huff. 'Fine.'

The tone went for a while as Caitlin's call moved through Arts Systems, then Elaine spoke, and Caitlin felt herself relax. The voice was familiar, warm, and asked, 'How are you, my dear?'

'Oh,' said Caitlin. 'Not bad. Just checking in.'

'We're all fine here. We're so proud of you.'

'That's good,' said Caitlin. 'Thanks.' She waited for Elaine to say something else, but nothing came. Really, she wanted her mentor to speak without Caitlin asking for it, to be given what she needed unprompted. 'Is everything okay with this job?' she finally asked. 'Is it legit?'

Elaine sounded confused. 'Of course it is. It's all official.'

'Did you know it was Kim Larson running it?'

'I didn't, no. How exciting! What an honour.'

'Yeah. I don't know, Elaine, it feels a little off, the whole thing.'

'I'm not sure ...' Elaine trailed off. 'I'm not sure where this is coming from, Caitlin. Is it cold feet because of the indefinite transferral? I thought it was strange, but I guessed you must be happy about it.'

'Indefinite transferral?'

'It came through the other day, all signed and proper and everything. Let me see.' You could hear her clicking away on some machine in the background. 'Here we go, yes. Indefinite transferral request for Caitlin Weir, blah blah blah, permission to transfer individual from Arts Systems, signed by HR, signed by individual, signed by me, of course. So you're not coming back?'

'It says *what*? Signed by individual?'

'Yes, I can see your wee name on there. I must admit, it was a bit of a shock to get it. I thought this would only be a secondment, but I don't like to hold my people back you know, I—'

'I'm sorry, Elaine,' she found herself saying, almost automatically. 'I'm going to have to let you go. I need to get back to it.'

'I bet you do. I can't believe you're working for *the* Kim Larson. You're really moving up in the world.'

Caitlin killed the line and let the mobile drop beside her. She looked out across the manicured gardens, the trimmed hedges and neat palm-style trees. None of this land was real, she realised. All of it was invented, cooked-up, artificial; between her feet and the deep, black ocean there was only a few metres of man-made turf to keep her from sinking.

Later, in the hotel room, she tried to call Alastair. The last time they spoke, she could tell from the quality of his voice that her ex was suffering. She'd thought about ditching the new job and taking a few days to get him back on his feet. But she knew a few days would turn into a few weeks, a few months perhaps. It would be difficult to maintain separate sleeping areas, especially with the space his junior took up. So she listened to his sad-sounding voice, then spoke back. She told him about this new situation she'd washed up in, about the terraformed west, about Kim actual Larson himself running the show. And then he'd gone quiet. He asked her to repeat herself, which she did, then he went quiet again. She said: *Hello? Hello?* And then he asked for her address, her work address, the hotel, because he wanted to send her an actual, old-fashion postcard, to make up for the bad times.

Now though, now he wouldn't answer. She wondered if he'd moved on, if he was shagging someone else. She turned the image over in her mind and found it didn't bother her much. She pictured him squeezed between thighs and felt nothing in her gut. The betrayal had been too severe, the way he gave up on their life. Once, he had been confident, and funny. He used to make jokes and they were good ones. They spoke to each other, late into the night, and when he talked and watched her, his attention was present, there in whatever room they shared. His focus reached out and connected to the perimeter of her love.

Perhaps Ursula or Roz would be around to chat. What could she say? I am trapped. I am in a trap and can't see its walls and don't understand its diameters? And probably those two would end up going down a conversational dead-end anyway, where they would tell Caitlin about the things going wrong for them. It made her guilty, but she felt worse after those calls. So instead of speaking, she lay still in the hotel room. She kept the lights turned off. She lay still in the dark and listened to people passing on the Uist boulevard, heels clicking, light chatter.

She lay still in the dark and she entered sleep, briefly, in a shallow fit of dreaming. In the dark, something came to her, something sleek and quiet. It moved around the room without friction, and she realised it stalked her. In the dark with her, an intelligence with movement; utter darkness, a white glint. Light glancing off teeth. Imagine that darkness, the pre-birth blank, imagine reaching out towards the light and your arms not responding because you are yet to have arms. Imagine urging yourself forward, before realising forward doesn't exist, not for you, not yet.

The intelligence slid around the room like a thought moving through a mind, a fingertip in water. She felt gripped by dread, couldn't move, couldn't shift the joints to spring away from the horror. Slowly, the thing in the room entered her bed. She felt its weight as four legs inched onto the covers, bit by bit. It slipped up beside her and before she woke, she saw a great tongue, ringed by fangs.

She went to the window and looked out. Now, no one passed. Now, it stood empty.

SIXTEEN

As quickly as it came, Alastair's connection to the junior went. He threw his head back against the car seat. He didn't know it was possible for them to communicate like that; perhaps no one did. But at least now the pair of them had a chance. Some small possibility of help, however slim.

'Who were you talking to?' the ghost asked, its voice coming from a few inches to his left.

They were in the back of the car, alone, the agents having left them maybe half an hour before. Of course, he'd tried the doors, but they were firmly locked. Before they went, the agents slipped something over his head, a black garment of some kind that clung to his face, shutting out his vision but allowing him to breathe freely. The agents had access to serious tech.

'My junior,' he said. 'He came through.'

'I didn't know we could do that.'

'No.'

You heard stories about the power these people had, such as the agents of Honey Bee. Serious tech and serious power. You heard stories about people disappearing, those who maybe saw the potential for stat-increases in running anti-establishment streams. He'd sampled one or two in anonymous mode – you wouldn't want that sort of thing lingering in your record – and they spoke some kind of sense. But it wasn't worth the risk to subscribe publicly. Some of them vanished off the field, their streams removed entirely, others, after a while, slowly changed their output to a more pro-system message. One or two hardliners called them out, but, again, for the majority it wasn't worth the risk. Serious tech, serious power, and now he felt himself tight in their grip.

Just let me go, he thought. Let me go and I'll be good. I promise. Let me go and I'll head home and put the hours in and spend my money wisely and watch the right streams, pay attention to the right content, if you'll just let me go. That's all he wanted: a second chance to be good and well-behaved and a model citizen.

'I don't know what I'm doing here,' he said.

'It'll be over soon,' said his father. 'Just wait.'

A while later, they heard footsteps, then the car doors opened. Fingers slipped inside the mask and a tone sounded and the material pulled away from his face, letting the light in. The agents were back.

'Sorry to keep you,' said the junior agent. 'Just had to sort a few things out.'

They got in front and started driving. The car moved through a tall wire gate, with a sentry posted by the side. She waved them through and the sleek black motor entered a warren of plain buildings, unremarkable, unsigned.

'We thought we might have to take you upstairs,' said the senior, 'but it turned out not to be necessary. You're not what we'd call high priority at this point.'

'What would be classed as high priority?' asked the junior agent.

'Oh, I don't know, someone who'd done something interesting with their life and didn't just shit-stir on the field for no good reason.'

The junior agent laughed as he drove, glancing back to meet Alastair's eye. 'I'd love to meet one of *them* someday.'

Fine. They would humiliate him. He could take all the humiliation they might throw at him, as long as it helped him survive. 'I don't know if it means anything,' he said, 'but I'm sorry.'

'He's sorry,' said the senior agent.

'Does that mean anything to you?' asked the junior.

'To me, it means exactly jack shit.'

They laughed loudly between themselves and kept on, creeping slowly among the low concrete, no sign of anyone outside in the darkness, no one he could call out to . . . as if they'd help if they heard.

'You can let me go,' he continued. He would beg if forced. 'I've been thinking about it and I don't care about being a whistle-blower anymore. You can let me go and I'll make my own way and just keep quiet for the rest of my life.'

They laughed again and ignored him. The motor continued its crawl.

'Please,' he said. 'Please don't kill me. You can take my stuff off the field, if you want. Wipe my profiles. I don't care.'

'We don't give a shiny toss about your profiles,' said the senior.

'They're *immaterial* to us,' said the junior, pleased with his word choice.

'Do my stats, then,' he said, his voice cracking. 'Please. Put them down. Give me a zero, whatever. Just do it.'

This seemed to impress them more, his recklessness with stats. They exchanged glances in the front seat, but didn't look back, or respond.

Soon, the buildings opened up and he realised they were by the water. Out beyond them, the Atlantic surged, crests lit up by the complex's floodlamps, a structure of some description way out across the waves.

253

He said, 'Oh God.'

They parked by the furthest building and killed the engine. The two agents shuffled round to stare at him.

'We were talking before,' said the senior agent, 'and we decided to let you in on how this is going to go.'

'We thought it would be fairer that way.'

'Because listen, we're not murderers, my colleague and I.'

'There are murderers out there in this world, and we're not it. Way beyond our pay grade.'

Alastair nodded. He needed this, badly. His stats, his profiles, his whatevers; they could take them all, as long as he got the chance to exist beyond this car, this night.

'So the purpose of this exercise,' said the senior, 'is to put the fear up you. Shake you up a bit.'

'Vietnam shit,' said the junior.

The senior agent did an accent. 'Di di mau.'

'Aye, di di mau,' the junior agreed. 'So here's what we'll do. In a second, we're going to let you out the motor, okay? We're going to let you out the motor and lead you across to the jetty there. It's right over the deep water and we're going to get you to kneel down on the side, with your head over the water.'

'Execution style,' said the senior. '*Pow.*'

'We'll ask you to put your head over the water and I'm going to say this now: we'll have a weapon out, okay? A gun. In the normal run of things, we'd be pretending we're about to blow you away. In the normal run of things, we're saying all this nasty shit to you, carrying on like we're about to shoot you in the back of the head, and—'

'But it's a game,' the senior agent interrupted.

'The gun's a dummy.'

'Because of the pay grade.'

Alastair was getting the picture. They'd been sent to scare

him, that was all. The guns weren't even real. These were low-level goons he'd been travelling with.

'And at the last second,' the senior continued, 'we let you go. We send you running and you've learned your lesson, cause you've come *this* close to death, see?'

He nodded. He saw.

The junior smiled. 'To be honest, my colleague and I don't have the stomach for that sort of psychic warfare. It's not our scene, really.'

'Good,' Alastair said. 'So I can go?'

They both laughed again.

'Oh, no,' said the junior. 'Not at all, no.' He knuckled his eye. 'We need to go through the motions, just to tick all the boxes, so to speak.'

'We wouldn't want you to go away thinking we're a pair of chumps,' said the senior. 'That's exactly the last thing we'd want.'

'Are you ready?' asked the junior.

He was ready. A surge of gratitude welled up inside him as he left the vehicle at the agents' insistence. They opened the door and ushered him out and they all walked together across the empty area, towards the sea. A wind blew in from the west, messing his beard and cooling his eyes. Soon, he would be back home, safe, and it wouldn't even cost him his stats. He looked to the structure out there, hovering above the horizon. He knew they blasted rockets out this way; perhaps it had something to do with that.

'We'll get you to go down just here,' said the junior agent, indicating an area of the harbour with the toe of his shoe. 'We need you near to the edge as possible.'

He did as he was told, kneeling on the hard concrete a foot away from the drop. In that position, sea air blew up and into his nostrils. He could see the flabby weeds stretching out into the water. There were no steps or ladders here; if he fell, he'd have to swim for it.

'That's perfect,' the senior said. 'Just like that. Now, in a few seconds, you're going to feel something touching you on the back of the head. I'm afraid to say that yes, this'll be a weapon, but remember, it's just for show. Think of it as a dress rehearsal.'

He nodded. 'Fine.'

The senior continued. 'I should say something, I suppose. Right. Here it goes.' He cleared his throat. 'You thought you could get away with it, didn't you? You thought you could shame Kim Larson all across the field and call his work into disrepute and then just walk away. You must be high, son, or stupid, if you think you can take on the system and walk away. We're going to kill you, understand? We're going to put a bullet in your brain and the last thing you'll think about is how it could've been avoided if you hadn't been such a smug little clype.'

The junior agent: 'That sounded good.'

'Thanks.'

'Maybe just a touch closer, if you don't mind,' said the junior.

Alastair shuffled forward. 'Better?'

'Much better.'

He waited for the gun to touch his skull. As he waited, he became aware of a tension behind him. The agents sounded like they were quietly arguing with each other, releasing little hisses of breath, the sound of clothes being tugged at. One of them coughed. 'Just a minute.'

More altercations, heels shuffling, then he heard the senior say, 'No, you do it.'

'I'm not doing it. You do it.'

And then he knew.

He glanced back. They were stood over him, wrestling the gun between them, this blackened piece of metal going from hand to hand. He swore, and leapt up. Their eyes widened and each stepped back. The junior pressed the weapon onto his colleague, pushing him forward by the shoulder. 'Do it,' he said. 'Just do it.'

The senior agent looked terrified as he fumbled with the gun. 'Right,' he said. 'Okay.'

Alastair held out his hands, showed them his bare palms. 'Please,' he said. 'Please don't.'

'Shut up,' the senior agent hissed. 'Give me a second.'

And then Alastair's mouth opened up. He couldn't believe it. Across the agents' shoulders, over by the car, someone was lurking. Someone came nearer to them, bent over for stealth, some shadowy figure, and he prayed. It must be. It had to be.

'Can I just say one thing?' he asked.

The senior agent blinked. His fingers trembled. 'Be quiet,' he said.

The shadowy figure passed under a floodlamp and Alastair felt the familiar eerie shiver at recognising himself, present in another body. The junior. He came.

'If you're going to do it for real, let me say something first.'

'Jesus Christ!' said the junior agent. 'What an effing saga. Here, give it to me.'

The gun passed between them and the senior looked ashamed.

His own junior came nearer in the dark. It was like seeing yourself on a home-recorded stream: always strange to be witnessing your actual dimensions, even in a moment of peril like this. His junior crouched only a few feet away, coming closer, silent. Alastair tried not to watch, didn't want to give the game away, so he focused on the agents instead, pleading at them with his eyes, still playing the role.

The junior agent brought up his weapon and pointed it at Alastair's face.

Their eyes met as the agent went flying, Alastair's junior

barrelling into the back of him. Alastair stepped aside to let the agent stumble forward, arms flapping, across and over the edge of the jetty. A huge splash followed. Meanwhile, the junior rounded on the other agent, who looked between them with an expression of disappointment.

'Great,' he said. 'This is just what I need.'

Together, they got him by the arms and wrestled with him. He was stronger, a big, solid man, but there was two of them and they thought as one. He went into the water too, after his friend, already front-crawling through the slight waves. They watched as the senior agent plunged in, then emerged gasping, hair plastered across his brow. He shouted wetly, then started to swim, heading after his friend in haste.

'You came back,' said Alastair, stepping away from the jetty.

'I had to,' said the junior. 'It's what I'm for.'

Alastair stared at his junior, at his copy, and sniffed. He wanted to say something, but wasn't able to. Neither spoke for a moment, then the discomfort of the moment nettled them. They went across to the car, where the ghost still sat inside. He faced the front, away from them, and appeared to have missed the fight.

'What now?' Alastair asked.

The junior shook his head. 'I don't know.'

'We could take the motor, head back.'

That made nearly no sense, even as he spoke it. Once the agents made land, they'd report Alastair, let the higher-ups know what he'd done. Home no longer meant home.

The junior opened his mouth to object, but Alastair said, 'Yeah, I know.'

'Let's keep going,' the junior whispered.

Alastair felt himself scowl. 'We can't. It's too much. They're going to beat us, and for what?' He pointed to the ghost in the car. 'He's not even real.'

'I'm real, amen't I?' said the junior. 'What's the difference?'

'They've got everything,' he said. 'We've got nothing.'

'Are you happy?' asked the junior.

'We don't have time. We—'

'Answer it. Are you happy?'

Alastair couldn't meet his junior's eye. 'No,' he said. 'Course I'm not. Ever since Caitlin went, I just couldn't—'

'Apart from Caitlin. Does any of it make you happy?'

He stared into his own face, looking back at him sternly. 'No. It doesn't. You know it doesn't. My head's screwed up. I can't think straight. Every morning I wake up and feel this pain.'

The junior nodded.

'I'm fucking miserable, man. Everything's always just so—' He prodded his fingers rapidly into his temples, the only way he knew to describe the feeling. '—and it's not just me, it's everywhere. Something comes on the flume or your stats get a wee bump and that helps but then you're used to that and you need something else. I'm sick of needing something. I really am. I hate wanting.'

He was sick of needing. He was sick to death of the things he'd wanted. Christ, the things he'd wanted. The viewing screens and gadgets and waiting for the flume to rumble and throw up whatever he'd been anticipating for hours, even days sometimes. The things he'd wanted. They were all stacked away inside the flat, down in the capital, and he could barely picture them, barely name them, but in distant hours they consumed him. The real fear was that if you took them away, those things he'd wanted, what would remain in their absence?

'I know,' said the junior. 'I remember.'

He stared at his junior and, for a moment, hated him, because he *was* him. That face looking back, his own face, and he hated it. Hated its weakness, its dependence on needing and wanting. Hated it and now, in a way, felt unbelievably sorry. Because he'd let the junior down too.

'You were one of them,' he said. 'Something I wanted. I wanted you so badly and then you came and it was just another hassle. Something else to stress about.' He laughed. 'I'm sorry.'

'Don't be. Let's go and get them.'

'Get who? Larson?'

'Whatever. We'll go and show them the ghost. We'll make them answer.'

Alastair nodded. They couldn't go back. Their home was no longer a home. There was no place for them in this world, not now. They hugged, briefly, and went to the motor; the idiots had left it running.

He drove, taking them back through the warren of buildings, towards the sentry by the main road. She waved them through without a second look and they were out in the open. As they went, he explained the events of the past few hours: pirating a Step-Stone uplift, then hitching, then getting picked up by the agents. The junior responded with his own version, revealing the things those 97ers put him through.

'They were about to wipe you,' Alastair said, shocked.

'I nearly let them,' the junior said. 'Almost. Then I gave you up, you and Dad. They think he was in on the disaster.'

'Fuck off.'

'Aye.'

Alastair glanced in the rear view. 'You hear that?'

The ghost's sad eyes met his in the mirror. 'I remember it happening,' he said. 'We were all so scared. All the machines were giving error codes and you could hear this whooshing sound from somewhere outside. The burner was going mental. You could see it from the windows, even. A mile high, the flame.'

'But you didn't know?' asked Alastair.

'Course I didn't know,' the ghost said. 'I died.'

'They think it was a conspiracy,' said the junior. 'Make the

260

field bigger, more powerful. If the whole world's on the field, no one's on gas.'

Alastair nodded. 'Makes sense.'

If there was one good thing about Larson's field, it kept power green. His oceans teemed with windmills and other apparatus to harness the movement of waves. Most of Alastair's childhood had been field-powered, but the old man's plant still processed the oil and shipped it to Antwerp, to places beyond. The ends justified the means, Larson would probably argue, and if Alastair hadn't lost his family in the disaster, he'd have been tempted to agree.

As they drove through the dark roads of Uist, across its terra-formed outreach, nearing town, he thought of the running boy again, the child of him, another kind of junior. For the first time, he felt proud of that kid. Over the past sixteen years, the only feeling he could give to that silent running child was a sort of embarrassment. Embarrassed of his gangly jogging, his fear of dogs, his teenage dimness. This boy, arriving into the camp half-dead, skipping round in the sand. This boy of him, needing to be fed from the camp's sachets by hand he was so exhausted, so dehydrated, so fucked. But now, a real pride there, an ownership of the running boy. Thinking: Christ, you made it, you wee bastard! You actually did it!

He found out later that everyone back home, those hiding out in the old school, they succumbed. The place went up in smoke that same morning and most were trapped inside, even Jayden's mum. A whole lot of guilt over that too, the fact he ran. But he didn't want to, did he? It wasn't a choice; it was only movement. The running boy survived. He did it. The running boy ran and delivered him to himself and he was allowed to feel proud of that child.

In the camp, for almost a day, he stayed with a bunch of

others his own age. They spoke with his voice, with the voice of the peninsula, and shared stories of how they arrived. One boy from way along the Neuk told how he'd slipped into his father's boat and paddled for it. A girl whose family ran stables had been out tending to horses in the early hours, saw an entire hillside erupt and went flying off on Candy, her favourite mare. There'd been another girl too, this curly-headed quiet one, who was his sort of favourite. From the way she told it, it seemed like she'd fought her way to the coast, battering whoever got in her way, powered by the grief of seeing her home sink beneath a landslide. He slept badly that night, too amped up on adrenaline, his legs full of aches, and they stayed up in the tent, him and Maya, talking through the disaster. They were split up on the hovercrafts and he never saw her again.

Lochmaddy was dark. Beside him, the junior sat in its sleep equivalent, utterly still. The ghost lounged in the back, mumbling now and then, getting more and more distant from them. But he couldn't think about that; it wouldn't help them to dwell. Instead, he thought about Caitlin; her hotel was just across the road from where he now parked.

He said to the ghost, 'I'm going. Let him know if he wakes up.'

A man was doing the night shift on front desk. He wore a paisley shirt and watched an old music stream on his small screen. Alastair got the room number from him by saying it was a Step-Stone issue; he carried a company pass inside his wallet. He took the lift upstairs to Caitlin's floor and quickly found her room. As he came up in the lift, he rehearsed what to tell her. The full story. He'd give it to her breathless, excited, try to get her on side.

He knocked and it took a few minutes for her to answer. Her hair was all over the place, her eyes creased almost closed.

She said, 'What.' It wasn't a question.

'I'm sorry,' he said.

She rubbed at her nose with a knuckle. 'I must be dreaming,' she said. 'Tell me this is a dream.'

All he wanted to do was reach out and hold her, but he didn't. It wasn't like that, not anymore. 'I'm sorry,' he said. 'I had to come.'

'No,' she said. She looked a little scared. 'It's good. I needed someone.'

'It's not like that.'

She stepped back. 'Just come in.'

The room was lived-in but neat. Caitlin had always been one for neatness. It kept her thoughts straight, she said. There were clothes hanging on the back of the chair and the bed was unmade, naturally. He didn't want to sit on it. That would be an intrusion.

She fell down in her empty space, tucking her feet below the blanket. 'Sit down, would you. We're not strangers.'

He perched on the edge of the bed. He could feel heat from the mattress.

'So what's the story?' she asked. 'Have you finally lost it?'

'No,' he said. 'Not really.'

'That's a shame,' she teased. 'So why are you showing up in my hotel three hundred miles from the flat? Why are you showing up in the middle of the night? You could've called, mate. We spoke the other day.'

He looked around the room. 'I just had to see you. I had to. It's been bad since you went.'

'Come here,' she said.

He edged up the bed beside her and lay down. She pulled his head into her and put her palm against his ear, making the shell effect; he heard the ocean against her skin. Now, he might sleep.

'I keep needing to apologise lately,' he said.

'That's good.'

'I am sorry, Caitlin. You know that. I couldn't see the full picture.'

She rubbed her palm against his ear, fingers in the short hairs above. The ocean inside her hand hushed.

'Look at me,' she said. 'I'm like your mother.'

He laughed. He said, 'Oh God.'

'It's bad,' she asked, 'isn't it?'

He nodded, smiling. 'I miss how it used to be. What happened?'

'We're just different. That's all.'

'Tell me about your new life,' he said, and she slapped him a little bit for his cheek.

'I told you who the boss is, didn't I? Kim effing Larson. He's crackers by the way, but I suppose they all are. In his office, he had this …' She trailed away. 'Anyway, it's been interesting. We're working on the optics for a big announcement.'

'Aye?'

'Yeah. I shouldn't say.'

'Go on,' he said. 'Who am I going to tell?'

'I shouldn't.'

He turned over to face her. She smiled down at him. 'For old times' sake?'

She bit her lip, then pushed his face back down. 'They're blasting off, the lot of them.'

'They're what?'

'They're blasting off, Larson and these other big business dudes. They're going off from Scolpaig, any day now.'

He tried to remain still. He let Caitlin worry his warm ear and stared into the magnolia wallpaper. They were blasting off? Leaving?

'What for?' he asked. 'A day trip to Mars?'

'It's crazy,' she said. 'I guess they're getting frozen or whatever. They're blasting off and heading out for another planet. I couldn't believe it when they first said.'

Another planet. Another fucking planet. If Larson went then the whole thing would be pointless, totally pointless.

'That *is* crazy,' he agreed, his voice flat. 'These billionaires, you can't predict them, can you?'

'They've been messing with my contract. To tell you the truth, I'm scared. I spoke to Elaine and I've been transferred here permanently. It's probably just HR being HR. I keep telling myself that.'

He sat up. He needed to speak, properly now. 'Caitlin,' he said. 'I haven't been honest. I didn't come here to see you.'

'No?'

'No.'

He did his best to explain. He went back to the flat with her, spoke her through the bad days after she left, and the discovery of his father. At first, she refused to believe. She said it was nonsense, asked him if he'd lost it, but he explained the ghost sat outside in the car and something in his conviction seemed to persuade her. She nodded along as he said how he thought it worked, and hadn't everyone always wondered where your data went when you died? All those empty profiles existing beyond you? He spoke about the junior's disappearance and relayed what happened after and Caitlin had heard one or two things about the 97ers in her time and could believe the story.

'So what'll you do?' she asked.

'We're going to confront Larson,' he said. 'We're going to show him what he's done in front of everyone. We're going to film it, stream it, and show everyone.'

'You're mad,' she said. 'He's surrounded by security. You won't get close.'

'We don't need to. All we need is for him to see.'

'My advice would be,' she sighed, 'get yourself home. Forget the whole thing. I don't want to see you hurt.'

'I can't go home. They know where we ... where I live.'

She shook her head. He knew he was losing her.

'Promise me, Alastair. Promise me you'll go home.'

'I promise,' he said.

Outside, the sleek black motor sat below a streetlamp. He jogged across the road towards it and got in. The junior was awake.

'You went to see her,' he said. 'I thought we decided to wait.'

'We did, but I changed my mind.'

'And what did she say?'

Another round of filling someone in. The junior nodded along, then his eyes bulged at the new information. 'What the fuck?' he asked.

'I know.'

They saw how it worked. Everyone knew the weather kept getting worse; you couldn't deny it. Everyone did their best to ignore the protests, the upset. Constant, but you ignored it all, and now Larson and the others were giving up. They'd taken all they could, squeezed them dry, and were leaving the scene of the crime. A hit and run, in other words.

'So time's against us,' said Alastair. 'Caitlin says it could be any day now.'

His junior nodded grimly. They didn't need to discuss it any further; between them, they knew.

He started the engine and moved the car through the empty streets, passing under the palm trees and closed-up shops. They headed for the edge of town. Around them, between tall buildings, the sky began to hint at the sun's rising; one or two businesses showed signs of life within. Morning would soon come.

SEVENTEEN

A little over half his face felt warm. The rest of it was cold. When the air entered his nostrils, it was cold. When it left, it was warm. He kept his eyes closed and he breathed and tried to empty his mind. He tried his best, he really did. When pain came to him, he dismissed it as merely a sensation, nothing that could truly harm him. When his mind wandered onto the logistics of his endeavour, he tried to pull it back. But it did no good. In his lap, his hands touched themselves. He plucked at the ropey veins beneath his thinning skin, ran thumbpads over the dice of his anxious knuckles.

When a bell chimed, it came as a relief: an excuse to open his eyes and get himself plugged back in, into another distraction.

The caller's name was Neil. He was someone high up in Honey Bee.

'What can I do for you?' Larson asked Neil's stream, now showing on the large display.

'Nothing too enormous, Mr Larson,' said this Neil, middle-aged, droopy-browed, grey. 'It's to do with a remnant.'

A little taste of sick charged into the back of his mouth; he dismissed it. 'Well?' he asked, standing briefly to check that no one except his animal lurked in the sub-office.

'There was this guy, I don't know if you remember. He was

making a lot of noise on the field, trying to post footage of one of them. I think it's meant to be his father.'

It was just one thing after another. 'That's right,' he said. 'I guess you'll have taken care of it?'

'Well, not so much actually.' The apparition in the screen had the gall to chuckle. 'You would think we would've, but no. I'm afraid to say my latest report suggests a few of our men lost the fellow out in the wilds somewhere.'

Larson nodded. Slowly, the nodding turned into a shaking of his head. He couldn't help it. 'I see,' he said.

On a scale of one to ten, this news was merely a three. A measly little three hardly made him break a sweat. He could eat a bowl of threes for breakfast with lashings of liquefied fours. The remnants: something else he'd be glad to see the back of. They started showing up a few years after juniors began entering the world and workforce in large numbers. It didn't take long for a certain number of seniors to pass away, snuffing out their juniors' lives at the same time. Not every junior came back, but some did. A tiny percentage returned. There was no rhyme or reason to the process, as far as his JNR people could tell. Sometimes it happened instantly, at the point of their demise. Other times the remnants would resurface years later, often at a point of stress in the lives of those they left behind. People were upset about it, sure. People made calls, they wrote emails, but it didn't take much to shut them up. At any other time, this latest crank would've been observed, then sent a gift basket of warm currency and Larson could close the file on the whole dilemma. Now, it was one headache among many he was expected to deal with.

'I suppose I want to apologise,' said Neil, nervously.

'Fine,' sighed Larson. 'If he resurfaces, Honey Bee will deal with him, yes?'

Neil agreed that yes, if this person showed their face again, on the field or elsewhere, they would be processed. Most likely, they'd have skulked back to their Edinburgh digs and would be picked up later on, once they re-emerged upon the field. The temptation would be far too strong. Larson ended the call without much of a goodbye. Someone like Neil wasn't, in the strictest definition of the word, a person. An image on a screen, an avatar, one of many icons that appeared now and then to deliver him information, but not a person, so didn't require courtesy.

In all the confusion and hassle of transporting the entire operation into Scotland and subsequently across to its western extremity, it had been a long time since he'd had time to sit down with Deborah. There were scant private quarters to make use of in this Uist HQ and subsequently he now felt the absence of their nightly rendezvous. He simply had too much to do: the rockets needed to be supervised; the logistics of getting everyone who mattered to this one small city at the exact same time were a nightmare; the PR gurus and field experts who'd spin the journey into something positive needed constant monitoring.

And now, today, yet another problem suddenly flashed across his screen, his devices: there are murmurs on the field, Kim. Coming in from Stock now, too, saying someone calling themselves Carly Bailey is going to be appearing on the streams tomorrow, has a big secret about you she's going to break.

He stared at the message for a long time. He wiped his mouth and found the lips were drying out; a few grains of skin came away from the friction applied. So Mrs Bailey would be breaking her contract. Fine. That was her prerogative. She could go around spreading her lies as far as she desired. She would probably paint him as an abandoner, a bastard of a man who brought life into the world and didn't hang around to deal with the results. But that would be BS, wouldn't it? Because he'd looked after Junior his entire existence, perhaps not personally but certainly financially. They could get him for lots of things, but not for that.

On a scale of one to ten, this would be a six, maybe a seven. He couldn't stomach a seven in the way he could a three, but he could consume it all the same.

He found Deborah down on the lower floors, dealing with some employees tasked with arranging transport for the lucky few they were obliged to carry with them. Where necessary, they worked closely with visa companies around the globe; most of their colleagues were easily able to sidestep that sort of antiquated red tape. He watched through a window as she moved among them, short and sturdy, one with her profession. Her dimensions reached out to the limits of her profession and filled them entirely. He liked it. He liked to see her work. After a moment, he rapped on the glass. She looked up and their eyes met. He gestured for her to come over.

Out in the quiet of a stairwell, he spoke. 'I saw your message,' he said. 'The one about the Bailey woman.'

'That's right,' she said. 'It feels big, Kim. A lot of big names are getting excited about this.'

'Do you know what she's going to say?'

Deborah shrugged. 'I don't know. I don't want to know, but I smell people smelling blood.'

Somewhere, somewhere deep in his mind, almost in the back of his own throat, he could hear the tinny voice. *You'll look after me*, it spoke. *You'll look after me, won't you, Daddy?*

Deborah looked at him intently. He could see a great deal of care in the expression. 'Where have you gone, Kim?' she asked.

'I want to bring it forward,' he announced. He said the words before he realised he believed them.

'You want to bring *what* forward?'

'The departure. We're going to go sooner. We're going to go tomorrow.'

Deborah chuckled. She smiled, then realised he was serious. '*Tomorrow?* Tomorrow, Kim? We were struggling to pull this together inside the week. It isn't possible.'

His precious Deborah was certainly a human being. Nothing like Neil of Honey Bee fame. He knew she was human because he could feel the heat coming off her face. She smelled human. But still.

'Saying something isn't possible is the same as saying I don't want to try,' he said.

'This isn't one of your inventions,' she replied. 'This isn't something I can pull out my ass. We're talking about going to space, Kim. We're talking about collecting the leaders of the world into your old back garden. We're talking—'

'You *do* want to come, don't you?'

The expression of hurried irritation melted away. Her plump lower lip flipped down. He was a master of it: the pull-back and reveal.

'You're threatening me?' she asked. '*Me?*'

'I'm asking a question, is what I'm doing.'

'You're asking me a question?'

'Isn't it obvious?'

'But what's the actual question you're asking, Kim? That's the bigger question.'

He shrugged. He smiled. 'So you can make it happen.'

Deborah ran a hand through her hair, turned away for a moment, then turned back. 'I can try,' she sighed.

'That's exactly what I wanted to hear,' he said. 'And are you free this evening?'

'What do you mean?'

He came close, stepping near her on the tiles. He said, 'Baby's hungry.'

She walked away from him. She did not once look back.

Somewhere down the hall, an alarm sounded.

In the office, he sat in his ergonomic chair and looked out at the ocean, trying to ignore the alarm. Much darker, this ocean, much choppier than the one he was used to. Way out in the distance, its base lost to haze, the blasting apparatus jutted from the horizon. Back when he came out this way as a kid, with his aunts and their friends, this technology did not exist. Much of the work done on reclaiming the land from the sea had yet to be completed, so they were granted access to the old, true coast. Everyone brought tents with them and they wild camped. Usually the groups would be formed of six to ten, not including himself. Some were couples, others travelled solo. They went on beach walks during the day. He caught hermit crabs in the low surf and encouraged them to upgrade shells by trapping them in plastic buckets with roomier samples. He loved to watch spindly legs creep out of the openings, the crabs' antennae searching the bucket's water for threat. Sometimes they took the opportunity and shuffled themselves into the larger shells he provided. When that happened, a little pop went off in his head. He liked it, but couldn't explain why.

The alarm rang every few seconds. Every few seconds, a sharp burst of sound came from down the hallway, one that he ignored; someone would resolve it soon enough.

Generally he got left alone by the aunts and their friends. It didn't bother him. They spoke about an adult world he had no access to, so he made his own fun. He played with the hermit crabs in the low surf. He imagined an ocean that extended into the sky, one he could walk around in. He wanted to change his perspective. He wanted to look up and see rays and eels flying above him. Later, he explained his field in the same way: an ocean in the air, a water you can breathe and walk around inside.

One night, he wasn't sure at what age, he couldn't sleep. They ate poorly on these trips: lots of white bread rolls and cans of soft drink, plus booze for the adults. As a result, he went to bed hyperactive, listening to the ocean sounds through his tent, using a torch to read his comics. One night he wanted to see the water under the moon, so he went out. No one ever told him not to do this, but he knew it was illicit. It turned out the moon's reflection was not hugely interesting, so he crept among the groups' camp instead, standing near them and simply listening. In time, he came to the tent he understood to be shared by Fiona and Claire, his aunts. Within that tent, unlike the rest, he could hear certain sounds. He heard the small sounds of bodies, liquid slaps, the glitter of rustling sleeping bags. What else to do but kneel on the well-trodden earth and slowly, gently ease open the zip, millimetre by millimetre, rocking the slider across its teeth one by one, until a gap formed he could slip his head inside.

That alarm. What the hell did he pay people for, if it wasn't to monitor this kind of thing? In a minute, he'd go out and see for himself.

What he saw inside the tent wasn't particularly shocking. Perhaps a five on all-time, lifelong moments of shock. Up at the top of the tent sat his aunt Claire. She had her top off. One of the men from the group lay with her. He thought his name might've been Gary. Gary had his head on Claire's chest, holding her nipple inside his mouth. Gary used his mouth on the aunt's nipple. Both of their eyes were closed; they didn't see him, they didn't hear him. The young Kim felt something cold inside himself. He watched them for a little while, then closed the zip back up. Once back in his own tent, he turned the image over in his mind: the chewing jaw, the hidden nipple. He began to understand precisely how much had been taken from him in those early years, all the resources that he'd lost.

It was just one of those things though. They happened now and then.

The alarm's sound had become untenable. He stood up and walked across his office, resolving to find the person responsible for monitoring the alarm and give them some special attention. How were they supposed to pull off this plan if people refused to accept personal responsibility? He managed, didn't he?

Out in the hallway, a few people stood around in a triangle. They were talking together and looking at their devices.

'Can one of you sort that out?' he asked.

As a trio, they looked up at him, then blanched. Their devices perceptibly drooped.

'Well?' he asked.

One of them had the nerve to answer, some young kid. 'What do you mean, Mr Larson?'

'That noise. I'm trying to work in here.'

The kid looked to his colleagues. He smiled. 'What noise, sir?'

'The alarm,' he said. 'The fucking alarm!'

They all shook their heads. 'What alarm?' asked the kid.

He stared at them for a moment, then closed himself inside.

His animal lay out on the floor of the space he kept separate for meetings. People came up here, he explained what he wanted from them, they left. He enjoyed seeing new faces react to his animal. They didn't know what to do when they saw it, this creature they'd never experienced before. She looked up as he slid down the wall beside her. The experts told him he shouldn't get close, that its behaviour couldn't be predicted, but he didn't listen. Her yellow eyes were slits; she was barely awake. He held out his fingertips and she edged closer, brushing her spiky muzzle against his pads.

'They're going to ruin me,' he told her.

Her big mouth opened up in a yawn. The flesh inside shone brightly.

'Can you believe it?' he asked. 'I gave them everything, my dear. Everything they have, it came from me. I worked my whole life, every moment of it, all in their service, and now they want to tear me down. I don't understand it, really I don't. You didn't meet Junior, but you would've liked him, yes you would.' He stroked the skin of her head. 'I looked after him too, didn't I? I looked after everyone, and see where it got me? See what it cost me?'

With his free hand, Larson reached inside his collar and brought out his weapon, the shiny black button he felt press gently against his sternum every moment of every day. He looked down at it, this puck of machined metal resting on his chest, full of potential.

Just then, the animal bit his other hand, but only gently. She wanted to explore.

Caitlin barely slept in the hours after Alastair left. She couldn't believe he'd turned up like that, spouting all his crazy notions about ghosts and 97ers, but there had been an earnestness in his voice that forced her to believe. He wasn't one to lie, Alastair, or be prone to fantasies. Depressive, anxious, perhaps, but not a dreamer in that way. She couldn't remember a single fib he'd told her in their relationship. In many ways he'd have been the ideal partner, if he hadn't become so obsessed with stats and juniors and the dream of pulling himself up.

She washed and dressed groggily, getting her bag sorted, using her mobile to accept a few messages from colleagues.

Overnight, a meeting had appeared in her calendar for that day and she saw the whole team on the list. Another one of Larson's updates, no doubt.

Downstairs, she passed right by the dining room, assuming it to be off limits, then noticed it was completely empty. The foyer was deserted too, apart from a young couple checking in at the front desk. Every other morning, she manoeuvred through crowds to get out, but today, nothing. She went out into the morning and made for the tram. Again, Sarah waited for her on the platform and she was just as surprised about this overnight emergency meeting. They couldn't work it out, although Caitlin suspected the departure might be taking place sooner than expected; all those hotel guests vanishing in the early hours made her suspicious.

'I think they're going now,' she said, leaning in to Sarah to stop anyone overhearing. 'I had all these bigwigs in my hotel and this morning, gone.'

Sarah looked confused. 'Surely not.'

Caitlin shrugged. She said, 'Maybe.'

Her theory was all but confirmed when they reached HQ and departed the tram, finding the entire place alive with activity. Dozens of cars were parked up outside of the building, some bumped up onto the pedestrianised areas. Drivers stood around aimlessly, huffing on nicotine, laughing in small groups. All across the place people moved, some going into HQ, others barging through in a state of confusion. Their tram's arrival didn't help things and the pair soon got separated in the crush of bodies. Caitlin made her way as best she could to the entrance and went to scan in. She searched in her wallet, in her bag, but realised she must've left her pass at home, the little card with all her biometrics in. At the desk, they issued her a temporary replacement; the boy on reception was too busy to make much of a fuss.

She could feel her heart going in her throat. This was it, then. Project's end.

Sarah waited for her outside the office, and there were others there too: all the team she'd been assigned to work with. The atmosphere of the day was similar to a national disaster, when the usual order of things goes out the window and everyone feels free to talk to those they would normally ignore. As she walked towards Sarah, Caitlin overheard the discussions: what was going on? Who were all these people?

'So this is it?' she said.

Sarah nodded. 'I guess so.'

Being nominally in charge, certainly within their pairing, Caitlin opted to keep things as normal as possible, leading Sarah into their office while the rest loitered outside. They'd work on their draft announcement now and have something decent ready for the big meeting. That way, whatever got announced, they would be prepared. So far, they could be proud of the work done in crafting news of Larson's departure.

'I think it's good,' said Sarah. 'Not excellent, but alright.'

Caitlin nodded. 'Decent.'

'Exactly.'

The research had been invaluable. Their script did its best to reflect the excitement and intrigue of meeting James Partridge, combined with the hard-nosed defiance of the Retraction of State. Listen, it might have said: nothing is easy, nothing is fair, but in this life, you must admit that some of us are better qualified for certain tasks than others. We are at the dawn of a new era, it suggested. Right now, a new era beckons, and to make the most of it, we need to ensure that the brightest and best act as our emissaries. Think of it as a show of bravery. Think of Larson et al. as soldiers moving beyond the next frontier, putting aside their own personal safety in the name of our species' future. And if you don't like it, the script suggested, then that's your own fault. Why be such a crybaby about everything? Why not dry your eyes, pet?

For a while, they worked it over and discussed how best to present it at this big meeting. Caitlin began to get butterflies in her stomach, not helped by the increasing sense of excitement from outside, where people still lingered by the big windows. She started to read aloud, to make sure the text sounded good off the page as well as on, then faltered. The other workers had pushed their backs tight to the glass. She went over and peered through. They were making way, it turned out, for a long crocodile of men and women, most of them aged and decrepit, but all of them nicely dressed and tanned, strolling through the office space. Caitlin could see their heads and shoulders through the bodies lined up outside and she spoke to Sarah. 'I suppose this is them,' she said. 'The travellers.'

'We should go,' said Sarah.

Caitlin nodded. 'I suppose so.'

The atmosphere of stress and excitement followed them throughout their journey inside HQ. They took the stairs and, at all levels, desks and work stations lay abandoned. People sat on surfaces usually reserved for cups and screens, others leaned against walls. Most stared as Caitlin and Sarah came through, knowing these were individuals destined for the big meet.

They went to the Strugatsky Room, the same place as induction, and Caitlin didn't expect the actual travellers to be present. The fact they walked through the office itself was surprising enough. She started to recognise other team heads as they approached, nodding to those she'd spoken to, and soon enough they were all inside, helping themselves to decaf and fancy little morning cakes and Junior Meals. No one spoke much, though they shared meaningful glances with each other, little eyebrow raisers that showed they were all on the same page.

Sarah and Caitlin sat and waited. Soon enough, the door flew open and in came the main attraction: Larson and Stock and a few security guys, one of them taking a position with his back to the door. Whatever murmuring the room contained before, it instantly vanished. Everyone watched as Kim Larson sorted himself a decaf and Stock found herself a chair in the front row, her eyes glued to her tablet.

'Here we go,' Sarah said. Caitlin was surprised to see her colleague smile in a way that seemed entirely genuine.

Larson came to the front of the room. He pulled a table over and did his business with the baseball cap. He looked tired, and Caitlin was reminded of his actual age, somewhere in the nineties. You couldn't tell though. The best of the best in anti-age technologies and exercises and lotions, she presumed.

Doing his best to smile, he asked, 'So how are we all today?'

No one responded.

'Great,' he said. 'That's excellent. Thank you. Thank you all for making it to such an impromptu meet but, as with any big project, circumstances are liable to change and I really appreciate everyone's willingness to think on their feet and be flexible. I don't want to get into too much of the nitty-gritty with this, but essentially the headline is we're leaving now. Today.'

People around Caitlin began to chatter. She thought: hadn't they realised? Didn't they see the writing on the wall?

Larson paused, watching them all through narrowed eyes, probably trying to read the room. You didn't get to his level without mastering the art of public speaking.

'It's a shock, isn't it? But it's true. I've spent the night with the engineers out at the launch site and they've confirmed it's doable, so we're going to. I'm seeing a few sceptical faces before me and I must say that I respect that. You're right to feel sceptical because I'm honestly asking a lot, I realise that. I do. But I want to tell you a little quote that's always inspired me. This is a quote from a long time ago and I can't remember right now who said it, but basically it goes that the reasonable man changes himself for the world. Opposed to that is the unreasonable man, who adapts the world to him. Therefore all progress is because of the unreasonable man.'

Ahead of Caitlin, someone put their hand up. They held it aloft all through Larson's quote.

'Let me just ... The quote is saying that nothing happens unless someone sticks their neck out. I'm making sense?'

The hand remained in the air. Larson glared at it.

'Okay,' he said. 'Go.'

The person spoke. 'I'm sorry to interrupt but I wanted to ask what's the reasoning for the change?'

Larson nodded. 'No one needs to know that, except me.'

The hand went down. You couldn't tell if the asker thought this a fair response.

He smiled at them all benevolently. 'Right. Down to business.' He began focusing on certain members of the crowd, helped by Stock who seemed to have their images pulled up on her tablet. He questioned whether they were good to go now, whether they foresaw any holdups or issues that might stop the project finalising that very day. Sarah glanced at her, looking nervous. Soon, they'd be asked to present their own work.

'You two,' he said, pointing to them.

'Weir and Lovett,' said Stock.

'That's right, I remember. How goes the progress?'

Caitlin stood, clearing her throat. 'We've put together a draft script proposal for the announcement, to be released after the fact, obviously. What we did was take a look at other sources and try to pull out some—'

'What's that?' asked Larson. 'An announcement?'

'Yes.'

'What announcement? What—'

Stock interrupted him. 'Announcing the project.'

Larson shook his head. 'We don't need it. It's redundant.'

Caitlin waited to see if he would elaborate, but already he was moving on to the next team on his list, a few project managers who were arranging logistics. Just like that, passed over. Sarah looked livid and Caitlin could understand why. Days and days of work rejected, but somehow, she struggled to care. She watched her colleagues answer Larson's questions and soon the entire room had spoken.

'Great,' said Larson. 'Excellent work everyone. For the next stage of the meeting, I'm going to ask you to change venues a little. We're going to reconvene next door in about five minutes. Help yourselves to decafs and whatever else. Thanks. Thank you.'

At this, Stock opened the other door behind Larson and stood beside it, waiting for them to file through. A few filled up at the refreshment table, but Caitlin went right in. Just get it over with, whatever it was. Signing NDAs, some sort of debrief; she didn't care.

The entrance to the next room was its only doorway. There were chairs inside but no windows and the space was lit entirely by overhead lights. The rest of Larson's security guys stood around the walls. They found a space at the back of the room, no longer excited to be part of the team.

'I can't believe it,' said Sarah. 'All that work for nothing.'

'I know,' said Caitlin.

'I can't believe I gave up a gig in England to come up here to this shit hole,' said Sarah. 'We should've phoned it in. I can't believe we bothered making good copy.'

Caitlin sighed. 'That's the way it goes,' she said.

Soon, everyone was inside, sipping decaf, chatting among

themselves. From what she could overhear, it seemed the general mood was positive. People seemed excited that the project had been pushed forward. Caitlin didn't pay attention. She was miles away. She was dreaming of writing a note to Elaine, handing in her notice, being free. Bar work was obviously a stupid idea but there had to be things to do in the world outside of this. Down near the border, her old man made a go of it, growing his drugs and using a ramshackle field uplink to sell it to contacts in the city. He worked the land. He seemed happy, didn't he? Last time she was down, he showed her the new fields being processed, stomping round in his big dirty boots. There are other ways, she thought. There are other ways to live.

Pretty quickly, Larson reappeared. He closed the room's doors and stood in front of them. This time, he didn't remove his cap. He watched them all and Caitlin wished he would get it over with. Stop wasting my time and tell me what this is about, let me sign the effing forms and move on.

'Thanks for decamping, guys. I really appreciate it. We just wanted to make sure we got all the information down properly before we started talking about this next stage of the process. I have some complex news for you.'

He paused to let this information sink in. A thick silence greeted him. You could see heads turning rapidly among the assembled people, faces blinking to colleagues.

'What do you mean?' asked a man close to Larson.

'What I mean is, in the interests of confidentiality, I need you all to stay inside this room for a certain period of time. A long period of time.'

The same man stood up. 'I'm sorry,' he said. 'I don't want to be disrespectful, but I can't imagine any of us want to do that.'

Larson scowled. 'All I'm asking for is a little compliance. Surely you can grant me that much, given all I've done for you.'

'I'm sorry,' said the man. 'But I *am* saying no. Excuse me.'

He moved down his aisle of seats and crossed the floor towards Larson. Larson stood between him and the door, hands behind back, his cap nearly covering his eyes.

'Excuse me,' he said again.

'I really, really can't imagine anyone saying no to this,' Larson repeated.

'I want to get out,' said the man. 'Can you let me past, please?'

Larson didn't budge. 'You can exit at any time.'

The room watched this tense stand-off, and at first it seemed incidental. Larson wouldn't stop the man from leaving. There would be a short dick-measuring contest, then the man would leave, allowing the rest to follow.

'If anyone wants to leave,' smiled Larson, 'they're free to do so.'

The man tried to get past, but Larson didn't budge. He looked up from below his cap and smiled.

And then the man raised his hand, for what reason Caitlin didn't know. Perhaps to strike Larson or move him aside or squeeze past his shoulder. Whatever the motivation, the gesture wasn't allowed to continue. One of Larson's security guys appeared and held onto the man's hand. He brought him back and put him down in a seat and the process appeared to take the security guy zero physical effort.

'There we go,' said Larson.

Again, the room erupted. People shouted, they cried out. Groups of people stood and attempted to get close to the door, but security were on them, and now they didn't even need to lay on hands. 'You're holding us against our will,' someone shouted.

'I think it must be in your will or else you would do something to stop it,' said Larson. 'All the evidence I'm seeing suggests you're as excited about the prospect as I am.'

Among the confusion, the two women found each other. Sarah asked was it real, was it really happening? Caitlin felt a measure of responsibility for Sarah, but didn't know what to say. 'I'm not sure,' she admitted. She couldn't believe it, not really. Some sort of mind game, perhaps. A test, to scare out the sceptics? It took a lot to make it to the top of the world, but he wasn't evil in that sense, was he? He wasn't a true villain. 'Just stay close,' she said, as others round them panicked and pushed past, all to no avail because none had the ability to take on Larson's security.

She could hear his voice, but too many were around her now and she couldn't see his face. 'This is good,' he called. 'Finally, some obedience.'

Caitlin felt herself become very, very still. A survival mechanism of hers, to get still in moments of stress. Parts of her vision clouded up and only a narrow beam of motion remained to her. She held onto Sarah's hand and saw the hand grasp her own.

'That's enough!' Larson yelled and the room went quiet. A few sat down and he appeared to her again: shrunken, ancient, bitter. 'Judging from the fact that none of you have left, I'm going to proceed with that as confirmation of consent, and I thank you for it. There's still lots to be done from my end, so I'm going to leave you now. I assume someone will come to you, eventually.'

Flanked by two security guys, he left, and behind him a group fell upon the door, hammering it and pulling at the handle; the remaining security guys in the room didn't even bother to stop them. Instead, they watched from the side, smiling behind their shades.

'What are we going to do?' asked Sarah. 'It's a joke or something, isn't it? A test?'

Caitlin shook her head. She watched the doors. 'I don't think it is,' she said. 'I think it's real.'

How long they stayed in the room, she wasn't sure. It took the more energetic members of the group some time to leave the door alone and return to their seats. She half expected the outrage to continue, but it wasn't like that. Instead, everyone sat in their places, more or less, and spoke to those around them. Naturally, once Larson left, they all reached for mobiles and tablets and devices, but quickly found their data was blocked. It made sense. He probably had the ability to shut it off in certain areas, why not here? Even Caitlin started to panic. She felt her stillness ebb away and all the energy flowed into her and jangled around, clashing like metal in her ears. They were off the field's data. Zero access to the outside world, to anything worthwhile.

'We've got to do something,' she said to Sarah, close beside her.

'There's nothing to do. We're trapped.'

Caitlin gripped her eyes tighter and turned. 'I'm not going to sleepwalk into this, Sarah,' she said. 'I won't. I've done too much on autopilot. I won't do it.'

Sarah nodded, a little bit.

'Let's get close to the doors,' she whispered, 'and play it by ear.'

Sarah's eyes scanned the room, picking out, it seemed, the three security guys.

'It doesn't matter,' said Caitlin. 'When we get the chance, we run for it. He's counting on us not being brave.'

Earlier, one of the security guys, the biggest, had opened up a big pack of bottled waters and now they gingerly made their way towards him, passing through groups of workers in hushed conversation. They asked for a bottle and the security guy smirked as he handed one over. The bottle was warm in her hand.

'Thanks,' Caitlin said, leading Sarah away.

They circled the room, pausing by different groups, hearing snippets of panicky reasoning. Neither woman joined in, only skirting the edges, slowly making their way to the big double doors, sealed tight, which the guards didn't bother to monitor. They seemed bored, as if this detail was low priority.

'Let's relax,' said Caitlin, leaning herself against the wall there.

Sarah followed suit, but she was in a bad way. Cooling liquid sprung out on her face as she stared wildly into space.

'Hey,' said Caitlin, finding confidence. 'It's alright. Just breathe. We'll get through it.'

Sarah nodded.

'You know what?' said Caitlin. 'Everyone's probably right, I reckon. I think it probably is some sort of test or a joke or they don't want us talking to the press. That must be it, has to be. Listen. It's fine. We'll be out soon enough and we'll find out it's all a big joke and we can hire a car or take a bus or whatever and head off tonight. That sounds good, doesn't it?'

She kept talking, staring into Sarah's eyes, letting them be the only things visible to her. If she could keep talking, they would be safe.

'What are you going to do when we're done? I tell you what I'm going to do. I'm going to visit my family. I haven't seen them in months and months and I'm going to head down there tonight, once we're out. We're fine, Sarah. Listen. There's a great big river down there and after we're out I'm going to drive down there and you can come and we'll be safe. How does that sound? Good? Does it sound good, Sarah? Just focus, please. Please, for me, just pay attention.'

EIGHTEEN

In horror, they watched the mess carry on outside HQ. All around them people were milling, limos edging past the motor. Alastair looked to his junior in confusion. What was going on? He supposed this place probably got busy enough, but the scene here could only be described as chaos, pure chaos. No one spotted their car or their presence though; there was simply too much commotion.

'What'll we do?' the junior asked.

'Give me a second,' he said, leaning forward to peer through the tinted windows.

Drivers were hauling luggage out the backs of other motors. Trams were coming in from Lochmaddy every few minutes, depositing confused workers; the whole plaza outside HQ looked like the protests back in Edinburgh.

'It's good in a way,' he announced. He looked back at the ghost, then to the junior. 'Makes us less noticeable.'

The junior nodded. The ghost did not respond. He grew weaker every hour, and even his outline began to fade here and there. Tiny sparks flew from his edges and he barely spoke; even the mumbling was over with.

'Alastair,' said the junior. 'I think we have to go. If we're going to do it, we have to go.'

From the glove box, they dug out the remnants of the agents' kits: extra shades and a pair of wallets. As the junior went to exit the vehicle, Alastair caught him. 'Whatever happens,' he said, 'I just wanted to say . . .'

The junior nodded. 'I know. Obviously, I know.'

'Right,' he said. 'Well then.'

With all the confidence they could muster, they got out, round to the back of the vehicle where they ushered out their father's ghost. He fizzled in the daylight and they held what remained of him by the elbows. They walked on.

'Act like you belong,' Alastair said. 'Don't look anyone in the eye.'

They made their way through the busy plaza, dodging people when they came close by. No one seemed to notice their cargo and, if anyone looked, it was only for a brief second. The big glass doors of the HQ came closer. They could see more people inside, more movement, more confusion.

'Keep going,' he said.

'I am,' said the junior. 'I am.'

Outside, he took a moment to look around as he pulled Caitlin's pass out from his pocket. They'd made it this far at least. The noise here deafened you, all these people shouting out to each other, horns blaring in the car park. He supposed this must be the day of departure, otherwise why the rush?

'Alright,' he said. 'Let's go in, nice and easy. See there? The lad on the front desk? We'll have a word with him.'

Inside, they walked across the marble floor, and at least here the crush felt lighter. Less bodies, less heat. They ushered the ghost forward and towards the reception boy, who spoke animatedly to someone via his headset. He glanced up at them briefly with a scowl, then his eyes fell on the ghost between them. The boy swallowed. He said, 'Excuse me, I'll call you right back.' He clicked a button on the headset. 'Can I help you?' he asked, staring at the ghost.

Alastair nodded. 'Yes, you can. We've been given strict instructions to bring this specimen directly to Mr Kim Larson himself. It's a highly urgent matter. Can you let us know where he is, please?'

The boy stared a while longer, then said, 'Just a minute.'

It was working! It was fucking working. Alastair could not believe it.

'I'll be with you two in a moment,' the boy added, glancing to Alastair's right.

Alastair turned. One of the agents stood there. The senior. He looked both furious and excited. There was a little piece of seaweed poking out the chest pocket of his fleece.

Alastair turned again to see the other agent at his junior's left.

The senior agent spoke. 'We can take it from here,' he said. 'We've been expecting these gentlemen.'

Through corridors they marched, and at first they didn't speak. There were too many people around, too many eyes, too many folk turning, expecting information from these new faces. They brought them along hallways and through open-plan office spaces and squeezed them through packs of excited workers. Now, the ghost did cause a distraction. Workers watched open-mouthed as this unknown phenomenon went by and the agents did their best to keep the pace up.

Soon, they found themselves in a private corridor and the senior agent spoke. He pushed Alastair along by the small of his back, and said, 'You must think you're really fucking smart, son.'

'You got us, we admit it,' said the junior agent.

'But we were too clever for you,' said his colleague. 'Too clever by half.'

'You think we wouldn't guess where you were heading? A chimp in a hat would know you'd come running here.'

Alastair didn't bother to reply. He'd begged once and wouldn't do it again.

'It could've been so simple,' said the senior agent. 'Bang, just like that, and all your problems would've been solved.'

'What have you got to live for anyway?' asked the junior agent. 'Some shitty life working at, where was it, *Step-Stone*? Jesus.'

'I'd take death over that.'

'Me too.'

They pushed them on, and Alastair noticed they were being particularly rough on his junior, needling him in the back with sharp fists and using boots on his legs when he slowed. They came, in time, to a large meeting room. On the door, a brass panel read *Strugatsky*. Alastair looked through the windows and saw no one inside, just vacant chairs and the leftovers of a snack table. The agents led them in, looking around in apparent confusion. On the far wall was another set of doors and a tall, curved piece of glass that looked out across the water, where evening was drawing in.

'Where is he?' the junior agent said.

'No idea. There's meant to be some big meeting going on here.'

'Right, well it's clearly not going on now.'

'You think I can't see that?'

As the agents argued, Alastair noticed something outside. It was a drone, hovering on the far side of the window. It flew around in crazy patterns, bumping against the glass as though it wanted to come inside. He could vaguely hear its propellers whirr and, from where he stood, it sounded almost like crying.

The agents didn't notice the machine. They resolved to escort the prisoners upstairs, directly to Larson's office suite. He wouldn't want to wait, they were sure.

They led them onwards, past another vast bank of windows, looking out across the water, and again Alastair saw the blast equipment over there, jutting above the horizon. They came to a door and he saw the name itself taped to the wood; just paper and sellotape and it didn't look as grand as he'd expected.

All five of them halted outside.

'Here we are,' said the junior agent. 'Now you're really for it. Give them a knock, would you?'

The senior agent bristled. 'You do it.'

'Just hurry up and knock, I was going to give them a little speech.'

'I'm not going to—'

Alastair reached forward, his arm pushing past both agents, and he hammered his fist against the door. They stared at him for a few seconds then turned to listen. Through the door, you could hear very faintly the sound of a person talking, just one person, and at first no response came.

'Give it another go,' said the senior agent, so Alastair did. He rapped again on the door's wood.

You heard the voice inside pause, then footsteps crossed the floor. The door opened up and a burly man stuck his head out. His head was shaved and he wore an earpiece. 'What do you want?'

'We need to see Mr Larson,' said the junior agent. 'We have an understanding that the individuals we're transporting,' he flicked his head back to the three of them, 'are a high priority.'

The security guy looked at Alastair, the junior, and the ghost in turn. His face showed no emotion. 'Give me a sec,' he said.

He went back inside, shutting the door behind him.

'Wow,' said the senior agent. 'You're really in for it now.'

'Sad, in a way,' said his colleague.

Alastair nodded. He didn't care. They were speaking to a different version of himself, one he recently left behind.

Soon, the door reopened, and the security guy ushered them

in. As they passed, he whispered, 'Better make it quick. He's under a lot of pressure.'

Inside, a wee old man stood behind a desk. A bank of viewing screens behind him showed dozens of other faces. He turned as they entered and fiddled with the controls to instantly kill the videos.

'What's this then?' he asked.

Alastair recognised him at once. A presence on the streams ever since boyhood, he'd seen Larson interviewed too many times to count, watched documentaries on his work, read reviews of his products. The World's Father, in the flesh.

The agents pushed them forward, across the floor of this fancy office suite, watched by the two security guys standing by the door and window.

'Hello, sir,' said the junior agent. 'Can I just say what an honour it is to finally—'

'I'm sorry,' interrupted Larson. 'I don't want to be rude, but I really don't have the time.'

The junior agent coughed, then said, 'We wanted to come along and basically say, ta-da! This lot here. It's the guys we knew you wanted. The one putting this *thing* onto the field. A whistle-blower.'

'Uh-huh,' said Larson mildly. He watched them all from behind his desk, eyeing each from below his baseball cap. No one spoke. They all waited for his reaction, but none was forthcoming. He kept very still, the old man, still and watchful, then he left the desk behind and padded over towards them. Up close, you realised how small he was. He barely came up to Alastair's shoulder.

'So this is the one,' he said, staring into Alastair's eyes. No one confirmed it; it wasn't a question. He measured Alastair up, then moved on to the junior. 'Nice model,' he said. 'A good match.' Finally, he came to the ghost, Alastair's dad, only just visible beneath the room's strong lights. 'And here's what caused all the trouble.'

This was it. This was what it had all been leading up to. Larson and the ghost, present together. Alastair reached into his pocket and brought his mobile up to the fabric's edge. Flicking his eyes downwards, he turned it on, then selected the video and started to record.

'It's a bit less defined than some of the others,' Larson noted. 'You should've seen some of the first ones. My goodness. Living, breathing beings they were. It's a pity, a real pity. I suppose everything has its downsides.' He stared at the ghost, a slight smile twitching his mouth's corners. 'So, my next question is ... what do you expect me to do about this?'

Alastair felt the agents around him stiffen. Clearly, they didn't expect this kind of reaction.

'Well,' stammered the junior agent. 'We knew this was a high priority issue. We got word from the chain of command to keep an eye on the senior and we knew you didn't want anything about the remnants getting out.'

'That was before,' said Larson. 'Do you imagine the issue with the remnants is still on my radar?'

'Maybe?' suggested the senior agent.

'And you thought it would be good to bring them here, to my office, where I'm trying to negotiate the logistical nightmare of the century, hours before I'm going to leave the *fucking* planet?'

Immediately, the tension in the room rose. Alastair kept a grip of the mobile, did his best to position it to capture everything that occurred.

'Maybe,' the senior agent repeated, a little quieter.

'Maybe,' Larson said. 'Maybe, maybe, maybe. Maybe you two should've taken one second to think this through and realise what a pair of morons you are. Get out! Get out of my sight.'

He turned away from them and marched back to his desk.

Alastair felt one of the agents tug on his shirt, but he stayed still. He didn't think it was over for him yet.

'Leave them,' said Larson, without turning round. 'You two go, leave the others.'

The agents looked at Alastair with an expression that approached sympathy. Not for long though, as they instantly backed out of the office, slamming the door shut behind them. No doubt they would be sprinting down the corridor now, getting themselves as far away as possible. Alastair looked to the junior; the junior looked back. They shared something unspoken. It didn't require voices what they said to each other.

'It might be a good idea,' said Larson, 'to lose the mobile. It's not going to be any use to you, soon.'

His stomach contracted. His legs weakened. Larson didn't even look back.

'I'm not going to stop,' said Alastair. 'This is evidence of what you've done.'

Larson whipped round. 'Is it really?'

'Yes.'

'And what is it I'm supposed to have done? You can hold the mobile up if you like, I'm happy to talk on the record. Good. Come over. Come and stand here.'

They approached the desk and Alastair held his mobile aloft, getting Larson properly in frame.

'Tell me what a bad person I am,' said Larson.

'Well,' he said, a little unsure of himself. 'It's everything, isn't it? This ghost, everything. The disaster in Fife. These things shouldn't have been allowed to happen.'

Larson smiled, his whole face wrinkling up. 'This is what gets me. It's so easy for you, in hindsight, to look back and say I made mistakes. Maybe I did. Who knows? But at least I tried something. What's your name, son?' he asked. Alastair told him. 'Alastair. Hello, Alastair. Hi. Let me explain something to you. I'll put it plainly. You are a nobody, Alastair. In the history of this planet you will be unremembered. Ford, Jobs, Musk, Huang, Anand, Larson: these are the names that people will remember for whatever time they have left. These are the names we'll be taking with us, to the next life. Alastair . . . No. We won't recall that one, I'm afraid.'

Alastair felt his lip tremble. This fighting, he didn't have the guts for it. 'So why did you let it happen?'

'We did our best,' said Larson, rubbing his eyes. 'We did our best to mitigate against remnants occurring, but regrettably, here and there, the data stored in our systems finds itself reanimating on the field, using its power to sustain a kind of life. I'm sorry about it, okay? I didn't want it to happen. What else? The *disaster*? Yes, of course we engineered that. How else could we stop you idiots from killing yourselves? You were like greedy children, using my field and still messing around with oil. It had to be done. They did it in China, they did it in Brazil. I was nothing special.'

He could see now, it was useless. Nothing this man could tell him would make him feel any different. Sighing, he killed the mobile and put it in his pocket. He turned, the junior following as he walked away, the ghost trailing after. They made their way towards the door and Alastair began to wonder what would come next. In a short period of time, he'd thrown everything away. His job, his home, his girlfriend, and his stats. He nearly laughed. Stats! He hadn't even thought about his stats since he offered them up to the agents. No doubt one of their colleagues would've been on the field long before, docking his points, rearranging his details, and then certain connections would've dropped off the map. He found he didn't care. Seeing inside the centre of the operation . . . He just didn't care.

In the doorway, he stopped. He turned and said, 'You were supposed to look after us. They called you our father.'

Nothing he'd said so far had seemed to touch Larson, but this certainly did. His expression darkened. He came out from behind the table, and as he did so, Alastair noticed him reach down into his collar to pull out some kind of necklace. 'What did you say?'

Alastair repeated himself. 'You were meant to look after us.'

'Look after you?' the old man asked. 'Look fucking *after* you? And didn't I?' As he hissed, Larson gripped at the necklace so hard, the chain around his neck broke. Now he was holding the little black charm, whatever it was.

Alastair shook his head. 'No, you didn't. You didn't care.'

'I cared so much, son,' said Larson, pointing now with the hand holding the necklace. His eyes became shiny, red. 'I cared so much that I changed the fucking world for you. I made a new earth for you, and what thanks did I get? I got zero. I worked my fingers to the bone for ungrateful children and all they can say is: it wasn't perfect. Well what is? And who looked after me, eh? Who could I go crying to? No one.'

Alastair sighed. 'Fine,' he said, then to the others: 'Come on, we're going.'

'Stay where you are,' Larson said, looking down at the object in his hand. 'I want you to watch something. If you think I didn't care for you, see how well you do without me.'

The old man raised his thumb. A thought appeared to pass through his mind, then he nodded and pressed the device.

All the room's lights went off. The computer died. Alastair heard a dull thud as the two security guys fell to the floor.

'What's going on?' he said.

His junior made a strange expression. His face turned pale. Behind the junior, in an instant, the ghost of his father vanished.

'It's your precious field,' explained Larson.

'The fie—'

But he didn't finish. Instead, he rushed to reach for his junior as he too began to fall, his eyes staring wildly.

And oh Lord the junior saw stars. He saw bright lights across his vision and all the room's colours morphed into a blurred kaleidoscope as he went down. His head rocked back and his knees buckled and the room upended and threw him off and all the colours morphed and bled. He hung in the air for a while. Static rang in his ears. Oh Lord. He tried to speak but nothing came. He tried to speak but whatever controlled his mouth was offline. Everything flew past him and he realised: I'm still in motion. I'm still falling.

All darkness. The room's colours muted to greys and navies, deep reds. A faint light from the window: the blue of seas. Deeper he went, falling still, his eyelids rapidly blinking outside his control. Like a gentle kiss, the back of his head touched the floor and the two surfaces met for a brief moment. He felt the floor's tension push back against his own head's tension, two objects coming together in unison, the floor lurching to him as much as him crashing to the floor.

Two futures occurred to him. There were two paths laid out ahead. He knew he would not die. He would not die because he didn't exist, not really. The personality inside him would live on, in his senior, where it belonged. He remembered the time before he existed, when his senior wondered what old age would bring. He remembered that wondering as if it was his own. He is me and I am him. I won't die unless he does. But a second future existed, the one where his body would go. In the plant, they made him. They grew him out of plastic and metals and formed him in the shape of a man. They moulded his face and tended his hair in darkened rooms and his brain grew up around wire and solder and alloys. This is not me. I am not this body, this body crumpling slowly into the floor and looking up into the darkened ceiling and seeing the face of my senior look over me: I am not it.

But wasn't that the same for seniors too? Didn't they also say to the body: you are not me?

Oh Lord, the exhaustion. He was down now, really down, really pressing into the carpet and seeing stars and the edges of his vision began to darken. He felt his senior lay hands on him, press fingertips into parts of his face, tug at his clothing. He could almost imagine it was him, himself touching another version of himself lying on the floor. What a mindfuck. He knew exactly how his senior felt right now, because he was his senior too.

He could get the smell. It came in strong now that Alastair leaned over him. It gave him pictures, the smell, things he remembered but never lived. Being at home, in the flat, with Caitlin. The days spent sharing with Marcin, the early pub days, the laughs. Back beyond the disaster, being small. He remembered the running boy, just as Alastair did, and shared out his compassion to him. What a thing to go through, he thought. Thanks for getting me here. Thank you, son.

The junior lay out on the floor. His eyes were open and he seemed to be functional, just. Something inside remained.

'Stop it,' Alastair said. 'Put it back on.'

He heard Larson's footsteps coming closer. He felt the old man's presence loom over him, then a faint shadow fell across the junior's face.

'I'm not going to put it back on,' said Larson. 'They're finished, the old ways. You're going to have to get used to doing more with less.'

The temptation was to perform CPR, or a muddled version of it, but he knew the junior owned no heart. He had no lungs to inflate. The junior's mouth moved slightly; his eyelids flickered.

'You're killing him,' Alastair said. He turned on his knee to look up at Larson. 'It's me, you're killing me.'

Larson shook his head. 'I'm abandoning you, just like you said. Well, live with it, son. You chose it, so live with it.'

The ghost too. He remembered the ghost: gone, vanished. His old man, away for the second time. Something thick appeared inside his throat. He wanted to spit.

'Please,' he said.

'Aha!' said Larson, and with that, he bounded away from Alastair and the junior. He marched across the floor to the windows and put his palms to the glass. Out in the water, beneath the darkening sky, many boats were crossing, heading away towards the apparatus on the horizon. 'It's starting,' he said. 'Excellent.'

He made his way to the desk and pulled a small bag out from a drawer. He began filling it up with electronics from around the desk. 'Good luck with handling life on your own.' He continued to rifle through drawers as he spoke, pulling things out and stuffing them into the bag. 'I hope it's everything you wanted.'

I could stop him, Alastair thought. I could run across and tackle the old man and maybe lose myself in the process. This person represented everything bad in his life: the source of the disaster, the end of his childhood. But the junior. He needed to do something for his junior. He made the decision there, kneeling on the floor, cupping his junior's head. I am going to help you. Alastair slid his hand below the junior's skull, cradling it, and shoved the other beneath his knees. He heaved.

'Oh,' said Larson, voice oily with mock sentiment. 'Look at that. He's picking up his boy.'

And the junior felt hands slip beneath him and grip him by the legs and neck. He felt held and realised he was still alive, technically. Still alive, just. As his senior pulled him up, the junior gasped. It wasn't pain; it was the bloom of colours all around, the dark room, the dying sun in the big empty window frame. He wanted to hold his head up strong and see it all proper, but the workings of his neck, his shoulders, his back, were slipping away. He wanted to see something of the world before he went, just once. Slowly, slowly, he felt himself rise in his senior's arms and even though time moved at half-speed, he still couldn't turn his face to look.

A year. That's all they gave him: a measly year. What a swindle. What a scam. He remembered the plant, that little star of light that appeared to him and was the first thing his body knew. Before that, the memory of his senior going to bed on some anonymous evening. He couldn't square it. At least for seniors, your life got bookended by birth and death. Before and after, just the same. The same nothing before as the same nothing after. But for him, he did live before life. So he knew it: he could not die.

At the apex of his being hauled up, the movement threw the junior into the air for perhaps a half second, but for him, he hung there indefinitely. He hung in the air, millimetres out of his senior's grip and felt suspended in space and time. This would be fine, to exist in this moment forever, as a location of perfect peace; like being in space, he thought, or even the womb. I'll let myself be here and watch the present moment forever and if it can go on like this, then I'll be happy.

He came down. He returned to the arms and felt the buckle in his senior's knees as they took his weight. Thank you, he thought. Thank you for this. He didn't feel guilt anymore. Giving his senior away had been survival and he had to survive to reach this moment. Just like the running boy, who needed to survive to deliver the boy to the man. We're all surviving, he knew, as a favour, as a gift. It had been easy to acknowledge the running boy and thank him, but it took so much longer to recognise himself. But he said it anyway: thank you.

Alastair didn't know if Larson would try to stop him as he made for the door. He heard the old man whistling as he readied himself for departure and wondered if there might be further tricks up his sleeve. Alastair moved with difficulty, the junior weighing heavy in his arms, and paused by the door to look back. The old man did not see him. Not at all.

By leaning his junior against the wood, he managed to slip his hand underneath for the handle. It opened up. Outside, the hallway lay in entire darkness. All lights were gone, both in the building and beyond. He stepped out and looked back one more time. Larson glanced up through the doorway and noticed him leaving. He hiked the bag onto his shoulder and waved cheerily to Alastair as the door swung shut.

Not long to go, the junior knew. His system, messed up as it was, provided him with some scant data. You're in a bad way, it suggested. Time is short and getting shorter. We're for the scrapyard soon. Okay, he replied, I understand. It didn't even give him the option of an out this time. His system was as knackered as he was. But in the main, he felt cheerful. He felt relaxed as his senior guided him out the doorway, calmed by the hall's darkness. At least they were alone now, to tackle whatever came next. But then, as they walked away, he felt a shadow. He sensed something, or smelt it, or his system detected it with the last remains of its power. An evil presence was coming close to them, near in the dark. A power that he recognised marched towards them and would do them harm if they encountered it.

With the last of his energy, he tried to speak. It was hard. Harder than anything he'd ever done. He needed to consciously move the parts of his body that created speech, piece by piece. He whispered it hoarsely. 'Hide.'

He couldn't tell where his senior was in relation to him, but he heard the response. 'What?'

Louder, harsher, urgent: '*Hide.*'

NINETEEN

The crowds in front of HQ, spread out across the plaza, were in a state of panic. Daylight was slipping away and most of them were tasked with making sure their superiors made it into the building in time for departure. All around, people hustled, they ran sometimes, they elbowed and shoved, ushering their bosses to where they needed to be. As such, hardly anyone noticed the strangers in their midst, because most here were strangers to each other. Hardly anyone noticed the crowd parting, until it came to them. A few smaller individuals, looking the other way, only perceived the large shadow fall across them at the same moment its owner pushed them aside. More and more stepped back to let the three strangers pass, an empty corridor forming on the plaza, and at its head, Spencer. Behind him, Hirst and Mandelson took the rear and together they made their way through the crowd.

They came to the building's front and stared inside.

'He's in here?' Mandelson asked.

Hirst cupped his eyes against the glass and said, 'That's what the drone said.'

His two deputies had spent the day avoiding Hirst's ire, barely talking, lying low until they heard word of the runaway junior's location. Now they were here, and it was good, Hirst thought. The junior, the senior and Larson, all in one pot.

'We're going to do it,' he said. 'This is it. This is where it all changes for us.'

'What's the plan?' asked Spencer.

'See the lad on desk?' said Hirst. 'We convince him of our good intentions.'

Spencer sighed. 'Right.'

When someone opened the door, they barged inside, drawing stares in their bizarre outfits. They didn't look back. They had no time for folk such as these. At the desk, the boy seemed busy. He spoke into a headset twenty-to-the-dozen, flicking away on his machine, ignoring them.

'Hello,' said Hirst.

The boy glanced up. 'Give me a second.'

'Alright,' said Hirst sweetly. He leaned over the counter and drummed his fingers, then went on one elbow. 'Spencer, my friend – have a word, would you?'

Spencer moved. They all felt it as his hand came down onto the reception desk. They saw cracks form in the artificial wood as he pushed, as he heaved himself up, his long coat trailing. He went across the desk and a great crash came as his boots met tile and Spencer looked back to see all eyes in the foyer turn to him.

He had his personal ways and means; it didn't matter now who witnessed them. The things he could do with the human body and his own two hands. The little areas of weakness that existed on the human head that only he knew about, only he knew how to exploit. You touch those in a certain way, it feels like your skull's about to cave. He laughed as he worked the kid's head, stifling most of the screams. All around him people watched, impotent. Once, folk like this, they'd looked down their noses at Spencer. These posh-cunts, they thought they knew how the world worked, thought they knew its rules and its limits. Did they fuck. They pushed their monocles up against a keyhole, peering into a room owned, managed and operated by Spencer himself. None of them would take him on. Just try it, he thought. In that moment, he knew he could subdue an entire building, entirely solo.

But he didn't want to go too far. It'd be a mistake to damage the lad; they needed his help to find the junior. He released his hands and the boy blinked. He coughed.

'It's a certain room,' Spencer repeated, putting his hands to work again. 'We know what it looks like, we just need to know where it is.'

He gave the boy the description again and the boy nodded, in between Spencer's clutching fingers. That felt good. You applied a certain pressure and got back a certain information. One in, one out. Still small fry though; just a kid really. He looked forward to the end of Hirst's daft plans. He looked forward to being back in the capital where he could find himself some real trouble.

'Get up then,' he said. 'Stand.'

The boy stood. He walked. Spencer eyed his colleagues, as in: was there ever any doubt?

The boy took them away from the foyer, loping forward, maybe a little concussed in the aftermath. He kept looking back and flinching. Spencer had to laugh. If he wanted the boy dead, the boy would be dead!

Mandelson thought she might spew, but she kept up with the others. She hurried into the building's depths, avoiding eye contact with those who gaped at them, but in her mind she was escaping. Spencer was nasty; Hirst was worse. At least with Spencer it was physical. He bullied and tortured, but there was no acid below the surface. With Hirst, a different story. He would see them all killed, as long as it meant his ends were met.

She understood it now, could see the inevitable endgame in his mad excitement.

She tailed them as the reception lad jogged through corridors, towards the place their drone reported. That boy from the camp; the very same. She didn't know what she'd do when they caught up with him. All she knew was she could not let it proceed.

They were so, so close. Hirst could smell it. All the elements of his life's work were coming together like some magic fucking constellation. These stars and moons across the vast galaxy, edging themselves into alignment, spelling out a future for him that was all gravy. Everything gravy. He clapped his hands as they followed the boy, swiping at his heels every so often, keeping him sharp.

'Hurry up,' he said. 'If it takes much longer, my friend here will finish the job.'

'We're near,' coughed the boy. You could already see fingermark bruises on the back of his neck.

The junior. The ghost. Larson. When everyone saw ... You were right, they would have to say. Well done, Hirst; you were right. Those stars and planets and galaxies in the blackened sky would shift themselves, crunching bit by bit into alignment, until they formed a starry alphabet, spelling out the words: Hirst was right.

He could feel the old days calling. But the proper old days, way back beyond his own shitty life messing round on the fens, scrabbling for lost fish in the bloated ex-farmlands – getting his head kicked in off the old man, fungal infections inside his breached welly boots, streaming music from the golden age in his single bed, and this was a Hirst in his twenties, mind. Hirst wasn't an original 97er, not by a long shot, but when he heard of them, the idea resonated with a tone that'd been ringing in his own mind for years and years. The proper old days, the last few puffs of the second millennium – why couldn't they go back? Back when times were good. Back when you could have a job of work and gangmasters couldn't bus in juniors and run you out of business. What a time, and he knew they could bring it back. Blair and Brown, Oasis, *Urban Hymns*, Swampy, the Dome – the majesty of the Dome! – *FHM* and *Loaded*, Zoe Ball and Sara Cox, France '98, Dolly the sheep, Guy Ritchie, all that mad art of beds and sharks, a pint of lager and a pack of fags, *Trainspotting*, Richard fucking Curtis films, 'Roll With It' versus 'Country House', proper seasons, the big snows, actual weather, Club 18-30, Ibiza, eccies, rollies, Hooch.

He knew his history well. He read diligently and knew the pathway history took from there to him. Back then, they had no Amazon, no Facebook, none of the other small fry that sprung up on the far side of the dividing 2000, and no field – barely any internet even! – and no flume and no stats and no, absolutely no, fucking *juniors*.

The boy brought them to the door they sought. Its insides were empty of seniors or juniors or Kim Larsons. Spencer felt a small flush of anger and he placed a few fingers across the lad's pressure points – below his thumb, right under the eye.

'I don't know!' the boy screamed. 'They're supposed to be here.'

'It's a shame for you that they're not,' said Spencer and he gave a squeeze. The boy went a wee touch spooky. A double chin formed in his neck and he turned green.

'Stop,' said Mandelson, not far from Spencer's elbow.

He turned to see her. She was staring at the boy and he noticed tears in her eyes. 'Why?' he asked.

'Just please stop,' she said. 'He's not done anything.'

'He's part of the system,' barked Hirst. 'Do as you will, Spencer.'

But Spencer did stop, out of respect for his colleague. He released the boy and told him that if he moved a muscle, he would find him. He would swell up and fill the entire building until he crushed the boy completely. 'Understand?'

Mandelson went in first, scanning the room for signs of life, and she prayed they would find nothing, that they would search the room, search the building, and come up short. Hirst would be furious, but she could deal with Hirst and his anger. If they found her old friend ... She didn't know if she could deal with that.

'Let's try in here,' said Hirst, eyeing a set of doors at the far end of the room.

All three of them approached and Hirst knocked. On the far side: a gasp of breath. The 97ers looked at each other. What was going on here, then?

Spencer tried the handle, but it was locked, and Mandelson felt relief. He shouted, 'Anyone in there?' and she was sure she heard shuffling footsteps inside.

'Try it again,' said Hirst, 'and give it some juice.'

Spencer tried again. Nothing. Mandelson watched him consider the handle, then take a few steps back. His boots shook the room as he heaved himself forward, putting his shoulder against the door, and it almost came off its hinges. Almost, but not quite.

Take that, she thought. Something you can't destroy.

Is this what it would come to? A piece of wood standing between Hirst and his destiny? Fuck that. Absolute fuck that.

'Again,' he commanded Spencer. 'And I mean *juice*.'

Again Spencer tried, charging against the door and

slamming into it and this time some definite sound inside: a muffled scream.

'Get inside there, you brute!' he said.

Again, another charge, another knockback.

'It's solid,' breathed Spencer, bending and clutching his knees. 'It's not giving.'

Hirst looked at Spencer, at the door, at Mandelson. He gave them all his eye, then he snapped round and marched across the room to stand in the corner, alone. He felt his body twitch in its fury, felt the inside of his skull strain with pure anger. He chewed at the skin of a knuckle. Motherfucker, he thought. Christ, he thought. If he spoke, the words would be high-pitched and tremulous.

I won't have this, he told the world. I will not suffer it. A single fucking door and we can't get through. No chance. No bloody way. He didn't have access to a God because he was a child of atheists, but he prayed to one anyway. He swore and threatened and sent up a jagged message of outrage to a Higher Power, full of bile and spite, and he felt spittle land on his chin as he raged.

And then the lights went out. A loud, low hum, and the lights died. He stared through the window at the corridor outside, at the boy, now doubly afraid. The lights were off, and he had no frame of reference for lights going out.

He turned to his colleagues and they too wore expressions of confusion.

'What's going on?' asked Mandelson. 'Where's the field?'

Hirst shook his head. 'I don't know.' But he did know. He knew his prayer had been answered, that the Higher Power above looked down on him with pride and had blessed its favourite son.

Spencer was confused right enough, but also excited. The lights were off. What did that mean? He knew that a person like him could profit in darkness. He did his best tricks in the shade of the Pit, chewing through rat lads with ease. He enjoyed the capital's streets in the night, outside of control, outside of others' vision.

As he pictured it, something pressed against his back. He turned and saw the door had come open. Must've been field-powered too. The door had come open and a face looked out from within. A woman's face, staring through the gap, and he said, 'Hello, hello, hello.'

Hirst rushed forward to grab the other side of the door and press the woman back inside, the three of them piling into the room after her.

Mandelson's Head Thing came rushing on powerful as they entered. Hirst motioned for her to guard the door, which she did, standing with her shoulders to it, surveying the room: twenty or thirty business-looking folk, some standing, some collapsed, all scared, and a couple of juniors in suits and shades lying out on the floor too.

One man leant over a collapsed junior, a colleague, feeling its chest and face, and he looked up at them and asked, 'What have you done? What's happened to the lights?'

'We've done fuck all to the lights,' announced Hirst grandly, marching through the people. 'Does someone want to explain how come you're all locked up in this room?'

Nothing was forthcoming. They were all too scared, Mandelson realised. Scared of the field dying and scared of them too. She noticed many faces stuck on Spencer, his head craned to account for the low roof.

'Alright,' said Hirst. 'Fair enough. Then does someone want to explain how come all these juniors are crashed out on the floor?'

'They collapsed when you switched off the lights,' said the

first man. 'You have to turn the field back on. The juniors need it, you maniacs.'

Hirst ignored the man and continued to step around the room with obvious pleasure. 'Alright,' he said. 'Fair enough. Then does someone want to let me know the whereabouts of a man and his junior, name of Alastair Buchanan?'

He didn't notice the woman's face, but Mandelson did. That first woman who'd stuck her head through the door and now stood cowering against the wall. At the name, she'd paled, and Mandelson saw. The woman placed a few fingers against her own neck and put her head down. When she brought it back up, their eyes met and Mandelson did a headshake to her: *don't.*

'No?' asked Hirst. 'Nothing?'

The woman stared back, questioning. Another movement of Mandelson's head: *really, don't.*

'That's a pity,' said Hirst. 'Because we know he's been here. We have it on good authority, and I really don't want to get my large companion here involved.'

Mandelson could see the woman want to speak and she tried to urge against it with her eyes, straining them open, turning down her lips. *Please, don't.*

But the woman spoke. She said, 'What about Kim Larson?'

Hirst paused, turned. You could see this mean light dance in his eyes. 'Excuse me?'

'I don't know this Alastair person, but I could take you to Larson. If that's any use?'

Hirst came to her briskly, looking like a hungry dog. He pushed past others, stepped over fallen juniors, and stood close to the woman. He said, 'That would be ideal.'

The Head Thing operated at a record high, all her body's blood rising to live behind her eyes, pulsing, and she thought her organs might fail at any moment.

They brought the woman out of the room and Mandelson

asked her name. It was Caitlin. All the others followed shyly, leaving behind the fallen juniors, and once they were in the hallway, everyone ran. They sprinted past Caitlin and the 97ers, along the darkened corridor, and she noticed the lad from reception running with them. So much fear there, and she felt every drop of it herself. So much fear, but none of it in this Caitlin. She led them on without looking back, walking with a purpose that Mandelson couldn't help but admire.

If Spencer thought HQ's outside had been manic, it was nothing to the building now. In the dark, people screamed; they called out names. The 97ers saw people hide under desks and no one was sure, but it seemed to be true: the field's dead. The field's been killed. He laughed as he walked. He loved seeing posh-cunts get their comeuppance. This is what you got for living so high and mighty and above the scum, looking down your noses, living the good life while it lasted. Well now you're down here with the rest of us, he thought. Now you're down here in the dark, with me. Already he could envision possibilities opening up before him, if it was true, if the field really was dead and wasn't just a local fuck-up. He pictured all sorts of avenues for profit and pleasure in the capital's blackened alleys, plenty of ways to settle old scores.

'Is it gone then?' he asked Hirst, his ex-boss.

'I don't know,' admitted Hirst. 'Maybe. This might be our time, son.'

'It might just be.'

The daft bastard seemed to be getting emotional, but then he'd been fighting this longer than Spencer. One of the old-timers, Hirst. If the field was dead, there'd be old-timers like Hirst up and down the land popping bottles right now.

'How much further?' Spencer asked the wee lassie guiding them.

'One minute,' she said. 'His office is round this corner.'

Hirst nodded to himself. Fine, he thought. It didn't matter that his best-laid plans had drifted away, that they'd lost the junior, the ghosts. All that was a crock of shite anyway, because when it came down to it, direct action was best. They would kill Larson, simple as that. Nice and easy, seal that deal and welcome the return of their golden years.

'Here we go,' said the woman as they turned into the final corridor. A row of doors ran along the side, with a single exit at the corridor's end. 'That's him in there.'

He didn't meet her eye, but he clapped her on the shoulder. 'Well done, Caitlin,' he said. 'You'll be remembered in the new age.'

They walked on, leaving the woman there, but as they passed one of the doorways, Spencer halted. His big giant back twitched. 'Did you see that?'

'What?' asked Hirst.

'That door moved,' Spencer said, 'I think.'

'Who gives a monkey's if it moved?' Hirst snapped. 'Keep going.'

And the big shoulders shrugged and they kept going, just as he said. There was so much strength in Hirst now, so much certainty. He spoke and the world responded. He asked for a favour and the Power above reached down to pluck out the lights.

Except, where was Mandelson?

Mandelson's lamp shone brightly. Despite the darkness, despite the lack of field, the lack of light, the whole corridor was shrill with the brightness of her invisible lamp. It told her to continue. It made calculations for her and said: you've come this far, so continue. It's safer with them, it's safer to be with those you know, so continue.

But she felt herself stuck to the spot, rooted beside this

Caitlin, and she would not take a further step. For once, for the first time in years, she used her own mind and said: no. I will not. I won't allow it.

Hirst turned. Mandelson was standing back there, with the lass.

'Come on,' he said. 'We're doing this.'

'I'm not going,' she said.

'Very funny, Mandelson. Get a move on.'

She shook her head. 'I'm really not,' she said. 'I'm not going in there.'

'Go and get her, Spencer,' he commanded. 'No soldier left behind, even if she has gone nuts.'

He saw her stiffen a little, but she would be fine. In the new age, they'd probably get married, he realised; him and Mandelson, together forever.

'Go and get her,' he said.

'Nah,' said Spencer simply. 'Not if she doesn't want to.'

'Well then,' he said.

He wondered about the possibilities of his abilities then, about what he could achieve if he wanted to. Could he summon the Higher Power's hand from out of the sky and use it to move Mandelson forward? He could stamp and scream and the universe would align itself just so, turning its weight to his desire, but instead, he surprised himself with his own magnanimity. He said, 'I've not got time for this. We'll deal with you later.'

Together, him and Spencer went forward. They came to the door. 'Ready, son?' he asked.

Spencer smiled. 'I am.'

'You'll do it, will you? Go all the way?'

'I will.'

'Right.'

He opened up.

*

Spencer's instincts kicked in as soon as they entered. His senses flew round the office, noting doorways and windows and lives. He saw a couple of doors leading out, this huge window showing the water and all these boats streaming across it, and a couple of juniors on the floor, making short gasping sounds where they lay. The only true living, breathing human in there was a little old bloke behind the desk, up to his elbow in a bag. He didn't look up, this old man, but said, 'Back again?'

Him and Hirst gave each other a quizzical look.

Hirst spoke first. He said, 'We're here to perform a citizen's arrest.'

The old man looked up. Spencer recognised him; you couldn't *not* know this face. 'Who the fuck are you?'

Hirst approached the desk slowly. 'We're representatives of a certain group,' he explained. 'We're tasked with bringing you to justice.'

Larson peered at them. 'I really am a cretin-magnet tonight.'

'We're here to let you answer for your crimes,' Hirst said. 'We want to give you a fair trial.'

The old man continued messing with his bag. 'You're not the first person to call me a criminal tonight,' he said.

'We charge you,' announced Hirst, 'with destroying the balance of this world. We charge you with corrupting and despoiling a way of life.'

Something clicked inside Larson's face. He said, 'I'm sorry gentlemen, but you're a little late. You see those boats? I'm due on one.'

Hirst glanced up at Spencer and gave him a look. It was one that meant: *be ready.*

'You have to answer to the people,' said Hirst. 'You have to face the justice that men like you have been running from forever.' Spencer recognised the tone in that voice. It was the one he used on new recruits. 'The nineties will never die,' Hirst added.

'I'm afraid to say,' said Larson, 'that I don't have to do anything I don't want to.' He zipped his bag closed and hiked it
onto his shoulder. 'Let me show you something. It'll help you
make sense of this.'

He walked out from behind the desk.

'Stop right there,' said Hirst.

'Please. Just a second.'

'Get him,' Hirst hissed. 'Fucking get him.'

Spencer sprung into action. He felt himself at the end of a
journey with only one small task to complete before his return
home. Deal with this single old man, then back to the capital.
Shrug off Hirst, say cheerio to Mandelson and the others, then
cash in the chips he'd spent so long accumulating.

'You'll want to see this,' said Larson, and he opened up one of
the doorways before Spencer could get to him. He spoke some
words in an unknown language, calling into this other room.
Spencer stopped there in his tracks.

An animal slunk out through the doorway, passing by
Larson, reaching up to nearly his chest. It was pure black, utter
dark: a hole in the room that stalked towards them.

Hirst felt something slip away from him. He felt a certain
colour leave his system as the monster slunk into the room. It
padded across the floor, raising its muzzle to sniff at the air.
Some kind of cat; some kind of big tiger-thing, but bald, earless,
tailless, utterly black.

'What is it?' he asked, quietly.

Larson watched the animal with a slight smile. 'It's an invention,' he said.

'Spencer,' whispered Hirst. '*What is it?*'

The big man didn't reply. Like Hirst, he was gazing intently
at the animal, though it didn't look like fear in him.

'Spencer,' he said. 'Do something.'

The animal walked lazily. Its shoulders rolled as it went, its mouth opening to pant. You could see a tongue and the ends of fangs.

'What is it?' he said again. 'What is it?'

He backed away as slowly as he could, never turning his face away. He realised now that it was him the monster observed, him that it approached. Its eyes were flat on its face and Hirst remembered from his schooling what that suggested. A predator. There was an almost-humanness to those eyes; this unnerved him the most.

'Call it off,' he said. 'Larson. Call it off!'

But Larson didn't listen. He was already skirting the edge of the room and making for the exit.

It was close now, the monster. Close enough to lunge. It kept pace with Hirst as he backed away, until he felt a wall at his back. Where was Spencer? Why did he just watch this occur?

'Spencer,' he said. 'I mean it, son. I mean it.'

But there was no one to help. He was alone now; one man in the world. They didn't understand, not any of them. None of the freaks back in Summerfield knew how much love he'd felt for each and every one of them. Why else would he have done it all? Why else would he have lived this life? He lived it for his sons and daughters; for a better world.

In the end, it didn't even pounce. It didn't judge him worthy. Instead, it raised itself on hind legs and pinned him against the wall with heavy paws. It tickled, when the muzzle brushed his neck. He almost laughed. Then he felt teeth rest against his skin, just for a second.

None of them knew. Not one. What he would've sacrificed, just to give his children what he never owned.

He felt the teeth against his skin, then they came in.

*

A burst of darkness flew out from Hirst's neck and spattered the wall above him, spraying like a wing. The animal held his throat for a few moments, then lowered itself. It placed him down gently and didn't do any further damage, content to lap at the wound.

Spencer listened to the rasp of its tongue, the dry slick as it worried Hirst's exploded gullet. His grandad kept cats when Spencer was wee and he remembered the roughness of the kittens' tongues, tasting his offered hand and fingers. If he wanted to, he could slip away. He could edge round the room like Larson and be gone and probably the animal wouldn't notice. In the new dark, he could vanish. Looking into that future, he saw himself walking easily across the land, heading for the capital, watching it from the outer hills before descending. But for now, that option looked less attractive. The city, from this perspective, looked like a waste of his precious time. All the fighting and pit matches and the rat lads, they could wait. He saw he'd been spinning wheels his whole life, looking for something that now, in this room, he had found.

A true opponent.

He took a step nearer and the animal's head turned. Around its mouth the skin shone, its teeth stained by Hirst's blood. Inside its eyes was something both ancient and brand new. He took another step towards it and it moved a paw round to face him, leaning its weight forward. If he listened hard enough, he could almost hear the sound of gravel crunching beneath its paws. Huh, he thought, just the same.

Spencer hunched himself over. He squared his shoulders, ground his heels down into the floor. Christ, he felt big. Never bigger. He pushed a breath out through his nostrils. Everything inside felt balanced and tight. As he breathed, he swelled up. The surface of his scalp expanded outwards and might even brush the ceiling if he allowed it enough give.

'Hello,' he said.

The animal crept forward, up now and walking. It stayed low, its chin barely off the ground. Its rear hips swayed and Spencer knew he was inside a dance from before his own time, before modernity, before speech. Finally, he had a match he'd been built for, he'd trained for, lived for. Survival didn't matter; nothing mattered except the fight.

In a flurry, the darkness moved and leapt towards him and he was ready, braced, hungry. He felt muscles in his grip, felt flesh give way beneath his hands. Fangs and claws slashed, but he was quick. They smashed around the room, the two of them tight together, hugging. Spencer used his mouth too. He bit and tore and who knew which of them the noises came from – the screaming and yowling and barks.

In time, he lost sense of himself. Lost sense of all senses. All he knew was exertion and pressure and the need to destroy whatever he might touch.

TWENTY

Alastair waited until the heavy footsteps passed and he heard a door open and close; then he emerged. He strained under the junior's weight but carried on, out into the corridor, thinking only of getting the junior to a place of safety, somewhere where the field still ran. He looked down at his face, at his own face, the eyes closed, the mouth just open. He looked down and nearly ran into the people stood at the far end.

'Sorry,' he said, pushing by the two women.

He was a few steps away when one of them said, 'Al?'

He turned and almost let himself slip. Caitlin. She was there.

'What's going on, Al?' she asked.

'He's dying,' he said. 'It's the field. I need to get help.'

They went with him, Caitlin and this other woman; a colleague, he guessed.

'People were looking for you,' said Caitlin. 'I took them to Larson's office instead.'

He nodded, unable to focus. 'Okay.'

He didn't believe the field would be gone outright. No way. Larson wouldn't do it. It might just be this building. Outside, the field would still run, and if he could get the junior inside it, he would be safe. The office was largely empty, except for the occasional dying junior, slumped at a desk or sprawled by a wall. All the seniors were gone. The ship was truly abandoned.

They descended a back staircase, carefully edging down the steps in the dark, and Alastair said, 'Check your mobile.'

Caitlin reported everything was gone: data, power, all dead.

'Outside will be safe,' he said. 'They'll have it outside.'

He looked at the other women, at Caitlin's colleague, and felt a shock of recognition: a person he knew. But from where? In the mobile's waning light, she glared back at him. He couldn't think.

'Keep going,' he said. 'We're nearly there. Just keep going.'

They came to the building's vast foyer, deserted now, and from here they could look to the plaza. When he saw it, Alastair nearly fell from shock. Even outside, the field was gone. Up the slight hill, a tram sat empty. All over, cars and limos with their doors open, no lights, no engines. On the ground, juniors. He couldn't even speak to swear or cry. He couldn't process it, didn't know how to understand a landscape without the field, without the hum of electricity and data enriching everything inside.

'It's gone,' said Caitlin. 'It's really gone.'

Alastair felt his fingers weaken, so he yanked the junior up, closer to his chest. Inside the body, he could hear something whirr. The eyes came open for a second and he saw the pupils widen, then narrow.

'Where's the canteen?' he asked.

'What?'

'The canteen. Food, water?'

Caitlin pointed to the doors on the far end of the foyer. 'In there, but Alastair, he can't . . .'

He took off at a jog, hearing his shoes slap on the tiles, kicking aside the hands and feet of juniors lying below. He pushed through the double doors and into the empty canteen; loads of tables with chairs upended beside them, fridges with the sachets inside, unlit.

'Stay with me,' he said. 'Just a minute more. A wee minute.'

He found a table nearly free of debris and laid out his junior, then ran for sustenance.

The lights and stars were gone now. All the junior saw as he blinked was a creamy roof, some strip lights, a familiar face coming and going. Around his vision, a deeper dark formed, a bruising that crept inwards, bit by bit. His sight narrowed and soon it was like looking into a tunnel, with his senior there at the far end. He heard words but his system couldn't process them. No energy for language. Something pulled at his lips and tugged them open. There was wetness on his teeth, moisture pooling under his gums. There was nowhere for it to go, but he appreciated it all the same. It felt good to be looked after, as his vision narrowed and he sunk deeper into this well.

Soon, he was at the bottom, right at its base, looking up to the sky through an aperture the width of a coin. One pale moon in his personal night sky. Its warmth lay across the skin of his face and he closed his eyes to enjoy it. The disc remained, despite his eyelids. It tightened further and became a star, one tiny speck of light that moved with him. There was no panic here, no grief. One star shone for him, offering protection.

Alastair held the junior's head up off the table, tilting it at the neck, and fed water to its lips. Drink, he thought. Just take a drink. If the junior could do it, could change his system in some way, the water would be as good as any power off the field. It didn't matter, because they were here, together, close, and hadn't they connected themselves before? Hadn't they spoke across distance?

'Drink it,' he said.

The water spilled out the corners of the junior's mouth.

'Please,' he said. 'You have to drink. You have to get better. I'm going to look after you.'

The water wasn't going anywhere. It didn't seem to cause him any discomfort, but he couldn't swallow. Alastair let the junior's head down to the table and realised he was cold.

He felt himself flung through air and land and wind. Later, he felt himself shrink down to a unit measuring *one*.

One human, one thought, one star.

And gone.

Caitlin and the stranger were near him and Caitlin was crying. She said, 'I didn't know it would be like this. It's you, isn't it? It's you.'

She seemed to feel the need to arrange the body, straightening up the limbs, palming down the shirt and jeans. She combed his hair with her fingers and looked between the two of them. She said, 'I told you not to get him. I said, didn't I?'

Looking down on his own body, he felt nothing but gratitude.

Thank you, he thought. Thank you for this. He didn't feel guilt anymore. Leaving the junior behind, back in the capital: pure survival, pure instinct, and he had to survive to reach this moment. Just like the running boy, who needed to survive to deliver the boy to the man. We're all surviving as a favour, as a gift. It had been easy to acknowledge the running boy and thank him, but it took so much longer to recognise himself. But he said it anyway.

He said, 'Thank you.'

Caitlin didn't want to leave the junior behind. 'But it's you,' she said. 'It's you.'

He shook his head; there was nothing of the junior remaining. They left him laid on the table, among others like him.

*

323

Outside, they were not alone. Little bands huddled together here and there, all of them looking wrecked, haunted. On the ground were many juniors, now fully departed.

'Look,' said the stranger. She pointed up at a nearby hillside.

Alastair moved aside to see. Near the top of the hill, some small lights were showing, moving as if swung by human arms. They headed towards them, stepping off the plaza and onto manicured grass. They found footprints, which they followed, and others from the building came up alongside them.

'Look at the sky,' said Caitlin.

She was right. When he craned his neck, Alastair saw such clusters of stars, things he'd never known. He'd never been in the true night dark, and now he saw milk spattered across the sky. He saw light like dust suspended above.

'I know,' he replied. 'I see.'

It took them ten minutes to clamber up, helping each other over humps in the land, helping other escapees as they came closer. They kept going, up and up, climbing higher, jumping onto rocks and across small ravines. At the top, there were many others, perhaps everyone from inside. The lights they used came from the last of the power inside their mobiles. They waved them back and forth as some kind of signal.

'What's going on?' asked Caitlin, speaking to someone Alastair guessed she knew.

This man spoke back. 'It's for help,' he said. 'We need assistance.' He waved his arms back and forth, the screen's light leaving a trace behind it as he swung.

Who did he think might be out there, looking back?

The three of them moved across the crowded hilltop, dodging arms as they lurched back and forth. They kept close to each other and Alastair stole glances at this stranger, who he felt sure he knew. She bobbed around in his memories like a friend from school.

'Over there,' he heard someone shout. 'Smoke!'

They were now high enough to look out across the top of the building, to the ocean beyond. Nothing out there except perhaps St Kilda and the lonely structure that now released a plume of smoke, a ribbon of it streaming from one lanky tower.

They paused to watch. The smoke grew stronger, big clouds bursting from the structure, banks of it rising from the land below. Something fell away, a pillar or scaffold of some kind. It fell away, down into the mushrooming whiteness beneath. He thought, they've knackered it. Something's gone wrong with the launch and it's broken down. That would be a consolation, to sit here and watch them burn up, out there above the ocean. The smoke continued to billow though, expanding in all directions, and a deep orange glow lit it up from inside. He saw an egg poaching in air. He saw flashes of fire.

But then, a nub poked through the top; a little white cap. A slim needle broke free, piercing the darkness, lifting itself up. Half of it was white, the other pure fire, wavering at the edges. Around the rocket's nose, pale light formed a ring. It forged a pathway upwards, impossibly straight and true. A direct line to the heavens, and it looked as though the machine was pushed upwards by its burning tail, rather than the other way round. It looked as though the fire below was active, a separate energy that hoisted the rocket up. They watched it ascend, all their necks creeping back to see it rise and rise and rise and grow smaller and skinnier and more like a sea creature streaming through water; some kind of octopus or jellyfish with all its toxic limbs flying out behind. Gradually, it began to arc. Its nose edged leftward and the white plume hooked itself round, doglegging at the edge of the atmosphere. Soon, it blinked away.

'I can't believe they did it,' said Caitlin quietly.

'The field's dead,' said Alastair. 'He shut it off before he went.' He saw Caitlin's face darken. 'Everything's done. It's all finished.' She laughed as she spoke, shaking her head, still watching the empty sky.

The stranger stood a few feet away from them. She didn't keep her eye on the sky. Instead, she watched the building below them. He could see her brow furrow as she stared downward.

He asked her simply, 'Who are you?'

She looked a little surprised. 'Who am I?'

'Aye. I'm sure I know you. You're not from down there, are you?'

Caitlin interjected. 'She was with them, the nutters.'

The stranger sniffed. 'Aye,' she said. 'I was with them. We took your junior, before.'

'Really?' said Alastair.

She nodded. 'Yep. We tricked him into coming with us. We were going to wipe him.'

Alastair surprised himself by how little anger he felt towards this woman. The actions she spoke about felt like they came from another life, from out of a stream he once saw.

'I know *you*, though,' said the stranger.

'Me?' said Alastair.

'Aye. I knew you as soon as we got your junior. I recognised the face, even though it was so long ago. I couldn't stick with them, cause I knew you from a long time back.'

He squinted at her, making out her features in the mobile lights. Something clicked. Picturing the hair shorter, the face less gaunt, something clicked. 'The camp,' he said.

In the camp, the running boy was near knackered. His knees met in the middle when they knocked, his eyes gave everyone the horrors. They could get no sound out of him, nothing except heavy breaths and a sort of growling. A few there were too spooked to approach, watching him from the edge of the place, thinking him an omen of something ill. He arrived early

326

in the morning, running straight into the area they used for cooking, where the handful of Honey Bee peacekeepers administered first aid and distributed rations. He kept running when he arrived, jogging round the open area, round the makeshift tents, through the hands of those trying to stop him. When they caught him and laid him down, his legs kept moving, kept jerking at the hip.

In the end, it was the young ones who looked out for him, the others who made their way to the safety of camp solo. Someone who paddled, someone who rode horses and someone who fought their way inside. She shared a tent with the running boy, let him have the sleeping bag on the first night, the only night, because she didn't need it really; even out there on the coast, considerable heat still radiated from the inner peninsula. He slept fitfully, jerking awake near constantly, shouting and crying in his sleep. She watched him. She soothed him when he needed it. They were only bairns, the two of them, but she watched him and soothed him when required. Later, he seemed better. He spoke for the first time and asked where he was, what was happening. She explained what she knew from the peacekeepers, that hovercrafts across the water were being arranged. There were other camps dotted along the south coast of the land and, across in Edinburgh, people were waiting for them.

He nodded as she spoke, then told her his family were dead. Crushed dead under their home. Same for her, she explained. Everyone she knew was gone. They didn't know how to say it except baldly like that. It felt good to keep it open and raw. They pushed fingertips into their wounds.

He wasn't there long, the running boy. The hovercrafts came roaring through the surf, dozens and dozens of them, beaching themselves on the sand below the camp. Pure hysteria after that, pure madness. Everyone shouting and running, despite what the peacekeepers said; folk helping what remained of their families, others sticking with the new ones made in camp. One baby cried out. One old man died in his tent. Everyone else stampeded across the beach, lights from the peacekeepers' helmets guiding the way, and in the scrum they lost each other, the running boy and his friend. They were hoisted onto different crafts and didn't know if the other was searching.

Even from the beach, you could see the lights of the capital beckoning. The Firth sprayed them as they drove through it, but the lights stayed on, the dark hull of Arthur's Seat rising above.

'You were there,' he said. 'You looked after me in the camp.'

'I did,' she said.

He turned to Caitlin. 'Back after the disaster. Mind I told you? I was in this camp for a night before we came across.'

Caitlin said she remembered. Caitlin said she remembered him saying about the lassie that looked after him.

'Well . . .' he said, but didn't know what came after.

'Well,' she agreed.

'What was your name?' he asked.

She took a while to answer. 'My name was Maya.'

They stayed up on the hill for a while, waiting to see if anything further would happen with the rocket, whether it would fall back out the sky if they gave it enough time. They waited a while, then descended away from HQ. Others stayed behind, still signalling with their mobiles, asking for something from the empty night sky.

Looking back on this first journey months later, Alastair found it strange they never even discussed Maya coming with them. They didn't discuss with one another that they'd stick together either. They simply came down from the hill and went east, aiming for Lochmaddy, rarely speaking, and Alastair thought they must've been too shell-shocked to process everything they'd seen. Sometimes they came across others running from HQ. Sometimes Caitlin recognised them and similar conversations took place.

'Can you believe it? The field went down at work.'

'It'll be fine further east, though.'

'It was probably something to do with the launch. The launch probably messed things up.'

Alastair kept quiet in these conversations. He didn't feel like squashing their hopes, and besides, they might even be right. He listened to their theories and predictions, these seniors trudging through the hills and said, 'Aye, maybe. Maybe that's true.'

Except he couldn't call them seniors anymore, could he? If he was right and the field really had gone, then there would be no need for a word like *senior* anymore. That would be defining yourself against what you weren't, when the thing you weren't no longer existed. He wasn't a senior if he didn't have his junior. These were humans he spoke to, nothing more or less.

They saw the towers of Lochmaddy from on high and descended into its outer limits. Here, more people walked in the road. The doors of people's homes hung open, their innards shadowed. Trams sat empty, stuck between stations. More than once, they came across someone carrying a junior in their arms, just as Alastair had done. People were shocked, appalled. They said, 'This is an outrage what's been done to us. We were promised a lifetime guarantee.'

Already fires broke out in certain places, some buildings releasing smoke and rising ash. Caitlin led them down a busy street and said this took them towards the centre of town. Buildings surged in height, but everything remained dead, dark, powerless. On the wide boulevards of the city proper, so many people milled around. A huge volume of chatter and shouting and far-off yells. He couldn't help but remember that first morning after the disaster, that first hectic morning. The strangeness of seeing a man walk on tarmac without his shoes, some folk topless and bleeding and speaking strange words.

There was no field there, just as he suspected. There would be no field anywhere on the planet, not now. He knew that across the world it would be the same story repeated in cities and villages and towns: people walking out of their homes to see what had happened, people walking in the street, people moving in bands. When something went wrong, you needed to go out in the road; that was universal. Your home no longer felt like a protection to you when power went, when data went, when structure went. You needed to be close to others in the same position, to walk with them and ask: what happened?

'This is pointless,' said Caitlin. 'There's nothing here.'

She took them to the same hotel she'd been in, out of habit. They needed a place to sleep for what remained of the night.

Inside, they found more of the same. No sign of the owner and most rooms standing empty, some with juniors lying in the beds. They managed to find a handful near to each other that weren't badly spoiled. All three were dead on their feet, sleeping where they stood. Maya went into one of the rooms and closed the door. He wondered if she would be there in the morning, or if she'd run.

Him and Caitlin said goodnight to each other. They didn't share a room and he didn't ask either.

In the bed, he prayed for sleep, but it failed to arrive. He lay in one position for hours with his eyes closed and, towards the end, knew the light of morning was on the other side of his lids. Despite this, he didn't get up. He lay still and there were too many thoughts to fully slip away. He thought about all the things that would be gone now. He thought about the things he'd wanted. All the viewing screens and mobiles and computers would be gone. All the streams he'd watched, gone. What would power the flume and the trams and the Step-Stone lorries? Back in the day, you plugged something into a wall and that connected it to cables inside the wall which connected it to other cables running through the land and air. The cables fed backwards into ... what? Into the earth, somehow?

He got up. He tried to wash. Cold water trickled from the showerhead, so he made do. He put his head under and it hurt the top of his skull, but he made do. He got dressed into his dirty clothes and it felt sort of disgusting and they smelled weird, but he made do. He found a complimentary tube of toothpaste but no brush, so he made do, scraping at his teeth with a fingernail, swilling water round his mouth.

Caitlin and Maya were downstairs already, sitting together in the big breakfast room. Yesterday's pastries were piled up on the table, a huge spread of croissants and danishes all shiny and sugared. They drank cold water from jugs and ate the sweets until they felt sickened.

'Was there anything else around?' he asked.

'We went down to the kitchens,' said Caitlin.

'There was bread and stuff,' said Maya. 'And tins. We should take as much as we can carry.'

Caitlin and Alastair both nodded. Again, down the line, he noticed that they never once discussed their plans in those initial days. They seemed to cooperate as a necessity, pulling together resources for survival, knowing everything they needed.

'We should get going soon,' said Caitlin. 'Let's go down the kitchens now and stock up.'

They did just that. Alastair remembered a left-behind suitcase in a nearby corridor which they filled with tins of chickpeas, kidney beans, Heinz.

'What about water?' he asked.

They wouldn't be able to carry much of it, but once they got past the terraformed west there would be burns and lochs to use. A few big jugs were enough for now, Maya thought.

So they were stocked up, full of pastry, high on sugar, scared and alone.

They left town in much the same way they found it, although it was quieter in the morning. He guessed folk must've returned to their homes when no solution presented itself through the night. He pictured them huddled in their beds, the food spoiling in their kitchens as yet another sunrise arrived. How would they spend this first day, he wondered. How would they find a way to live?

Maya said it would be best to avoid the roads for now, and they trusted her, respecting the time she'd spent living in her cell. They weren't as tough as her and were happy to accept her prediction. 'People might be watching the roads,' she said. 'They might rob us, or worse.' Alastair knew that in times of trouble, there were those that saw chaos as an opportunity.

They left the town behind and soon found themselves walking through the artificial countryside stretching between old Uist and old Skye. It was all arable, all fields. You could walk this land and not realise the change in the air. The only difference they noticed came at farm buildings, where the field bulbs were no longer lit. In some places, animals stood out in the fields, horses and llamas and also long-haired show pigs in sheds. The animals watched them passing with friendly eyes and he thought that soon they would break down their fencing and run free.

After a few hours, they came across a couple walking in the opposite direction, a man and woman in middle age, wearing hiking gear. They seemed quite chipper and waved as they approached. The woman seemed to notice something off in Alastair and the others, and asked 'Everything alright?' as they passed. She ogled the heavy jugs of water that he carried.

They'd been out in the wilds overnight and didn't know. They probably thought their mobiles were faulty and were looking forward to getting home and having them sorted.

He couldn't think of what to say, so nodded to them and smiled right back.

When it got dark, they camped out beside a river on a bank of spongy grass. They didn't need cover because it didn't get cold at nights, not really. Alastair ate gritty kidney beans straight out the tin, scooping them up along with their red juice.

'That stuff won't last us long,' said Maya. 'We'll need to be careful.'

'I know,' he said.

Again, they marvelled at the stars. He couldn't believe how bonkers they were. You heard about the old times on streams, or saw them in photos and paintings at Caitlin's work. Cold winters with snow on the land, ancient sandy beaches that grew up organically from erosion or whatever. Plus night skies.

Maya fell asleep first, huddled in the grass a little way off from them.

He asked Caitlin, 'What'll happen, do you think?'

She shook her head, looking up. 'I don't know, Al. I don't know.'

'We'll try for the city, I suppose,' he said. 'See how the flat's doing?'

'Maybe,' she said.

'I don't mean like—'

'I know what you meant.'

Alastair stayed up for a long time after Caitlin nodded off. He lay on his back and wondered what might have happened to his old man, in the moment the field went. He wondered where that mind went to, if his data still existed. Could it have vanished into the air, or did it reside somewhere else?

He pictured the particles of his father thrown out across the ocean, bits of him blown on the wind and perhaps carried to the launch site, perhaps sucked into the workings of the rocket engines, settling on machinery and in combustible places. He pictured the engines roaring into life, a riot of fire and energy and heat, with pieces of his old man blasted into something new. The dust settled onto the rocket's sheet metal sides, collected in tight corners, and went upwards with it, pushed beyond gravity into the empty space beyond. His father clung to the rocket like skin and went with it.

After touchdown, the pieces of his father would shed themselves, would sprinkle themselves here and there on the surface of whatever place they found, mingling with unknown chemicals, pollinating alien fruit.

TWENTY-ONE

It turned out the hardest thing to lay your hands on was sun cream. In all the shops, Maya rushed to the cosmetic shelves and found them swiped clean, just hair dyes and deodorants remaining. Without protection, the three of them kept to the shadows and only walked when the sun was cool. In the heat of day, they sheltered inside abandoned buildings, supping on loch water and eating from tins. Their pace picked up after they found an SPF cache in one empty farmhouse near Mallaig, but the year was progressing anyway, the sun losing its ferocity.

They walked a few hours in the morning, a few in the afternoon, but they didn't rush it. If they went too fast and became hungry or thirsty, resources would soon run out. Sometimes they slept outside, sometimes they entered properties with open doors. They were constantly falling into step with other walkers, other travellers, who discussed their own routes and plans. Nearly everyone headed for the cities, for Glasgow and Edinburgh, where they were convinced the field still held out, thinking of its loss as a rural phenomenon.

Maya agreed with them; she couldn't bear to argue.

In the night, she grew panicky. She sometimes struggled to sleep in the open and felt sure that enemies were closing in. Her heart raced and she would walk around whatever place they were in, keeping her head in one piece. In other people's homes, she looked at the dead viewing screens and the empty cupboards. During her shallow sleeps, she experienced nightmares of Hirst and Spencer, pursuing her across the land, and you didn't need a psychologist to tell you what that represented, did you?

She told herself to keep it together. Keep going. She mustn't think about the future, or the past. Now, these were merely distractions.

A few weeks in and they found themselves skirting the edges of the disaster's violence. They came across a field which remained brown and barren, and they looked out across the ruined earth there, smoke climbing from the ash. You got this sickness in your stomach. You knew you looked at something wrong, something unnatural. But they kept on, walking alongside the destruction's high-water mark. There were less people here, less places to sleep at night, but they knew it guided them south.

Bizarre rainstorms came upon them in this zone. One minute they'd be trudging along beneath a midday sun, next they'd spy a bank of black clouds on their tail. Rain fell hot against their necks and Maya would get dribbles down her collar. Once, she led them beneath a blackened tree. It didn't have leaves, but its thick branches provided shelter and they took the opportunity to share some chocolate from Caitlin's bag.

The rain continued and after a few moments, Maya noticed something on the horizon. Standing, watching them, were a pair of dogs. They were dark and shaggy, with open mouths. The hairs on her neck stiffened and, to her shame, her first thought was to run. She wanted to throw down her chocolate and take off, leaving Alastair and Caitlin behind. But she didn't. She kept watch on the dogs until one of them lay down in the ashes. The other kept standing, bringing its head low to the ground, taking in their scent.

'Look,' she said.

The others turned to see what she pointed at.

'It's dogs,' said Alastair, with a tremble in his throat.

When the rain stopped, they continued their walking and the dogs followed. As they went on, she became aware of the animals coming closer, bringing up their pace, and soon they were travelling abreast of them, a few metres uphill. They didn't look towards the humans, but when the humans stopped, so did the dogs. That night, she found some tinfoil-sealed pork-approximate and brought it over, laying it on the ground and stepping back. They watched her for a moment, then approached, sniffing round the pink meat before devouring it. When their meal was finished, the dogs came over to the place where Caitlin and Alastair sat. Maya thought they might be of the same litter; the pair were nearly identical and wore proper collars. Caitlin held out her fingers to be sniffed and licked and, after a while, the dogs fell asleep inside their camp. Later, Caitlin drew pictures of them in the little notebook she carried with her.

Maya felt better with them there. She couldn't explain it to herself. By rights, she should've been terrified, but it felt good to have them curled up nearby when she bedded down. They stayed close for the journey, waking whenever the sun rose, at the same time as the humans. They drank water from the ground and would sometimes stiffen, rushing out into high grasses to bring back squealing rabbits. You heard tiny bones snapping as the dogs crunched them down, guts and all. Eventually, they felt relaxed enough to play and Alastair would torment them with his hands, pushing their mouths away and roughing them up. He too spoke of having lost his long-term fear.

*

Weeks later, at the edge of the city, their plans changed. They came across a band of people emerging from the Edinburgh suburbs, bruised and bloodied, one of them carried upon a makeshift stretcher. They calmed the dogs and shared food with the city people, sitting on bonnets in a car park.

'It's a wreck in there,' one of the strangers said. 'It's gone to hell. Everyone's fighting. Everyone's killing each other, all the time.'

They spoke of the giant man running things, stockpiling resources, and all the wee bams who did his bidding. They spoke of the torched buildings, of the terror, of the violence. Maya listened to the descriptions of the city's master, and she knew. She didn't need it explained to her, where Spencer had washed up. The guy on the stretcher said he'd been forced to fight another man and ended up with his leg all busted. They said: don't go in. Keep out if you can avoid it. The strangers were hoping to reach Falkirk, if they could get the broken man up and walking soon.

They left the strangers behind and edged round the city limits, agreeing to wait and see, check whatever signs presented themselves. That night they set up in an empty bungalow and were awakened by roars and bellows from the north. They saw the lower skies lit up red from fires within the city. In the middle of the night, Maya heard loud footsteps and she snuck to a front window. She saw a band of people march through the street, banging drums, playing on whistles, wearing masks. At the head of the parade stumbled a person with their hands tied; when he slowed, those at the front kicked out, forcing him onwards.

In the morning, they agreed: Edinburgh was done.

A few days later, they crossed a golf course as the light was dying. Its greens were overgrown, while the roughs sprung up like miniature forests. Caitlin knew a place nearby, remembered it from her childhood.

'There's no signs,' she said. 'But it's in the woods someplace.'

Nearly full dark when they found it, hidden among trees to the east of the course. First, an ancient-looking bridge, nearly falling into the burn below. Proper medieval, but still standing. They crossed over and found the castle ruins up a short path. Crumbling stone and weird windows and arches were all that remained. Caitlin urged them on. There was an underground bit somewhere close by, the perfect place to set up camp for the night.

They passed under a wall and went downhill. Among high grasses, the dogs found an entrance to the castle's vaults: a tunnel they all crept through, into the vaulted basement that felt like something right out of a historical stream. You could imagine kings doing banquets down there.

'I remember it,' said Caitlin. 'It's all the same.'

They set up camp right there in the cellar, moonlight creeping in through a high window. On the walls, people had scratched graffiti: *SATAN LIVES* and *THE BIG ONE IS NIGH*. Maya felt frightened but comfortable. There was old wood left behind, dry enough for a fire and they built it up in the centre, sitting around it on fallen masonry, the dogs nearby. They decided to break out the beer bottles they'd been saving.

'There's this legend,' Caitlin explained. 'The laird was a wizard and he summoned a demon army to build the castle for him.'

She looked at the others across the campfire and they all started to laugh at the spookiness.

'I won't be able to sleep now,' Alastair said.

'They say he used to do his magic down here,' added Caitlin, smiling over the top of her bottle.

She woke to see only embers left inside the fire. They provided a small heat to her cheek and her face felt dry. In the tiny light, she could see the others were awake, sitting on stones, watching the smouldering wood.

'Do you know what day it is?' Caitlin whispered.

Alastair replied that he didn't know. Maya understood. You lost count of days when they stopped being useful. But Caitlin knew, apparently. She'd been writing them down in her book.

'It's Christmas Eve,' she said.

'No way,' he said. 'It can't be.'

'It is. Look.'

Maya watched her show him the days in her book's pages. Caitlin was right, and it made sense when Maya counted out the weeks they'd been walking. She considered all that time passing and realised she was no longer afraid. Spencer and Hirst were gone from her dreams. The panic of her Head Thing remained a distant memory. Back in that corridor, she'd extinguished her lamp, once and for all.

Alastair said, 'Merry Christmas,' and Caitlin said it back, then they sat together and he used a stick on the embers, poking them into brief life. From her distance, Maya watched them watch each other. Caitlin was looking right at him, right into him, and her eyes were wobbly and wet. Maya decided to leave them in peace, turning over and closing her eyes.

'I'm sorry,' she heard him say. 'I really am.'

'I know you are.'

'I didn't realise what I was doing. I was so mad. I was so full up.'

'I know.'

They were nearly there. Maya could feel it now. They were getting close.

The next day, they did the walk all in one. Seven hours walking from when they woke, and none of them spoke about the night before. Soon, they would make their destination and the days of walking would be behind them. They walked in the middle of the road. They walked across fields and into bits of forest. They passed bodies of water. When they got hungry, they ate. When they needed the toilet, they hid themselves.

Caitlin squealed when she started seeing signs with the name; the name of her village. Alastair spoke about it, remembering the place from other Christmases, coming in with heaps of presents for the family. He loved it down there. He didn't have a home, but they offered him one. Maya wondered. Would it be the same, the same for her?

They soon arrived in the village's centre. Lots of the houses had fires on inside; you could tell from the smoking chimneys.

'This is it,' said Caitlin. 'We're here.'

The day was ending as they crossed the river. There was the house on the far side, just like Caitlin described it, and from inside, a light shone out. They stepped into the water and it ran over their feet, wetting their shoes and socks. At the other side, they climbed up the embankment and she knew they were finally home. A man was standing in the overgrown garden. He gasped when he saw them, then shouted out, 'We've been waiting.'

Acknowledgements

Luke Smithson, Alex Ewart, Dean Reid, Sarah Fulton, Ross Jamieson, Marianne MacRae, Lara Williams, Timothea Armour & the Goblins (for showing me Yester Castle), David Bishop, El Lam, Sam Boyce, Rachel Humphries, Angela Cran, Olivia Hutchings and everyone at Corsair, Cathryn Summerhayes and everyone at Curtis Brown, and most of all, Janey Crichton.